*The A*1

The Awakening

ANITA AGNIHOTRI

Translated from the Bengali by
NANDINI GUHA

To
Dear Runuli!
Love
Nandini (Tuya)

zubaan

The Awakening
First Published in English in 2009 by
Zubaan
an imprint of Kali for Women
128B Shahpur Jat
1st Floor
New Delhi 110049
Email: zubaanwbooks@vsnl.net and zubaan@gmail.com
Website: www.zubaanbooks.com

ISBN 978-81-89884-08-6

Zubaan is an independent feminist publishing house based in New Delhi, India, with a strong academic and general list. It was set up as an imprint of the well known feminist house Kali for Women, and carries forward Kali's tradition of publishing world quality books to high editorial and production standards. "Zubaan" means tongue, voice, language, speech in Hindustani. Zubaan is a non-profit publisher, working in the areas of the humanities, social sciences, as well as in fiction, general non-fiction, and books for young adults that celebrate difference, diversity and equality, especially for and about the children of India and South Asia under its imprint Young Zubaan.

Typset at Tulika Print Communication Services
35A/1, third floor, Shahpur Jat, New Delhi - 110 049
Printed at Raj Press, R 3 Inderpuri, New Delhi 110 012

To Ma and Babu
ॐ

I sincerely thank the author Anita Agnihotri
for having so much faith in me and Preeti Gill
for giving the book its final form.

To my son Sameer, whose unstinting support I
have at all times and my grandson Dyujoy,
who is the delight of my life, I dedicate this
translation of Akal Bodhon

1

1972. It was early morning in the month of Kartik. The sky, the colour of slate was covered with clouds. The sun was still to rise yet faint streaks of light indicated that the night was over. It was chilly because of the heavy rains in the month of Ashwin. People were sure that the winter would be severe. A procession celebrating the Chhat or sun festival was moving along Christopher Road towards Number Three Bridge. Preparations to worship the sun god were underway well before sunrise. At the head of the procession, girls could be seen rubbing their noses in the dust as they prostrated themselves. The rhythmic beat of a copper gong reverberated in the air. Bringing up the rear was a pushcart laden with bananas covered with thin red cotton. Biju, the little boy who had been pushing the cart, was drenched in sweat. His shirt was soaked through. As he stopped to wipe his streaming face his eyes fell on the tarpaulin covered structure beside the road. The towel remained suspended in midair as his eyes popped open in shock. Sarayuprasad, the leader of the procession had gone far ahead. Seeing Biju he took a few steps back and asked "What's up Biju?" Biju couldn't say a word. Following Biju's pointed finger Sarayuprasad ran to the edge of the road.

On a bare wooden cot under the tarpaulin slept two figures wrapped up in sheets. Sarayuprasad tried to shake them awake shouting, in Hindi, "*Arrey* wake up, wake up. A fire has broken out, a fire. . . ".

As soon as one of the men awoke Sarayuprasad left. He had done what he had to. The girls were far ahead, the pushcart had stopped, it was not possible for him to wait any longer.

Bishu was a young boy. He woke up but covered himself again and promptly went back to sleep. He and Arjun da had slept very late last night, their bodies aching, their heads heavy. Aware of the back breaking labour awaiting him in the morning, Bishu's eyes still unfocussed and sticky with sleep were about to close again. Arjun who'd also woken up hurriedly was sitting up like one who doesn't know where he is. Throwing off the sheet covering him, Arjun stared at the darkened workshop for a while.

This bamboo framed space with a thatch of dry coconut leaves was Arjun's studio. Next to it stood a festering pond, the reason why the owner Bansi Manna charged a lower rent. In this small space were packed all the clay gods. On top of the broken elephant of Lord Vishwakarma, the architect of the world, lay a rolled up mat and a tattered pillow. From the hand of Saraswati, the goddess of knowledge and learning, hung Bishu's lungi and vest. Unsold, awe-inspiring figurines of Durga, Kali and Lakshmi were there as well. Piles of straw, bamboo and clay cluttered the doorway. The big idols had to be kept outside, there was no where else to keep them.

Four enormous idols of the goddess Jagaddhatri, the protector of the world, sitting astride lions were on fire. The straw stuffing inside the idols had caught fire and the glow was visible through the thin clay cover. The lions were still wrapped in cool clay. It was a strange supernatural sight, the unearthly procession of blazing devis, harbingers of calamitous happenings. Saturday was Jagaddhatri puja and the idols were being prepared for this. But there had been no sun to dry them so Arjun and Bishu had to hang strings of fireballs made of a mixture of earth and coal and dry them with a lamp. These small balls were to be strung on sticks and placed on the neck, stomach and hands. The coal was then lit to dry the clay. Once the idols were painted the decorations would be put on them before delivery on Thursday. Holding that lamp all day and all night had exhausted them so completely that Arjun did not realize that some embers left in the dry straw had caused the fire to spread through the whole structure. All night the straw, covered by the clay, had smouldered.

What an amazing, wondrous sight! Completely forgetting the puja, the delivery deadline or that the fire could engulf his whole studio – Arjun continued to stare with open- mouthed awe. In the process, the heat from the fire went into his blood. On the outside cool Ganges clay and inside raging fire!

It was only many, many days later that it struck Arjun that he had seen his Didi smoulder in just that way. She had smouldered as long as she lived but she had never allowed the heat of the fire within her to touch anyone physically. The result was that after burning a long time it had finally consumed her whole frame and reduced her to ashes.

But on that early morning in 1972, Arjun had not been so philosophical. That blinding unusual yellow-orange glow could have swallowed his shelter because Bishu's deep slumber had not been disturbed by the heat or smell of the fire. Kunti, Arjun's Didi, who had gone to fetch the family's drinking water suddenly stopped seeing the flames. She screamed and shouted to wake Bishu and then shook Arjun out of his exhausted slumber before organizing the colony residents to get water to douse the flames. With the help of some young boys Bishu and Arjun threw water on the burning idols. The air inside the shelter was thick with the smell of burnt straw and damp smoke. Arjun cracked open the plaster coat of the idols and pulled out the burning straw from stomachs and chests and hands. Blisters broke out on his and Bishu's ash-blackened hands. He had not allowed Didi to touch the straw. Poor thing! After the housework, the cooking, the cleaning, and the washing of clothes she would make time to come to the shelter and sit in a corner on her haunches, working with the clay for hours. Her slim soft fingers could make magical impressions with the moulds, better than anyone else. She would gently press the clay into every corner of the mould to take out the most perfect impressions. Arjun did not want the fire to touch Didi's artistic fingers.

Baba came running from their Daspara shanty dwelling and so did Ma a while later, on unsteady legs. Arjun and the others were busy patting the cracked plaster with soft cloth, repairing damaged fingers and noses.

The tea had become cold like water and the puffed rice Ma had sent was soggy. A searing pain shot through Arjun and Bishu's shoulders. Their chests were dripping with sweat. Didi, her head half covered, her face stern, her jaw set and sombre handed them wet pieces of cloth with steady concentration.

People from the colony came and stood at the entrance, watching. Elders came from their gossip stations. One idol was to go to Mallik Bazaar, another to Chandannagar. The members of the Puja Committee would arrive in the afternoon. How would Arjun manage to get the idols ready in time? Would he be able to free the frames from the fire, cover them with clay, paint them and finish the decorations? He wouldn't be able to do it even if he worked all day and all night. Not unless there was a fire or the sun shone brightly again.

Balai who owned the grocery store in front and remained bare bodied through the year would constantly massage his smooth belly and say, "*Chha*. Does Aju mould the gods? No it is his didi! First of all she is a low class chamar, the daughter of a shoe maker, then a widow, how else will this whole inauspicious cycle come full circle and cross all limits?"

He now stood a little way off. He hadn't come close like the others but neither had he stayed in his shop. His tongue had leapt up like the flames. He wanted to be heard by all the residents of the colony, "The hands that strip the hide off cows now touch the body of the goddess. They will not only burn themselves but the entire colony. Where is the sanctity of society? See the excesses of the low castes. . . ."

Arjun's father Rupen Das, alias Rupen Chamar, was listening with his eyes lowered. Short, jet black, nose and eyes carved out of stone, full head of thick grey hair, eye lashes prematurely grey, the old man looked like a black horse down whose trembling muscles the insults were rapidly sliding down. Didi did not raise her head, her face was impassive. When she sat at work lifting impressions, or sculpting fingers and crowns, her head remained uncovered, she did not turn her back to the door. Just like a chamar's daughter she would sit on her haunches as though to repair shoes with awl and leather and work for hours on end, unmoving. She sat in the same posture today – unmoving. The collected breath of the crowd around her failed to raise even a ripple on the hair falling over her forehead.

Everyone heard what Balai said. The barely clothed children of Daspara nudged each other without comprehending the meaning of the words. The elders and the youth were silent. Balancing on a rough handmade ladder Arjun was repairing the Howrah Goddess's arm. Sweat poured down his bare body. His taut spine strained with every movement. Everyone stared at his back as though it would actually speak. It was just for a few moments. Suddenly Arjun jumped off the ladder, the crowd parted and he stood in front of Balai. "This hand will now strip off your skin as well, do you understand? Do you really have no idea what the low castes are capable of?" he said.

Unable to say a word, Balai stepped back. The sudden

retaliation caused his tongue to get stuck between his teeth. "Now I know from where the fire started." Returning to his shed Arjun shouted to the crowd, "Come, come all of you and see for yourselves who are the ones responsible for starting the fire."

Immediately Balai slunk into his shop. He had never imagined the boy would confront him like this. The words 'chamar's daughter and that too a widow' had reached Arjun's ears almost as soon as they were uttered – after all he did not lack friends in Daspara.

Rupen Das's back was bent. Maybe it was a consequence of long years of sitting and working with leather. Or perhaps fate intended it to be bent. Anyway it made him look even shorter. After the trouble with Balai he went home and returned again in the afternoon. He carried food for his daughter, Aju and the assistant Bishu who belonged to Harowa. He was a labourer's son. He lived here during the season, got his wages and ate at Arjun's house. The workshop had a loft which was piled high with hair, jewellery, a tool box and the boys' beddings. They ate coarse red grains of rice along with some vegetable and a boiled potato. Once in fifteen days they got dal and thrice a month Bacha fish. Aju said they would eat mutton the day they got paid for the Jagaddhati idols. Aju's mother sent onions and green chillies with the food. This was the custom in the season. Her son forgot everything but work even if the heaped plate was placed in front of him. Kunti was the same. Even if Bishu or the other workmen were hungry they wouldn't dare eat if the master hadn't put a morsel in his mouth!

Rupen Das had never faced such pressure. He always came home to eat in the afternoon. His work, cutting up leather to make shoes was not something that could cost you your life. If there was greater demand, the owners Asgar Ali or Ling Pen simply employed more people. The markets were flooded with shoes during festivals, Puja, Id, Christmas but shoes always looked the same. Rupen Das also worked with wood – people in the colony were fascinated with the lotus flowers he carved out of teak. The bed in his rented shanty room was made by Rupen. It was large enough to accommodate him, his wife and their children. He looked back to the year when his daughter, newly widowed, had to return to the parental home. And to the first time he saw his son Arjun outline the eyes of the Devi with a thin brush dipped in paint mixed on the back of his hand. Arjun was a stranger to him. His older son Bheem made shoes – the intricacies of painting were beyond him. Rupen was well aware of the life of the pat painter. He knew that the pressure of work would make the artist forget food and water. He would forget to bathe, to change his clothes, to oil his hair. Burnt ends of beedis would stack up on the floor and his shirt would hang endlessly from a horizontal pole while his dirty lungi remained unwashed for days on end.

At first, Ma tried to plead and cajole and threaten, "Why leave your ancestral profession for idol making?"

"We should not be doing this baba. We are chamars, low caste."

"What will happen if we make idols?"

"We commit a sin. What else?"

The fourteen year old boy would bunk school. He would run away to Kumortuli, the potters' colony. Ten years back, Ram Pal from Bangladesh had his workspace on the right side just before the end of the road. Seeing the young uniform clad boy there he tried to shoo him off, but the boy sat patiently at the door moulding birds and animals out of clay with his artistic fingers. Some days Ram Pal looked at him, on others he ignored him. Each day he thought the boy would not return and each day Arjun returned. One day before Durga Puja when time was short and one of Ram Pal's artisans had not come to work, the other two quietly put Arjun to work. Not on the

main goddess but on painting the smaller figures on the side.
The owner didn't notice – he was concentrating with single-
minded attention on an open-mouthed lion.

"The boy's hand is good," Gana remarked, his beedi between
his teeth. "*Aaye* boy don't get us into trouble," he said gesturing
with his hands to show the putting down of a paint brush,
"don't let the old man know."

Arjun's childhood was spent thus, giving life to clay images
without any payment. Surapati, the second worker at Ram
Pal's studio, did not speak to him at all. He was old and ill and
his eyes seemed to bore into Arjun's back constantly. Surapati
did not like Arjun. He was jealous. One day he caught Arjun's
right hand and twisted his fingers viciously. Arjun groaned
with pain, fearful he would be heard. Everything came to a
standstill in the semi darkness of the studio: in the gathering
dusk he could see through the open back door, the large kettle
of tea for everyone, the mess of Bonomali Sarkar Street, littered
with straw and incomplete frames, the studio walls covered
with row upon row of Durga images, open mouthed lions,
swaying heads of *asuras* and demons, horns of buffalo-like
soldiers going to war.

This battalion of soldiers seemed to sway somewhat before
his pain-filled eyes when Surapati released his fingers. In that
instant it dawned on him that he would never be able to retrace
his steps, for the path back from Kumortuli could no longer be
seen.

☙ 2 ☙

Bare-chested, Ram Pal would oversee the work of the artisans.
His ancestral home was in Mymensingh and his Bangla accent
amused Arjun. It did indeed sound strange in Bonomali Lane,

Kolkata, somewhat like rice mixed with sharp kasaundi, mango. Ram Pal told Arjun wondrous stories of tigers that came down from the Garo Hills and Arjun heard every word, completely enthralled by the erstwhile Bangal. He hung on his every word as he gave directions to the artisans.

"You left a crack on the elbow, did you? Am I supposed to patch that up? Come on, move."

Gana must have missed that particular crack on the elbow of the right hand. He went away in shame but returned again to take the cloth dipped in clay water from the master's hand. It was the demon Asura's hand, a very important part and Gana told Arjun later that if the crack had gone unrepaired, the hand would have hung loose.

Ram Pal went without sleep for the seven days and nights before the delivery of the large idol. Everyone at Kumortuli was in the same state – the sleepless nights were reflected in their unruly hair, red eyes, body aches and the endless rounds of tea in small earthen tumblers.

Arjun recalled that in the late fifties and early sixties, the eyes of the goddess Durga and the demon Asura were focused on each other and that this exchange of looks continued for many years, until the early eighties, in fact. In the seventies, Gorachand Pal too drew the eyeballs of the storm- tossed wild haired goddess in such a way that they met the Asura's eyes. Yet, even though her eyes slanted downward it seemed as though she was looking deep into her own heart. Arjun too had modelled many such idols.

But just how precisely the head was to be placed on the neck so that the eyes would meet the Asura's, was an intricate art that Arjun learnt by observing Ram Pal from the shadows. Once the Asura was complete, sitting with his mouth open, ready for war, the head of the Durga idol which was still in its mould, had to be lifted up and placed on the bamboo sticking

out of the neck of the statue. It had to be placed at an angle
such that even without turning completely, her full gaze was
on the Asura. The unfailing deftness and precision with which
Ram Pal executed this was something that Arjun stood and
observed hour after hour standing in Bonomali lane. The
passionate absorption often made his neck throb with pain
but his eyes remained focused, unblinking.

After the sari was draped, just before delivery, began the
ritual of fixing the sari border with glue mixed copper sulphate.
At the feet of the idols were pots of glue, rolls of borders selected
by the master and arranged systematically according to size
and colour. But even so there was much last minute fretting
and fussing.

"It is hanging, the sari border is hanging! Gana what is
wrong with your eyes? Move over now, move!"

This meant that the glue had not been applied evenly, causing
the border to hang or to look wrinkled or puffy. The master
would drape the sari on the main idol himself but he wouldn't
tolerate shoddy work on the smaller idols of Saraswati,
Lakshmi, Ganesh and Kartik either.

Each sari pleat would be held up separately and small
invisible nails would fix it onto the frame. Ram Pal would yell
and scream till each nail and each placement was correct. The
lower half of Durga's sari had to fall artistically on the back of
the singha, the lion, like the petals of a lotus – as though it was
a piece of art by itself! Arjun, the chamar's son who lived in the
midst of the stench of leather, whose forefathers had grown
hunchbacked, old and frayed before they died, having
breathed the acid fumes of tanneries all their lives, was
completely won over by the fragrance of straw and earth. With
all his senses, his big eyes, his nose, his strong hands, skin and
brains all together, he secretly and stealthily gained all the
knowledge and skills of his mentor, his guru.

The twin blobs of Durga's red mouth light up into a smile as soon as the lips are outlined but this alone is not enough to complete the picture. Parallel to the conjunction of the two lips, a fine curved line has to be drawn. And midway between the lips, tiny crimson lines express pain and sorrow. But is it only sorrow or is it also the petulance of a girl leaving her parental home? But even before he had quite figured this out Arjun had learnt to draw the required strokes.

One day, as he worked in secret Arjun got caught. In a way it was Surapati who engineered this. Of course the master would have found out anyway.

It was the dawn of Mahalaya and Ram Pal had climbed up the scaffolding to draw the eyes. Surapati was handing him the cloth brush from below. This was the Hathibagan Netaji Club idol. It was a very Bengali rendition of the goddess decorated with sola or pith which reigned supreme as decoration material even in 1961-62. She had huge eyes painted outward, almost to the ears, on a yellow face.

Ram Pal had dipped his brush and drawn two powerful eyes on the Devi's face. With his tongue protruding slightly he was now wiping off the extra paint on the edge of the pot when suddenly there was a sound behind him. Startled, the brush fell out of his hand and slipped to the ground.

Eagerly Surapati craned his neck. A glance at the back and he knew what had happened. "That chamar's son has cast his evil eye, how can any auspicious work be done like this? His evil eye can take the skin off an animal, here it has fallen on Ma Durga's face! His inauspicious glance!"

Ram Pal's curly white hair was plastered with sweat on his forehead. His heavy body was no longer agile and flexible. Stroking the white hair on his chest, Ram Pal tried to understand what had happened.

Arjun had been hiding behind the tin door on the other side

of the workshop. Maybe he'd got excited, or may be a mosquito bit him but he had managed to overturn an old paint tin which had rolled out of the door onto the street.

Arjun turned white with fear, his ears were thudding with the sound of his own heart, his throat was parched, as dry as wood. Last evening Surapati had caught him in the dark alley and it was only by fighting desperately, turning and twisting, that he had managed to save himself. Surapati smelt of dry leather and burnt hair. It was nauseous to stand near him. He was totally out of place in this land of scented earth.

A sound like the roar of a tiger arose from the scaffolding.

"Hey you Sura, you yourself are the son of a weaver so why do you keep on about chamars eh?"

Surapati was bent over trying to retrieve the paint brush. Like a fox who cowers at the sound of a tiger, he stood hunchbacked trying to see what the fuss was about.

"Come, come little artist come," called Ram Pal softly to Arjun. From the confusion of paint tins and pieces of wood, rose up a slender small tree. It would break in a storm but not bend, was the language clearly visible on its visage. Either that, or seeing that there was no need to hide anymore, a singular courage had entered his being. "Come you will paint Ma's eyes today."

"Come on, hold my hand." The master was holding out his hand, bending down from the scaffolding but Arjun still stood as if turned to stone. The inside of his mouth was dry, his chest was pounding loudly right up to his throat. Was this a reprimand, a punishment? A final flourish before an irrevocable farewell? Fourteen year old Arjun was to paint the Netaji Club idol's eyes? Suppose they refused to accept the idol? Would the two hundred rupee idol then lie rejected in the workshop? Yet, to refuse would be another kind of rejection for someone who had withstood Surapati's blows and worked for days in secret, unmindful of the burning heat of the sun. If the master was not happy would anyone bother to teach him the work?

It had taken an hour. One full hour, Arjun remembered. His back ached in unbearable agony, his body was soaking wet, like a sponge, yet Arjun carried on. Everything appeared hazy, Ram Pal standing next to him, Surapati below, the row upon row of warriors standing lifeless in the studio. The young boy could see only the one face, its sorrowful forehead like the terrace of a temple. The expectant look on the sightless face seemed to possess him completely as each stroke flew effortlessly from his fingers to fill it. They seemed to be outside the boy's control. His hands seemed to be moving of their own accord, with a volition and direction all their own. Whose hands were these? What unbelievable speed – as though they were the dancing limbs of some drunken old Santhals. The black strokes with their lightening speed were teasing and playing with Arjun. Eyebrows, eyes appeared in this way, distinct, different, fluid. The boy then painted a blood red artery over the dried veins of the whites of the eyes. At the core of the warrior goddess, a little sign of weariness had to be made visible and so he drew a web of fine lines that ended quite far away from the iris.

In the deep black pupil of the eye, a yellowish brown spherical ball was then painted, over which came an even finer dark dot and immediately the clay image came to life and gazed at her low-born creator. His grazed elbows and knees continued to sting, his stomach was contracting, burning with hunger.

Seeing him so completely engrossed, Ram Pal gave him a little push and said, "The third eye? Who is going to paint that? How come you are sitting silently?"

Words finally emerged from Arjun's dry palate. "I can't do any more. My hands are aching. You paint the eye on the forehead."

Ram Pal had painted the third eye, and had praised Arjun

by slapping his back heartily. "You have the passion to go deep into your work, eh?" From tomorrow come early and I will show you what real work is!"

Many days later, Arjun told Bishe that his mother would have given him a third eye too, given a chance. "The master let me go only after he'd fed me a meal. Ma was livid because the rice at home was wasted. Then, hearing that I'd painted the idol's eyes, she threw a stick at my forehead . . . how much blood flowed, how much blood."

"How much blood, how much blood," suddenly Kunti looked up and made faces at Arjun. Her hands were covered with clay, she was moulding a finger. Her face seemed etched from stone, so rarely did she smile. That day some strange breeze touched it and caused her to show her pearly white teeth for a second.

"Liar, Ma never beat you with a stick. She barely touched you with Baba's wooden clogs – that was enough to make you bleed."

Rupen Das wore his home made wooden clogs all the time since the heels of his feet tended to crack otherwise. "You have to understand, Bishu those shoes were lying under the bed and that's why Ma lifted them."

Ma hadn't wanted to hit him on the forehead, but the clogs had flown out of her hand. "Oh enemy of mine, you have painted the eyes of the goddess on a moonless amavasya night. As it is we have no peace or happiness, surely now this household will be destroyed!"

Seeing the blood flowing from her son's forehead, however, Jadumoni was frightened. She pressed her sari aanchal to his forehead.

"Where were you, Didi?" asked Bishu.

"I was in that house," Kunti said pointing in the direction of her sasural.

"If Didi was there would this have happened to me? Would Ma have hit me?"

Rupen Das was a quiet man. Seeing Arjun's condition when he returned home, he became extremely restless. Arjun's forehead was painful, his body feverish. His stressful labour of the morning and his severe beating of the afternoon were taking their toll on him now. They couldn't even call a doctor – where was the money for that? All he was being given was a sick person's diet of watery milk and sago. Rupen Das who worked in coarse leather all day couldn't bear to see his son's agony. He stayed awake by his side all night. He refused to eat or to speak to his wife.

Dr Biswas from Kamardanga came and prescribed medicines for the fever and the wound. Of course Jadumoni hadn't eaten anything either. In the swinging unsteady light of the lamp she saw the traumatised face of her husband and her breast throbbed with pain.

Silently she vowed to make offerings to Annapurna, Shiva, Kali and other gods. But her mind remained plagued by apprehension. Whatever anyone might say she was convinced that her son had committed a sin. The old man from East Bengal would encourage the boy and then go away, leaving a raging fire to scorch Jadumoni's family. How could he do this?

A chamar's son would paint the eyes of the mother goddess? And that goddess would then be worshipped? Could this ever happen? The Lord Shivshanker would burn this mud hut of theirs with the holy fire from his forehead.

Trains passed under Bridge Number Three in those days just as they do today. At dawn the next day as the train whistled past, Arjun was sleeping peacefully, his hand on his chest.

"Lucky hands," Arjun's father said touching his fingers lightly. "My son is very talented. But lord knows whether he will be allowed to survive by these class and caste- ridden

people." Jadumoni had been lying on her side on a straw mat
on the floor. She hadn't slept the whole night. Her eyes were
red, her hair was rough as sun dried grass. Rupen Das did not
look at her. Staring out at the newly dawning day, he said
loudly, "You are his mother. You must take his side. You must
speak in his favour. Let the world do whatever they want. If
you hit him, to whom will he turn? He didn't go to paint the
eyes himself, it was Ram Pal who called him. Could he disobey
his master? Could he come away?"

"And what if we are cursed? Our household burnt down?"
Jadumoni had bitten her lips to stem the tears. Again the early
morning train arrived and along with it the early morning
stench. The Durga Puja fortnight had begun. Under a tiny,
bent Sheuli tree lay scattered the aromatic flowers of the tree.
The lovely perfume wafted to the houses in Daspara. In Rupen
Das's home the smell of the flowers mingled with the smell of
the medicines that lay heavy in the air. Maybe it was to smell
the early morning perfume that Rupen Das had gone to stand
by the open window. Turning his back to the barred window
he said, "If a fire is ignited, let it be lit. Will the master serve
your son with rice on a golden platter, if he doesn't paint the
goddess's eyes? Will they serve him water? Will they allow him
to sit on their beds? Whether he does carpentry or idol making,
a chamar will always remain a chamar."

Did his words filter into his sleeping son's ears? Rupen had
no idea. Nor was Arjun aware, he was still half asleep. But
somewhere in his blood the words struck a chord. Otherwise
on this morning in 1972, covered with straw and clay, his hands
blackened with ash and scorched by fire, why did Arjun say,
with his back to Balai, "Let the fire be lit. I don't need to be told
who lit it."

Over the years, the fears in Jadumoni's heart had got buried
under life's small joys and sorrows and lay quietly asleep. Now

they rose up again like hissing snakes. If the house was not on fire, the workshop certainly was. Instead of fascinating her, the supernatural sight of the burning Jagaddhatri idols, had filled her with fear and panic. However, she had learnt to keep quiet now. The deep one-inch long scar on Arjun's forehead served as an eloquent reminder to keep silent.

She kept her thoughts to herself as she got busy sending early ripened rice to the workshop. 'My son had said mutton would be cooked after he got his payment. That will obviously not happen now,' she thought.

Three days and three nights. No one could remember how time had sped by in those few days. Pulling out the burning straw, applying thick coats of clay, drying the wet clay again with coal held in their hands. Painting the clay as it dried, making the jewellery and adorning the goddess, fixing the sari borders and tufts of hair again. The work had been delayed by 24 hours but in the short time left to them it seemed much more. The workshop would lose its reputation if the delivery was not on schedule. As long as Bishu carried the balls of fire, Arjun continued with his painting, Kunti filled the cracks with clay and Jadumoni arranged the tufts of hair on the goddess along with the children of the para. No one could afford the luxury of sitting down to eat. Instead food was gulped down hurriedly in a half squat. Just before evening, if one felt sleepy, then one stretched out for half an hour. In the last 24 hours this was the only sleep permitted to master and workmen. They had two small pots of tea in the evening and then battled on. By early morning, their backs throbbed and one of them was definitely feverish. Instead of Thursday, the idol was delivered on Friday evening. The Howrah Puja Committee deducted Rupees fifty from their payment saying that the paint was still wet in some places. People came to the para and heard the wonderous story of the smouldering straw all lighted up inside the clay covering.

The Secretary of Mallikbazar, Robin Bose, stamping out his cigarette under his foot said, "But isn't it your fault? The weather can always change, so what stops you from starting your work earlier? Instead of waiting till Tuesday night you could have started to dry the idol earlier."

Arjun was standing behind the lorry and supervising the loading of the idol. It was a slightly grey Kartik evening. Venus shone in the sky. The blue darkness of the sky was like a covering. The idol's incomparable eyes were painted by Arjun Das on a sorrowful-serious face. There was no fault. Arjun had made no mistakes. Not even in the white spots on the deerskin leather shoes of Asura.

Under the leather, the blue veins on Asura's hands shone clearly even in this failing light. Seeing the image that had emerged from his heart should have left Arjun speechless but seeing Bishu's torn half pant and his mud covered body a vein in Arjun's temple burst into flame. Mentally crushing the Secretary's cigarette with his own foot, he said, "Two Puja Committees have taken their Durga idols, I have yet to be paid. You too will not give me any payment. My father doesn't have so much money that I can pay for things from my own home. I got money for delivering idols for the Kali puja and with that I bought the ornaments and decorations for these Jagaddhatri idols. Even the gods above persecute those that are ill-fated. What can I do?"

As the last lorry disappeared around the corner, Arjun slapped Bishu on the back, "You have worked really hard. Shabash! Have a bath and go to the bazaar. Today we will have mutton." One whole kilo of mutton worth eight rupees was cooked with lots of onions and chilli and eaten with great enthusiasm late at night. Kunti had cooked with generosity. Arjun laughed and joked a great deal. But he ate very little. For someone who ate voraciously when he was hungry he seemed to be playing with a piece of meat held between his fingers. Kunti saw this but said nothing. She knew this brother of hers, who was eight years her junior, better than she would know her own son. Early on Thursday morning, as he toiled in the workshop, Arjun had gone out to urinate in the drain outside. Suddenly his head seemed to swing to one side of its own accord and he'd stood and thought for a minute and then gone to stand at the window. Kunti who woke up very early, before her parents, had changed and was sitting now in front of her gods. Hearing her brother's call, she opened the door gently and asked, "What's happened?"

"Come out Didi, will you?"

The sky was still dark. It had rained in the night. The grass at the edge of the drain was wet with dew.

Under the concrete cover of the drain lay a torn leg. Fair, slightly hairy, torn from above the knee, it was lying there. Meaninglessly. Looking at his sister Arjun whispered, "Tapesh da?"

Silently, Kunti covered her eyes with her hands. Later that morning the local Puja Committee informed the police. After that Arjun was neck deep in work. The news of Tapesh Mukerjee's murder after whirling around in the wind had subsided by mid afternoon. The image of that torn limb buzzed like a bee in the cavity of Arjun's head. But he'd been unable to stop working. He had no time to breathe. Kunti had gone to Mitra da's house. On getting the news, Mitra, a member of the Puja Committee had informed the police.

Arjun Das was not a weak man who would feel nauseated and throw up at the sight of food. After all, no one had eaten any food since Kali puja. But it was not easy to forget that leg. Man hunting man. A black and white image of that lay in the drain. Before Jagaddhatri puja, on that very night Arjun had scrubbed his hands and washed them for a long time. He had sniffed at his hands, holding them close to his nose. Over the smell of the onion, garlic and spices came the dull stench of blood. Growing steadily stronger. He had never skinned a cow or been covered with blood, only mud and straw. His work was with mud and bamboo and straw. Why then did the blood flowing in a vein cut through them? His hands wrung with pain. Why did this happen to Arjun? Why was he so sensitive to these things?

3

Trains rattled by in front of the house all day, so close in fact that tea cups shook with the sound. A jungle of dust covered weeds stood on the embankment bordering the train track. The rusty skeleton of a tempo van lay propped against it. Close to it lay the lifeless limbs of a hand-pulled rickshaw that someone had abandoned there years ago. At the corner of the road, passing right in front of the house was the overhead bridge. It was thrilling to hear the trains thundering past. Even today, on his way to and from the workshop Arjun would stand for a few moments and listen silently when a train passed overhead. The sound excited his blood just as it had in his childhood. Today too, it called to him in the same way.

The path was rough, it wound up and down meandering along like an uneven ribbon of worn out tar. An offshoot of the busy CIT road with its speeding traffic, diesel fumes and crowds of people, the road emerged twisting and turning past the leather market, up Number Three Bridge and plunged downward again. Then turning almost in a semicircle, it passed in front of the protruding limbs of the railway quarters and then went down under the bridge.

Standing atop the bridge one could see the tracks shining or twinkling in the light of the day or night. Saraswati Puja was over. The breeze was different now. Its wild restlessness heralded the imminent arrival of spring. There was a shed just after you crossed the bridge. This was the paan shop which only opened at night. On its roof lay scattered the yellow brown dust of millions of mango florets. Under the tree sat an old cobbler. His salt and pepper hair was full of bits of twigs, mango blossom, feathers and such-like. God knows where they came from but the old man was oblivious of them.

Was there a slight smell of kerosene in the air of this colony? No! Surely that was a figment of the imagination. How is it possible that the smell of Amal Kundu's house could be found here in the air around the rail bridge? That young girl had burnt to death. Death was a reprieve for her. Amal Kundu had gone to file a case about his missing wife. Along with him went 10 or 12 of his friends. There was Bunty, Kanu, Ashish – all his drinking companions. A newly wed bride was missing. Perhaps she had a paramour and had kept quiet about him. Her jewellery, expensive clothes, nothing could be found. Amal Kundu gave all these details to the police. Didn't he also push his nails into his eyes and produce a few tears? Red, red eyes because of lack of sleep, hair standing on end, uncombed. The second officer had been very sympathetic. But the in-laws had created trouble. With not a paise to their name, unable to produce even a hundred rupees , they now overflowed with concern and care. Who would have married that skinny, dried up, squint-eyed girl except Amal Kundu? Part time maids didn't last in his house because of the piles of utensils to be cleaned and clothes to be washed. Once married all that work was done by Putul. As soon as she returned after the first ritual visit home on the eighth day after the wedding the maid was sacked. Amal Kundu's mother refused to eat the food cooked by her bou, her daughter-in-law. Mago, her fingers are so like the antennae of a cockroach, let her cook for the others, she would boil her own rice.

Putul's brother, Bhagirath came running when he heard of her death. The stench of kerosene hit him as soon as he entered the room. Of course when he mentioned this, Putul's mother-in-law came rushing out in a rage. Amal Kundu had looked stunned and sorrowful. He didn't speak much. First find out where your sister has run off to, dear boy, and then sniff the air in our house. Do you think your girl is so valuable, that we would pour litres of oil on her and burn her! For the last six months you have kept us dangling on the promise of a good watch. We even bore the medical expenses when she lost the baby in her womb. Waiting at the police station proved to be an exercise in futility. Bhagirath's house was in Duttapukur. He had no resourceful friends, no one spoke to him. Bhagirath stood for a long time on top of Number Three Bridge, resting his elbows and looking down at the trains coming and going. Then, suddenly feeling nauseated, he fell down on the road, his head spinning. In the darkness of the night some people had come there with a sack. They were outsiders and had no idea that there was an old bamboo and wood platform right below the railway tracks. It must have been constructed to do repair work on the bridge. Putul's half burnt body wrapped in the open sack fell on the platform and got stuck.

Bhagirath's screams brought people from the Railway Colony and from around Number Three Bridge running. They went together to the police station. However by the time the policemen dressed up, armed themselves and arrived, Amal and his mother were not to be found.

The disorderly spring breeze was scattering tiny bits of mango blossom and simul seeds – the hopes, desires, joys and sorrows of a girl called Putul – indistinctly smelling of kerosene seemed to mingle with the other scents in the air. Arjun had

never seen Putul. He wasn't even supposed to. Yet it was not
very difficult to imagine her as a small built, dark, plain looking
girl. People said she had a squint and her upper teeth protruded.
However she must have liked dressing up just as much as any
pretty girl. So having been given in marriage without warning
to Amal Kundu would have pleased her. Therefore she wore
vermillion sindhoor from her forehead all the way up the
parting in her hair. In the evenings she applied pink lipstick
and cream, wore a flowery synthetic sari and sat down in the
kitchen to roll out the chappatis and clean the rice.

The girl was fated to lose her life despite scouring utensils in
her in-laws home, washing their clothes and looking after the
house. She died even before the lipstick, snow and powder given
in her dowry were used up. Standing on top of the bridge Arjun
was contemplating the new dawn, this Magh morning. A thorn
of anxiety had embedded itself in his mind. Before him lay
impoverishment from which there was no escape and within
these mountains of trouble were some indistinct, inauspicious
thoughts.

The 8.50 passenger train passed under the bridge with its
low rumble, towards Lakshmikantapur. From the residential
colony on the other side could be heard the sounds of clothes
being beaten clean and of utensils being scoured. There were
other sounds too, of dented buckets and broken tins being
pulled along in the queue for water. Strains of songs from
television sets were floating in the smoke from portable stoves.
All these sounds, and the mild smells of the morning, in which
were mingled the smell of broken coal, dung cakes, washing
soap and the odour of boiled dal surrounded him every day.
Arjun never stepped out of his house at this time. If he hadn't
been to the money-lender this morning he would have been
able to have a bath with tap water. Standing atop the bridge,
Arjun recalled Putul's death.

The flowery synthetic sari.

Last night, some local boys had brought up the topic at the doctor's clinic in the corner. The sari was a gift to Putul from her husband and he'd said that she would look very nice in it.

Of late, Putul's husband had started playing a new game. He was not getting any money from his father-in-law. If he demanded a thousand rupees, a hundred would appear after six months. His mother spewed venom relentlessly but how long can one flog a dead horse? Better than that was his new tamasha. Bring out the wife all dolled up into the evening drinking sessions and let her be teased and mauled by his friends. If she couldn't provide any money at least she could be a source of entertainment. Putul Rani, unfortunately, was useless even at this. The first couple of days she had just got up and run away. She had cried at night and begun screaming if she was forced. In the deep dusk of the evening of the third day of the lunar fortnight, the drunk Amal had become stubborn and spirited. How long could one tolerate the tremors of a plucked chicken? Who could have known that Putul would fall face down unconscious in the corner of the room after a few slaps and kicks? Kanu, Ashish, Bholu were all quite drunk by then, Kanu was very irritated; here they were at home, playing around with a bony wife while there was no dearth of beautiful women if you had the money to pay. He was the one who said, "Shala let's finish her off, instead of carrying on with this daily farce!"

Putul was unconscious then. Even the strong smell did not bring her to her senses. The flowery synthetic sari had burst into flames, like a dry twig or light plastic. The drunken haze lifted somewhat, but only when the flames had almost completed their task. Then there were a thousand hassles. People from another locality had to be procured, the body had to be removed, the room had to be cleaned, and Ma's scolding had to be heard. The stench and smoke emanating from Putul's story was probably still floating around from locality to locality.

The rumbling sound of the train made Arjun tremble in fear. The train would pass through his daughter's in-law's place. Bonu now lived there. How was she now, who knew? If his reserved, proud, serious faced daughter was suffering and in pain – Arjun would never get to know. What if they were to suddenly engulf her in flames? Or hang her? Chhi chhi, what frightening thoughts were these in Arjun's mind? Quiet and as cool as the silvery moon, his son-in-law was poor but he lived in a reasonably neat house. Bonu's mother-in-law and sister-in-law too did not appear to be wicked . . . what were these thoughts then . . . coming to him early in the morning . . . why were his eyes repeatedly brimming with tears? Arjun stood for a while in front of the broken gate. Pradeep was coming down the stairs, his sandals making a slapping sound. He wore a dirty t-shirt over his jeans and had wrapped a light cotton shawl over himself.

"I have taken your shawl Baba."

"What's new about that? Where are you off to?"

"To the workshop."

Pradeep noticed his father's pale face as he spoke. Pradeep was twenty, the moustache above his lips starting to mature, a light beard making its appearance on his chin and cheeks. He was slim, dark, with a head full of dark hair. He seemed to have inherited his mother's eyes, but not quite.

Sarayu's eyes were large and brimming over with the compassion of Shravan. They looked as if tears would flow out of them in a burst at any moment. Pradeep had not inherited the language of those eyes. His eyes, though large, were dumb, immobile, expressionless. It was only when he laughed that it seemed the sunshine had fallen on them. A simple boy who did not understand complications, his father had brought him up with great care and affection. From his childhood he had been protected from any difficulties. Such a simple boy in this day and age may find it difficult to survive. Every day Arjun's doubts about his son ever being able to earn a living increased. He was forever immersed in his own thoughts and pleasures but today the look on his father's face was evident even to him.

Pradeep had been about to leave for the factory having eaten his lunch early. He had just managed to avoid a bickering session with his mother about the food – why was there no fish, no eggs etc. Some large frames had to be set up today and he had to get the bamboos and wood together for that. Yet he was aware that Baba hadn't come home, hadn't gone to the workshop, his face looked wan as though he had just recovered from a long bout of fever.

"Come along upstairs."

Pradeep turned and began to climb up the stairs ahead of his father.

The verandah was long and narrow. Two people couldn't walk abreast. Rows of rooms ran along the length of the verandah. At the edge of a drain someone was getting a child to urinate while another was grinding spices on a flat mortar slab. At one end was visible a whole pile of utensils.

This was an everyday picture of life in the quarters. Strangers from different parts of the country lived together here side by side. Unless there was a strain on their supply of food and water, there were no fights or quarrels. In this drab poverty-stricken hole, there was a kind of peaceful community living that they had all become used to.

Sarayu had looked out of the door and seen Pradeep, seen the boy climb up the stairs followed by his father. Immediately she filled a bell metal jar full of water and stood there waiting silently. She knew that Arjun would wash his feet and hands before entering.

The way the man sat down on the chair, instead of climbing onto the bed as on other days, made Sarayu think that he looked like an empty shell, with nothing inside. Arjun's throat was so parched that even two-three glasses of water were not enough. There was sweat on his forehead and he seemed to be leaning slightly forward.

The mother who'd known every little detail about her son was not around anymore but Sarayu knew no less about this man. If anyone had looked at her they would have seen the reflection of that tired face leaning slightly forward in her own nut brown eyes. Leaning against the door frame with her hands on her hip Sarayu let fall the ghomta from her head saying, "Ki, did the mahajan refuse you?"

For an instant Arjun raised his face as though someone had slapped it. He did not reply.

Pradeep had climbed up on the bed and sat down. He seemed to be finally absorbing the fact of the imminent disaster looming over them. He sat up, lowering his legs from the high bed. If Ma would only serve a little tea now, he thought, the air in the room would become a little lighter.

"Badribabu said, 'Ajju, I won't be able to help you this time, do you understand?' He asked me to leave. It seems his son is expanding his business and his daughter is building her in-law's home. So I am out this year. And yet I have been paying fifty percent interest all these twenty years."

From the kitchen came Sarayu's soft, yet sharp voice, "So is there only one mahajan in this country?" The dust in the grains of sugar had floated up to the surface and she was carefully spooning them out.

Arjun leaned back in his chair and lit a beedi. The bitter strong smoke entered his lungs. The early morning breeze of spring flowed through his veins and arteries and he leaned back a little more comfortably. Gradually the smell of kerosene that had lingered on the bridge melted away.

Arjun started to laugh.

"I do have another mahajan, dear. But she does not deal in capital. She only takes interest and that too very high interest."

"Deepu, come and have your tea."

Hearing his mother's tone Pradeep got down and went to the kitchen. He'd thought he would be served his tea in bed.

Arjun was sitting with his eyes closed, his hands clasped behind his head. As soon as Sarayu came and placed the cup beside him, he opened his eyes and sat up straight. He did so although Sarayu hadn't made a sound. There had been no flash of white conch shells or iron and glass bangles.

Like the aroma of fresh herbs or the fragrance of warm sunrays that linger in the forest in the afternoon, there was about Sarayu a sweet scent that was uniquely hers. So that even if one's eyes were shut her presence, her movements, her expressions, the look in her eyes were all encapsulated in this fragrance.

"Don't you know what you should say and what you shouldn't in front of Deepu?" Startled, Arjun opened his eyes and looked at Sarayu. Despite working at the hot stove all day Sarayu had not lost her soft, dark cream colouring. Right now there was a paan leaf stuck inside her mouth and as long as it stayed in her cheek, her lips would be stained a deep rich red. Like other women Sarayu did not elongate the line of vermillion sindhoor right down to her forehead. It stayed in the parting of her hair. A hint of silver had begun to show now at her forehead but even today her red nose ring gleamed and twinkled when light fell on it. With a large bun twisted at the nape of her neck, the aanchal of her printed cotton sari wrapped around her, Sarayu came in, took out two biscuits from the tin and placed them on a saucer.

"I do. But sometimes I do forget. If only you dealt in the principal, partner, would I then have to roam the streets?"

"Did you learn that just now? Didn't you know that before?" As soon as Arjun detected the hint of tears in Sarayu's eyelids, he became alert and changed the subject.

"No big deity will be made this time Deepu *re*. We will have to sit idle till Vishwakarma day. Crows and sparrows will make their homes in our workshop." Arjun stared vacant-eyed at the approaching afternoon. For the very first time, his personal world of earth and straw had stopped rotating. It had come to a grinding halt.

Saraswati puja was over. There would be very few orders in the months of Phalgun and Chaitra. Perhaps a couple of orders for Chaitra Kali, and because these days Annpurna pujas were so popular in order to propitiate the goddess Durga, some orders may come in for Durga idols as well. Kali pujas were performed the year through for personal reasons. Some workshops also moulded idols of Panchanan, the five faced avtaar of Shiva. Arjun had never done this. However what really took up time were preparations for the big puja. The frames of the smaller deities, Lakshmi, Saraswati, Ganesh and Kartik had to be got ready. The bamboo and wood to make the large frame for the goddess too had to be procured at wholesale rates. Some even made Kalis and Lakshmis in advance in order to expedite their work. The inaugural puja for the frames was done on the day of the snanjatra when Lord Jagannath sallied forth in a ceremonial procession for a bath. But all this preparation of course depended on one's pocket and Arjun had been sent back empty handed by the mahajan, Badribabu. He had given him no warning, no hint even though they had met recently on Lord Jagannath's immersion day. If only he had at least warned him!

"Even if he had warned you what would you have done?

Would anyone but an old associate have lent you this money?"
asked Sarayu, putting the rice to boil. "Earlier customers used
to pay advances, you told me. So why don't you get hold of
one such?"

Bonu's marriage had been in Shravan and after the pujas he
had suffered two bouts of malaria. Not being able to mould
any Kali Thakurs, or get any orders had been the beginning of
a spell of bad luck, whose large frightening face had reared up
before him this morning. Arjun's savings were at a low. He
was barely able to keep himself afloat. Any slight tilt would
unbalance him and he would be stripped and eaten by
crocodiles and tortoises.

Hadn't he thought of taking an advance? All the way back
he'd thought of various options. If one took an advance – the
money certainly came in useful but the customer would deduct
it from the final payment. For a Thakur that was worth Rs
20,000 the customer would then pay just Rs 12,000. Arjun had
not learned to treat his work as merely a job. The Bangal Ram
Pal had prohibited slipshod work and so as a result his labour
and materials had to be impeccable. This was not economically
viable. Even if his desire to mould idols was fulfilled he often
had to starve in order to generate funds. Hence to swallow the
bait of an advance at this age was nothing short of foolhardiness.

Deepu had planned to visit Baghbazaar Ghat in the
afternoon after lunch. Boats full of straw would be coming to
the ghat and the father and son would buy the straw they
required for the season. It was not just the buying that kept
them engrossed but also the gossip as they went from boat to
boat. The river bank resounded with the loud calls and cries of
the petty traders and wholesalers.

But now he wasn't in the mood. He felt empty and vacant.
How could he go to the straw boats when all he could see ahead
was an endless stretch of want and scarcity. Deepu was young,

but not Arjun! In this month of Ashar he would complete 54 years. Already the hair on his head was stark white, in total contrast to his dark skin. Ma used to say, hair turns white from the fire burning in the stomach.

Fried uchche, bitter goud, arhar dal, and potato peels. Serving the steaming rice on a plate Sarayu said, "Do not lie down after your lunch today. That will make you even more unhappy. It is better that the two of you go to the ghat. You'll see the trains, the boatmen. It will cheer you up."

Rows of boats carrying straw from the Sundarbans were moored there. The water of the river shone in the rays of the afternoon sun. From the heat of the earth, 64 elements of various colours and shapes are procured in order to make the clay idol of the Devi, the mother goddess. The boatmen carry the straw down risking their lives, the labourers dive under water holding their breath and bring up the clay. While all these activities for the big puja went on Arjun would have to stand a mute spectator on the bank, staring blankly. But even that was a better option that sitting at home and dying of claustrophobia.

Quickly Deepu got up and changed his dirty t-shirt for a clean shirt.

Serving herself rice, Sarayu said, "A person came with a letter from Bonu's father-in-law in the morning when you weren't here."

"Ae? Why did he come? Why did he come again?" unconsciously Arjun reacted with apprehension. The fear that had grown on the bridge gripped him again. "What does Bonu's father-in-law want?"

"Oh ma! Look at the man's reaction! Why are you behaving like this? Your daughter is well."

Deepu leaned over to his father and whispered in his ear, "My nephew is about to arrive! Your grandson! Good news."

"You didn't tell me all this while!" Arjun was quite aggrieved.

"How could he tell you? You were busy raising a noise about the mahajan!"

"Why a grandson, why not a granddaughter?"

"A lovely, little, bouncy haired girl. With her hands covered in clay, she will play on the floor of the workshop just as her mother did. She will paint Kartik's peacock and Thakur's budding fingers. Before Saraswati puja she will help her dadu to fix the sari borders the whole night through."

Ish, how a man turns strange when plagued by money problems! This news was worth distributing sweets for and yet Arjun sat like a gloomy owl.

The large river that lay along the city from south to north never proclaimed its presence. So no one even glanced at it. Arjun went to the river along with Deepu. In the gradually sloping, broken down path there was the fragrance of spring. Spring was around the corner. The strong breeze was scattering the leaves from the mango tree and the kadam flowers in great flurries across the stone paved footpath. The sound was grating. As Arjun walked along he remembered Bonu's face as she looked at her wedding. A wood nymph with two swollen red eyes, wet with tears.

"Ma mine, do not cry for us anymore."

Happy, Arjun spoke to himself, aware that somewhere in his happiness was mixed a deep pain. The hint of a grey-black sandy sea shore on the horizon.

☞ 4 ☜

Down Adhar Banerjee Street, at its very end, was the river. If one stood on the verandah, one could see a grey expanse of water. The houses and factories on the far shore, soiled by the smoke from open ovens and chimneys, were bathed in the evening light. Rows of boats filled with straw were anchored along the ghat. Boatmen thronged the tea stall and sat on the steps of the mandir. Across the road stood the straw godown. The air was heavy with the scent of straw and the comings and goings of people.

Hridayballabh stood on the verandah for some time. "Ayee Shambhu", he called from the top of the stairs. He'd come home a little earlier than expected today. There was mud on his right elbow as well as between his fingers. Since one couldn't do away with clothes he wore a bright blue vest. His dhoti too was new, bought during the Ras festival held in honour of Lord Krishna.

He was panting, he'd just climbed up to the third floor. Now he needed water to drink, and some tea. He was not usually upset by minor irritants but today he was feeling uncomfortable and annoyed.

Shambhu, his old retainer, came up in a short while carrying a tea kettle and biscuits wrapped in paper. He realized something was amiss as soon as he saw his master. There was mud stuck on his hands.

"Isn't there any water?"

"If there was any, would I be standing on the verandah? You all have scraped the bottom of the tank. It's empty! Do you think water will grow out of it? Does water have hands and legs?"

"I'll just get some water from downstairs. The pump was not switched on, it will take time for the tank to fill."

Irritation writ large on his face, Hridayballabh Pal remained standing on the verandah. He couldn't enter his home with the dirt of the street on his feet. The first floor pump should have been switched on. If people neglected to do the jobs assigned to them how could such a large house run efficiently?"

Putting two buckets of water in the bathroom, Shambhu said, "Chhoto Bouma, has gone to watch a movie. Mejo Bouma has taken her daughter to the music school. If I'd known earlier, I'd have switched on the pump!"

Vagabonds used the footpath in front of the house for sleeping. Dogs barked incessantly. Groups of people used it for their card sessions. When the house slumbered in the afternoon Shambhu found time to rest, to catch his breath. He found a place for himself in some corner. If the master was home it was different. There were still some ancestral traditions observed in the afternoons. There was good food, sour mango broth, or putti-fish curry – these were never made except on holidays. The master was now at the ripe old age of eighty. He'd begun to stoop a little. He walked really slowly. But each day after his tea and breakfast, he would go to sit in the workshop. He had been sitting in the same place for the last 50 years. Under the same roof he continued to mix his soft, wet clay and mud. Ever since they'd come to this house it was only the route that had changed, nothing else.

Hridayballabh had not married. Having weathered one difficult situation after another, traumatized by numerous tragedies, caught up in celebrations of auspicious events, the years went by and he didn't even realize that he'd passed the marriageable age.

When he came to Kolkata from Dhaka he'd had to make a living with just this tiny plot of land for his workshop. A year later he had to start sending money home. He was saved because the land belonged to the Bhagyakul Rays who had left the land vacant because they'd wanted to build a hospital there. Taking small portions of this land on rent, Hridayballabh had started to make idols. Initially he'd taken on the lease alone, then his second brother's sons also joined him and later his elder uncle's sons too started working with him. With independence came the partition of the country and he had to bring across all the family women and other dependants. The ancestral home was sold off for a pittance. Now began the struggle for survival in Kolkata.

His thirst had, by now, spread from his throat to his chest. Washing off the mud from his limbs, Hridayballabh realized that no one had ever spoken to him of marriage. Just Ma. When she passed away, he was all of 35. The age of marriage hadn't completely passed him by as yet. He had large eyes, a fair complexion, soft skin, big moustache and looked younger than his age. But after Ma's death no one had bothered. Why didn't they? Obviously all of them were afraid that if their dada married at this age, his bonds with his family would become weak and they wouldn't be able to demand from him the pampering and spoiling they did now.

It had been almost 30 years since he'd moved to this rented house on Adhar Banerji Street. And just as what happens when a tree keeps growing and from the knots of its branches new leaves emerge and older leaves and branches silently break off and fall away, he too never got to know what those living on his bounty thought of him. Just as the parent tree, engrossed in the play of sun and shade, never got to know what those living on its branches and leaves thought of the aged tree, he who had no family of his own allowed his wealth and his time to become family property. A girl's wedding Banarsi sari had to be bought, a boy's fees had to paid – tell Boro Dada or tell Jetha Moshai, the eldest uncle. The attitude was, he has so much money and who is going to spend it if not us?

After buying the rented house and renovating it somewhat, a new three storied house was constructed. On the first and second floors lived the families of his nephews. Manab and Sahdeb, his brothers had died. They hadn't inherited Hriday's long life. Jagatballabh had died as the house was being constructed. His family was very different and they lived in another area.

Hridayballabh couldn't refuse anyone. He was incapable of refusing his customers so there was no question of refusing his family. His own savings had dwindled and were at a low. He had never economized, and neither had the others. He'd never bothered to see where all the money had gone to! He was a little worried today, anxious, as if these were his last moments. He felt very much like the residue left behind in a tank, spent and depleted as if all the care and love of mankind was over.

Ruma returned at six in the evening. All her friends belonged to the colony and had already gone home. Wearing a black sari with a gold border and a cheap red satin ribbon in her hair, Ruma made a dazzling entry. She was humming Tagore's *Rabindra Sangeet*, she'd just heard it at the cinema. She couldn't sing and yet the lyrics aroused a blend of joy and pain in her heart which she loved, "It's all right if you never understand me . . . that's best, that's best". As soon as she entered the bathroom she realized that the pump had not been switched on. Ish . . . today was her turn, Wednesday. So what if she wasn't here, Bor di, Shambhu, someone should have switched it on. People in this house were strange! They had given an old man the room on the top floor. Wrapping an ordinary sari around her, Ruma went to the kitchen and saw Shambhu entering the house with a shopping bag.

"Oh Shambhu da what have you bought?"

"Potatoes and onions." Shambhu was very grumpy. He never spoke more than was necessary. Why should a paid servant feel so much love and concern for his master, while not an iota of it was felt by the members of his own family? The daughters-in-law of this house seemed to be constantly on the move – they even entered the puja room with dusty feet!

"Shambhu, didn't you switch on the pump? Obviously, Boro Thakur did not get any water, did he?"

Staring straight in front of him, Shambhu said, "I was playing cards."

He wanted to see what Ruma would say to that. If she said, 'Why were you playing cards?' then Shambhu would reply, 'Why did you go off to the cinema without letting me know?' Ruma, however, bypassed all that. Twisting the edge of her faded yellow sari aanchal around her fingers she climbed nimble footed up to the third floor.

The door to Hridayballabh's room was shut. A tiny light was burning. He was lying on the high bedstead, a hand over his eyes.

Next to his room was the store and then the kitchen. It was here that Shambhu would prepare the potatoes and onions. Maybe there was just nothing else to cook.

Compelled by habit, Ruma peered in but then retreated. She then softly knocked on the door and called "Thakur Dada!" this was her personal endearment for him.

Hridayballabh was floating in a light doze. Next to him lay an upturned volume of Sri Ramkrishna's *Kathamrita*. He read a few lines every evening. In his sleep the steamer on the ghat was blowing its horn as it passed along. The river was making lapping sounds as it hit against the anchored boats. The still shadow of Rohini seemed to come alive at such times and move from one corner of the room to another. You could hear her soft breath. Sometimes she came and sat on his high bed. She placed her fair, soft hand on the master's chest. In the dim light, the cupboards, clothes stand, wall clock all appeared hazy and strange. They did not seem to belong to the present, but like characters from his youth in Kolkata. Rohini too belonged to that era.

His nephew's wife was calling to him. Her voice was powerful yet soft. The veil of sleep that enfolded Hridayballabh started to lift.

The hand which covered his eyes slipped and he sat up with a start.

"Who is it? Oh Chhoto Bouma, come in."

Instead of a full ghomta covering her head, she had only partially covered it following the traditional custom when in the presence of the elder uncle-in-law. In a house without a mother-in-law, such liberties could be taken. Ruma stood for a while holding the door.

"You must have had a lot of trouble today isn't it Dadu?"

Hriday swung his feet off the bed and yawned.

"Well, one is bound to have some trouble or the other."

Both his Ma and Thakuma, his paternal grandmother belonged to Jessore and had been married into Dhaka families. His childhood had been spent in the laps of both women. The Jessore dialect was still on the tip of his tongue but the Dhaka dialect had somehow got coated with the Kolkata lingo. One's mother tongue lived in one's blood.

"What did you see at the cinema?"

Ruma raised her eyes and thought for a bit.

The film had a lot about present day women. Bengali girls were shown smoking cigarettes and dancing. One even turned around and slapped her husband. Good for her! Such a husband needed to be beaten. Ruma had quite enjoyed the film although standing in front of Samarballabh half of what she wanted to say sank to the pit of her stomach out of fear. This was so despite the fact that their son would turn nine in the month of Ashar. Ruma felt she would have looked smarter had she cut her hair short, worn skirts and blouses and smoked cigarettes in long filters.

Chhi, chhi, how could one say all this to Jetha Moshai! Ruma thought a little, "It wasn't about gods and saints. I forgot to tell Shambhu da and I see that Didi has also gone out with her daughter so no one switched on the pump today. How could this happen!"

From the kitchen came the aroma of potatoes and spices.

"Should I bring some dhhoka dalna for you?"

Hridayballabh shook his head in satisfaction. Mixed in the aromas wafting in from the kitchen were memories of his childhood. It was to relive his lost childhood that he often asked Shambhu to cook this particular potato chhechki dish.

Rohini stood near the closed window on the north. She would be about twenty years old. A clay statue, she had not developed a single blemish or crack. Once in a while the master restored her colour. He wiped off the dust and cobwebs with his own hands, using a soft cloth and repaired her ornaments. He wore his reading glasses and worked on her with such utter concentration that even a loud drum beating in the vicinity could not distract him.

The statue was not a goddess but an ordinary human figure.

Her flowing tresses spread over her back. She wore a thinly striped sari, some light jewellery on her neck and hands and delicate adornments hung from her ears. Her paan shaped face looked just a little too broad. She had large calm eyes, a narrow forehead and the barest hint of a smile played on her lips. Ruma had seen this statue when she first came to this house as a bride and she was curious to know who it was. Samar however had no curiosity at all. Jetha was setting up frames and moulding clay idols night and day. Thousands of clay goddesses had been made and immersed in the water of the Ganges, which of these was he to look at?

A very beautiful peaceful looking woman stood near the bed. She may not have stood out among the furniture in a family home but if one came upon her all of a sudden a shiver went up one's spine. How could something that looked so commonplace in a workshop look so out of place inside a room?

Ruma had been to Hridayballabh's studio very often. They used that lane all the time. Heaps of straw, mud, wood, planks and spikes were piled high on both sides of Bonomali road. Everywhere there were half moulded mud plastered idols, both large and small. In Hridayballabh's studio one could see huge statues of Durga, Kali and Jagaddhatri as well as images of Chaitrakali, Sheetala and even statues of Mother India. The demon god Asura too came in different poses. The master climbed up a spiral staircase and sat on the second floor. Just above his seat of authority was an old idol of Bonodurga, the resident goddess of the forest with a dried flower garland wrapped around it and next to it was Mansa the snake goddess. The master himself regularly worshipped these goddesses. They had large wide eyes drawn above their cheeks with a fine brush and yellow faces. They were quite unlike the goddesses being moulded these days.

Ruma's father was a cloth merchant. Samar's business was to do with wood. In his childhood Samar had played with mud and clay as was the tradition in the Pal household. But neither his heart nor soul was in this. His father Aghor Pal used to work with Jetha. The two workshops were joined together. Ruma had heard that her Jetha-in-law was a famous and formidably talented man. For the last forty years all the big pandals had idols created by him. People crowded to see these idols. Even when Ruma was a child she remembered how people thronged to see the idols even though the lighting and decorations were not so bright and eye catching. But people came and stared at the goddess. The big idols and the smaller ones, where was Ganesh? They would ask. What of the owl, Lakshmi's carrier? And where had the image of Shiva been put? At which point had the trident pierced Asura's chest? How had the neck of the bull been cut? Exactly where?

From the beginning of the seventies, the faces of the Devi sculpted by Hridayballabh in his special mould had won the hearts of the Bengalis. Later through his brothers and nephews his fame had spread far and wide. Sometimes the decorations were made of tinsel, sometimes sola, sometimes with one single backdrop, at others with individual backdrops but the face remained the same, the beauty was of the same essence.

"Why did you sculpt that doll?" Suddenly and rather impertinently Ruma asked. Yet she had folded her finger even as she pointed at the figure, just as one should when pointing at a Thakur.

"That doll." Shaking his head Hridayballabh laughed. "That is a naughty female doll."

"Tell me, why don't you tell me her story?"

Did words rise up to his throat? The way tide waters touch the first steps of the ghats and then recede?

Ruma's delicate voice, her pouting lips, her laughter which brimmed out of the pupils of her eyes – in another moment Hridayballabh would have capitulated. Controlling himself, however, he said rather loudly,

"I will tell you another day. Go now. Let me rest a little longer."

No one was your own. And now even more so. Just as Jagat was already separate while in the same city, Ruma, Samar and the others too would one day begin a fight on some pretext or the other and go away. Meanwhile the only worthwhile secret he had would be in everyone's possession, circulating among them. There was no point in opening one's mouth!

The doll was a clay doll. And yet it had a life of its own.

Once Ruma had left, Hridayballabh walked slowly up to Rohini and stood staring at her. Minutely he examined her nose, eyes and chin. In the same meticulous way as one had to on the morning of Mahalaya, before the ceremony of Chakhhudaan, investing the goddess Durga with sight. The colour of the left pupil had got rubbed off somewhat and a small feather was fluttering, entwined in her earring. In the eyes of her creator, however, she appeared as magical and mysterious as always.

Rohini was not her name. For some strange reason her real name had got completely wiped out from Hridayballabh's mind. In fact he could no longer even remember when it had got lost.

She had come one afternoon in the midst of heavy rain. Autumnal showers had that year brought in an early winter. The strong gusts of wind made the frames in the workshop sway from side to side. It was an afternoon long ago. Had it all been a dream or had it been real, he couldn't remember. She'd got drenched on the way, her broken umbrella shaking like a half dead crow. Even as his middle-aged heart delighted in the sight of her wet body, what had really dazzled his eyes was her moist visage, her slightly wide mouth, a soft smile held back and her large eyes. Her wet hair plastered to her forehead seemed to outline her face even more sharply.

Hriday was busy applying soft and slippery mud on the neck of Kartik's peacock. One of his artisans was asleep on a hammock and another had not returned from his village.

She had come to order a Kartik idol, this girl from Harkata Lane. "The thakur you are moulding, that's the one I want." Hriday had trembled as she pulled out a few wet notes from between her breasts and came forward. Whose money was it, from where had it been procured, he couldn't be certain. Prostitutes always came for the god Kartik. It was a day of great joy for them when this celibate god was worshipped. However normally they just spoke to the artisans outside the shop and left. No one had ever come inside like this.

"Wait. The money can come later. Do you know the price for such a big thakur?"

"What's the point of knowing the price? This is the one I want."

Like a small little wet girl she stood there staring at the throat of the huge idol, at the sweep of his hair, his muscled arms. Hriday's heart was taken.

She took the thakur as it was. Hridayballabh had been unable to take any money from her. Like a fish that was irrevocably hooked on a line, this simple quiet potter had walked from one end of Harkata Lane to the other trying to avoid prying eyes till late at night. If anyone found out, he would be disgraced at home. After all he was the eldest son, respected like a father.

He had seen her only on two occasions, in dim light. Like the memory of bathing in waterfalls in the summer, even today the memory of those two meetings beckoned to him. Time, existence, family, honour, the earth, everything had got mixed together and formed into a red ball of fire. His heart had wanted to run there and many a time he had gone half way only to turn back. The attraction was strong yet somehow shameful. His heart was full of pain.

Many days later Hriday returned utterly crestfallen. She had vacated her room and gone away somewhere. The landlady did not know where. The Shiv-Durga calendar on the wall, the pat painting of Lakshmi, her crockery, the old locked trunk – she had left everything and gone. Hridayballabh stood like one destitute, his blood infused with the shape of her unforgettable face, her two eyes and the barely suppressed smile on her lips.

From the end of the sixties to the mid seventies, this style of the Hridayballabh school was adopted by various puja pandals. From his hands to those of his brothers and from the brothers to the nephews – year after year with the dedication of the heart and the soul the lighted lamp passed from one to another.

The Devi to whom man paid obeisance with crown, decorations and lights looked like a doll in this room for here she stood without rituals and ceremonies. Only an expert could detect that the two images were of the same person – Rohini. It was a name Hridayballabh liked. No one would ever know even if he were to secretly call out to her in his heart.

The face of the girl who was continuously persecuted and abused was replicated in a clay mould. The popularity of this girl's image spread like wildfire in the puja pandals in Bengal. His heart aflame, Hridayballabh continued his work of lighting the festival lamp.

No one would ever know. And if in the dead of the night his heart stopped beating, this story too would come to an end. His life would come to an end along with hers. He would never be able to let anyone else into this magic spell. Like the sting of a scorpion the secret would fester within him to his last day, lacerating his inner being.

Carrying a plate piled with 4 rotis, potato chhechki and curd Shambhu came and stood at the door.

The door was closed. He tapped on it at first and then knocked softly.

Why wasn't the master opening the door?

Unable to bear the silence from the other side, Shambhu left the plate and ran downstairs.

5

Ready for office, Debika stood in front of the mirror. She saw Andi arrive. She could see a reflection of the main road in the window pane – the movement of buses, trams and cars – hazy but perfect like a miniature painting. A kurta worn with jeans, a head full of shaggy hair, it was none other than 'our Andi budi' as Debika fondly referred to her.

Urmi had fancifully named her daughter Anandi. However, no one called her by that name except her college friends. Anandi brought the morning's newspapers and sometimes a favourite novel along with her in her bag although there was no need to do so. There were countless books in this house and from among them Anandi could choose whatever she liked.

Debika was leaving for office. She would return by 6.30 in the evening. The sun would have set and an orange glow would bathe the sky over the metropolis. As soon as it was evening the streets were a tangle of buses, trams, cycles and pedestrians. No one stopped for anything, there was total mayhem on the roads and so even if Debika left office at 5.30 it would take her an hour to get home.

Of course Andi left much before she got home. These days she was learning to sing and so she had to get home before her tutor did. The day stretched before her as clear as an open book, as free as a bird with its wings outspread.

In this house there were no restrictions on her movements. She could come and go as she pleased.

Sudhamoni lived on the ground floor, in a small room on the right. She had to be propped up to be fed, have her mouth washed and then helped to lie back again. She had a rheumatic heart. Gradually her health had deteriorated so much that the blood circulation in her legs had ceased, and now she was unable to move.

A few days ago, a young girl had been employed to look after her during the day. But Debika was not very comfortable about leaving her mother-in-law in the care of a part-timer. There was no full-time help. Her son Shankho was quite old but he had to run out on frequent errands. Suddenly the phone would ring and the boy would leave the house. Andi had herself solved the problem. She had recently resigned from her last job and was now applying for others. She did not like any of the offers she'd received and needless to say the employers too didn't like her.

Anandi had said, using her own pet name for Debika, "Ranga Mashi, I'm free the whole day. I will come and look after Didu."

Debika's husband, Bikram, was often away on work. He knew that many household decisions were taken in his absence. Even so he said, "Don't allow Andi to come without asking Urmi first. Can we really demand so much of her?"

Urmi's eyebrows were permanently creased.

She'd said, "This battle is totally between you all and Andi. If she suddenly gets bored with the whole thing don't come to me."

Who would blame whom?

Neither mother nor daughter paid any heed to one another. Yet they teased each other like sisters.

Standing in front of the mirror, Debika once again adjusted the placement of the pretty decorative teep on her forehead. She picked up the perfume only to put it back on the dressing table. Patting her hair into place she came down to find Andi sitting at the dining table banging a spoon on her plate. She was already 27 but thanks to her slim build and shaggy hair she looked younger. The girl, it seems, had decided she just wouldn't grow up.

"Are you leaving? Give me my food before you go."

"Haven't you had any breakfast?"

"Nothing was made. Ma ate porridge and milk and left."

"Aiee re. There is some roti and gourd poshto, would you like to eat that?"

Anandi started eating without wasting any words.

It was time for Debika's chartered bus. Sudhamoni had just

gone to sleep after her bath. The soft sound of her breathing was audible. The maid on duty was dozing as she leaned against the bedpost. The muscles of the house would remain slack, in this way, for some time.

After eating the vegetable and roti Anandi once again peeped into Sudhamoni's room. Then, humming a tune she marched into the kitchen to make some tea. "You remain happy looking at my face . . . " she hummed – the song made her happy even as she sang it. The music tutor was balding. He wore silver framed spectacles and he was getting peptic ulcers worrying about his job since his company had changed owners. It made him cry to sing "You remain happy . . . " Anandi sang every song in her own individual way. She would secretly insert a new note or add some new strokes to the rhythm often breaking all rules. Listening to these unconventional songs the tutor would get really agitated and the cloud of exhaustion on his face seemed to darken. Urmi was trying to find some more students for him.

Placing the saucepan on the gas flame Anandi said to herself 'just one cup of tea?' She felt very selfish so she went across the passage and knocked on Shankho's door. The door was not locked.

Lying on the bed Shankho replied, "Who is it?"

"Do you want a cup of tea?"

"Are you making tea? Then yes, give me a cup." But even as he spoke, Shankho changed his mind, "No, let it be. Not now!"

Anandi returned to her room. On another day she may have forced herself into the room but today it seemed that she detected in his voice an attempt to hide something. Normally Shankho had no qualms about inviting her into his room so why hadn't he done so today?

After drinking her tea, Anandi inspected the arrangements in the sleeping Sudhamoni's room and then settled down to her books. She removed a plate with orange peels and seeds which was lying there. She cleaned the water jug and brought it back to the room. She gave the bolster cover to Moyna to wash. The maid had resented Anandi initially but now actually liked her a lot.

From Ranaghat to Sealdah. From Sealdah to Ballygunge station. From there in a bus. In this peaceful house in Jodhpur Park you could hear the koel sing the year through. It was Spring and an unruly breeze beckoned the leaves to emerge from their hibernation. Moyna felt sleepiest at about 10 am when Sudhamoni had been given a bath and was fast asleep. It was at this time that her sleepless nights hit Moyna like the swing of a hooked pole. In one corner of her one-roomed place was the kitchen. Moyna would leave the night's cooked rice there for the children to eat the next morning. If it was winter she'd leave some vegetables as well. But in summer the food would often turn rancid. Her son and daughter kicked through the night, they put their legs over her in their sleep and searched for her dried up breasts by force of habit. On their one small cot slept her husband his mouth slightly open. His snores filled the room disturbing even the cockroaches hiding in the corners.

Yet before he went to sleep how he lorded over them, showing his terrible authority. Bhat debai bhatan noi, kil marar gosain. (He was no food providing husband, he was an expert boxer!) He did not even earn half as much as Moyna did and yet he yanked her hair and threw her down whenever he liked. He slapped her and kicked her for no reason. Unless he beat her a little everyday, his bangla smoke-clouded brain did not clear up it seemed. "A slut who always wants to be out of the house – she is travelling in trains and buses to earn money she says. Would you believe that?" Bhaben loved saying such things. A commute of two and a half hours each way for a mere fifty rupees, another ten might have made it more worthwhile.

But unless you registered at the Centre it was difficult to get regular work. Of course registration meant the Centre would cut ten rupees per day. In this area there was as yet very little demand for nursemaids. You had to go to Kolkata to get work. When she got home from work completely exhausted she had to cook for the family. Boil rice for the next day. The children too would be tired having played out in the streets all day. By the time she finished feeding and cleaning them it would be time for Bhaben to return home. A cat and mouse game would go on between them for some time. Bhaben would discover new ways of beating her daily. Moyna tried her best to take the beatings silently without protest so that the ordeal would be done with quickly. Bhaben would then eat his food in a dirty uncouth manner, sometimes he'd even vomit. Moyna would stare at him with unwavering eyes and say, "Please hurry up. I'm very sleepy."

Bhaben's hunger could engulf the whole world. Moyna thought that the beating was preferable. After an hour, torn, scratched and mutilated when Moyna came to lie down between her children she was not herself, she was a skeleton. The skeleton of Moynamati.

Chubby cheeks, hair tied in a pony-tail, her frock a little soiled, she'd been the adored daughter of her parents. Her father had a tea shop at Shinthi corner. Ma too sat at the shop. All she had to do was to come to the shop and make circular movements with her hands and she would be rewarded with semolina biscuits and rusks. How quickly that beloved daughter had turned into the skeleton Moynamati.

She'd had just four hours of sleep.

Out of the house at five in the morning she had to walk to the station to catch the 5.20 passenger train to Sealdah. Through the day her body accumulated filth and sweat; clots of blood gathered under her skin. The smell of beedis settled into her dry oil-less hair. How many male hands, in various ways, flicked over the exposed parts of her body. After 10 am however, an overwhelming sleep descended on Moyna in which all these things mixed and tangled together in knots.

Sleeping in this house was comfortable. There was no fear. No one to scratch or poke you. She'd begin to doze leaning against the bedpost and then tumble onto the mat on the floor. On several days Sudhamoni had woken up asking for water in her thin voice. That voice would penetrate the congested lanes of her dreams. Maybe Shankho passed by the room and woke her. The daughter-in-law went to office but each day before she left for work she fed her mother-in-law breakfast and gave her her medicines. It was Moyna who fed her a light lunch. It was an extremely comfortable working environment and when suddenly Anandi appeared on the scene, Moyna was somewhat irritated by the girl in her pants and shirt. Within a few days she realized that Anandi was more concerned about Sudhamoni, she wasn't really concerned with supervising Moyna's work. In fact she helped Moyna a great deal. As soon as Sudhamoni woke up she'd pull up a chair next to the bed and talk to her. She even teased Moyna lightheartedly. Anandi had forbidden her from bringing rice from home. She thought it would create additional problems if the rice were to spoil and Moyna fell sick.

For the last thirty years the Mukherjee household had been trying to get over a painful loss. Although the fire had died down so as to be almost invisible yet it still seemed to hang over every corner of the house like a mist, along the staircase, on the ceiling. There was no photograph of Tapesh on the wall. Even today Sudhamoni couldn't bear it. It was Debika who took care of these details. She made sure nobody brought up this topic that would hurt her mother-in-law. She didn't want Sudhamoni's frail and withered 80-year-old bones to suffer

any more pain. Bikram's success took him away from the house
more and more as he became even busier with each passing
day. A Zonal Head now, he had to travel to look after smaller
offices on a regular basis.

Debika worked out of habit. The sudden death of her
brother-in-law had almost killed her. The child growing in
her womb had been destroyed by the blow but she herself had
inexplicably come back from the jaws of death.

Tapesh had been a year or so younger than Debika. All his
antics, tantrums and outbursts were shared with his boudi.
The typically spoilt behaviour of the youngest member of the
household had awoken in Debika a deeply protective love and
care.

The distance between Tapesh and his brother, older to him
by four years had not diminished. Dada had tried to teach him
Algebra just once when he was in class seven, never after that.
When new clothes were bought, it was Bikram who swooped
down and chose the best colours for himself. Every new pen
was first used by him and then handed over to Tapu. Stories of
Tapu's misdemeanors in school were relayed at home even
before he got home. "Ma do you know what Tapu did today?",
saying this Bikram would tell tales of his brother who couldn't
walk as fast as he could. Once they were out of school the
situation eased a bit since they attended different colleges. But,
of course, it was the peace of distance. Mentally, Bikram was
already far away by then. Tapan's wildness, impatience and
restlessness was not something Bikram could understand. The
rift between the two boys was something only Sudhmoni knew
about. Her best efforts to bridge the gap, to distract and divert
them, to feed them from the same plate, to rock them to sleep
on either side of her did not succeed in bringing the two boys
together. Fed up of his mother's stifling love Bikram might get
up and leave but not so Tapesh. He would remain with his face

buried in his mother's lap and even finish the food on his plate by himself.

After his boudi came to the house, Tapesh tried to maintain some distance and behave with circumspection but that was not his nature. He couldn't pretend to be something he wasn't. As a result his awkward efforts at pride were easily visible to Debika whose eyes caught him out at every step.

Bikram and Tapesh's father, Jagannath was still alive then. Both he and Sudhamoni enjoyed listening to the gramophone. As soon as their meal was over, the elderly couple would retire to their room with their paan and other ingredients and settle down to listen to their records. Bikram would lie in bed with a crossword puzzle, a book or magazine. Tapesh came home late. His dinner would be left on the table by the maid. Sudhamoni would tell Debika, "You go to sleep Bouma, who knows when Tapu will return." Debika could, however, never sleep. She had her own fears. In their ancestral home in Entally, even with two sons, their parents and a new bride, one or two rooms were always vacant. Jethu, their eldest uncle, also used to go out early in the morning and his room was mostly vacant. Debika's heart skipped a beat whenever the windows and doors of that empty room rattled. Her parents' house was on the Bhawanipore Tramline Road. There, even in the middle of the night, it was difficult to sleep with the clamour of various metallic sounds and the harsh streetlights blazing. More significantly, things were gradually changing all over the city.

Christopher Road went past the cemetery and towards the Chinese colony. Parts of it remained in darkness and jackals could be heard calling out at night. The streetlights were dim. After dusk the shops downed their shutters and people peered out through peepholes made in their doors. They didn't trust anyone, after all what if there was a police raid and uncomfortable questions were asked?

Revolution was spreading through the villages. It had a logic and spirit all its own. Waves of this movement touched the cities too. No one in the cities was bothered that in a certain village because of the high price of rice people were boiling jute leaves and eating them with salt. The class struggles in rural areas, the persecution of class enemies, who were the power brokers, who were those against extermination, who were the revisionists — no one in the cities wanted to talk about these things. They were too cautious and as scared of vacant places as they were of crowded ones. If they saw strangers they feared they were intelligence agents or assassins. Before dusk descended, the city downed its shutters and sealed its lips.

The middle class people of Kolkata had not heard of Brazil's 'Urban Guerrilla' theory but still, looking at the anarchy around them, they were petrified. With the tensions reaching schools and colleges, the aborted exams, bloodshed on the streets, the smashing of statues — no one knew where the next generation was headed. Police trucks continued their patrols in the middle of the night. In a sudden swoop white uniformed policemen picked up any young man found loitering and took him away. The victims of these warrant-less arrests returned after questioning sometimes without an eye or with their backbones permanently damaged. Some did not come back at all.

On one such winter evening in 1972, in the month of Agraharjen, young Debika had fallen asleep after having waited endlessly for her brother-in-law to return. Suddenly the faint call of a jackal woke her. It was midnight and Tapesh was still not home. At one-thirty she finally woke her husband, poking him with light fingers. Ma and Baba were sleeping downstairs but it was better to be cautious. For a while Bikram stared at her, his eyes red with sleep and then he fell back, fast asleep again. With a start he woke up again and scrambled upright.

"Oof, that scoundrel hasn't come back as yet? Where does he go to everyday? Does he tell you?"

Debika went cold with fear. She began to shake from top to toe as though she was a slender tree struck by a storm. There were so many things Tapesh told her everyday. Things he wouldn't dream of telling Baba-Ma, and definitely not his Dada. Yet with this almost unknown girl from another family Tapesh was like a fearless child. He laughed easily and told her little details about the Party, relating interesting events to her in an amusing way. He enacted the disputes the leaders had, gesturing with his rice covered fingers as he ate. He made frequent trips to the rural areas and set up many primary units in places like Burdwan, Hoogly, Mednipore. He had no equal, this even his enemies would admit. At these times he stayed away from Kolkata for long periods. Baba-Ma-Dada chose to believe that it was his love for theatre that took him to all these places. The politics of bloodshed was unacceptable to them. Maybe that is why they were sure its flames would never touch their cheerful, ever-smiling, theatre-mad son.

"Does he tell you when he goes away?"

Bikram's question let loose a storm in Debika's mind. Had she never cautioned Tapesh? Had she never said to him, "Tapesh, leave all this. Live only for theatre"? Had she never said, "Hang on. I'll tell Ma. Tell Dada. They will take charge and put a stop to all these revolutionary activities of yours"?

Had her wide-eyed attention, her reserving the largest piece of fish for him encouraged him? Conveyed the wrong message to him?

Now they would have to call the police station, enquire at the hospitals. Irritated Bikram was splashing water in his eyes and wrapping a warm shawl around himself. Debika shivered. "God forbid, what are you saying? Why the hospitals?"

The first blow of that terrible time struck Sudhamoni at

about eight the next morning. Two members of the Puja
Committee were desperately looking for Bikram. Not finding
him, and with a complete lack of sensitivity, they said to
Sudhamoni, "A member of your family has been murdered –
come to the police station."

Like a scorched tree Sudhamoni collapsed. Debika was right
behind her. As she put out her two arms and held her mother-
in-law to her breast, she too blacked out. A strange pain
wrenched through her stomach. Only one name jumped out
at her like a bolt of lightening from the darkness engulfing her
mind. Urmi, Urmi, Urmi. Very beloved of Tapesh. His
treasure, his wealth. "Urmi what will become of you?"

A pyjama clad, disheveled looking, agitated Bikram came
hurrying down the stairs, his shawl trailing behind him.

⟫ 6 ⟪

Pain affects people in different ways. Tapesh's death
completely paralyzed Sudhamoni and Jagannath. What shook
them even more than his death was the post mortem that
followed and the bloody sequence of the events after that.
Suddenly both became silent, as if turned to stone. There were
no tears in their eyes, no hunger and no sleep. Like two imbeciles
they remained seated immobile on their beds. They had to be
cajoled to bathe, change their clothes, to eat. It was impossible
to force food past their tightly compressed lips.

Bikram's job was new yet he found himself chasing all over
the place leaving his office work. The trail to find the remains
of Tapesh's mutilated body after his torn leg was found was
difficult and fraught with pain. The body was discovered three
days later from the pond in front of Slum Number 13. By this
time Bikram's ears had become numb hearing the word 'corpse'

repeated over and over again. Watching the delight exuding from the spittle accumulating at the corner of the investigating officer's mouth, Bikram continued to answer endless questions. Co-operate with the investigations! What was any responsible citizen expected to do except co-operate? Especially someone who had a brother like Tapesh. The police stunned him with the evidence that they had against his brother which they now laid out on a table before him – pictures from his past, things identified with him, various bits and pieces of evidence which would be valid in a court of law. His admission that he had no idea about all this they found incredible.

Staring blankly at the ceiling of Bhawani Bhawan, Bikram wondered why he didn't know anything at all. He felt no anguish. There was no grief at such times. The sudden dismemberment of his brother, who was a complete stranger, though he lived in the same house, was causing him irritation rather like the slow gathering of clouds. Yet at the same time he was flooded with memories of their shared childhood. Keeping all the insinuations, insults and cruelties he suffered through the day to himself, Bikram tried to sleep. He needed sleeping pills. They at least made him sleep even if that sleep was filled with nightmares.

Initially Debika tried in her own way to apply a healing salve to the family's wounds. She saw to it that her in-laws had their baths and meals and at the end of the day, when Bikram returned, he had to be cared for as well. There was no one to care for Debika. The unending silence of the house weighed her down like a millstone trying to kill her. Bikram did not want any relatives to come to the house. He seemed to believe that in this sorrow there was also shame. Debika felt that if someone came to stay it would be a good thing. Perhaps one of Sudhamoni's sisters or maybe one of Bikram's first cousins. Debika did not think there was any disgrace or shame in the way Tapesh had died, instead it was Bikram's reaction that made her angry. Bikram had never really known his brother. Who was he to be so ashamed? Her daily effort to protect and care for her in-laws whose grief had left them so devastated was, in fact, corroding Debika inside. But whom could she say all this to? Everyone was lost in their own private hells.

Debika had not gauged the extent to which she herself had been affected by Tapesh's departure. She had not recognized this acute sorrow as being akin to that of losing one's own child. Maybe by keeping herself very busy Debika had learnt to think that it was not so terrible. There had been someone who had spoken to her every day, who had opened himself to her, who laughed at his own stupidities, who when talking of his frustrations contained his words and whose eyes became strangely shadowed when he talked about his love life. He did so every day, almost everyday in various ways. He was no more. No more would Debika have to wait up for him, his food on a plate, covered. No more would she have to go down shivering on winter nights to open the door for him. So what if he was gone? Debika's own child was about to be born. There was not much time left, it was due in the middle of May, early Jaisthya. An offspring etched in flames who would make Debika forget, who would surely wipe out the mutilation, the grief and sorrow of this house, with soft hands smelling of milk.

In the depth of one's existence, one's body, one has an inner consciousness and on this falls the reflection of all external events, all sorrows and joys. This inner consciousness shatters and then comes alive again. In Debika's subconscious the memory of Tapesh remained enshrined.

Within fifteen days of Tapesh's terrible death, the seed growing in Debika's womb was uprooted. An innocent life was washed away in streams of blood. With Debika in hospital, the house came to a grinding halt. Bikram brought his Chotto

Masi, his mother's younger sister to the house and somehow saved the tragic situation.

No one had the time to worry about Urmimala or to console her. Bikram had only heard about Urmi from Debika but Sudhamoni had met her. Urmi had visited the house twice. A head full of thick, short curls, a chin carved out of stone, thin lips. She did not speak much yet her eyes and animated body showed she was an eager listener. Sudhamoni had noticed that she was not given to rituals like touching elder's feet etc., yet there was no trace of insincerity in her behaviour. Urmi had moved around freely in the house. She had done so under the assumption that she would be coming to this home one day. Once she'd gone to the kitchen and once even into Sudhamoni's bedroom. After looking at the shelf full of records she had given her own opinion on the collection. On both these days Bikram hadn't been home. Tapesh's face had been a mix of anxiety and embarrassment. He'd been incapable of sitting in one place. He moved around restlessly, following either Urmi or Debika. Finally after Debika scolded him, he went to sit in his own room. Seeing this side of the boy who was a Master of Political Philosophy and a playwright and who commanded such respect among the masses, was a revelation to Debika. Yet it would not be seemly to tease him in front of her mother-in-law she thought.

That Urmi! After Tapesh's death she seemed to have suddenly turned into smoke and vanished. No one asked her to come and identify the stitched up corpse in the morgue. It is doubtful if she'd have come even if they'd asked her to do so. The news of his death had been conveyed to her by a common friend, Tanmoy Chaudhuri. He'd sent her a letter through a friend, not met her in person. By then of course it was common knowledge, the newspapers, the gossips of the locality all were full of the news of his death. It was still not clear who his killers were. A handwritten letter neatly covered in polythene, found in his abandoned shoulder bag said, 'I have killed you by mistake. I did not recognize you, I ask forgiveness.' Of course there was no reason to think that this letter was from his killers. People died this way in police custody as well. Getting such a letter written and planting it in the bag was all very possible. The evening before he died, Tapesh had not visited Urmi. If he had been killed on his way back from her house, the police would have traced the trail of blood and have found her. They wouldn't have spared her then. If Tapesh had come, it would have been so good. This thought plagued Urmi for the rest of her life. It would have been really good. After all she was now carrying their child. She'd been unable to give this crucial bit of news to Tapesh. He hadn't known.

Almost as if mocking the killers, Urmi became increasingly joyful and lively as the little life within her grew. The glint of steel in her eyes and chin was invisible except to those with very sharp observation. Bringing her child into the world was now her only goal – it became, in fact, her own method to challenge death.

Initially no one knew, not Ma, not Dada, no one. Urmi had lost her father when she was a child.

As soon as her pregnancy started to show, her mother asked her fearfully, "What is this Urmi? What will you do?"

"There is nothing to be done now. The date is far away – September. I have a check up next month."

Urmi's Dada, Sanjoy, knew Tapesh. They had been in opposing camps but it was impossible not to like Tapesh. On top of which he was also Urmi's beloved.

Since she was a child Urmi had always relied on her brother and her Dada had always protected his little sister.

Sandwiched between a fearful mother and a hard as stone Urmi, Sanjoy became brittle and broken-up like the earth that cracks under the constant onslaught of heat and sun.

"Sanju, please try and reason with her. There is still time. Any more delay and it will be a danger to life."

Who was Sanjoy to reason with? The girl whose body had absorbed the shadow of death, and who was taking out her old swing from the attic, looking for old dhotis to make into baby kanthas, and humming old nursery rhymes long forgotten in the seabed of childhood memories?

"Ki re Dada?" Urmi would say and then run back from the window, her eyes full of the sunshine of another world, the shadows of other trees and shrubs.

"Just see Baburam has pulled out the swing today. Will you get it polished please?"

She never uttered Tapesh's name. It was as though by some magic Tapesh had been transformed into the child in her womb. Now all she talked about was the child, all her dreams, her songs were of the child.

Sanjoy did not know what to say. What one could and could not say to a sister eight years his junior was something his mind was aware of. It was within these constraints that he had to ask questions.

"Khuku, with Tapesh did you have, what I mean is, any kind of registry done? Or was there any notice or something given . . . ?"

Did a shadow flit across Urmi's sunny face? Laughing lightly she said, "Not really, we never talked of marriage."

"Oh!" Sanjoy was a little embarrassed. What was he to tell people about the father of the child. The question became complicated. If only Urmi could have been passed off as a widow, then Sanjoy would not have to be a party to a plot to destroy a life.

How many babies were born in this country every day? On railway platforms, to beggar mothers, raped women, prostitutes. There was nothing that stopped the births; certainly not the fact that their father's identities were unknown. The mothers carried them in their wombs for nine months, as they worked hard, constantly on their feet. One day they gave birth on the streets of the city or town. Urmi had often seen mothers leave their newborns on the footpath when they went to scour utensils in someone's house. The baby would be guarded lovingly by its brothers and sisters while a street dog stood nearby awaiting his chance. During the Indo-Pak war the skeletal children of refugees had lain on these same footpaths on which had been born the children of the famine struck areas of rural Bengal. They were all here to find refuge. There was life after all. A tiny heart beat under the skin and bones. Tiny lungs. When the killer days beckoned, they crossed the opening of the womb. The only thing they were aware of was hunger. There was no bed under their sleeping bodies. They picked up crumbs from the street and became expert at salvaging from dustbins, or they learnt to roll beedis. Those who didn't learn were lured by conflicting ideologies into planting bombs.

'Urmi won't you be able to give birth? Care for and bring up the baby with your love and strength? You are a literate mother, you have been educated, you have stood on your own feet, you might even get a job. I'm leaving our baby inside you. What I have to say is not over yet Urmi. I had still to show my love for humanity. I never told you anything either. Yet see how quickly they tore me up and then sewed me together . . . '

Tapesh kept saying these words, standing at a distance, evoking deep compassion. An unhurt, handsome, smiling Tapesh. He was visible only to Urmi. During the day and night, in her sleep, at work. Just like a big moon stays awake behind the leaves and branches of trees. Hidden from everyone, Urmi's eyes brimmed with tears, which washed over her dark creamy cheeks. Urmi promised to herself, "I will be able to, I will Tapu. Just you watch."

Afraid of local gossip, Urmi's mother became gloomy. Without getting into arguments, Sanjoy started looking around for doctors and hospitals. He accompanied his sister for her medical check ups. When she walked down the road Urmi did not even look at those who loudly spat into the drains to insult her. At the corner, at the bazaar square, boys made catcalls at her like dogs and jackals, but Urmi just smiled slightly and passed by these gangs. At other times the colony would be quiet and well behaved and a neighbour might even venture to inquire, "Ki Urmi, how are you?" The reason for the concern being that just a little earlier Khona-Deba-Taposh had just patrolled the area. They were still not in the police net. As long as they were around just a look from them was enough to chill the neighbourhood. Although they were not responsible for Tapesh's death, their mortification and distress at not being able to prevent it was visible in their every word and action. They remained at a distance from Urmi but their awe and respect was evident. As though the halo of light surrounding Tapesh now encircled Urmi's head.

In this way, on one hot Bhadra day when the sky was upturning bucketfuls of rain, Anandi arrived. There she lay wrapped in the kanthas stitched by her mother and crying her lungs out. A complexion like her mother, lots of hair on her head, shiny eyes, a small nose and loud cries emanating from her small open mouth. The creases on Urmi's mother's anxious face eased out and softened. Sanjoy was very busy tidying up the house and arranging for additional help. The neighbours who had turned up their noses at Urmi now arrived to look at Anandi, with a mixture of joy and curiosity. They fought to carry the little child in their arms. Everyone had just one thought in their heads, 'Wow! What courage the girl has displayed.' This was a grand show for an unmarried mother. This was something that made the middle class cringe but here was Urmi proudly parading her child. Wiping out Tapesh's death, Urmi filled her lap with life.

The first time Debika came and took Anandi to their house Urmi was a little frightened. It was not in her nature to warn her daughter and anyway what would she say to the four-year-old? She wouldn't understand anything and would get confused. Having learnt to speak at a very young age she would display her tiny lower teeth and lisp, 'Mal naam Ulmi, babal naam Tapech'. (My mother's name is Urmi, father's name is Tapesh.) Maybe Sanjoy had taught her to say this. Urmi knew that even if the people in the house were overwhelmed hearing her lisp, Sudhamoni would not be pleased. Along with her pain she would also be angry with Urmi for her audacity. This was to be expected. Still when Anandi went to the Jodhpur Park house with Debika, Urmi did not want to stop her. How much Debika cared for her, the reserved Urmi had already gauged. In these four years Debika had come to Urmi innumerable times, posted letters to her filled with details about Tapesh. After all there was no one else Debika could speak to about these things.

Anandi was too small to know Debika's actual relationship with her. She was happy knowing that she was her mother's friend, mashi. Anandi loved going out and did not differentiate between the familiar and the strange. It was a year now that Sudhamoni and the others had shifted to the Jodhpur Park house. There was neither a photograph of Tapesh on the wall nor any other evidence visible. And yet, as she stepped through the entrance door and walked with tiny steps round the hall, uncannily, Anandi called out "Ta-pe-ch" in her baby voice.

Sudhamoni was descending the staircase. After ages, in fact for the first time since his death, she heard her younger son's name in an unknown little girl's voice. She did not ask Debika who the child was. She hurried down and took Anandi into her lap and hugging her began to cry. At this unexpected emotional outburst, Anandi, who was bathed in sweat, too, began to wail at the top of her voice.

Anandi had never forgotten that incident. Each time she entered this house she was reminded of it. The only thing that had changed was that unlike that day she could never enter the house and call out to her father.

Filled with pain at having lost her first child Debika drew Anandi closer to herself. Shankho was about five years younger than Anandi. Almost as soon as Anandi had first stepped into this house, Debika had stared expecting her second baby. That was another reason why Anandi was such a favourite in the house.

Shankho pulled Anandi's hair on his way out to the university.

"Instead of boring everyone, go and relax in my room."

Shouting back, "That's what I always do," Anandi immediately thought, Sankho's door had been shut. Maybe that's why she was feeling somewhat diffident today. Otherwise on how many occasions had she sprawled on his bed and listened to songs while Shankho sat on the bed reading. Today she thought she'd sit in Mashi's room and read her own book.

There was something mysterious in Shankho's room – it seemed eerie. It was as if someone had left the secret of Anandi's life locked in a box in that room. It was a small twelve by fifteen feet room, painted white. There was a small divan on which Shankho slept or read or lay and listened to songs. Next to the bed was a tall cabinet with five drawers. On top of this were kept Shankho's numerous belongings, a pen stand and a photo frame. In one drawer were his clothes. The underside of the divan was made into a box in which were kept many papers, Shankho's notes, his old books, and other things.

When Anandi was twelve, she had once come to the house, entered a room and found a black and white photograph while rummaging through the things in a drawer. Shankho was very young then and did not have his own room. In this room were the clothes kept for ironing and a book shelf. The photograph was under the newspaper lining the second drawer. Black framed glasses, hair brushed back, a thin moustache above pleasant lips – this was not a face unknown to Anandi. In her mother's album that always remained inside her cupboard she had seen this photograph many times. Her mother had shown her the photograph when she was quite small when she would sit on her mother's lap and look at pictures. Stuffing her hand into her mouth she would rub her saliva over the picture over and over again to test whether the person was real or not and to see if she could feel the contours of that face. Involuntarily her mother's arms would squeeze her tightly at such times. If she turned around to look she would perhaps have seen tears in the depth of her mother's eyes. What even she could clearly detect was the change in her mother's voice, which would become a low, broken croak.

The photograph had appeared when her finger poked at the newspaper lining and lifted it. Baba's photograph. Suddenly Anandi had experienced intense pain and left the room. Later she had returned secretly and looked at it again. As she used to in her childhood, she once again rubbed her fingers on the photograph. Suppose Baba had disappeared without telling anybody it would have been really great. At the age of twelve that is what she thought. Then she would go and search for him once she grew up. But Baba had not got lost. Baba had been killed. Those who had killed him were all living very comfortably, breathing free air. At the time of the shooting, it was easy for the police to put the blame on someone else. One day this game of looking for the needle had come to an end.

The Mukherji family burnt to cinders with sorrow and grief did not have the strength to keep looking for the killers. Yet no one had thought about Urmi or Anandi. Anandi wanted to find the killers. The people who'd prevented her from seeing her Baba's face.

Times had changed. The 1965 newspapers in the drawers became 1967, then 1970 and now they had reached 1999. In the maze of murders, deaths, kidnappings, price rises and news of many conflagrations, the details of the ideological movement for which her father's friends had walked through rural areas, dug trenches in Kolkata, written songs, done theatre in villages, told the people about the impending revolution and returned bloodied, had gradually faded away until now they were lost from sight.

There was now a new dawn. The world of globalization, Macdonalds, high yielding cotton seeds, mass suicides by farmers. The middle class had opened themselves to a world of dollar embellished software and in the life of young men and women were joint entrance exams, night clubs, gyms, luxuries, health, personal success. The more one's desires and wishes were fulfilled the more grew the tide of new desires. And so also grew the angry writings on the wall. Various flags decorated roundabouts and street crossings, the closed hospitals and factories. The villages were taken over repeatedly in order to gain control over a few skeletal bodies. In every household two flags were kept, of both parties and these were hung up as required so that peace could be maintained.

Where was Anandi to search for the assassins in this dark tunnel of disintegration and destruction?

"Didibhai! O Didibhai! Come and eat."

Moyna was calling. Her rice induced sleep was broken. Her voice pierced through the house like the whistle of a train.

Closing the door once again, Anandi came downstairs.

⌐ 7 ⌐

It was only when you came to the river that the boats became
visible. Because they were anchored so close to the bank they
were virtually invisible from a distance. Deepu counted one,
two . . . four, five . . . and a little further on the right, six, seven
boats.

In the evening the river looked calm, the tide had come in.
Clusters of water weeds, flower garlands, clumps of hair from
the immersed idols and god alone knows what else had been
washed to the top of the stairs and were lying around mixed
with mud. The Phalgun breeze was trying to soften the
scorching effect of the sun's rays, waves were swirling up every
once in a while sparkling with sunlight. When a river is this
close to the sea it acquires a salty tang from the sea breeze. The
salty sea water began to enter through the estuary into the
river's very blood. The presence of the sea made the river
behave as a pregnant woman might, careless and assured. Sleep
seemed to weigh down the river's movements, as if it were
pushing aside the piled silt and mud with great difficulty and
making its way towards its inevitable destination.

The city was so used to seeing the river that the changing
patterns of light did not attract it any more. The scent of the
waters, its moist breeze, nothing affected the city's rhythm.
The city's attitude was: so okay this river flows beside me, let it,
where else will it go?

Near the river was a tarred road. Parallel to the road, in fact
along its curve, ran the railway track. It obviously had no self
respect. Which is why through the open mouth of its level
crossing rolled rickshaws piled high with pots and pans, and
stumbling, tottering three wheelers and one eyed tempos. The
trains twisted and turned on their way up the track keeping
the river to one side. On the other side stood houses that had

not been painted for ages, their fancy glass windows festooned with cobwebs. There was a time when lights from the windowpanes dazzled the boats midstream. At that time the town had honour and dignity. The grandeur of the wealthy was considered a reflection of the town's well-being and health. The poor of course lived no differently than they do today. If a history of their survival were to be written it would be the same down the ages – they fought for survival either standing tall or crawling on all fours.

The person hurrying along the bank was an old hunchback. The 'Bharat Shakti' launch had blown its horn and was about to leave without him. The sound of the horn stayed suspended in the air for a long time much like a paper balloon in the river breeze.

Standing at a distance from the bank Arjun was surveying the boats. Ancient, deep black moulded wood boats that still retained the smell of the salty soil of Geonkhali and which now lay buried like crocodiles in the muddy bank of the river. It seemed they were unable to free themselves of the various joys and sorrows they had encountered on their long journey.

Arjun came almost every year. Apart from supplies for the big puja, he bought his year's requirement of straw from here as well. When he couldn't come himself he paid for an artisan to come instead from across the canal or from Beleghata. But this was only rarely. Just looking at this straw market at the start of the season was addictive; it was like watching sweets being made in a wedding house. The trading aspect was only a part of it, there was the gossip exchanged with the boatmen, the potters from different colonies, sitting endlessly at the tea shop and asking the Shivmandir purohit to give them charanamrit to drink. From the shop keepers of Borobazar to the carpenters of Gopalnagar there were many who came to buy the straw apart from the idol makers. The smell of their collective beedis, mixed with the scent of paan and tobacco always resulted in a large traders' party on the bank of the river.

From the half hidden faded black boat behind the old banyan tree emerged a man, his back bent. He was about to wash out his aluminum glass and brass plate in the water when he happened to see Arjun. His eyes widened. With his scarred eyebrows dancing on his forehead and his paan-stained teeth split in a wide grin, he left his plate and bowl on the boat and jumped down.

Shaking Deepu's chin with his food-soiled hands he said, "Ki re boy, don't you recognize me?" He looked at Arjun and exclaimed, "What a surprise! How did you grow so old Aju da? Grey hair, sunken cheeks, aa! You're like a doddering old man, aa! You do still have your teeth, or don't you?" Deepu thought Baba had only to open his shirt to the reveal his snake like muscles inside! Malaria, colds and fevers, all the loans and expenses for Didi's wedding – everything had come together to reduce Baba to this. But that did not mean that Baba was old. For not only could he do the work of four artisans single-handed, he didn't get out of breath while sifting soil with his feet or even when he had to set up straw frames.

Arjun just laughed and kept staring at Gaur Dhara's face. No the boatman's son did not dye his hair – his healthy crop was still jet black. Of course he ate river fish six months of the year!

Gaur had just returned from the Sunderbans with a boat piled high with straw. Once he'd sorted out business details with the wholesaler, he would go back to his home in Midnapore. He would see his wife and children after a long time. The monsoons would be here in a few days, the planting season would begin and Gaur the boatman would then concentrate on sowing paddy like a gentle farmer. He would

trim the overgrown sticky bushes of the thorny Babla trees in
the demarcating barriers between the fields and use this to feed
his cattle. Water and earth – how well Gaur had divided his
life between the two. Through the year he lived in this happy
blend of mobility and fixity. What if Arjun too could leave at
will like a boatman? There would be no burden on him then,
no interest to be paid to the mahajan, no days of sitting idle
because of lack of money, no need to sigh heavily each time he
saw Deepu's face dark with disappointment. He would float
on the river, day and night, night and day!

In the day the water looked a muddy red-ochre. As the boat
sailed, forests of palms and mangrove trees like Sundari were
visible on the banks alongside. Waves of wild parakeets soared
overhead and a blue-green Kingfisher streaked up from the
water. Their vibrant colours enchanted the eyes of the
boatman. The boat was not alone. No one travelled alone these
days for fear of pirates. There was no money, or gold and silver,
just straw. But so what – there were sails, fishing nets and at
least 30 seers of rice. In this bloodless battle whatever you could
get was good enough.

A big steamer would lead the way followed by four boats
filled with straw. During the day they sailed down the river,
dropped anchor at the onset of night. In this way with several
halts, the two day journey was completed in four days. Gaur
had been plying his boat for more than 15 years now. He carried
an earthen barrel filled with drinking water and a porcelain
jar containing lime pickle, crimson coloured rice and a fish
curry. In the Bada area the paddy had long stalks so the straw
from here was longer and there was great demand for it since it
was used for all sorts of purposes. He'd been just 25 when he
first sailed on the river, and his heart trembled. He could barely
look at his wife when he took leave of her. The river pirates, the
danger of fever and of course the great Master who with

thunderbolts of yellow and black could take a life at will, without warning – all this was in his heart. And then there were the crocodiles and tortoises whose home was the river. Despite all this Gaur had gone. The river held a magnetic attraction for him. Every year at this time his blood was excited by the call of the river, the boundaries of home, fields all became confining. Gaur would become irritable, his appetite would diminish and sleep would evade him. Then his wife Kajli would scold him with a wry face, "Go on. Go now, leave for the outdoors. I can see home cooked food is not suiting you any more. There's nothing for me to understand. So don't make any excuses. A strange sickness is what you have, honestly!" On a cloudy afternoon, or on an evening when the sun had set, Kajli's face would torment him to death as it floated up into the sky looming above the river.

Sipping from a glass at the tea shop, Arjun said, "If I have become old, then you have turned as black as ebony! And you call yourself by the fair name of Gaurchandra! An ordinary man should not meddle in large affairs but still tell me, how much is a kahon of straw?"

"Arrey dur, forget the kahon of straw, even if it were a thousand rupees a kahon, it wouldn't cover the cost of procuring it! Is it possible to pull in a boat piled high with supplies by a thunder bolt? After dropping anchor we couldn't sleep the whole night. I, Ganesh, Polu all sat wide awake. Suppose pirates attack? They would riddle our backs with our own double barrel guns . . . oof what an awful time we have had!"

Gaur stubbed out his beedi and turning around threw it far away looking in the direction of the hazy shore. His voice deep with yearning as he recalled the past he said, "What days those were, weren't they Dada aa! Boats used to be moored at the quay side right up to that distant curve. So many shopkeepers would come, looking for small quantities . . . this straw bazaar has dried up before our eyes! The wood of this boat is rotting but the owner pretends not to hear when I tell him. It means an expense of at least a lakh and a half to make a boat like this – who will invest so much money?"

"Honestly, there has been great scarcity this year!"

Arjun brought biscuits from another jar and gave them to Deepu. Why were people unwilling to invest – either in the straw business or in idol making. Bit by bit, the clay idol was created out of 64 ingredients from the earth. Would mankind actually pull out her very roots from the earth? If the mahajan was not willing to invest his money then why would the potter leave his usual tasks and run to the clay factory? Many new materials had come into the market but their tide had already ebbed – idols made of wood, glass, fiberglass, cards, match sticks. Wasting a lot of money these pujas had been celebrated at great cost but chhi, could artisans remain satisfied and fulfilled with these?

Once Ram Pal sir had told him, "I cast moulds all year round but only during the puja season when I feel the touch of soft clay do I feel really good, you understand Arjun. I feel as if I am in the lap of the Mother goddess, attached closely to this earth . . . "

Is there anything comparable to this earth? So soft, hankering for one's touch, light yet capable of assuming a bewitching shape at the slightest touch. It brings with it so many memories of childhood drenched in rain, the scent of dry earth which has got wet, like the innocent joy of newly hatched babies in a bird's nest.

"I am not making any idols this time Gaur. I have come to see your market empty-handed." Arjun suddenly spoke up.

The sigh that rose and fell immediately did not escape Gaurchandra's ears. He caught Arjun's hands with a worried look on his face, "Really? Then the market must be really down. Brother, I can get the straw for you from the warehouse; I can even put it down in my own name if that will help you in any way!"

Joyfully Deepu danced up saying, "Take it Baba, keep the straw." The sound of the horns as the boats left the ferry crossing seemed to cause the breeze to waver. Arjun did not move. His gaze was fixed on the other side of the circular rail crossing. . . .

"Dur mad fellow, will only straw do? We might even manage the wood, bamboo etc.; even get the clay on loan, but what about labour? The day Shravan begins, their rates will go up to a hundred, a hundred and fifty. Can people like us get our work done by keeping payments pending? Don't you remember how Shanker ran away the last time, in the month of Bhadra after taking an advance? I lost one thousand five hundred rupees right there!"

Gaur was silent, his head bent too. He was a farmer and knew that in this business one had to invest at least three-four thousand rupees for labour. Moreover payments had to be made every week, one couldn't keep them pending – small businessmen had a tough time in Shravan and Bhadra.

Across the road was the straw godown. Trade was slow, it was the end of the day. The scent of straw was in the air, fine straw dust blew around causing old men to cough. Small shopkeepers were leaving one by one, having loaded carts and tempos with their goods. Looking in their direction hungrily, Arjun spoke up, "Okay then you can give it to me Gaur, put it against your name. Let me take the straw. Let us, father and son, continue the battle. This time let us go without employing other artisans for the big puja."

Immediately Deepu's face fell. Suddenly, he looked weak and lifeless. Swallowing nervously he said, "Me and you? Can the two of us manage? Won't it be too much hard work . . .?"

Gaur came up and boxed him on the back. "I see the tiger cub is a mouse! The thought of work is making your heart sink. If you can't, your father will do it." But his light hearted remark did not affect Deepu. His face remained dark. He knew what hard labour was all about. Last time at the Jagaddhatri puja, barely recovered from malaria, his father had almost fallen off the scaffolding, his head spinning. His face and eyes had dark patches and one could almost count his ribs. He had continued to work, night and day – if he hadn't he would not have been able to deliver the idols! A cough accumulated in his chest, there was a metallic ring to it, while his chest and back remained drenched in sweat. All this only his father could do. Deepu would never be able to do it. It was not the question of one or two seasons, working like this throughout his life just wasn't possible for him. Deepu knew this but he'd never said this clearly to his father. Maybe it was not yet time to tell him. After all Baba had just about surfaced from the financial burden of Didi's wedding, when the mahajan's sword had descended on him. Deepu would be relieved once this season was over.

The father and son walked back through the streets of Kumortuli. Once the evening lights were lit, the city looked even more weary and pathetic. Although this was not the busy season yet some idols of Annapurna were kept outside. Some workers were applying clay to the ears of Shitala's donkey. Some old frames from last year's immersion that had been brought up by young swimmers lay around. These along with some old stuffed arms and legs lay upturned on both sides of the lane while straw and mud lay piled up at places. These were preparations for the work which would soon start. In Jagatballabh's studio a huge Kali stood ready along with an idol of Lakshmi. Straw was being tied up for Durga. Here the economics were very different. Jagatballabh had his own place at Ultadingi where too idols were made. Because there was so little time after Durga puja, they made their Kalis and Lakshmis in advance. These big houses kept to a completely different pattern.

Suppressing his sorrow, Arjun moved forward. His son had not inherited his broad shoulders, his expanse of chest. He was weak natured and rickety. He backed off as soon as he heard that there would be no artisans to help. Of course the path full of thorns that Arjun had treaded the last forty years had changed him completely. Deepu had hardly suffered from want in those years; Arjun had done his best to make sure of that. There was no doubt that the pain, the barriers of caste, the discrimination against untouchables that Arjun had faced in his youth would have destroyed Deepu if he had been subjected to them. Arjun's father Rupen Das had not been able to share his son's pain. Their relationship had changed a long time ago. It was Arjun alone who'd turned to cinders as a result of the fire smouldering within him.

At the curve of where the road almost entered Bonomali Naskar Road, Arjun stopped for a while in front of a large door that remained dark and deserted. His master, Ram Pal, had given him the address of this house. For a few days before his death the master had been tormented by breathlessness and had been unable to eat. Arjun had cared for him like a son, staying close to him through this time.

"You are a low caste boy. Whenever you sense trouble go to Hriday. I do not believe in caste distinctions, in gods and deities but people do. If anyone hurts you I too will suffer. Hriday is the son of a Pal. But his heart is good, soft as clay."

Why had master spoken of trouble? There was no smell of explosives in the air was there? There was courage in Arjun's eighteen-year-old heart. The world was at his feet then, wasn't it? Knowing that the man who warned him was about to depart from this life and that he had much experience behind him, Arjun still chose to ignore him. At that moment he was like a shining black horse and all he wanted to do was to toss his mane and enter the battlefield.

Many days later, Arjun had come running to Hridayballabh, his heart torn to shreds. At that time Hriday was like a famous, formidable magician who was enthralling the people of the cities and villages with his full, paan shaped, mysterious bride-devi's face. Many idols would be moulded in this image, perhaps by changing a feature or two. He was painting the mystical design of the blue lotus flower in the backdrop and filling the bangles on the arms with earth's fine web of secrets. Hridayballabh listened to Arjun calmly, patted him on the head and pointing to his own breast said, "The more this bleeds the more will your work captivate the eye of man. Who doesn't suffer? Some can speak of their pain, others cannot. . . "

This huge workshop lay dark and empty today. The door was slightly ajar. Some new work was visible inside along with some Kali idols lying unsold from the year before. A wood staircase went to the first floor. Hridayballabh sat and worked there.

'Why was the workshop closed?' Arjun asked himself after having peeped in. Deepu was talking to the owners of the instrument shops in front. One of them called out, "Haven't you heard, the master is sick? He was taken to hospital a day ago."

How strange! Even this door was now closed to him. Lord knows what else the fates had in store for him. Everything was closing in on him.

Arjun had never come with his burdens to this door but each time he went down this lane, his hand would rise automatically to his forehead in salutation.

Hridayballabh had suffered a cerebral stroke. Even if he survived would he ever be able to work like before? This illness caused loss of memory, mobility; the perşon was never the same again. The wound in his breast which had bled and caused his tears to flow, that wound too would disappear from Hridayballabh's mind. Then Hriday would not be able to recognize Arjun even if he saw him, just as Arjun was unable to recognize Deepu in the evening dusk with his long face, slack jaw and dissatisfied look. His own flesh and blood!

⟡ 8 ⟡

The workshop adjacent to the pond did not exist anymore. About fifteen years ago this new workshop had been constructed along the edge of the winding road. Yet God alone knows why Arjun could still see his Didi whenever he stood at the door. In his mind a corner of the workshop was reserved for Kunti. There, just there, Didi would be sitting on her haunches. A sharp nose and eyes, a wheatish complexion. Even if the eyes were not very large they were certainly very sharp. Her face was squarish, unlike most Bengali girls. Her lips used to be sealed tightly together when she worked, as if in an iron grip and clumps of hair would be plastered to her sweat soaked forehead. She would twist the knot of hair high on her head. Arjun had never asked her to come. Didi had come on her own to help her brother. She had an excellent hand for sculpting and could lift moulds with extreme neatness and care. If required she'd even help with the straw binding. Draping the sari, arranging swathes of hair and other womanly tasks were performed by her, without being asked.

When she returned home, a widow, her parents, her brothers, everyone who saw her was appalled to see her face and eyes, dry as cinders. There wouldn't have been a problem if she'd continued to stay with her in-laws for her mother-in-law was a soft hearted good person who loved Kunti like a daughter. However even before her husband's body was taken for cremation, Kunti stopped eating or drinking in that household. As soon as the pall bearers returned from the cremation ground, Kunti requested her father to come and take her away. Rupen Das had not been able to refuse his daughter.

Rupen Das had neglected his responsibilities as the father of the bride. The utensils, clothes etc., had been arranged for by her mother and aunts accompanied by neighbours. The proposal had been brought to them by a distant older cousin. The boy was known to be clever and smart and he worked in a British firm in Chowringhee. He would insert a word or two of English in his speech and this frightened Rupen even more. Relying on the older cousin, Rupen did not make adequate inquiries about the boy's family. This turned out to be a big mistake. Dinanath was a good boy, honest and hardworking but there was no love lost between the brothers. Dinanath was petrified of them. The older one would constantly be up to wicked tricks. Within three years of his marriage his chicken coop had caught fire. It did not even strike Kunti that someone might try to burn to death hundreds of dumb thin chickens which were anyway dying of disease. The burnt wood, the skeletons of the birds, the smell of charred flesh in the air had stunned Dinanath into silence. Kunti had followed her husband when he woke up and went to the coop. She was used to being called brazen by her sisters-in-law.

"They will not let you live here. Let us go away." Kunti whispered to the frightened Dinanath.

"Where can I go, wife?"

"Come let's go to Baba. You can start a new business."

Dinanath's insecurity changed to laughter on his dry, chapped lips. Dinanath's family had been villagers for generations. They lived in mud huts, their paddy, paan, hens were all here. He'd felt claustrophobic in Rupen Das's two room rented home on the one day he'd been there. Kolkata with its big cars whizzing past one's ears, houses crowding on one another, not a whiff of open air anywhere, tiny courtyards, bathrooms placed next to kitchens – how could one stay there?

His stubborn wife was a Kolkata girl. She was as proud as she was strong. It was evident that she couldn't stand her husband being harassed daily.

Within six months of this incident Dinanath was dead. There had been no tension between the brothers at that time, instead they had actually organised a feast together. The sisters too were involved. They had taken Dinu to the venue forcibly. Kunti had not gone, no one had even invited her. Dinanath had died at dawn after throwing up repeatedly and ultimately foaming at the mouth. Kunti had wanted a post mortem but no one heard her at her in-law's home. Before Rupen Das could arrive, Dinanath's last rites were over. The young doctor who had come from the dispensary at dawn had said there had been poison in Dina's stomach.

Since the day Kunti held her father's hand and returned to her home, she never looked back, never went back to her in-laws. Seeing their daughter silenced, like a tree struck by lightening, her Baba and Ma were unable to fathom what to do. Kunti had always been a quiet, grave girl. She never came out and spoke aggressively, never fought in the queues at the water tap. She was a strongly built girl and impossibly efficient. Her older brother, Bheem, was already married. His wife, Shyama did not like being involved in the family's problems. Bheem maintained a separate house, a one room shanty he had taken on rent in the same locality. He worked in the ancestral business, leather. He had also learnt woodwork from his father, Rupen Das, though his work was nowhere as good.

His designs did not 'speak' as did those of his father's, carved with his tired old fingers with their prominent arteries. But Bheem managed to run his household on the little money he earned. Once in a while he and Shyama came to meet Kunti but they were careful to stay aloof from her pain and sorrow. They did not want to get involved.

Seventeen-year-old Arjun had grown up healthy like a chhatim tree which had got plenty of rain water. Kunti had visited her parental home once in a while after she was married. But because she was newly married, had new desires and fancies and would keep looking at her reflection in the mirror staring at her own sindhoor, she had really not looked at her younger brother with any seriousness.

This brother had always been crazy. He did not want to go to school and was always running off to Kumortuli because he loved to get his hands full of clay. Ma had been afraid of this craze and had often told her, "You tell him Kunti. Unless you tell Aju, he will not listen. Does all this suit our caste? He is playing with the gods, bapre, playing with fire!"

Hearing this, a wave of love overwhelmed her. She'd wanted to laugh. It was all a game. The responsibilities of a family had yet to touch him, he still had the protection of a father, an older brother, that is why the little one of the family was able to run around in his craze for mud and straw. Could one do such work all one's life? Who would give Arjun orders? When he would have to stand on his own feet, he would automatically abandon everything and return. Why should Kunti stop him now? Arjun's face would fall, he would stand listening to Kunti with a stiff neck but he would not obey her, so what was the use of berating him now?

So long as her eyes were overshadowed by grief and pain Kunti noticed nothing. Each morning she awoke like an automaton at her mother's call, ate her breakfast and had a bath. Her knotted hair was combed out by Ma. By evening she'd again be lying silently on her bed and the night would pass in nightmare laden sleep. At times she wept aloud and told her father, "They poisoned him and we did nothing about it! Let's go to the police station Baba and lodge a complaint at least!"

Even a thorough gentleman like Rupen Das knew this was impossible. Someone who's been burnt to death, whose parents and siblings had not reported his death, who had instead observed his last rites with great pomp and show–would anyone listen to the complaints of the dead man's widow? It would make people laugh. It was easier to live with the wounds. There were no children, she was young, she could remarry if she so desired.

This was the only way to divert the mind. However, even in the middle of her grief, Kunti noticed that her brother had stopped coming home for meals. Ma was taking dal and rice in a plate to the workshop daily. Did this mean that the boy was eating and sleeping there? But he'd fall sick like this!

It was the month of Paush, the air was chilly even in the city. Lying on thin mats made one cold – did her brother stay outside on a night like this?

It was the season for making Saraswati idols and Arjun was singlehandedly making 45 thakurs. There was no time to bathe or eat. Some poor boys of the locality did help him occasionally but that was only to put things together. One would hold the bowl of paint, another would cover cracks with cloth. None of them felt the thrill of creating dreams in clay. No one had placed any orders so why was Arjun making so many thakurs? He wouldn't get a good price, his artistry would be sold for peanuts. He knew this and yet he was bent on doing this, fighting against all odds.

Once, having woken up at midnight, Kunti walked to the workshop door. She had lived in this locality since her childhood, she knew every lane, yet having stayed indoors for so long, the path seemed to undulate before her eyes like waves. In the pond was reflected the fragmented face of the moon, in fact it seemed as though a couple of stars too were immersed in the cold blue waters. If only Kunti too could sink into the water in the same way!

Because it was so cold, the door of the workshop was closed. That is if you could call it a door, it was a wooden frame wrapped in light bamboo matting. As soon as she pushed it open, her heart leapt up with emotion.

Just beneath the hundred petal lotus of the huge idol created for the Beleghata Youth Sangha, with one arm lifted towards the swan, her brother lay sleeping curled into a ball. His blanket was somewhere near his feet. If he laid out his bed as he did normally, then Arjun would wrap himself in it but today, he'd obviously had no time to make any arrangements and had simply fallen asleep where he lay.

The long hair on Her head would eventually be jet black, right now there were just bundles lying alongside. Her face appeared as peaceful as the moon, and as lacklustre. She seemed to be smiling, an invisible aura seemed to surround Her head. The swans looked as if about to take flight – it was as if Arjun had personally taken care to place every feather. But why would he do that? What bound him to Saraswati, the Goddess of Learning, in this way? The day he passed his seventh standard examination his connection with school was snapped. Lord knows what spell old Ram Pal had cast on him for the boy would spend day after day without any food, at the straw and bamboo godown. Okay, maybe he could have abandoned school, after all even Bheem had stopped studying at a very early age. But did it have to be like this? The leather craftsmen, the carpenters – they too slogged the whole day, but at least they returned home to a meal and a bed to sleep in each night.

All of a sudden, Kunti's eyes began to burn, they filled with tears. In one corner of the room, lay a used plate and bowl, unwashed. Ma had left some food after sunset.

What sort of profession was this? Like a beggar on the streets, no cover on your body, no pillow under your head when you slept! For whom were these lotus petals being crafted so artistically? The beak of the swan being moulded thus? The spectators were just locality kids afterall who sat in the pandals all day, with snot dripping down their faces; and some others who drifted from one pandal to another. Despite all his slogging if the delivery was delayed he would be roundly abused as well! It might be because of unseasonal rain, or lack of money to buy materials, when the reins of his work were not under his own control, how could he work for other people? He was still young. He had neither people to support him, nor any money, yet her brother was already addicted!

'He will die, kill himself and torture us to death as well!' Silently mouthing the words, Kunti covered Arjun with the blanket. She tried to tuck it in as far under him as possible, because his back lay on a cold wooden plank, which he must have placed for his work.

Exhausted, with the smell of mud in his hair, white paint from the Goddess smeared on his cheeks and hands; one could still see his dreams floating around under his half-closed eyelids.

Actually what had attracted Arjun was not the money, or the work or the thrill of making a delivery, but the overwhelming magic of clay – without being able to name it, or understand its shape and form, even Kunti could gauge that this was something unusual, a story in a different language. How many men had this addiction ruined, how many turned into paupers leading lives of renunciation, men who had finally grown old and tired and died, was something Kunti did not know. However, her ties with her younger brother were obviously very strong. For it was this bond which made her realize in the middle of the night, standing in the workshop, that the boy was obsessed and could not be brought back to sanity.

Wrapped only in the cotton aanchal of her sari, Kunti was shivering in the cold. Suddenly she remembered that she had left her own door unlocked. If a thief came he would carry away every pot, pan, shoe that he could lay his hands on. Kunti tip-toed back home.

The next day she woke up late. She drank a cup of tea, quickly ran a comb through her hair, and went to Arjun's workshop.

"Ki re Didibhai?" Arjun was quite surprised to see his Didi. Sorrow darkened Kunti's eyes and face.

Arjun thought Kunti might talk about the past. About her in-laws' home. Details about the complaint that the police had refused to lodge. She would tell her brother, "You, at least, do something." But Kunti did no such thing. Picking up the paint brush she sat down to work on the nails of the Goddess, on the orange beak of the swan, the sari border and other such details, as though she had been doing this work all her life.

After the month of Shravan, life took a huge turn.

Arjun was caught unawares. He had, somehow, managed to put things together on his own and made quite a few small idols – for Annapoorna, the festival of Shiva, and other pujas and even now in one corner of the lane he was engrossed in mixing a deep blue colour in a bowl, for the three and a half feet Kali he had moulded for Kartik puja. It was premature no doubt since he had no orders, no buyer. Yet his very fingers itched to work and so he carried on.

Tridib Basu had taken a taxi to his friend's house on Pottery Road. The friend, Ashim Sen, owned a printing press and since Tridib made advertisements their business relationship soon developed into friendship. At the entrance to Christopher Road his eyes fell on a partially soaked back, hurriedly covering some clay idols with jute sacks in order to save them from the unseasonal rain. Even from that distance Tridib's attention was caught by the single blue palm of a hand, within which was a red glow. He could see the flawlessly shaped fingers. Paying the cab driver, Tridib immediately alighted from the taxi.

The boy was still trying desperately to cover the idols with the torn sacks. His half-wet back was towards Tridib. He made no effort to look back. Gradually Tridib's neck and ears started to get warm, he could feel the heat creeping up.

⋐ 9 ⋑

Arjun did not look at him.

Despite the drizzle, Arjun could see the smoke curling from Tridib's cigarette but it still did not strike him that this impeccably dressed Saheb could possibly have any work with him.

Finally, Tridib had to speak, "Ayee listen, will you tell me your name?"

"My name is Arjun Das." Saying this Arjun pushed the bowl of blue paint under the platform the Goddess stood on.

"Will you make a big idol?"

"When?" Arjun still didn't look surprised. Of course if one was to look closely it was apparent that his nut brown eyes had widened slightly.

Flinging his cigarette to the ground, Tridib wiped his hands on a kerchief. "This Puja. Can you do it?"

Before Arjun could respond, Tridib had already carefully moved aside the torn jute sacking with one hand. The Kali idol was about two-and-a-half feet in height. With keen eyes he critically examined the shape of the face, the small forehead, the two unpainted eyes, the slight crinkles on the sides of the lips, the protruding tongue.

"Is the mould your own?"

"Yes, sir." Arjun's face seemed to glow.

Tridib was finding it difficult to believe him. Yet, in the young man standing before him, in his stance, in the self-confidence and conviction reflected from every muscle in his dark body, in the erect firmness of his backbone – Tridib saw a unique human being.

Every year at Puja time, Tridib had to visit Kumortuli to order the thakur. He was familiar with the famous and expensive elderly sculptors who'd been making idols for the Sanskriti Sansad for years – he knew their methods, their ways, their creations. He had been the President of the Puja Committee for the last ten years and more. Even if he'd wanted to resign, the Sanskriti Sansad was not willing to let him go. This boy was like a breath of much needed fresh air. "Is the mould your own?"

Tridib realized his mistake as soon as he asked the question a second time. In an instant Arjun's face became still, the light went out of it.

"The mould, the face, everything is inside. You can have a look."

Arjun raised his hand and pointed to the door of the studio at the edge of the pond.

"What does your father do?" Tridib was carefully scrutinizing every garland around the hands and waist of the Goddess.

"He makes shoes."

The words whizzed past Tridib's ears at full speed, like a brickbat.

The voice belonged to a high-spirited female.

The sun was trying to shine now that the rain had finally stopped.

Tridib turned around to see Kunti. She had just appeared around the turn in the lane. At her hip was a pile of washed utensils. Even if it was not clear that she was the boy's sister, the fact that the two were cast in the same strong mould, was not difficult to gauge. On the dark skin was etched a sharp nose and mouth. Thin lips. The shape of the face slightly square. Her forehead and hair parting were vacant and empty, yet there was the glow of health in her gait and posture.

"We are chamars, Babu. If you commission work, do so only after carefully weighing the pros and cons. Don't break the heart of a young boy."

Arjun had not looked at his Didi. Nor had he asked her to keep quiet. Therefore, one could conclude that he agreed with Kunti's statements. Only the line 'Don't break the heart of a young boy' had caused his shoulders to shake.

As soon as Tridib Basu looked at Arjun, he said, "My Didibhai".

Kunti did not wait. She was already making her way home with all the utensils. She had left, having lashed Tridib's face with an invisible whip.

"What is there to be worried about? I am the Puja Committee President. Arjun, this time you will mould our Durga idol. We are a very old club, Sanskriti Sansad, you must have heard the name? I draw pictures myself, commercial art. I will tell you roughly what kind of an idol we want. You will be paid a lump sum of Rupees Three Hundred, no advance."

Arjun's heart lost some of its zest on hearing that there would be no advance. Maybe the huge stars in his eyes dimmed a little. But then he really wasn't in the mood to calculate so much. That this was one of the greatest moments of his life, was something he was well aware of. The Sanskriti Sansad Puja was one of the oldest pujas, and a very grand one at that. In those days elaborate pandals and excessive lighting were not indications of pomp and grandeur. In fact coloured cellophane wrapped light bulbs were still to catch on. The Sanskriti Sansad had sitar and shehnai playing throughout the four Puja days. The recitation of the mantras and the performing of the rituals and ceremonies were as flawless as a traditional Bengali family puja. Occupying a large space around the pavilion were painting exhibitions, and highly reputed drummers would come from Midnapore to liven up the celebrations. Idols made by Dharanidhar Pal were ordered for this Puja, at least that had been the norm for the last three-four years. Last year, Arjun himself had gone and seen the Sanskriti Sansad Puja. Did this mean that Dharnidhar Pal would not be making the idol this time? What would the Puja Committee tell him then? So was this whole thing for real? Arjun almost wanted to pinch himself and see if it was true. Surely, someone had played a prank on him!

No, there lay the cigarette on the ground. The gentlemen had snuffed out the cigarette with his foot. Tridib Basu was going to return. He would personally come and draw pictures to make Arjun understand certain specific requirements in the idol that the Puja Committee wished for. He had only told Arjun to keep the matter secret. No one should get to know where the idol was going. Not even members of his own family.

On his way back, sitting in the taxi, Tridib Basu was thinking, how quickly he'd made a discovery today from such a delicate source. A living sculptor – working away at his craft at the corner of some lane, absorbed in his own world. Just suppose Tridib's eyes had not fallen on that blue palm? Each and every artist had his own patents, his exclusive trademark or hallmark. Without an artistic eye, it was difficult to search these out. The palms and arms of both Ramesh Pal and Jiten Pal's Durga idols were flawless, delicate. Each finger had life flowing through it. Yet even these moulded hands had the gravity of clay. It was the robustness of the female form and an amazing crimson glow, which had caught his eye even from a distance.

Tridib remembered that in his youth he had passed the entrance of Kumortuli Lane quite often as he travelled north in a bus. His paternal aunt, Pishima, used to stay near Hathibagan in those days. He had to teach Bangla to his aunt's daughter who'd just arrived from Patna. At the entrance to the lane was Gana Pal's workshop. He was poor but hardworking – Lord knows how many idols he moulded for a living. There would be no balance in the form, a slim waist would be wiped out by a heavy shoulder and neck. The most painful sight was to see rows of hands sticking out of the workshop – hands that had been moulded carelessly and in a hurry, their fingers joined together. Even if they were separated with a flat thin bamboo scalpel at the lower end, the top of the fingers remained stuck together. That this inexpert hand-moulding artist would be fighting a useless battle all his life was something Tridib had gauged as far back as that. Gana Pal had been obliterated at the beginning of the sixties. Maybe he had left to join in some other battle along with his whole family!

Arjun had only told Didi the news, no one else. He had already collected straw and clay. It would have been really good if he could have got some money as well. It went against Arjun's pride to even ask his father for money to buy materials. Most of what he had earned during the Chaitra trading season, was kept with Didi. He would have to take some of that for the time being

Arjun was ready with straw and string to fill the mould. He had got wood and bamboo for the frame. The month of Shravan was at its end yet Tridib had not returned. Arjun could feel a cloud of fear and disappointment gather inside him. He did not utter a word but Didi understood the situation. Lifting up a Kali face mould she said, "The whims and fancies of the rich! They come and disappear like the wind! After exciting you, he quickly went away." Didi's fingers were as firm as they were soft. There would be no trace of clay on the sides of the moulds, she lifted up the freshly moulded face with expertise.

Actually neither Arjun nor Kunti had any idea of the fight Tridib had to put up to plead his case before the Puja Committee.

Kunti had thrown a challenge to Tridib by mentioning their caste. Tridib was himself an artist, on top of which he was a thorough gentleman. If it had been anyone else, he would have withdrawn immediately. The deal would not have even reached the idol-ordering stage. He had seen the boy's work, he had liked it, he would have praised him, and come away. At the most he could have said, "Ish, is that true, brother? Achcha, then let me just first place the matter at a meeting, and if they agree, I will come and place the order."

Kunti's words had actually cut Tridib to the quick. 'Whatever you do, think over it seriously. Don't break the heart of a child.' With the pride and perception of the upper middle-class, Tridib had lapped up the words. He was after all the Puja Committee President. That too not out of choice, but under the insistence of others. Could there possibly be the fear that he might have to take back his promise?

Back in his neighbourhood, when the pulsating blood in his veins had calmed down a little, Tridib again thought over the whole matter. The first task was to ask Dharani Pal not to make the idol this time. Of course, the reason the order had not been placed at the end of the month of Ashar, was because Dharani Pal had not been in town. A businessman from Birbhum had taken Pal's whole team to Sheuri, to make a model of the story of the Mahabharata on the walls of the courtyard of his home. The epic was to be depicted in terracotta, the pictures had to be the kind that would remain etched in your mind for ever. What would he say to Dharani Pal?

For the present at least, Arjun's identity and background needed to be kept a secret. Tridib had no doubts that he would put his life and soul into making a unique idol, but suppose the Thakur did not ultimately impress the people? Then it would become difficult to procure Pal's services the next time round. The only reasons for hesitation Tridib had thought, was because Arjun was just a young, nameless artist. Even when he got back to his colony the matter of his caste did not enter Tridib's head. Mother earth was always pure. Once a clay idol had been ceremonially awakened, you could worship it. Who moulded the idol, what was his race, his identity were all secondary matters. What was important was life and beauty.

However, when he was about to broach the subject, he realized his arguments were not very powerful ones. He was also doubtful as to how socially acceptable the matter of his own belief and emotions would be to the people. The whole committee was not present, but still Tridib put up the proposal at the evening get-together.

"This time the Thakur will be in a completely different style, you understand! You will be totally awestruck."

Turning the pages of the *Basumati* in a dispirited manner, Montu Mitra, the Vice-President of the Puja Committee, had said, "They had gone to Dharani da."

"When?"

"Day before. Dharani da is back from Sheuri."

"No, no, not Dharani da. I am getting a new artist this time."

Montu Mitra did not even raise his eyes, of course even if he had, nothing would be revealed since his eyes were invisible under dark glasses.

"Dhoosh! Forget all that, will you!" Again there was the rustling of the *Basumati.*

"No, no, I have given my word."

"Take it back. It will not work."

"What do you mean, it won't work?"

Tridib Basu was irritated and agitated. What was this? If they didn't listen to him, he couldn't remain in the post of President, could he? He would have to step down.

"We cannot let go of Dharani Pal." Montu Mitra confidently made this statement and left.

On the other side of the room, a shaded lamp hung suspended from the ceiling. Its mellow buttery light softly enveloped the old carrom-board. Four elderly men sat on four sides; a game was in progress. Bijon Mukherji said, "What are you saying Tridib? You want to bring a new kind of Thakur this time – Bring one, do. Why don't you give a design to Dharani Pal – you are after all an artist yourself! He too can make it for you."

"That is not the point, Bijon da. I have discovered a very talented boy. He is very young. Just nineteen-twenty years old. This time we can try experimenting. . . ."

"One can't experiment, friend, with public money."

Saying which Bijon took the red counter in a trice. On the opposite side, Satyesh Nandi had been eyeing the red counter for a long time. Now he stuck his tongue between his teeth and lamented the loss. He had the habit of turning the nape of his neck and shoulders and cracking his bones, *mot, mot, mot,* as though someone was bending a clump of bamboos.

"Where else is the boy supplying idols?" asked Satyesh.

"Nowhere!"

"Nowhere! Ha ha ha!"

The laughter of the four old greyheads caused the yellow light to sway. Scratching his bald pate, Bijit Ray said "These matters can lead to scandals and things, you know Tridib! Who will make the idol and why. You are an artist, and understand only art. I have heard in many localities they take commission from the sculptor."

This tug of war continued for about fifteen days. Meetings were held. Montu Mitra banged on the table.

"You have to give us the boy's name. We will go and see his work."

But if Arjun's name and address was disclosed, their shanty, their workshop – everything might just disappear.

Across Montu Mitra's forehead was a deep scar. Last winter he had been beaten up and left lying in a drain. His hangers-on had not been able to come close out of fear. It may have been the work of those whom Montu Mitra defined as the offspring of Mao-Tse-Tung or Marx.

It would have been much simpler and more dignified to have resigned from the Committee, but then Tridib's obstinacy had grown, and so he had to stick on, persevere.

"The name can't be given."

"Why? Why?"

"Let that remain a surprise!"

At the end of Shravan, Tridib suddenly appeared one day. The taxi halted at the entrance of Christopher Road.

Arjun was not at the workshop. He was at home, wondering whether he should accompany his father to the leather mart. The naked and tremendously enthusiastic urchins of the lane came screaming to call him.

Tridib, the last time round had stood at the head of the lane just for ten minutes. But even that had not escaped the eyes of the children. They played the whole day, but they watched everything.

Today, placing his hand on Arjun's back, Tridib drew him closer by informally calling him tui.

"Mould such an idol, that ten other Clubs will be left looking at it in wonder. This is going to be a real challenge for us, you do understand, don't you? For you and for me!"

Arjun's eyes lit up with joy and enthusiasm.

Now he and Tridib Basu formed a separate group. Tridib had carried paper and pencil with him. He drew the way he wanted the Devi's fist to be. He showed him how the index-finger of the open hand and the little finger were to be moulded in a different style. The conchshell had to be made with clay, so too the serpent. Loose hair, a gold crown, with a moon on it.

Arjun heard and understood everything.

What Tridib did not describe, Arjun managed to create out of the depths of his own calm strength. A never before seen woman.

On the fifth day of the Durga festival, in the morning, bringing a truck to carry the idol, the Sanskriti Sansad saw the completely new, unique, awe inspiring sculpture.

Wearing a buttery yellow silk sari, with the same coloured aanchal flying in the wind, was a Bengali girl. Her face was a little squarish in shape, the complexion wheatish, sharp nose, compressed lips, her eye-brows like flying wings. It was impossible to gauge how much she had suffered in her in-laws' home before leaving it. After all, the one whom she had cherished fondly like a mother, that artist had placed a gold crown on her head, adorned with a curved moon.

Next to the cascade of buttery yellow, quite suddenly appeared dense black – not the Bangla buffalo – this girl was holding the horn of a wild African buffalo, her hand in a slightly curved gesture. The buffalo's neck was hanging broken. Emerging from this bleeding neck, the Asura appeared to have collapsed at the feet of that girl. What amazing movement! What a contrast between the black and buttery yellow! The whole method and style was pathbreaking in conception.

Montu Mitra, Bijit Ray, and Bijon Mukherji examined the

impeccable gestures of the fingers on the ten hands, the crimson
glow of the palms, the extraordinary details of the toe-nails,
the individual finish of every tooth inside the open-mouthed
lion. . . .

This was the first time educated gentlemen had stood in the
dirty hole called Christopher Road, and looked at such
wondrous beauty. Gradually their eyes lowered to take in the
reality of the narrow alley and the bodies of the naked urchins.
Standing amidst the cow dung cakes stuck on the walls, the
piles of garbage and the buzz of flies they suddenly realized –
this was not Kumortuli. The people who lived here were
untouchables, who were not even allowed to serve food to the
upper castes. And this strange dark boy – he had not even
greeted the gentlemen as yet, or even asked them to be seated.
Of course, where could he have offered to seat them? Were
there any chairs here, indeed could gentlemen sit here?

Arjun had to accompany the lorry. That was the custom.
After offloading the Thakur in the pandal, if it was found that
an elbow or an ear had broken, then these had to be repaired
immediately. Such damage was possible of course during the
course of transporting it in a rattling lorry, or even in the
loading and unloading process.

Arjun went along, carrying with him a little clay, his rag
cloth, brush and some paint.

Tridib Basu was not present. Arjun felt a little pang of
disappointment. The fear of disrespect too was threatening to
engulf him.

However, nothing had broken. Not the Thakur's hands,
nor the ears of their mounts. But just before making the
payment Montu Mitra and his young hangers-on decided they
wanted to have juslas and ice-cream sodas along with a tobacco
preparation and paan.

"Ayee, just give twenty-five rupees from that," called out

Montu Babu. "Why are you rummaging around for it, there it is in Nyapa's hands, take it."

Arjun was still waiting. An Arjun who had only eaten a little rice very early in the morning, who had been unable to bathe and was covered in dust.

"Here, take this brother, we have cut twenty-five rupees to eat paan etc."

Leaving the remaining amount in Nyapa's hand Arjun came away. Apart from the money he'd already spent for this work, he and Baba and Didi had put in two months of hard labour into this job. Yet it didn't take Arjun five seconds to form all of this into a ball and chuck it out of his consciousness.

Behind him, a hushed uproar broke out amidst the crowd.

Nyapa was stunned. In all this commotion, someone had thoughtfully gone and called Tridib from his house. Tridib was able to calm Arjun down, and he left after treating him to sweets from Shakti Moira's shop. Seeing the idol in the pandal, he was awed and overjoyed. Such revolutionary work had not come to this neighbourhood in a very long time. Tridib's detractors, unable to recover from their shock and awe, were temporarily silenced.

But the flames almost extinguished, did not die out completely.

On Ashtami, the morning of the eighth day a small child, who'd been sitting very close to the idol through the day exclaimed, "Oh wow, Asura is wearing leather garments."

The words were not very important, but they pricked the ears of the senior priest.

Now thanks to the garlands, the moonlike necklace and other religious offerings, could one actually make out, whether it was really animal leather? Or whether it was actually touching the Goddess' body?

Tridib arrived. He'd been summoned. Carefully Tridib

scrutinized the idol. Yes, it really was leather!

It was possible that Arjun hadn't even realized the implications. He was so far removed from religion and society that he was unaware that one could not use leather here.

"Where did the sculptor find leather?"

In answer to this question, Montu Mitra glibly informed them, "Over there, leather is available all around! It's a leather mart! Nyapa and all say skinning cows is the profession of this caste."

In seconds the Sanskriti Sansad pavilion began to seethe. The Hemanta Mukherji and Bismillah records stopped playing. Offerings to the Goddess dried up. Renouncing the attractions of a good remuneration, clothes, and silk dhotis, the senior priest said, he could not worship an idol made by a cow slayer. He left straight away.

The Puja was completed by somehow persuading the junior priest with various assurances, but there was no joy in the proceedings. The priest had to be literally begged to do the job. After all a Puja that had commenced, as soon as the ceremonial awakening had been performed, had to be completed!

Bijon Mukherji's elderly mother, who even at the age of eighty-five applied sindhoor in the parting between her grey hair, and sat next to the senior priest and performed puja work for all four days, was never able to stand up again. She took to her bed, she almost lost her speech, and on Ekadashi, the eleventh day her soul left her body.

A remorseful Tridib had rushed across, but an aunt waved her hand, warning him not to come close. There were tears falling constantly from her eyes. Boroma had just not been able to accept Tridib's beliefs and opinions – one who skinned animals, would never be forgiven by Bhagwati, the Goddess Durga, and to worship a Thakur made by one such. . . .

Tridib stepped down from the Puja Committee. But the collective feeling of guilt and fear at having sinned, and a mostly simulated anxiety did not abate. Who was going to absolve them of this great sin?

Sitting in his home in Uttarpara, the senior priest pronounced his ruling – Akal-bodhon, a reawakening. To save them from the sin of having allowed the idol to be moulded and touched by a cow-slayer and Shudra, a low caste untouchable, the Devi had to be awakened once more. In the month of Chaitra, by performing Basanti Durga Puja in spring, the sins would hopefully be absolved. This time the idol maker would not even be Dharani Pal – but Gopal Chakravarty, the son of a Brahmin.

Arjun bending over his luchi and meat curry feast on the Ashtami day, never even knew when the falchion had lowered itself over him.

In the month of Chaitra, the beats of the drums sounded, celebrating the Akal-bodhon, at the Sanskriti Sansad Basanti Puja. Arjun who was too busy concentrating on making small Chait-Kalis for personal prayer fulfillments, remained completely unaware of the significance. Why Tridib Basu had never returned was something he did wonder about once in a while. Of course, it was another matter, that Arjun may not have recognized the worn out and prematurely aged Tridib even if he had appeared.

☞ 10 ☜

One afternoon, in the month of Kartik, Swapnabha was stretched out on his mother's bed. He lay with his two hands clasped together under his head. It was a time when calm seemed to descend from the blue skies and the entire world seemed to be bathed in this. Swapnabha was imbibing the scents of the afternoon with his eyes shut and his ears alert. There was no noise anywhere. Not a sound of the trams and buses on the main road could be heard in their house. Old Ballygunge Road. Through the window was visible a deep blue afternoon sky, dazzling like steel. Occasionally a bird could be heard calling plaintively, continuously and then there was quiet again. Was it a dove? There was a picture too of a deserted homestead overrun by doves. Had Swapnabha's surroundings turned as silent and peaceful as that? There was the sound of rickshaws passing down the lane. From the body of these hand-drawn rickshaws emerged a kind of rasping and grating sound. It seemed as though some gigantic spider was walking along, it's bones creaking.

It was an old bed. Polished black. At its head placed against the wall was a flower, like the opening of a bolster-cover. The waves on the two flanks came down to the side posts of the bed. Swapnabha and the others called this rather heavy and high bed 'Mother's bed'. Swapnabha, however, had never seen his mother lying on it. Actually Swapnabha had never seen his mother at all. The name Swapnabha, meant that he was the dream that his mother had barely fulfilled on earth, and disappeared into thin air thereafter. In any case, before his birth at least Ma had been here, on this bed, in this house.

His maternal grandma, Didima, had brought him up. Fed him and lit wicker lamps for him. In between it had even occurred to his father's fancy to bring a new mother for him. Swapna was then eight or nine. The new Ma did not last in the house for more than a year. She had an important job, and was quite arrogant. Finally Baba and the new Ma had possibly fought each other on the issue of sending Swapna to boarding school. Baba was not agreeable to sending Swapna anywhere outside the home. The new Ma too left in a huff. Then began the divorce proceedings, paper work, court appearances – the way such things generally happened. Untying the knot of his tie, on his return from office, Swapna's father had pulled him close, saying "You are fated not to have anyone but your father, you poor idiot." Baba sometimes called Swapna an idiot, because he used to stare blankly out of the window into the far distance, instead of studying. Anyway, since then it had been just Baba and Swapna, Swapna and Baba.

When he lay silently on her bed, Swapna imagined he could sense his biological mother's aroma filling the whole room. He felt that suddenly his mother would appear in the room. Fearful that he might lose his Ma, Swapna would startle himself into opening his eyes every so often. Suppose Ma was to appear, today, what would she tell Swapna? Surely she would not have scolded or reproached him for having lost his job?

Swapna would have left the job anyway. Maybe in another week or so. But before he could do so Avinash Samtani had shown him the door. Just thinking of this made Swapnabha squirm in frustration. In life a sense of timing was very important. If you delayed even a little, the opposition would flatten you out. If Swapna had not gone to Delhi, his timing would have been absolutely perfect. But Avinash had laughingly said in Hindi, "Roy, this job can only be done by you. No one else. You'd better go to Delhi." Swapna had thought he would resign as soon as he returned from Delhi. The pride, that just before resigning he had successfully handled a difficult task for the company, would be concealed in the drama of his exit. But Avinash was no fledgling businessman, even though he might have been a second-rate engineer. The anxieties of those he had given jobs to, did not normally trouble him, as their existence never really affected any of his decisions. The minute the case had been successfully processed in Delhi,

Avinash had put together a cheque for Swapna's pay for twenty days and other dues, along with a formal letter.

This morning he had gone rather early to the office. Samtani was more or less free between nine and ten in the morning. That was when he called someone or the other to his office. Purchase, Sales, Export, Documentation – from all these different departments he summoned various executives. Once a week, on Wednesdays, there was a planning meeting, with all the departments present. From eleven onwards Samtani's phone would start ringing. He had yet to enjoy all the pleasures this city had to offer. At one time, he would get up only at one in the afternoon with a yawn. Now he sat up at ten. At eleven all the different phones both landlines and mobiles, of different colours and shapes, would start ringing. Avinash had four phones. One was an inter-com, one a tele-fax, the third just a phone, the fourth a mobile. As soon as you entered the room, on the right hand side was a wallpaper of the deep blue sea at Kovalam beach. The Kolkata sky and the shining top of high rise buildings were visible through the slats of the Venetian blinds behind the table. This high up, there was no greenery of trees. Maybe one or two eagles flew past as they split the sky with their mournful calls.

If anyone entered Avinash's room between eleven and one that person would have to face this kind of a situation. Initially it had happened to Swapnabha, now it didn't.

"Avinash, do you think the drawings. . . "

Phone. "Excuse me, please. . . .Yes, yes, Subburaj. . . ."

"Avinash, if we submit the drawings, then. . . ."

Phone. "Sorry, friend. Yes, Veenu, no, check it at the port. . ."

"If the drawings are submitted, there is still a risk, the production department has not cleared them as yet. . . "

Phone. "Excuse me. Vimla, my dear wife, please, I will call you – in five minutes – Yes Roy, what were you saying?"

After every word the phone rang. It was jarring. It completely destroyed one's line of thought. Then one had to pick up the threads again and proceed. Swapna found it very irritating. Nowadays, there was no place where the mobiles did not start ringing, no place where a mobile ring would not destroy the flow of thought. They rang in a doctor's chambers, cinema halls, poetry readings, in fact even at music concerts. Why, Swapna felt, did people who were chased everywhere by other voices, even look for entertainment or go to enjoy the fine arts? They obviously did not have the time.

Swapna now voluntarily never went to Avinash after eleven. It was another matter if he was summoned. To avoid the strident authority of the phones, the first thing Swapna did at nine-thirty, was to go to Avinash's room. He was going to first brief him on the Delhi matter. But, even before he could enter the room – something that had never happened before, Cecil, Avinash's secretary, with a telling expression on her lips, halted his entry. Meaning, do not enter!

"What's up?" Swapna was a little annoyed. "Is the boss still busy?"

Cecil pursed her blood-red painted lips, and said, "Return to your desk. You will be called back."

No explanation, not even an apologetic tone; Swapna got the impression, Cecil was giving him orders. She was, it seemed, softly rebuking a little boy.

He had always entered his own cubicle first thing every morning. He would drink a cup of black coffee, relaxing in his seat for a short while. Then he checked his previous day's mail, email and recorded phone messages. If Avinash did not call him, he immediately started doing the day's work.

Returning to his desk, he found the letter lying on top of his in-coming letter tray. The company name was printed on expensive paper, the envelope carried with it the stamp of gravity. It was a long envelope. Was it a little scented as well? For a moment Swapna had been a little perplexed by Cecil's blood-red lips, the irritation evident on her frowning forehead and the hint of intolerance. He lifted the envelope and sniffed it.

The envelope was sealed in such a way, that it opened as soon as he picked it up. On a folded white paper was a letter. It had been signed by Avinash himself in his usual way, 'Avi'. He had written one long statement – "From tomorrow, the company does not require your services any more." 'Avi', that is Avinash Samtani. In the beginning, when Swapna had seen letters, signed by him, this signature of Avinash's had seemed so very intimate and friendly. How it was possible to be spurned by a person in a friendly manner, was something one would never be able to understand except when it happened to oneself. Swapna, too understood that now, through his own experience. With the letter was a cheque. Stapled to it was a slip of paper detailing the particulars. Swapna's pay till the evening of his return from Delhi, along with other dues accrued to him. Swapna was initially tempted like the movie heroes of the forties, to tear the cheque into bits and throw it away. He then controlled himself. By doing this, Avinash in fact would actually save some money. It would make him quite happy. Swapnabha did not intend to give Avinash any cause for pleasure.

Carefully he placed the cheque in his briefcase. Folding the letter four times, he tore it up. Putting the shreds into an envelope, labeling it with Avinash Samtani's name, he left it in the Despatch Tray. Then softly, pushing the door open he entered the lobby. The sun, air, the blue sky outside seemed at this moment to be limitless. The company had made a minor mistake in calculating his dues. His cheque had about Rs 2500 less in it. This intensified Swapnabha's self-satisfaction. Let it be, Avinash could buy the production staff shoes and umbrellas with that money. Out in the lobby, his two eyes took some time to adjust to the normal blue lights. There were a variety of lights in the office. Neon, halogen, visible, hidden. Different kinds of shadows and lights played about the inner passages and cubicles. There were three offices on three sides of the lobby. However, in the space in-between, through the skylight at the staircase the golden light of day came streaming in. For the first time Swapnabha felt that the aim of these offices was to somehow obstruct this natural beauty.

Swapnabha walked to the lift. As soon as he stood in front of the door, it swung silently open. Normally many people hurtled out of it. This time there was only one girl. Initially Swapna could not recall the girl's name. Then he remembered – Anandi.

Swapna thought for a moment to ask her, 'where are you going?' But that may not seem appropriate. What if he asked if she was coming to see him? That too would not sound proper. Of the three offices, Anandi could have work in any one of them. In the beginning of course, Anandi had come to see him. At their office.

Putting an end to speculation, Anandi herself asked, "Are you going out somewhere?"

The answer to this question was neither yes nor no. He certainly was going out, forever. But if he said that it would sound too dramatic. Looking at him for a few moments, Anandi said, "I was coming to you."

Two large eyes faced him. Even if kohl had not been applied, the eyes looked as though traces of last night's kohl were still present. The girl had a very direct way of looking at people. As though she could pin them down.

Swapna said, "Let's go down."

There was no one else but them in the lift. The back of

reprimanded. He had always done whatever he had wanted to do at any given time. Once, when he was about ten years old, Swapna had expressed a wish to learn to play the fiddle. Baba had even bought him one. Not the clay one, but a real one. The fiddle did not play any tune when Swapna's fingers touched it, in fact within a few days it broke into pieces. Baba had packed up the broken pieces of the fiddle in its case and kept it away, yet had not scolded Swapna.

Swapna sorted out things in his own head in detail. Swapna's ethics had never matched those of Avinash Samtani's company, 'The Millenium Systems.' It had about it an eye-catching glow, yet within lay innumerable manipulations and a host of dishonest dealings. Documents were prepared according to requirements. The export documentations were full of lacunae. To push sales, agents were employed and cash deposits were entrusted to them – yet, how come none of the other executives seemed to have any worries regarding the company's work ethics. They were quite happy and satisfied as long as they managed to achieve their targets and preserve their outputs. Swapnabha realized that somehow he was just not being able to detach himself from these internal matters. All his work, his output, performance, everything seemed to be getting mixed up in the company's ethics. If he continued here, Swapnabha would not remain Swapnabha anymore, he would turn into a Vijay Aggarwal or a Neeta Arora or even a Biku Mukherji.

On his visit to Delhi, he realized how different in actuality external and internal matters were. The expert the company wanted to bring in next month for their license case, was to retire in six months but despite this his greed caused him to salivate. He would come and stay in a five-star hotel in Kolkata, that too under a false name, because service rules did not permit it. His job was to make false recommendations to the license committee, in order to pass the case. Swapna had no idea of the rate he had fixed with the company. In fact, Swapna had no idea that there *were* problems in their case. Then why the payment, and the hospitality? Swapna had carried all the drawings and documents with him in order to explain things to the expert. The expert heard him, understood everything, and putting his hand on Swapna's shoulder, said "Everything is okay, the rest I will discuss with Avinash." This obviously meant that Swapna's visit was either a cover up or a masquerade.

The last ten years had brought in globalization. It was being said that the license-raj which gave quotas, privileges and control to the chosen few would soon be a thing of the past. However, those who had guarded this huge fiefdom so jealously for so long were reluctant to let go. There seemed to be a rush to grab whatever little remained at the bottom of the pail. It was an ugly picture.

Anandi was looking for one man in this thick jungle. Actually, not the man himself but his forgotten story. And she was an intelligent girl, certainly not crazy.

Tomonash, a college friend of Swapna, had called to tell him about Anandi. Anandi would come to meet him one day, in the office. She wanted to speak to Amulya Jethu, his father's elder cousin, who used to be in the Special Branch at the end of the sixties. Swapna had remembered immediately but he did not even know where Amulya Jethu lived now. It was a long time since he had been in contact with any of his father's brothers. Let him first locate his Uncle, only then could Anandi meet him.

Anandi had come to Swapna's office with Tomonash's reference. She had come in so early one day that when Swapna entered his cubicle the first thing he saw was a head covered with shaggy hair and the check pattern on the back of her dress. Anandi was seated on his chair.

Some years ago, when Swapna's hair was not cropped so

short and he was much slimmer, possibly Swapna too had looked like Anandi when he sat on the chair. Since it was someone else's chair, Anandi sat on just half of it. Swapna brought in a chair from the next room and sat down. Why, he thought as he stood at the door, that was himself sitting on the chair! For a moment his heart had leapt up from within.

What Anandi had set out to look for was a truth she would never find. However, it was her search that had attracted Swapna. Anandi had grown up, she was independent; the man whose history she was looking for, her father, was someone she had never seen. But Anandi's own roots were buried in that unseen soil. Achcha. Swapna too had never seen his mother. How come he had never felt the need to search for her? Anandi's losing her father was so intricately mixed up in the process of deconstructing society and history that she just had to search for him. Swapna's mother was not taken away from him by time, that's why she was still with him.

Swapna knew that he was unconsciously involving Anandi in various ways with his own life, and looking at her from different perspectives.

☞ 11 ☜

Swapnabha had gone to sleep. He sat up with a start when his father called out to him. The clock showed it was four p.m. A yellowish-orange glow lit up the wall. It was a strange evening. Swapnabha suddenly realised, that he had never seen this light on the walls. It struck him that he was not supposed to be at home at this time.

Possibly it was Baba who had drawn a sheet over him. Wiping the sweat on his neck in a sleepy voice Swapnabha asked, "Have you eaten?"

"Long ago. Did you eat in office?"

Swapnabha was suddenly very hungry. He had not eaten in office as he usually did. When he'd returned home, he had seen the food kept on the table – it was his father's afternoon meal. He knew it would be their dinner as well, so, if he ate some now it may not suffice for their evening meal. He was now rolling on the bed with hunger. Of course it was also possible that the blow of losing his job had wiped out his hunger. Perhaps he himself hadn't realized this.

Baba came forward and placed a hand on his forehead. It was clear that he was very worried. Returning home in the afternoon, he had seen his son lying on his bed – this had never happened in Baba's life. To prove that he was well and strong, Swapna sat up straight and said "I am making some bread-omelette. You'll eat some?"

"Dur!" Baba's cheeks creased into a laugh, "Omelette at this time? Bolu fed me a lot."

Bolu was Baba's post-office agent.

For some strange, totally unnecessary reason Baba had distributed his savings in various post-office schemes and it was Bolu who kept track of them, for example when a Rs 3,200 savings scheme matured into Rs 8,700. On one monthly scheme Baba got Rs 377 from one pass book and Rs 550 from another. Bolu knew all this. Baba had a good handwriting but still all the papers were filled in by Bolu. Swapna knew that Baba had got himself entangled in these complicated schemes only to help his childhood friend. Baba seemed to enjoy standing in long serpentine queues on Saturdays and arguing with the eternally irritated staff at the counters in order to withdraw money! Despite the cobwebs and dirt that lay thick over piles of papers, the drone of ceiling fans, the need to give a day's notice to withdraw Rs 10,000, Baba's devotion to the post-office remained unshaken. He often said, "Do you know it is because such an institution exists that a two-rupee postcard can still be distributed."

How agitated Bolu and Baba got when the Central Government brought down the interest rate on postal savings!

How much anger and abuse was thrown at the invisible government! Why did they reduce the interest, what would happen to the fixed income group? Why had such an anti-people decision been taken? What would have been the harm in a dual interest scheme being maintained – all these and other questions were discussed by the two of them, through Sunday afternoon, over a meal of khichuri, rice and lentils cooked with lots of vegetables, along with a sweet chutney of dates and tomatoes. Swapna had already eaten his pizza. He'd found it very amusing – to watch the two old men making various calculations. Yet the very next day at an Exporters Meet at the Grand Hotel, Swapna's heart had suffered a jolt.

From Delhi had come officers of the Ministry of Finance and Commerce. Welcoming them the Chairman of the Traders Association, Sushil Jhunjhunwala began by saying, "After all these days, the Government has finally shown some good sense. By reducing the interest rate, they have proved that they have some business sense. Now trade will increase." Swapnabha was seated in a row at the back, as the representative of a small exporter. Avinash was then somewhere in Dubai or Moscow. Swapna suddenly realised that Avinash and Baba were on opposite sides of the interest rate, in two different worlds. Their ideas and decisions were completely in opposition to each other.

The Government was actually not on the side of the Bolus – even though he knew this very well in his mind and heart, Swapna was finding it very difficult to accept this.

The history of Avinash's rise was so new, that even Swapna knew almost all of it.

An ordinary student, he had become an engineer by paying a huge capitation fee. As recent as seven years back he'd been doing the rounds of offices carrying his briefcase in his hands. Then, along with a friend, he became an agent for exporters. From an agent he rose up to the ranks of an exporter. By then the fruit had already turned rotten. Avinash had become an expert at dishonest practices. On the other hand, Swapnabha had a degree in Economics, and he'd done his MBA by joining a course after office hours. He was also a computer wizard. He was not a production person but Avinash consulted him on many production matters. Swapnabha looked after the export planning and management but if a complicated case had to be explained to the Committee then he was sent. This was because Swapnabha's command over the English language was very good. At one or two places, Avinash had lied and said Swapnabha was an engineer. As a result, Swapnabha sometimes found himself in an awkward position being forced into embarrassing denials. By denying, of course, he lost his own credibility, not the company's.

The last five years had been a steady history of climbing up the ladder for Avinash. The deeper the roots of globalization extended, the more the laws of income became lax, generating widespread intrigue in the name of export activities. The person who brought foreign exchange home, was above all suspicion. Avinash had increased his margins by fooling everyone into following this code. Now one did not require intelligence, not even hard work. Even pride in one's pedigree was not of much use. Now all that was required was cunning, and speed, and dishonesty and fraudulent practices like benami and hawala.Once in a while there had been strained relations with Avinash regarding these matters. Avinash was the owner of the company, Swapnabha was only an employee. It was obvious that the company would not be run on his terms. But in spite of knowing this Swapnabha did not give up without argument. He had tried through reason and fact to make Avinash understand that he was going the wrong way. Avinash had listened to him with a stiff jaw and creased eyebrows. At such moments, Avinash had found Swapnabha unbearable. He had actually wanted to crush him under his shoes. Like one treats a cigarette butt thrown on the ground. But Avinash had surprisingly never protested. Unless he gave a person a long leash, how could he really judge him?

Avinash had employed a broker to get his work done in the license office. This agent would carry petty cash with him, offer baits to people here and there and then claim much more than what he'd paid. Swapnabha told him, "Why do you need him? The company is a small one, but for this job, you have at least three people. What will they do? Moreover there is no limit to what the broker will spend! Have you any idea how much he has put into his own pocket?"

Avinash waved his hand before his face in the manner of swatting a fly and said, "Do your own work, you don't have to bother your head over all this – there are other people to deal with all this filth."

The broker steadily began to overstep his limits.

What troubled Swapna the most was getting boys from government offices after working hours who would be paid to get the work in 'line' so that no objections were raised at the time of granting the license. A difficult individual was paid by the broker only to keep him quiet – so that he wouldn't raise objections and create problems.

Thanks to Swapna's stubborn attitude, one day the broker left, but he remained a thorn in Avinash's side. He became livid, whenever Avinash brought any problem to him. "Solve it yourselves! You are all there! Don't come and tell me your problems!" As a consequence Swapna had to run around much more and his responsibilities increased tremendously. He also became extremely unpopular with those who were lazy and inclined to do no work!

The only pleasant memories Swapna had of his days in that office were of the large river that was nearby. Avinash had sent him quite a few times to Phalta, the Export Processing Zone, from where some of their packaging material came. In the evening after work, on his way back, he would go and sit by the river. The new jetty had yet to be inaugurated. One had to leave the car at a wicker-gate and walk up a bit. The gravel path led to the concrete jetty. And at the end of this the deep peaceful river with its large expanse of water bathed in the colours of the sunset awaited Swapna. Here the river had almost merged with the sea. It was neither in a hurry nor restless. The ambivalence of city people, the fears in their blood were things it understood to a certain extent, having experienced them in the course of its long journey. Once in a while, near the jetty, a local madman was seen to loiter. He was middle aged, his beard peppered with grey, wearing tattered limp trousers, his head full of shaggy hair covered in mud. He laughed to himself and tore paper into shreds and threw them into the breeze from the river. Swapna's driver had found out from somewhere that he used to own land in what had now been turned into an Export Processing Zone, the women of the household now survived by working as domestic helps. The man, unable to bear all this, had gone mad.

Swapnabha had watched the madman with a lot of curiosity – he too after all was a man who had been uprooted!

Swapna had once or twice even bought shining Ganges Hilsa fish on his way back from the river. It had not escaped his notice, that after the maid Sarala di had cooked the fish and put it on the table, Baba would keep aside a few pieces of fried fish in a covered dish for Bolu. There was amazing compassion in Baba's heart. Even now, on a cold winter night he would come to check whether Swapna was covered with a blanket or not. Yet, regretfully Baba never found a partner to share his warmth with.

When the blows fell, they seemed to rain down from the skies. They came hurtling down one after another as though they had already arranged themselves in sequence. Swapna had been completely unprepared for the experiences he'd had in Delhi. The committee member Avinash had asked him to meet did not give him any importance. By hints and gestures he made it very clear that he had already discussed these details with Avinash yet he also acknowledged that Swapna had taken the trouble of coming himself. "I am convinced, this time I will be able to make the Committee pass this case." Swapna had been pleased to hear this but since he was not one to forget anything easily. An invisible thorn kept pricking the back of his mind. The day before he returned, he pulled out Sree's name and number from his diary and called her. And that was the biggest mistake he made.

Sree had in a way been lost to him – a friendship of his school days which had turned intense in Class Eleven. She was the girl-next-door and Swapna's heart overflowed with romance. Sree's two plaits, rosy lips, slightly blunt nose disturbed his night's sleep ever so often. In a frenzy Swapna wrote letters to her and Sree replied writing absolute gibberish and nonsense.

One day, the same Sree suddenly left home with a Punjabi man twice her age. The reproach of the whole locality, the curses of her parents on their fate, the complaints to the police – in the midst of all these obscenities, what had seemed to be the ugliest and most shameful had been Sree's letters kept in her drawer. They were the incoherent outpouring of a sixteen-year-old girl in love. However from the timing it was evident that while Sree had been openly reciprocating Swapna's love she had also at the same time secretly planned to run away with Sureen Kapoor. Had she run away or been abducted? No, she had actually run away. This was obvious because when she had left the house she had carried with her some clothes, even if they weren't too many, along with, funnily enough, a few school books. This could not have been possible in the event of an abduction.

He had no mother at home and it was impossible to tell his father anything. As a result for more than a month Swapna hovered around Sree's house like one possessed. He was almost about to fail his second terminals, having completely stopped studying. Even more unbearable than Sree's betrayal was her distasteful running away, and her decision to go for a loveless living together. Understanding nothing, unable to reconcile himself in any way, Swapnabha was drifting towards chronic dementia. Just then, thanks to Baba being diagnosed with typhoid, quite ironically, Swapna was saved.

One day, Baba returned with a fever almost as fatal as that of Harihar, the father of Apu, while in Kashi, in Bibhuti Bhushan's famous novel *Pather Panchali* . Then his eyes turned red, he became delirious and there were sores in his mouth. Baba became so weak and thin in a matter of days that Swapna was forced to discard the outer aura of his demented state. He sat by his father constantly, out of sheer fright. His fear was greater than his concern. Fearing that Baba too might leave him and depart this world, Swapna rushed across and brought Doctor Lahiri and his voluminous bag home. He went and bought medicines. He called his aunt, Boro Pishi, to come over and stay for a month. By the time Baba recovered, Sree's departure was reduced to a mere scar in Swapna's heart. Sree was no where.

Was there any point in going to look for that girl after fourteen years? Not really, just a little aggrieved curiosity remained in some corner of Swapna's mind. How was Sree, what kind of a household did she have, what was she doing now? Kiran Khanna from office was a relative of Sureen. It was through her, that he was able to obtain a telephone number. Otherwise, Swapna had no other source. But after he'd visited them he realized he had not done a good thing. Sureen was touching fifty, his cheeks were sunken, he was bald, his recent photograph showed eyes which were totally vacant. He was not even at home, he'd gone to Punjab. Just a day earlier, Sree's newborn son had died. He had some deadly virus.

Sree had borne an undesired, unwanted child alone, on her own. This meaningless death of the baby had completely broken her. Swapna stood and watched the frightening ebb and flow of that grief. It was difficult to gauge how much of her weeping was sorrow and how much self-reproach. The other members in Sree's house did not even ask him to sit, it was as though they hadn't even noticed him. There was a stone-faced elderly woman and a painfully skinny maid who appeared as shriveled as a dried up prune. In any case, they did not know Swapna. After a while, Sree raised her face amidst her tears and saw him. In her swollen, pale face there was no desire to return to her youth – her gaze was extremely dull and expressionless. Maybe, she too had not recognized Swapna. Swapna saw that Sree had put on weight, her hair had thinned, her pink lips and mischievous laughing eyes were now lifeless with sorrow and mirrored a life lacking in warmth and ardour. Swapna did not recognize this Sree. Realising that he had dedicated the precious years of his youth to this woman made Swapna shudder. The only feelings he could experience was relief at having been saved from falling into the hands of Sree. So it was in the shadow of a deep melancholy that Swapna left Delhi early the next morning.

He had gone by air but his return was by two-tier air-

conditioned coach on the Rajdhani Express. The company had
given these instructions. To catch the Committee Member it
was necessary to reach in time by air. However since there was
no need to hurry back, what was the point in spending money
on airfare? Avinash's economics were on these lines.
Swapnabha had never liked Delhi. That was why he had always
found excuses to avoid coming.

Almost empty, spread out, lifeless, polluted, this city showed
no traces of Durga Puja. Unlike Kolkata, where sal leaf plates
would be flying about and the shabby awnings of the pandals
would be evident along with open-ended bamboo poles – such
impropriety in the heart of Delhi was unthinkable. Here it
appeared as though some senseless old woman in a befuddled
state had chopped her hair off, and applying a dark lipstick
was getting ready to smear flour over her face – that was how
pointless the city's artificial décor was. There was no spirit, no
life at all.

As the train left the station, smoothly without its customary
jerk, initially Swapna found the journey quite pleasant. He
was very satisfied at having left Delhi. Soon after, however, the
yellow Kartik eventide, the chequered squares of crops in the
farmyards, the flat rich picture of rural life carried him to the
edges of another kind of depression. Overnight Kolkata had
somehow turned empty for Swapnabha. He had no one there.
The reason – Sree was no longer there for him. But, Sree was
never there in Kolkata anyway. Was it her shadow hovering
somewhere in Swapna's mind or some impression? Suddenly
Time seemed to have destroyed even that shadow, those few
impressions.

Swapnabha had visited Delhi once in his schooldays. On
that occasion he had been accompanied by Baba and his new
Ma. Throughout the journey, the new Ma read a thick tome
and did not speak more than a few words to Swapna. Baba had

kept Swapna busy. That train was unlike this glass enclosed one and forest breezes kept ruffling Swapna's hair.

Baba applied cream on his lips that kept getting dry. It was the first time Swapna had seen peacocks in a flat open unshaded field next to a jungle of wild grass. Seven, eight . . . countless peacocks were flying about almost like crows. On this journey, as the melancholy evening commenced, Swapna was unable to spot even a single peacock. He searched frantically – just in case they suddenly spread their huge feathers and shook the forest with the sound of their calls as they flew past. The world outside was like a brown sepia drawing. There were no peacocks. The whole sky was as pale and joyless as Sree's eyes and face had been.

☞ 12 ☜

It was inevitable that the market for Arjun's work was fairly well defined after the Basanti Durga Puja celebrations of the Sanskriti Sansad. Such incidents are never advertised and the newspapers did not carry any details but somehow word spread. Without any discussion, the Bhadra Bengali society succeeded in reaching a common concensus – and Arjun was never again able to venture into making an idol for any high-class locality. Arjun was really young then, one could say that he had barely even begun to make an effort to gain recognition. In his mind had been a vague expectation, that through Tridib Basu's contacts alone, his name and fame would spread to different Puja Committees. He had even thought of printing some posters in the local press, with pictures of the Sanskriti Sansad Durga idol, and sending them out. That was the one way an artist could hope to get an advance payment.

As he went about town looking for work, Arjun would also

go and see the Puja pavilions at Deshapriya Park, Sahajatri, Park Circus and College Square. He did this not just at Puja time but at other times as well. The roads would be empty in the month of Shravan, and the rains would be incessant. On such days, it was nice to think that soon pandals would be constructed in those lanes and the houses that stood on either side would be festooned with streamers and inside the pandal an idol made by Arjun Das would be installed. His name would appear in red near the head of the bull – Sri Arjun Das, Kamardanga.

Tridib Basu did not come again. Even at this young age Arjun had realized that going on his own initiative to people who deducted money from the payment to eat paan, who performed the Akal Bodhon puja if animal skin touched their Devis, would not be a pleasant experience. However, inspite of this, he got advances for the Mallikbazar and Dhakuria Traders Samity Lakshmi idols, for the pujas to be performed on the full moon day in the months of Aswin-Kartik. Unfortunately though, his dream of moulding a huge Durga idol for the large community puja pandals always remained beyond his reach. No one came to him from that side and Arjun out of a stubborn pride never thought of approaching anyone on his own. Instead, the strangely different world of the marginalised sections of society was now much closer to him. A world in which people were submerged in work all year round, who somehow managed to make ends meet, people who spent their life in a world of light and shade and yet continued to celebrate every festival or feast – they too celebrated Durga Puja even if it was on a smaller scale. Canal East Road, Benepukur, Bridge Number Three, Tiljala, Tangra . . . all of them suddenly discovered Arjun, and displayed their excitement and enthusiasm in their own way. The Thakurs in these localities were small – from two and a half to four and a half feet high, the pandals did not bear the stamp of tasteful design. On the Saptami day itself, barely two days after the celebrations had begun the white cotton ribbons wrapped around the red Shalu cotton cloth could be seen hanging thanks to the many urchins who stood around with their noses dripping. No dignified beauties in zari bordered saris and white flowers in their hair offered anjali in these puja pandals. Dirty, wet, black-coloured hands could be seen grabbing the prasad from the wooden trays. They soiled the cucumber and conchshell shaped Shankalu fruits being handed out.

Strange, inappropriate Hindi songs, discordant drum beats accompanied the gamboling of dancing children. No, there was no similarity between the pujas of these localities and the Sanskriti Sansad. And because there was no similarity, a Gopal Mandal could so easily sit beside a Kallu Rahmat eating the khichuri prasad. These people would never dream of subtracting even a tiny percentage of the artist's fee to eat snacks themselves.

Such Committees were also least bothered about what profession Arjun's father and grandfather belonged to. Instead they were delighted that just by going under the bridge, down the broken-down path to the Christopher Road slum, they could actually watch their own idol being moulded. One such group in the Bridge Number Three area, called Tetrish Palli or the thirty-third locality, had given Arjun Das an advance this year. It was in two installments, but in no way would the price be reduced. Their idol was normally quite a small-sized one so there would not be much opportunity to display one's craftsmanship here. Going by averages, the price was also low. This would result inevitably in a low profit margin as well. Yet at least it was some work. Even though it would be the only big idol he was moulding this year.

With the straw Arjun had bought on loan from Gaurchandra

Dhara, he had started to make the frames. Like in previous years, he had performed the frame puja on the day of the Rath Yatra of Lord Jagannath, when the deity went in a chariot for a sea bath. There was some wood left over from last year, along with some string and nails. A truck load of mud would have to be bought. Outside he could see the shadow of dark clouds as he stared out of the half-open door of the workshop. He could not concentrate. There were some serious reasons for this lack of concentration but yet Arjun was unable to determine what exactly was troubling him. Two repeated attacks of malaria, the hard work arranging his daughter's wedding, the shock given by the Mahajan, Arjun had had to absorb all these one by one. So far the difficulties he faced outside, the sorrows he suffered, had made him wary, but they hadn't broken him. However, this time the fire seemed to have reached inside and touched his very heart. The clay with which Arjun was moulding had begun to crack and it seemed that all the applications of wet mud were unable to control the damage.

The evening was overcast. There had been no rain in the past two days and the air had grown quite warm. Since this afternoon though, the earth somehow seemed cooler. Right now there was no work in the studio yet Arjun couldn't bear to stay at home. A few days back this lane had witnessed a hailstorm. The children had pushed each other in their endeavour to pick up the hailstones. That day Deepu had been sitting near the door. Young boys and girls were very fond of him. Amidst gurgling, fun-filled laughter they attacked him with hailstones, and climbing all over him with their wet bodies they tried to soak him as well. Today the children were laughing and playing by themselves. Perhaps they were expecting a hailstorm today as well. One tiny little bald-headed mite was banging his head repeatedly on the tin plank of a shop in anger, he wanted a biscuit right away. The child's mother was not there. As Arjun was contemplating whether to get up or not, the shopkeeper himself put two biscuits into the child's hands. Today Deepu was not there. Was that why Arjun was so depressed? No, that was not the case. There had been so many afternoons and evenings, before the harvest season or after it when Arjun had been alone in the workshop. He had ordered muri, puffed rice and fried savouries from Bhomla's shop, and tea from Keshto's. After doing some work or even when he had done nothing, very often Deepu would say, "Baba may I go now, and play a little?"

Arjun nodded without thinking. Deepu was the child of his later years and so his love for him was a little more. Sometimes Deepu may not say anything, his friends would stand at the door or come inside and help in the work. Some worked at the factory using lathe-machines, some at the tannery. Yet having watched claywork from their childhood, they had all learnt the skills – Bishai, Charu, Tarak, Badal. They could paint whole borders of the clay idol's saris, they knew how to colour the beaks of swans and peacocks, they were also able to spread out tufts of hair evenly and stick them on the idol's head with Fevicol. One or two of them even knew how to lift moulds. They would work for some time and then turn restive. "Kakababu, Uncle, may we leave? Could we take Deepu with us?"

Today Deepu's absence could not be attributed to this. It was an absence of greater significance, a completely different kind of absence. That was why Arjun's loneliness had increased manifold. The shop in front, the stone paved lane all appeared empty and formless to him. Arjun was aware that something had happened, the nature and appearance of which would never ever change again. Sarala entered, bending forward a little.

In her own home, Sarala's son had installed small gates,

and one had to bend while entering. Hence Sarala now instinctively bent a little, or made herself shorter whenever she saw a door.

"Why are you looking so glum? You don't have a fever do you?" Arjun turned his face, along with the beedi in his mouth, away in an irritated manner. He disliked the fuss involved in touching one's forehead to check whether there was a fever or not.

Saying "nothing has happened", he blew out smoke and laughed. Pointing to a stool covered in mud with his finger, he asked the budi to sit. Of course, one couldn't really call Sarala a budi – if he called her a budi, then he too was no less a budo, an old man. Sarala had given up wearing colourful saris, the half-soiled dhoti and white blouse did not suit her at all. In a household like theirs, how was a widow to maintain the aristocratic tradition of a mandatory white sari? On it, she was either wiping her hands smeared with halud, turmeric, or dung. One did not immediately notice her firm shape, because of her short peppery hair, cropped to the nape of her neck, and the skin of her face, which resembled sun-dried mud.

Sarala did not stay in this neighbourhood. After the leather mart when one crossed C.I.T. Road, her house lay on the opposite side, at the end of the lane leading to the bank. She no longer owned the small double-storeyed house in which she had lived for years. After Sarala's son's wedding, this qualified engineer had, on the advice of his father-in-law, found a shack for his mother. He dutifully paid for the rent and her upkeep. In this way peace was maintained in the family.

Sarala wanted to maintain peace. That is why she herself had reduced the reasons for visiting her own home to an almost non-existent level. Once in a while when the baby's ayah ran away, her son himself came to take his mother home. She then had to bend to enter the house. Even if she didn't exactly create chaos within the four walls of that house, Sarala was not one to keep her mouth shut either. Very often she sat in Arjun's workshop unburdening her resentful heart and discussing details at the top of her voice. Arjun listened to her silently while continuing with his work but the inhabitants of this slum —who could also hear what she said — wouldn't refrain from talking. "You yourself gave your house away to your son, so why are you crying now? Does anyone handover ownership in this way? Your husband is dead, you hardly have the means to cover your body or to make ends meet — now you can as good as go to hell!"

Very often, Sarala brought something or the other for Arjun. Sometimes it was food, at others a dhoti or vests. Even though these gifts did make her happy, Sarayu just could not stand the sight of Sarala. Secretly she stared at this self-styled sister of Arjun's with eyes that could kill her. Everything about Sarayu, her manner of speaking, her behaviour had always been very sophisticated and polished, quiet and mysterious so that even those who stood at the taps and fought twice a day, trading the most offensive insults, respected Sarayu.

During the work season, therefore, Sarala would hardly ever visit the workshop. Arjun invariably had to ask his wife to come and assist with the work. His daughter and wife, both came together. With the owner's family working inside the studio Sarala would only be termed an outsider there however much she may style herself as a sister.

Today the clouds of Ashar had gathered and there was no work. The workshop was empty therefore Sarala had come. Even if Arjun didn't really tell her anything she had many details of this household at her finger-tips.

"I think I saw Deepu near Salimbhai's office." Sarala's arrow did not miss its mark. Arjun seemed to start and shiver abstractedly.

Salimbhai was the local councilor. A peoples' representative of many years. At one time he enquired after the welfare of the people everytime he passed by. Now he had become distant, in the same way as stars are from the earth. Even so, he was a good soul and was polished in his behaviour.

In fact, Arjun had met him just this morning at the corner of the bazaar. He had been on his way back from the bazaar. Salimbhai had recognized him all right. He said, "In my time I did so much for so many people but you never came to me even once. Now when I try for Deepu, my recommendation will not have the same worth as before. You spent a good ten years sleeping. People have milked the Government dry."

Without looking at Sarala, Arjun told her, "There is a new scheme for leather work. Maybe he is applying for that."

Arjun looked with longing eyes at the almost empty interiors of his workshop. Just behind him was the platform and bamboo frame he would use this year. The work of tying up the straw stuffing had not begun as yet even though work always commenced in the name of the straw. He had not thought of how he would mould a Thakur of this height with the measly funds at his disposal, or how he was going to balance the Devi, Asura, bull and lion all on this tiny platform.

Arjun had first put his hand into clay at the age of fourteen, today he was fifty-two years old. How many times had the darkness of his workshop been adorned with lights? In a single season he had created ten Durga idols, eight or nine Kalis, and four Jagadhhatris. Arjun was so much in demand at the small and medium pujas to make the Saraswati and Vishwakarma idols that he could barely cope with the orders. The Thakurs in the workshop would overflow onto the lane. Two days before orders were expected, Arjun Das' studio would light up with the dazzle of tinsel and other golden wire decorations and bright radiant electric bulbs.

By then Didi had left and it was Sarayu who had stood in her place. Initially during the work season, he had had to call for her once or twice, but never after that. She had worked even with a babe in arms. Once the daughter and son had grown up, they too had voluntarily come in to help in the work. They had held paint brushes, they had assisted their mother in holding the sari pleats while she fixed the zari borders, and of course they had helped in the work that even the smallest children could do, open and arrange the tufts of hair.

Thirty-eight years. A confused cycle of four decades. A whole lifetime had passed by so quickly! It was as if it was over even before he had blinked. 'It was over', these words seemed to have pierced his head. They had never been there before!

A few days ago, while eating their meal Arjun had flexed the muscles of his hands and shown them to Deepu. The father and son had even laughed over this. He would have to work for at least another fifteen or twenty years, he would have to gain control of the market forces. One Mahajan had gone, he had no option now but to search for another one – these thoughts had been troubling his mind lately. This morning, however, his mind and heart seemed suddenly to have fallen by the wayside.

One thing was clear in Arjun's mind. All these years had not passed in sorrow. Only on the days he had not had to scrub the mud off his nails before sitting down to his afternoon meal, had he felt empty and purposeless. How he dressed, how many new clothes he had, whether his dhotis had been from the looms or from the mills – seen from this distance everything appeared hazy and confused. However, he did remember that money had come and gone like the flow of water through one's hands. All those loans from the Mahajan, the paying off of those loans, the profit from the sale of thakurs, the household expenses, every incident of the past had got submerged and disappeared from sight in this extended deluge. But Arjun had never forgotten to enhance Sarayu's beauty during the seasons. Nothing to be excessively proud about, of course.

The shades of green he had chosen for Sarayu were innumerable – all matching the colour of her skin. The green of Dhanekhali, Shantipur – paddy green, bottle green, grayish green, green mixed with yellow, green tinted with brown. Once he had bought her a pair of silver anklets from Amherst Street. At that time, in 1977, he had made a profit of a thousand rupees from the sale of a pair of Jagadhhatri idols. There was a slump in the market for idols, three political parties were fighting with each other in a poster war all over Kolkata. It was thanks to Nepal Sen of the Congress, that the Kumortuli Market had not gone into a decline. He had managed to buy her gold ornaments only twice – he had once bought gold pins for her bun in the midst of the monsoons – there had been knee-deep water under Number Three Bridge then. On receiving the first installment of the Mahajan's loan – he had thought of blowing it all up and adorning Sarayu's two eyelids with kohl, a black paint brush. Even at that time Sarayu was able to make a beautiful bun with a sweep of her thick hair. This was despite of being the mother of two children. It was 1980. There was no electricity in the house. Turning her around in the light of the lamp, he had seen a smile lighting up Sarayu's lips, but that had not spared him from getting scolded about his lack of common sense either.

Even if he had been unable to give her anything after the birth of Deepu, when his daughter was born he had bought her a fancy ring set with white stones. What little ornaments adorned Sarayu's body were still there, Arjun had never touched them.

Sitting in his workshop, on this heavy Ashar day, Arjun suddenly saw Sarayu's expressive face and eyes, and just as quickly the image disappeared along with the breeze. What remained was the cobweb covered walls of the workshop, and the mudsoiled fibres and bunches of discoloured strings suspended from the rope-line strung up on the wall.

"You have not touched my jewellery, what a great job you've done. A lamp must have been lit in heaven for me. . . . "

"This time I had thought of giving you sola ornaments. There is no money to buy gold and silver, my hands are empty – is that why I thought of it?"

No, that was not so. Instead he had thought, maybe the language of beauty could be altered with the passage of time.

Those who came to place orders for the big thakur, had asked for sola this time. They had asked him to give the goddess a new look.

This time the sola market was asleep. Last year's continuous rains had flooded the sola fields for too long, the harvest had been very meagre. The sola that looked like white bone, and could not take too much water nor too much sun revealed its actual appearance only when the outer cover was peeled off with a sharp knife. Sola was a material unique in quality – with its butter-soft texture, its conch-shell-like colour and its ability to cleave itself to the curve of a knife.

In his youth Arjun had enjoyed watching the craftsmen at work in the dress and decoration bazaar. He may have gone to make purchases, but after that his feet had remained fixed, and he had stood gaping.

Water crabs existed in low-lying areas. They sank their teeth so sharply into the sola plants that their marks remained even deep within. "Look at the teeth marks," the sola craftsman Shaktinath peeling the layers of sola before young Arjun's eyes, would finally reach the innermost flake. In every layer these bite marks appeared like brown scars on a white body.

"It will not do to just peel the layers, look how I lift this up . . . ", saying this he used a slim knife to slice off the scars at the heart of the sola. After he'd used his knife to cut out the correct shape, Shaktinath immersed himself in the making of the swan's throat.

This was where the craftsmen were at an advantage. Who was a buyer, who was a passerby, was not something they noticed. Just because some people were watching their work, did not mean they would chase them away or even feel irritated. You do your work, I will do mine.

The swiftness with which the steel knife had descended into the white breast of butter and sliced off the scar, removing its very traces, was a display of speed that Arjun had not forgotten even today. If only he could have similarly removed the scar that time had inflicted on Sarayu's heart! He had neither had the speed, nor the courage to do so. That was why, although he was so close to her, there had still remained a hairsbreadth gap between Sarayu and him, like a distance that could not be bridged, even when one stretched out one's hands to do so.

☙ 13 ❧

It was a small tiled house. There was a road on its left and a strip of land on its right. At one time paddy was cultivated on this land but now there was a forest of banana trees. All year Janardan Mandal's house had a surplus of bananas, banana leaves, banana stems and banana flowers. In his small shop by the side of the road he kept soap, biscuits and a cycle pump. Janardan wore holy tulsi beads and worshipped Lord Vishnu – he was a Vaishnavite. Fish and meat were never cooked in his house. Ever since his eldest son went missing the food in his house had become even more meagre. It barely kept body and soul together. About three years after losing his son, a daughter was born. Janardan had been once again eagerly awaiting the birth of a son. But instead a daughter arrived. The mother felt her heart fill up – its emptiness somewhat filled. Pujas had been done, stones tied to the aerial roots of trees, promises to deities had been made all in the hope that a son would be born. But now after the birth of the girl the mother was finally able to turn her attention to household matters.

The growth of the girl's hair was uncontrollable. At the age of two-and-a-half or three it had to be made into two plaits on either side of her head, otherwise she began to cry because the heat made her uncomfortable. After outlining her large eyes with kohl and dressing her in clean clothes the mother would go to the kitchen to get some food, in that short interval the girl would have vanished.

Coming out of the room Ma would call out, "Sarayu-yu-O Sarey Ma!" The banana leaves would make stirring sounds in the breeze. Outside there were cycles on the road, children walking to school, and a little calf – tied to a stake – that was slithering down the low embankment on the side of the road. If she raised her voice any further, it would reach the shop. Where had the girl gone? Wherever fish was being fried, the girl would be sure to be there. She'd never eaten fish, how then had she developed such a taste for it?

The Duttas had a large kitchen, it was according to the size of the family. During harvest season, food was sent to the labourers as well. There was a cook to make the meals.

Their daughter, Monisha, would sit down to eat before leaving for school.

"Will you eat fish, Sarayu?"

Sarayu would be ready and nodding her head, just like a greedy cat.

Monisha's mother would say "Now who is going to remove the bones for her? She will make a mess, and get something stuck in her throat."

Sarayu was an expert. In minutes she had removed the bones and finished eating the fish. And then she would run back home. On the way back she would even have wiped her mouth with her tiny hands. She was so naughty! However, she had not realized that one bone had got stuck to her forehead. If Janardan spotted it, he would get into a burning rage. Feeling guilty Sarayu's mother wouldn't scold her daughter, but instead, quickly wash her face and wipe it clean, so that she'd escape detection.

The girl did not want to eat on plantain leaves. She asked for her rice on a plate. There would be banana stem and flower cooked at home – but she would still ask for gourd or potol cooked in poppy-seed paste. Janardan did not like to give any money for vegetables. He got angry if any other vegetables were cooked. Sarayu would bury her face in her mother's lap and sulk. From birth she had been seeing rows of yellow and brown plantain leaves bending and swaying in the breeze. Leaves, flowers and peels lying rotting on the ground. Sarayu felt depressed. On the way back from school, she picked up the big fallen simul flowers, and entered the house. On her return from school, she never found her mother at the door to receive her. She would possibly be standing at the window at the back, staring out at an invisible sky, shut out by the thickly growing leaves of the drumstick and evergreen bakul trees. At other times she could be found weeping into a pillow, while pretending to be lying down on a mat on the floor. Sarayu was a quiet girl. She would lower her satchel of books and wash her face and hands with the water kept in a bucket outside. Silently she would sit and wonder, what it would be like if her lost

Dada were to return. Where did missing people stay? Maybe
Dada wasn't a human being, maybe he'd turned into a beast
or bird by now. Magicians wandered about in fair grounds,
thought Sarayu. Perhaps one of them had turned Dada into a
cat or bird. Sarayu was not frightened seeing small creatures
close to her, she did not even shoo them away. Still she kept her
imaginative thoughts to herself. She did not even have the
courage to tell her mother. Nowadays, Sarayu's mother, once
in a while in the afternoons boiled a duck's egg for her daughter
—on days Janardan was not at home. It was difficult to cook
fish, the smell would be everywhere, and people would get to
know. Better than that was to boil an egg and serve it with
steaming rice, mustard oil and green chillies.

Ma had never really spoken about it, but Sarayu knew that
what she was eating was not in her father's knowledge. She also
knew the trick of washing the plate in a hurry without dropping
a morsel. Aha re, only one child, but she could not even feed
her to her heart's desire. The excesses of this Vaishnava
household made Sarayu's mother, Giribala, resent her
husband. This was just miserliness. An excuse not to spend
money. Since there was no son Janardan did not think a girl-
child worthy of consideration. How could they even think of
fancy food for her! Giri had however heard that Janardan ate
non-vegetarian food in hotels whenever he was out on work.
He went to Chinsurah and Kolkata to make wholesale purchases
for his shop.

Here in Chapadanga, the monsoon was a time of great
difficulty. The roads were untarred and broken. Low-lying
areas got waterlogged, with the water almost reaching as high
as the door. Throughout the day, a rotten putrid smell of wet
plantain leaves came from the orchard outside. In the standing
water there were mosquitoes, snakes and the like. The whole

place looked somewhat eerie, shaded by trees and bushes. It was shadowy and dark. Even on sunny days it was late afternoon before the sun could push its way through the thick growth of trees.

Fearing snakes and other creatures, Giri was even more protective of her daughter on monsoon evenings. Her own sister had died of snake bite, standing chest-deep in paddy – when she was almost about to deliver a child. Within a month, her brother-in-law had got married, wearing the groom's conical sola hat – making the care of his two sons the excuse. Janardan would surely do the same thing if Giri died. Still, she did not feel like keeping her daughter anywhere but close to herself.

However, undetected by Giri, a snake had entered the house. Sixteen-year-old Sarayu, even if she could not be termed beautiful, was by the standards of her family background quite fair, and down her back cascaded a thick fall of black hair. Even if she tied a bun with a pin, her hair could not be contained, it burst its bounds and fell, pin and all. The girl roamed about, her plait of hair hanging python-like down her back. The miserly father was lucky enough to get a marriage proposal for his daughter where a dowry had not been demanded. Janardan was pleased. Rupen Das, accompanied by his elder brother, had come and seen Sarayu. Arjun worked with clay. He moulded idols. His artistic skills were well reputed. None of these details were very clear to Janardan. Someone or the other had to mould the thakurs, but why his son-in-law-to-be had to delve in straw and clay for this, was not very clear to him. What exactly was art, did one eat it or apply it to one's head, was something he could not understand. He only understood small business deals and cash transactions: the two questions sufficient to satisfy and end his curiosity, were whether the groom had any vices and what his monthly income was. Sarayu's opinion had not been asked for by the father. Neither had he asked for her mother's. Consequently, tying a plait instead of a bun, and dressed in a zari-bordered Tangail sari, Sarayu had had to stand before the visitors. The absent-minded Rupen Das had roared 'Ahaha'. By then the kohl in Sarayu's eyes was almost on the point of getting wiped out with her flood of tears. Who wanted to get married? Who was this boy from some alleyway in Kolkata who worked with straw and mud? Having been rebuked by her mother, Sarayu had finally dressed up and stood before the visitors. But in her eyes was a different dream.

Bappa, the son of the Boses, desired her, was calling her, sending her letters through other people. What was all this caste business? All that did not exist any more. For lovers – there were no deterrents in anything. "What thick hair you have – it can't be held in both hands." They were meeting in the brick-kilns, in the ramshackle Basak house. Sarayu often returned home with the smell of cigarettes in her hair. Her simpleton mother did not understand what was going on. Sarayu had failed Class Nine twice. Her studies were to end as soon as she completed her Matriculation – this had been decided at some stage. She took tuitions thrice a week. While trying to extricate the broken teeth of her comb, entangled in the glow of her darkly glowing river of hair, Sarayu would say "Oof, the boys at the coaching class smoke so much!"

Sarayu never realized that she was even more stupid than her mother.

"What do you like to eat, Sarri?"

Shyly she'd replied to Bappa's question, "Fish fry. Kaviraji cutlet."

With very little investment and even less effort, Bappa continued to play with her body day after day. The aroma of his cigarette smoke, the cheap strong perfumes he used all

turned Sarayu's head completely. She ate the fish fry, threw
the paper bag in the bushes and came home having wiped her
mouth just as she had done as a child. Having cheaply
surrendered her newly blossomed lips, resembling the beautiful
red palash blooms of spring and her body to loveless lust, the
girl spent whole nights in restlessness.

"Ma, Ma, I don't want to marry now. I never want to leave
you." The answer to these affectations was a slap on the back
from her mother's oily, smelly hands. Everyone thought she
was a fool, a dolt, her opinions were not worth considering.
Only Bappa understood her. He looked at her sad eyes, and
continued his own activities with his hands.

"Soon you will leave me and go. Won't you come to me at
least once before that Sarayu?"

Ma did not let her leave the house nowadays. However,
taking advantage of her mother's absence when she had gone
to the bazaar to make purchases, the girl had managed to run
away. Today her favourite food was not to be found anymore
in the green aroma of the bushes around the dilapidated Basak
house. Instead Bappa had invited two of his friends to also
come and enjoy his prey for the final time.

The darkness had been pierced with terrified shrieks.

The deer realised she had been playing with a python all these
days, that in reality she had meant no more to it than food.

With great difficulty Badal Mukherji, the comrade of the
Chapadanga field workers union had managed to get her to sit
on his cycle and taken her home. He had lifted her mud-soaked
sari and somehow wrapped it around her half-unconscious
body, her chest and neck covered in cigarette burns.

Janardan would have burnt his daughter alive if he could.
Stuffing cloth into her mouth, her stupid mother was weeping
inside the room.

Even though Badal was underground, he had advised them

to inform the police. Janardan had not agreed. In his worldly head, it was very clear to him that the little honour still left to his daughter too would be lost if he did this. For the Boses, it would not be too difficult to embroil a rebel like Badal in the incident.

Before the cigarette burns could heal, Sarayu's marriage had been consummated. The marriage was held 15 days earlier. It was a a little inconvenient and awkward for Rupen and all but the joyous celebrations of a wedding could succeed in covering up a lot.

A sweep of thick hair, black like the river at night. It was difficult to imprison such hair even within a net held down with silver hairpins. Sinking his clay-scented fingers into the cloud of hair, Arjun had turned to stone.

The new bride had let out a scream as piercing as that of a dumb animal. Did hair have nerves? Did they hurt when touched? How could Arjun have possibly known how much blood remained clotted in the still waters of this dark river?

* * *

Almost overnight the simple girl who talked nineteen to the dozen within the confines of her home became a quiet, mysterious and extremely mature woman. Sarayu had heard that her widowed elder sister-in-law used to go to the clay factory to oversee the work. In their bedroom hung the red lac-dye imprint of a pair of feet, traditionally taken before a person's final journey. Kunti, Arjun's Didi, had passed away about a year before their marriage. Arjun would call his wife over during the lull in the afternoon of the work season. He would tease her by wiping his paint brushes on the back of her hands. While painting the Devi's two lips, taking the blood-red colour from the saucer she herself held for him, he would ask.

"Sarayu, there is some pain deep within you, can't I know what it is?"

"I will tell you before I die, don't worry," saying this, Sarayu would suppress her laughter.

"Before whose death? Yours or mine?" Instead of being startled at Arjun's mocking words, Sarayu had covered Arjun's body with the paint on her hands. Those who had expected that the arrival of a new bride in the house, would light up the doors and windows – were fated to be disappointed. The rustle of new saris, the scent of hair oil, the tinkling of ornaments – initially all this was evident. However, the movements of this new person who was walking about the house, seemed to lack gaiety. Lack life. Newly married girls came to their in-laws' homes and cried, they were nostalgic for the parental homes they had left behind. Such tears evoked a lot of teasing as well. However, Sarayu had not wept in this manner. She was not over eager to return to her parental home. But a deeply suppressed darkness, a pain kept her tightly encircled. If no one else, Arjun had understood that. And having done so, he had laughed a little ironically to himself. The train of good fortune never jumped off the rail-tracks at sea-level and climbed up the mountainside. At the most, after crossing the holes and ditches, it started climbing up the bridge. The luck of the Rupen Das family too, did not suddenly change its path.

Sometimes his heart swelled up in hurt pride against his newly wedded bride. Yet the actual cause for this hurt pride, never became clear even to himself. Theirs was a household riddled with sorrows and problems. The two years prior to his marriage had not been happy ones. Sarayu should have brought a wave of joy with her. Her presence should have lit up the whole house. Instead, Sarayu was so entangled in her own personal sorrows that she never managed to look up and notice Arjun's family at all. If it had been Bheem and not Arjun,

he would have forced an explanation from his wife either by
poking her with questions or by screaming and shouting at
her.

He would have blotted himself out in beedi-smoke and
hollered: "What is your problem, hey? A new bride, with no
smile on your face, who gets startled when you see people? Ma
is taking such good care of you and feeding you, and inspite of
all this you are drying up. Can you tell me what is wrong?"

Sarayu had to be dragged to the kitchen on festivals and
celebrations. Then maybe a few words would gradually emerge
from her mouth. One day, in the intimacies of the night, she
possibly even voiced her secrets. Many girls did so.

The touch of clay, the world of wet-earth, neither cold nor
warm, had changed Arjun completely. He was different from
his father and brother. He was an artist, a creator of beauty.
He moulded bodies, he broke clay with the pressure of his hands,
and created different shapes. He created moulds, and from
deep within them he lifted out faces. On the headless bodies he
placed faces carved out of clay. Spending all his days amidst
silent forms, his own words had dried up, and his thoughts
and ideas had changed appreciably. He was very much part of
this world, involved in its materialistic aspects, but his mind
was elsewhere. Inside the earth. The anger, malice and aversions
of worldly individuals were not really evident in Arjun. He
was a quiet man, who had learnt very early in life how to play
the game of adjusting to one's surroundings.

His personal pride vis-a-vis other people, was something
Arjun had never put into words. Possibly from the age of
fourteen whenever anger and grief overwhelmed him, Arjun,
with the scalpel in his hands and the artistry of his fingers,
transformed his anger into pictures on clay. Next to the
peaceful Lakshmi idol, would be created a storm-tossed owl its
eye-brows crinkled up in a frown. Or the lion's mane would

embody the velocity of a tempest. Since the time Arjun could transform and mould beautiful shapes, he had never had to come home to the drudgery of cooking his own meals.

For two or three years before his marriage their small family had undergone many ups and downs. Arjun knew that he could only provide his Didi with some solace, care and shelter in his workshop. Just by keeping her close like a friend with no questions asked and no overbearing sympathy. That was all he wanted to do. However, even then Didi did not stay.

The first to go was Didi's mother-in-law. That too had been very surprising. . . . A completely shrunken old woman, she had arrived at the house of her dead son's in-laws, unable to survive in her own household. All she had brought with her was a small bundle.

Kunti had not kept any connection with her in-laws after the death of her husband. Still, rumours were rife in the breeze. Like the seeds of the simul, gossip came and alighted on its own on the cobweb covered tin roof of the kitchen.

Kunti's husband was gone, in fact according to her he had been poisoned to death. Now the effect of that poison was spreading. The brothers were now tearing each other's hair over the property. Her mother-in-law, unable to bear all this any more, had one day just left home.

She was standing on the road at the end of the lane, in front of the grocer's store at the corner. A local boy called Shasha Maity, proper name Shashadhar, came to inform Arjun. Embarrassed and hesitant, the old woman had possibly not been able to progress beyond the shop, and just stood there silently. God knows how long she would have kept standing there! The old woman finally entered the house along with Kunti.

Although she was a little taken aback, Rupen Das' wife had looked after her daughter's mother-in-law.

Even without interacting too much with her initially, Kunti's common sense told her that there would be no point in bearing old grudges in her mind. This old woman had borne a lot of pain before she was forced to leave her home. In their kind of families a mother suddenly arriving to stay at her dead son's in-laws' home was unheard of. Now, if Kunti too avoided her, she might again take to the road out of sheer sorrow and suffering.

Actually with the arrival of her mother-in-law, Kunti enjoyed even greater care and affection than before. She braided Kunti's hair for her. In winter she applied oil to Kunti's hands. Kunti too crushed paan leaves for the old woman. She washed her pillow cases and sheets and put them in the sun to dry.

Even in a humble household like theirs, it did not seem right to allow a mother-in-law to do any work. The question of letting her sit near the stove did not arise. Yet Kunti's old mother-in-law refused to sit idle. In that tiny two-roomed house, she pottered around constantly. She tidied the clothes, chopped the vegetables, grated coconut. When she got tired, she spread out a mat in the corner, and took a little rest. It is very difficult to deal with the people who have lost their will to live. They look strong from outside, but from within their bones have turned brittle and dry. That is what had happened to the old lady, but no one had realized it. She had almost lost the desire to eat, her night's sleep had quite evaporated, she lay on the ground tossing and turning.

Then, one day, just before the Vishwakarma Puja, she suddenly disappeared while out shopping in the market. She never returned. Places close by were searched. The news was conveyed to Kunti's in-laws' house. How long could those who laboured for their daily bread possibly leave their work and look around? Finally, everyone just went back to doing their own work. But Kunti once in a while still went to search the neighbourhood, it had become a habit. Sometimes she asked her brother, "Tell me, what could possibly have happened? Did she truly get lost?"

Six months later, just before Saraswati Puja, his eyes burning with smoke, bitten by mosquitoes, Arjun returned home to suddenly freeze at the door-frame. Ma had gone to her own Uncle's place. Baba was not at home. The soles of two feet were visible behind the half-shut door. Didi lay fallen, stretched out on the floor. Her hair was spread out on the ground, some of it wrapped around the nape of her neck. Maybe it had been tied up. The comb had apparently been thrown off and landed on the ground in the corner. The light in the room had not been lit. She appeared to be sleeping peacefully. If blackish blood had not coagulated under her nose, it would not have appeared to be anything more cold and severe than sleep. It was the lac-red imprint of this pair of feet which had been framed and hung on the wall, in the larger of the two rooms. Even when Arjun looked in that direction absentmindedly, it was as if a knife pierced his heart.

ෙ 14 ෙ

Dearest Ma,
Not having heard your voice in a long time, I was really worried. I feel much better today. Let me know how Baba is, he should not get wet in the rains and get a cold or fever. It is evident that you have not received two of my letters in the meantime. It was so difficult to procure those postcards, and they were written after so much thought. Please don't feel sad, do not think yourself alone, dearest Ma! All of us here look up to you and gain strength, gain courage. After independence, it is no more lawful to fight for freedom. That is why Dada had

to leave us so early in life. Like Dada, we too have been born in this unfortunate country Ma, our shoulders weighed down by a burden of debt. The Harijan Tamil girl who bore the physical torture of ten men, the landless who were unable to face the famine and died, the girl who sold her body everyday on the streets of the city in order to feed her child, their debts will have to be paid back with our lives, this is the lifelong burden we have acquired. I know how painful your daily life must be. Still, do not neglect any attempt or efforts in order to stay well. My body is now completely healed. The medicines you sent are not yet over. Both you and Baba, please accept my love and lal salaam.

From
Your own
Baba

PS. You wrote to say you had found my childhood bowl and feeder, and my leaf-shaped kohl case in the lower most drawer. This time when you come bring them with you. I really want to see them.

Yours
Babu

Arunima had gone for a bath. The letter file was kept on top of the desk, tied up loosely. A thin dusting cloth lay nearby to dust the pages. Tirthankar had just lowered the shopping bag on the kitchen floor. That is why the maid had not been able to see the injury and blood on his thumb. He had washed the soles of his feet under the tap even though this was banned in the kitchen.

Tirthankar lovingly touched the letter paper. Much like moonlight, the paper too seemed to be full of Babu – his look, his tenderness, his wishes and desires. The large sheets were not many. Letters had been written, on narrow strips of paper, on thin white cigarette paper covers and smuggled out of jail. Arunima subsequently wrote out all the letters on big sheets in her own handwriting. Then she arranged the original papers and their copies chronologically. This was how the files had been prepared. Even twenty-five years later, Arunima with the same dedication and care used a clean cloth to wipe and lovingly preserve Khokon and Babu's letters, the books, copies and geometry boxes of their school days. Their clothes were regularly washed at home, ironed and kept back. Their shoes shone with polish and care.

Of course, this task was not undertaken by Arunima alone. The maid helped her as much as she could, as did Tirthankar to the best of his ability, especially when she was sick. A large portion of all this loving care and preservation work had also to be undertaken by Tirthankar.

Today was Babu's birthday. In their childhood, the fashion of feeding people or having a party as is done nowadays, did not exist. A birthday meant lighting a lamp, sitting on an embroidered mat and eating sweet payesh, made of rice, milk and dry fruits. When they grew a little older, both Babu and Khokon collected the whole rice grains and durba, three-pronged blades of grass, required for the elders to shower blessings on the young. Only once in a while did they get new clothes. Sometimes maybe Babu would pick out one of the new clothes bought for the Pujas, and wear it earlier on his birthday. Actually the Puja clothes were never bought that early. Khokon's birthday was just before Mahalaya, the new moon day immediately preceding the autumnal worship of Goddess Durga. Khokon would not wear new clothes on his birthday, because his brother couldn't wear them on his. The bonding between the two was extremely strong.

Babu was born during the heavy monsoon rains. Arunima

and Tirthankar had got wet just returning home from the hospital carrying their three-day-old baby in their arms. However, the red-faced baby, with frowning eyebrows and half open fists didn't even get slightly wet. Under the protection of his mother's sari, enjoying the warmth of her body, the baby had reached home absolutely unharmed.

If on this morning Tirthankar had become absentminded for even a few seconds, then the memory of that first homecoming may have somehow got entwined in his thoughts. Both his hands held shopping bags, more than ordinarily heavy, because it was Babu's birthday. This bazaar had hectic sales till eleven in the morning, so much so that pedestrians could not walk on the footpaths. As a result banana leaves, polythene strings and other garbage piled up in spaces between the footpath and road. One would definitely slip if one stepped on them. Tirthankar always walked carefully. Because of Arunima he would be very careful now. A speeding Tata Sumo had almost hit Tirthankar today before it braked hurriedly. The people who sat in such cars, women wearing sleeveless dresses or shorts, and T-shirt wearing upstart babus never parked their cars in the right place. They wanted to sit in their cars and buy the cheap stuff available on the footpath. As a consequence, in this clash between two opposing forces, the ordinary pedestrians were in danger of losing their lives. The car having hurtled almost on to him, Tirthankar's line of thought had snapped. The memory of Babu's tiny red face got all shaken up and was almost lost, while the letters on the walls suddenly became very sharp and seemed to be hitting his head – all at once Tirthankar realized that he had fallen on the road, his weight balanced on the palms of his two hands. As a result his wrists were throbbing in agony. His spectacles had not fallen, but were hanging from one ear. His big toe had jerked out of its ringed hold on his sandal. It had hit the edge of the footpath. Its corner had been crushed and blood had soaked the front portion of his foot.

While he was trying to somehow pick himself up by placing his whole weight on his two injured hands, Tirthankar suddenly realized that a young man, wearing a striped shirt and jeans, was collecting all the articles that had scattered onto the ground from his bag. The petty shopkeepers sitting on the footpath had also lent a hand. Tirthankar first set his spectacles right. He felt lost if his spectacles were hanging awry. The tiny paper packets of cashewnuts and raisins had opened up and spilt their contents onto the road. The packet of butter was covered with dust. Of course, the dust on the vegetables could be washed off once he reached home.

After quickly picking up and arranging the scattered shopping, the young man, then began to brush the dust off Tirthankar's body with his handkerchief. He turned and examined his elbows, and his scraped palms.

"Where are you hurt, Uncle?"

Tirthankar stared at him open-mouthed. Dark complexioned, the handsome young man was very well dressed.

"Where are you hurt, Uncle?"

"Ish, the toe is gone, it is bleeding. Come on, I will take you to that dispensary . . . "

Impossible! He could not go now to a doctor's clinic. If he did, dettol, mercuro-chrome, bandage, tetanus vaccination – the dispensary would raise these and seventeen other fusses. It would really delay his return home too much. Arunima would get extremely anxious and worried. As soon as he asked the question for the second time, his eyes fell to his feet. Maybe this was his way of examining him from top to bottom.

"No, no my house is very close by."

His throat felt parched. In spite of that, Tirthankar offered the information in a strong, yet calm voice.

"You want to apply some medicine at home? Achcha, let's go. I will accompany you."

Tirthankar had not noticed, but the young man had alighted from a taxi. The taxi-driver had been waiting impatiently for some time.

The two bags had already been lifted into the taxi.

"Come with me now, please."

"It is a short distance, I can walk it, baba."

"I am going in that direction, come along."

The young man looked rather uncomfortably at the shopping bags on the front seat of the taxi.

"I don't think it is right for you to be carrying so much weight."

Tirthankar was amused at the young man's diffident manner of speaking. He actually laughed.

"I don't do this everyday. It's only because today is Babu's birthday. . . ."

"It's your son's birthday today?" The young man was eager to know.

Finally standing beside him, Tirthankar examined the nut-brown iris of his eyes with great intensity; his face was simple as though even at his age he did not understand complexities. He was listening very attentively to what Tirthankar was saying.

"Here it is, this is the house – three by thirteen; you must come in the evening – we will feel happy."

Tirthankar did not permit the young man to even climb the stairs with the bags – "I'll manage myself. Don't wait anymore." Just before the taxi moved away, Tirthankar raised his voice a little and called out, "Do come in the evening though; Babu's friends will be coming . . ."

Did anyone, that too almost a complete stranger, come home on such an invitation? He might, speculated Tirthankar.

Of course, here people were rather busy, their days divided

into slots. Something had appeared in the pupils of the young man's eyes, which was more than mere curiosity, something closer to a deep empathy and compassion.

Arunima was now quite exhausted, but she still would not allow anyone else to cook the food for Khokon or Babu's birthdays. Earlier she had not even allowed the cutting and chopping to be done by anyone else, but now the maid had forcibly taken over that task. Both cauliflower and cabbage had to be cooked today. Babu loved cauliflower and Khokon, cabbage. If only one was cooked, they would sulk. So let both be cooked. Pulao with cashew and raisins. Plain white rice. Moong daal. Either mango or tomato chutney. Four or five friends came. The old local electrician, Gopal, also came. There would be a lot of reminiscences, a lot of stories about Babu and Khokon's childhood and college days.

Arunima had just emerged from her bath. There was a thud of the bolt being pulled back in the bathroom. In one hand were her washed clothes and towel, down her back cascaded her wet, uncombed hair. She had left her spectacles behind before entering the bathroom, hence she now screwed up her eyebrows to look at Tirthankar, "What are you doing sitting down? Why don't you pick up Babu's letter file!"

As soon as she had hung up her clothes to dry, Arunima wore her spectacles and looked towards Tirthankar's feet. Maybe a thin line of pain had been evident either on Tirthankar's forehead or face. Or perhaps there had been a slight change in his gait. The always absent-minded Arunima, had gained a sharp, keen and all pervasive vision since 1975. In her youth, she had spent whole afternoons lying on the bed reading story books, she had looked after the household, but had not been very neat and tidy. Her two sons thought the world of their mother. Whatever she cooked was wonderful to them. Yet, she never made any sustained effort to keep her cupboards or clothes-stands neatly ordered. As long as the house was reasonably clean and tidy, it would do; and the household was running routinely. When the pastime of her neighbours was to spend hours making cigarette packets into narrow mouthed dogs or flower vases out of buttons, Arunima was merrily reading Premendra Mitra's poetry or Sayyad Muztaba Ali's prose. She would, however, have tied up her hair and been ready as soon as the boys returned from school. She would listen wide-eyed to all their tales of the whole day's activities at school, every minute detail, all the fun and laughter. The boys would never get such a wonderful audience as their mother.

That same Arunima today, wiped and arranged every shelf and table beautifully. Every fortnight, she examined Babu and Khokon's clothes, books and stationery, cleaned and tidied them. After wiping the letter file, she spread them out in the sun for some time. Much more stress surrounded her life now, than in her youth – yet it had not overwhelmed her. Arunima did not appear encumbered with any heavy burden. She seemed always busy, extremely eager and attentive. She seemed to have encircled her emptiness like a bird's nest, in a ring of loving care.

"Have you washed your foot properly? No, you haven't. Go immediately, I am getting the Dettol."

While applying the antiseptic to his foot, Tirthankar described the details of his fall in the market. He mentioned the stranger who had brought him home in a taxi – "I have invited him home this evening."

Arunima was happy to hear this. Maybe she was also a little embarrassed.

Even today their housekeeping was as simple as before, as unencumbered. Yet, Babu-Khokon's friends still came. Tanmoy, Boltu, Bonu Hazra, Somnath – definitely came on their birthdays. They, in fact, found various excuses to

surround Arunima and Tirthankar with their presence. Taking
them to the doctor, solving any problems with their electricity
bills, calling the plumber when their water pipes got choked –
they helped with everything. After Khokon's death, when Babu
was still in jail, they even wrote letters to Arunima and
Tirthankar, once in a while. After Babu's death, they had
wanted to wrap Arunima in a huge wing made up of their
letters. To lose them both within four years. Who knows what
would have happened to any mother, but Arunima lay
shattered in bed for a few days, both times. However, she had
then arisen, and regularly attended court whenever her sons'
revolutionary friends were slated to appear. Alighting from
the prison van, they would invariably see Arunima and
Tirthankar standing silently on one side. They had visited them
in jail as well, carrying food in boxes, for the boys and girls.
Most of the time that food had been wasted, it had not been
given to them. In this way they had created a world of their
own, the boys and girls inside jail and Arunima and Tirthankar
outside. The young people inside ensured that Arunima forgot
her pain by keeping her busy with their various requests, whims
and fancies. Arunima too became closely involved with all their
family and friends, and in all the events in their lives, both
good and bad. Gopa had written from jail – "Why don't you
write, mother of mine? Don't you love us any more? Are you
forgetting us?. . . . You must wear that sky blue sari when you
come next time, you look very beautiful in it. . . ."

Arunima was no party worker steeped in political
philosophy, she revealed no visible manifestations of
revolutionary consciousness. She was the very incarnation of
a simple housewife, who regularly performed Lakshmi Puja
every Thursday. Even till the day Khokon was arrested, she
was not very clear as to what extent her two sons were involved
in this revolutionary battle. Yet, Tirthankar had never seen

Arunima remorseful, saying 'Oh, how did this happen, why did only I have to lose my sons' or anything else to that effect.

After Babu passed away, there was a long time when Arunima was unable to sleep at all. Like one demented, she would go from one room to another, and repeatedly drink water. In this way the sky would lighten in colour and dawn would break. Even during those days, Arunima had done all her household duties. The lady downstairs had left her small daughter with her and gone to office. During the delivery of the girl next-door, she had sat in the hospital along with the other family members. She had done so not because she was suppressing anything, in fact it was more the great desire enveloping her, to dedicate herself to public welfare. What would Babu or Khokon have said, if they had been there at such times?

"Ma, please go, won't you?"

"Ma, go and see what can be done to help."

Having considered their mother as a friend, both brothers had made all sorts of demands on her, in fact everything they wanted to say, was said to her. When they wanted money, it was Ma. However untidy their mother maybe in her housekeeping – whenever people required help, she would jump into the fray and take charge -- that was something Babu and Khokon had always believed. Now that they were no more, Arunima still pictured their invisible smiling faces and continued to think of herself as every bit as courageous and strong as her sons had imagined her to be. It was a long time, many years since Arunima had worn a new sari for the Pujas. Even if relatives presented her with saris, these lay unworn on various shelves in her almirah, still wrapped in their unopened packets.

Khokon and Babu had been taken away from home, by the police on Shasthi, the first day of the five day Durga Puja

festival. On Navami, the penultimate day, they were brought
to the courts. During the three days in between, indescribable
and horrifying tortures had been perpetrated on them in the
police station. They had cracked Babu's nose and jawbone.
They had walked over Khokon's stomach wearing boots. They
had been beaten all over with sticks. Aha! Hadn't the bricks
and woodwork of the police station, the air in its surroundings
turned blue with disgust, shattered into bits! Even today, thirty
years later, Arunima would absentmindedly, unknown to
herself, tremble and stroke her whole body with her fingers –
as though she was soothing not her own, but the bodies of her
two sons with fear and love – Aha re! How much they must
have suffered! Their noses and mouths had got covered with
their own blood! Swollen to such an extent, their own faces
were unrecognisable to themselves! They had beaten them,
cursed them – these people in the police station! How easily
they had done this! To two thin bespectacled boys who had
secured three Distinction Letters each in their Higher
Secondary exams, and were always at the top half of the
academic merit lists! Today, when after embezzling crores of
rupees, a Hawala accused, writes a daily 'column' in the
newspapers, when ministers and mafia dons are captured on
camera together – how do you feel Arunima? On the final day
of the Pujas, Vijaya Dashami, the skies had pelted down. Rain
had been accompanied by storm, thunder and lightening!
Along with one of Arunima's brothers, Tirthankar went to
the Central Jail, having heard that the boys had been taken
there. Khokon was in a critical condition, they were informed
at the jail. He had been removed to hospital. 'They have almost
finished him and taken him away.' This frightening statement
by the Jail Superintendent almost stopped Tirthankar's
heartbeats, but he was a father, he could not stop, he could not
give up, he had no time to rest.

He ran around searching everywhere in that corridor of
Sarkhel Ward. This corpse, horrifying, mutilated, bloated up
– this was Khokon? No, no even if he was lying like that, Khokon
was still not a corpse. Cursing the police and their erstwhile
fathers at every step, the doctors did try their best even
afterwards. It rained ceaselessly that night. A chilly wind came
through the broken blinds. Arunima's brother had gone home
to inform her, Tirthankar kept waiting. He kept sitting on the
bench. There was a strong smell of medicine in the ward.
Doctors, wardboys, nurses came and went. It was as though
Khokon's Higher Secondary Physics Exam was on – and
Tirthankar was waiting for him outside. As though very soon
Khokon would emerge from the left door of the ward. His hair
would be slightly ruffled, there would be sweat on his forehead,
and his spectacles would have slid down his nose.

"How was it Khoka? Tough?"

"No. I'll surely get a Letter. I won't have the fresh coconut
water. Give me the sandesh."

In his hand would be the question paper scribbled over with
pen markings. Mutilated. On the margin he would have made
various calculations.

"How many scratches and crosses you have made!"

Awakening from the depths of some obscure drowsy spell
with great difficulty, Tirthankar came floating to the surface.

The doctor was leaving. The senior doctor. The house
surgeon was standing silently. The haemorrhage could not be
controlled. They were now covering it all up! They were
covering up Tirthankar's first born! How well they had wiped
clean Tirthankar's dream and very existence, created and
developed, little by little with love and care, song and play.
How easy, how harmless appeared the operation designed to
obliterate this truth!

There lay Arunima, fallen on the bed like an uprooted tree,

the mother of the boys. If you went close she either began to
tremble like a mountain shattered by an earthquake – or
already a stone, she would turn even more stone-like. She may
not awaken ever again.

The next few months had been unbearable. Tirthankar
found he was reluctant to go visit the Central Jail. He lied. He
had to lie to Babu.

"Dada's treatment is going on. The internal wounds are
taking long to heal." Sometimes he said, "Another infection
has again attacked his upper respiratory tract. He has a terrible
cough and fever."   ·

Tirthankar's insides had shattered and turned numb, as
though he was a tree struck by lightening. His feet did not
want to move forward. It was the same on the way back. There
was a jail within the jail. In it too, the weak suffered everyday,
there was robbery and pilferage, torture and trickery and
cheating. Even here the women had attempted to plant flower
trees, and were engrossed in making the flowers bloom while
the children, like vagabonds, were growing up hearing curses
twice a day and being beaten up. It seems man's real test was
within a jail, when he really and truly discovered himself –
Babu had written so to his mother.

For about two months this game of hide-and-seek
continued. Then one day Babu got to know. One of the fellow
prisoners who must have learnt the news through a friend of
Khokon's informed him. Maybe he was unaware, that this news
had not reached Babu as yet. Babu had felt the air around him
in the cell turning into strong steel, as though his limbs were
being taken away even while he still had life. Dada had passed
away. His lifelong friend, comrade and confidant.

Arunima had spent part of her life without the
companionship of the boys, before they were born. Babu, on
the other hand, had never known life without Khokon or his

parents. Even then, for the things one couldn't tell Baba-Ma, for the fun one couldn't have with Baba-Ma – for all that Dada had been everything for Babu. Dada had taught him Maths, made him practice his handwriting, tied his shoelaces, it was Dada who had initiated Babu into the new war of independence. Since Dada was the one to inspire him, what then was there to be afraid of? Crossing the barriers of fire, passing through the garden paths of glass and nails, Babu was capable of walking all the way to the horizon.

That Dada had passed away. That too, not just the other day, but many months ago. Dada had been sent to the hospital by the police and jail authorities, only when they had almost killed him. Just the day after he was taken away from the jail, Dada had passed away.

Babu too had been beaten up. When Dada was taken away, Babu too had suffered two fractures and was burning with high fever. Then, for how long must Baba have kept the news of Dada's death from Babu. Aha re! he too must have suffered so much in the process.

What was Ma doing? Hadn't she wept all these days and yet hidden her tears and written letters to Babu!

The three years in between had passed by constantly compromising with danger. Carrying the burden of sorrow for Khokon's death in her breast, Arunima had come yet again to Central Jail. She had again tried to give him washing soap, his favourite fried aubergine, the fabric whitener, medicines. The bald-headed vagabond children inside the jail had become very fond of Babu. In order to improve their living conditions Babu and his comrades found something or the other for them to do daily. The Jailor was going mad with this group, yet somehow a bond of love had also been created. Still, suddenly, without any rhyme or reason whatsoever, some of Babu's group were taken away to Howrah Jail. How was Arunima to go so

far with her shattered mind and body? But they would have
to! They put in a petition. It had no effect. Opportunities to
meet his parents became few and far between. They did not
allow interviews as they used to before. Did they fear even a
mother? What about the rumours then, that within the jail
the boys had hoarded arms, cartridges and bombs!

Early one morning, the curtains came down on the fears
and anxiety with which Arunima and Tirthankar had passed
their days ever since Babu was removed to Howrah Jail. The
clamour of crows heralded the dawn with the news of the killing
of prisoners in Howrah Jail.

It seems Babu and his comrades had tied up the guards,
beaten them up and attempted a jailbreak. As a result without
a lathi-charge and the firing of numerous bullets it had not
been possible to bring them under control. Five or six bullets
had got embedded in Babu's body. Every visible bone in his
body had been broken with lathis. His face and body had been
disfigured by pokes and digs. To identify him even his mother
had had to search desperately to find some part of him which
was untouched – in the mutilated, bloated, decomposed body
of Babu, she attempted to locate an island which carried some
tiny sign worthy of identification like a little skin, a black spot,
some childhood scar!

Arunima and Tirthankar had not only gone to make the
identification but had also returned after doing this. They were
in fact still alive; even today they were running a household,
going to the market and shopping. They carried on much like
a tree whose heart had been emptied when the birds flew away
but had still spread its branches in all directions. Even today,
people came to sit in the shade of the tree and small plants
dreamed of living and growing bigger by entwining themselves
in the tree's branches.

In some Bengali papers, a letter written by a mother had

appeared suddenly like silent drops of blood. A letter written
to Justice Chaudhuri by a mother. A copy of that letter was in
the file even today. The paper was a little worn out, a little
yellowish, yet that letter still flickered like starlight and
throbbed as did human hearts.

╒ 15 ╕

It was a rich neighbourhood, with aristocratic roads and
pathways. A new shopping mall had come up almost overnight.
Riding up in the escalator one could see merchandise in
profusion on every floor. Chinaware, glass home decorations,
nightclothes, curtain material, soft toys. So many people, so
many things. Those who came to shop here must have homes
with similar interiors. They must also possess the same glasstop
tables, almirahs, box-beds and toys brought from all over the
country and abroad. They nevertheless came again to these
markets, to buy more to stuff their homes; did not that make
the houses look even more similar to the shops. In any case,
where did they find space to keep all these things?

Kitty, Swapnabha's Bithhi Mashi's daughter, had two
almirahs full of clothes – many dresses had not even been
touched in months. Yet, Swapnabha had seen Kitty sweating it
out buying more clothes. He felt tired. The thoughtless,
illogical shelves piled with merchandise created countless weary
white corpuscles in Swapnabha's blood.

The lower portion of this Mall had initially been empty.
This multi-storeyed building's upper floors had been decorated
and arranged at the very outset. Lastly, the underground
parking for cars had been completed. On the two sides of the
gate those food stalls that had been leased out, had set up their
shops. The footpath was on the road itself. There was no place

left on it for pedestrians. The shop owners themselves had arranged moulded plastic chairs and tables on the footpath because there was no place to eat inside. Carrying plates of phuchkas, dahi-bara, bhelpuri, and pao-bhaji, customers were walking back and forth. This place had self-service. One had to pay for coupons, which when presented, gave you food which you had to carry back to your table. Those who had come shopping had descended in great numbers to partake of these tasty snacks. Some had yoghurt on their moustaches, some had savouries stuck to their hair. Swapnabha was not averse to food. But this style of eating with shopping bags stuffed between one's legs, and eyebrows raised high on foreheads, irritated him a lot. The fatter the people, the more greedy their attitude – as though they had never eaten such food before.

However, Swapnabha still came here once in a while. His interest was in the bookstore on the fourth floor. Initially there were only books then a whole cassette section was added on. Now there were even soft toys, games and household items. Still, just browsing through the books and stationery section made one feel good. What a varied selection of notebooks there was, diaries, beautiful wrapping paper. In a special section, all the new publications had been displayed – what were known as New Arrivals. Swapnabha loved walking around this garden of new books. Most of the new English books bore unreal prices, there was no question of buying them. Yet just picking them up and flipping through them, aroused the feeling of an old desire in his mind. In his childhood, Baba used to bring many books from the library. They were in Bengali mostly. English detective stories, adventure and classics too came every month. There was no question of buying hardbound books from the stores. However, memories of going to the shops and buying books still remained vivid in Swapnabha's mind. He would select a small, slim volume out of a whole collection of books.

Maybe the book was not something he really wanted, maybe
he had told his father he wanted to buy the book because it was
cheap. Maybe Baba knew that, yet to him this game they played
had a different meaning. Even today when he touched a new
book, Swapnabha recalled those early days.

Just a few days ago Swapnabha had met Anandi in the New
Arrivals section. Swapnabha had not bought a book, Anandi
had. They had chatted for sometime standing around on the
ground floor. Anandi was to come today as well. Swapnabha
was feeling quite thrilled at the thought, that Anandi would be
coming especially for him. Talk of the devil and there she was !
Though the statement was on the tip of his tongue, Swapnabha
swallowed it hurriedly. Suppose Anandi was offended, suppose
she didn't realize that it was a joke!

Shaking her head full of thick curls, Anandi said "You've
been waiting for a long time, haven't you? While I was in the
taxi, there was such an awful jam that I finally just got off. I
have been walking from the street corner – not for too long,
lets go upstairs!"

Anandi delved into her bag, "Ma had made chicken
sandwiches in the evening – will you eat one?"

Swapnabha was really amused by Anandi's little school-girl
manner of taking out her tiffin-box. Anandi seemed a little
worried – could one ask Swapnabha to eat something in this
way – standing on the roadside. One couldn't carry food inside
this Mall.

"Very nice," Swapnabha responded with a shake of his head,
his mouth full of food.

Anandi was pleased. "Ma was making them – I quickly picked
up two."

"Have you told Ma?"

"What?"

"About me."

"Not yet. You will come home won't you!"

"I don't have a job." Swapnabha felt embarrassed as soon as he uttered the words. Before Anandi's eyes could cloud over with sadness, he quickly apologized – "Sorry! Very sorry!"

"You are very formal." Anandi rebuked him with her eyes. "As though you would have turned into someone stupendous if you had one." As soon as the button for the lift was pressed, the door opened. There had been such a crowd till then around the door – but inside the lift, the two of them were suddenly alone.

"I don't have a job either!" Anandi suppressed a laugh. Swapnabha was watching her reflection in the wall-mirror with total concentration.

There was no place to sit in the bookstore. However, while looking at the books one could walk side by side and talk in soft tones. They were neither of them looking at the other now – both were near the Classics shelf. A little ahead on the left-hand side was the collection of new Bengali books.

Anandi had picked up Ajay Home's *Banglar Pakhi*, the Bird of Bengal, and was flipping through it. Swapnabha's breath was falling on Anandi's cheeks. "Ajay Home – was Kaka's pet raven, it used to walk all over his dining table."

Anandi turned round and stared, her eyes partly laughing, partly disbelieving.

"You yourself are a raven."

Anandi bent down to put the book back.

"Did you read your father's letters again?"

Straightening up, and unwinding the knot at her waist – Anandi half-turned around.

Gradually the crowd in the shop was lessening. A group of small children were creating a racket at the gate. Anandi was searching every corner inside the shop with great eagerness. Nowadays, she felt restless at home. A serious and sorrowful mother, the sick grandma of the other house, along with Kaka-Kakima, Shankho – in the love of all these people there seemed to be drawn a watermark belonging to some special time. That mark never got wiped out. Anandi would never find her father, yet she would never be able to wipe out his absence either. The death of a father, who had left not a trace, would create within her a new series of ever-amplifying trauma – like the Madhabilata creeper, which grew huge with leaves and flowers, on absorbing the monsoon rains. Anandi was like a butterfly, whose wings were patterned in black. However much she wished to fly towards the sunny blue sky, the dark marks of sorrow would always remain on her wings!

Standing amidst strange people, Anandi still felt somewhat light. Their laughter, talk, bits of hilarity aroused a sharp jealousy within her and at the same time showed her dreams of another world. A world Anandi would have found maybe, if she had not lost her father. Anandi would never acknowledge to herself that she felt light, even if she did so. Immediately a feeling of remorse would prick her mind like a thorn. No, Anandi did not want to forget her father's death. Yet, she had to live a life of her own! Just a little while ago, Swapnabha's breath had wafted over her cheeks and neck. Swapnabha had been talking of a raven. And within moments, Anandi had mentally reached a different world along with Swapnabha!

Swapnabha was with her, yet only he could take Anandi across this bridge of pain to some other place. Today while she had been standing in the kitchen and putting sandwiches into her tiffin-box hidden from her mother's eyes, she had been thinking rather cautiously about meeting Swapnabha. Yet how swiftly her own fingers had worked, as though they had definitely been programmed from before.

"I have seen Baba's letters." Anandi took herself back to the

watermark of that special period. "Khokon is mentioned, the
Khokon of Moni Sen Lane."

"You must come with me one day. You will really like them,
I'm telling you. Mashima and Meshomoshai, are a completely
different kind of people. The way they made me sit down and
eat . . . as though they had known me for ages – yet it was only
that morning that, I had met them."

Anandi and Swapnabha were moving ahead side by side.
Sometimes, Swapna would fall back a little and watch the white
lights playing on her thick hair.

" . . . Their whole day is taken up with the two boys . . . yet
not just with their memories . . . they are doing everything,
looking after their friends, showering affection with smiling
faces, but they have forgotten nothing – the police torture,
their death – how can people overcome their grief, without
forgetting any detail – was something I saw for the first time."

That day Swapnabha had taken Tirthankar, along with his
shopping bags, straight to his house. Tirthankar had told him,
"Today is my son's birthday, do come in the evening."

An unknown boy, couldn't be very young, seeing
Tirthankar's age one could gauge that much. To go for his
birthday, should he carry a gift Swapnabha wondered. There
was only one reason why he wanted to go, a deep instinctive
feeling of warm regard for Tirthankar. Such feelings were not
possible in such a short time. Swapnabha had been reminded
of his own father. He had actually felt a little anger towards
the old man's son. What a way to send their father to shop for
the birthday, carrying those two bags. A leg-wound without a
bandage, Lord knows whether he had blood-sugar or not,
suppose by the evening the pain had brought on a fever!
Swapnabha held roses in his hand in a bouquet. He had
thought that only flowers could easily be given to a stranger.
Tirthankar had affectionately called him in from the door,

and introduced him to Arunima. Side by side on the table in the bedroom, were photographs of Babu and Khokon. Although there was no garland on Babu's photograph, that it had been very carefully arranged on the table, was clearly evident. If Swapnabha at that moment could somehow have hidden the flowers in his hands, he would have felt saved. He had begun sweating, from an acute sense of embarrassment. Tirthankar himself arranged the flowers in a glass vase with water.

By that time a couple of Babu-Khokon's friends had arrived. From their conversation it was clear, that they knew all the details of this household. Blood tests, pacemaker, the electricity bill, the chemist shop etc., were being mentioned on and off in their talk. Boltu studied with Babu in school, Somnath used to earlier live in the neighbourhood, now he stayed in Shyam bazar, Tanmoy had been in jail with Babu. Babu had died, Tanmoy had bullet wounds in his arms and shoulder. He had recovered only after prolonged treatment. On coming out of jail, he had started his own small business. Initially it was a radio shop, then after failing as a tour operator etc., he was now into catering.

Tanmoy was tall and dark, his hair was cut very short and he had a square determined chin. His eyes had a piercing look. On first sight he appeared to be a plainsclothes police officer or a retired army major. Tanmoy who was not keen to get acquainted so quickly with a stranger, was watching Swapnabha silently. Between them there was almost a generation gap. If one were to consider the difference in beliefs between the two ages, the gap was more than that of a generation. Tanmoy and others had gone to fight for freedom. Many of their invaluable lives had been destroyed, crushed, rendered meaningless. Many had become victims of political affiliations and ideals, many were abroad. Those like Tanmoy, who had tried to survive normally by getting jobs or taking up

business, just could not understand this generation that
Swapnabha belonged to. They had no ideals, no beliefs, no
dreams. They only understood money, and what they
understood even better was dollars. These girls and boys knew
nothing else but consumables and more consumables – more
articles to better their standard of living.

Even though Tirthankar introduced Swapnabha, Tanmoy
remained stiff-lipped while looking at him. Why was this boy
here? What did he have to do in this house? Would he be able
to understand anything? Would Babu-Khokon's photographs
mean anything more than portraits to him? This Tirthankar-
Arunima, who were today serving them with fried rice,
cauliflower, payesh, brinjal fry – could Swapnabha and his
generation even imagine the time when the same two were
searching the morgue to identify the bodies of their sons? Did
they have any sense of gratitude or debt?

Babu's other friends were comparatively easy-going.

Bonu Hazra had set up an electric light and accessory shop
in the neighbourhood. He was over fifty years of age now.
Whenever he came to this house, he had a hearty meal. Wearing
short pyjamas and sitting with one leg raised over the other,
he was enjoying the meal served to him with complete
animation, continuously praising Mashima's cooking.

Swapnabha felt uncomfortable with Tanmoy. He was simply
unable to wipe out from his mind the shame of having walked
in carrying roses in his hands. Arunima and Tirthankar of
course were feeding him with great care – Swapnabha was the
youngest person in the group. Tirthankar knew Tanmoy very
well. At some point, he had possibly even called Tanmoy aside
and told him something. As a result, after the meal, Swapnabha
found Tanmoy's gaze to have softened somewhat.

That day, Tanmoy had even accompanyed Swapnabha quite

a distance down Moni Sen Lane, and on to the main road as well.

Trams were plying through the rain-wrapped evening like destiny, grave and detached. If there was a jam, cars blocked the tram lines. No one gave way to them. Never having allowed their insults to affect them, the trams developed a kind of unmindful, disinterested look. Apart from this, quite often there was an uproar demanding 'Remove them, remove them.' From here and there people did remove the tramlines. Still the trams remained – like moving ancient artifacts! Seeing these empty halogen illuminated trams, Swapnabha had been reminded of Anandi. At that moment Tanmoy was asking, "Should we take a tram? What do you say?"

Swapnabha's house was quite close by. However it would be quite nice to travel in an empty tram. On one side of the second class compartment, was Tanmoy, the Conductor and himself. On the other were colourful people from the villages returning from the Maidan. They had gone right up to the Depot and returned. The city was almost asleep, the streets were almost deserted, they were wet yet lukewarm – what did one call it – something belonging to a distant past, a story of days which were almost extinct – this city pulled at Swapnabha in a variety of ways. It was as though the city was trying to tell him that "You were in my lap, you grew up here; not once, many times. . . ."

Plucking up courage, Swapnabha had himself asked about Tapesh Mukherji.

A deep crease had appeared between Tanmoy's brows, as though even now, it was his own major responsibility to save Tapesh Mukherji from the rest of the world.

"How do you know him?"

Suddenly Swapnabha realized that maybe it would not be

right to talk about Anandi. Not straight away at least. He said, "I know Urmi's Kakima. She is a family friend."

Tanmoy sat up straight and turning his head began to look at the street.

Standing in the wealth and illumination of the book shop, Swapnabha mentally decided that he would not talk of Tanmoy here. One couldn't talk about this unyielding, difficult, sharply intelligent man in this way. What Tanmoy had said about Tapesh Mukherji might also flow into the conversation. Anandi may find it difficult to handle the blow her story of the past was about to give her, in this strange place. Both *Anna Karenina* and *To Kill a Mockingbird* – were favourite books of Swapnabha. Anandi had bought both – again there was some bickering at the payment counter. Anandi would not accept the books if Swapnabha paid for them, as she was gifting the books to someone, not keeping them for herself.

"Who are you giving them to? Tell me – won't you?"

Anandi laughed and shook her head.

"Uhhu, I can't tell you now at all."

The books were being wrapped in different kinds of paper at the counter, and Swapnabha burning with jealousy had to watch. Whether Anandi would stand for so much irritation – within so few days of their acquaintance, was a fear that was turning and twisting playfully through his mind. However, at that moment a baseless jealousy was what he felt most. Since his return from Delhi, Anandi's comings and goings were slowly pulling him out of the strange feelings for Sree that had been overwhelming Swapnabha, and the battle with emptiness which he had felt would never end. Yet, they had met only a few times and nothing had been said about love. Swapnabha knew deep in his heart that Anandi and he were very similar. Their two eyes, shape of the face, complexion and aroma were the same – even the way of speaking. It was as though they were

friends who had played together with mud in their childhood
– or why did it feel that way? Anandi had no father from the
moment of her birth – Swapnabha no mother. Anandi was
searching for her father through many sources – perhaps she
actually wanted to reach Swapnabha himself. Was the search
then only a pretext? No, that wasn't so – Anandi's belief was
that, she had to find out the details surrounding the
disappearance of her father. Whatever Anandi did, she did
out of her beliefs and she liked to do things with care.

That he understood Anandi so well was something
Swapnabha would never have admitted to himself. Yet his alter
ego stood apart from him and kept telling him, "Yes, I know,
you understand Anandi very well, and she is coming to you
only." Nowadays Swapnabha did not want to fight with his
alter ego. He felt lazy. Taking that opportunity, this alter ego
was becoming like a tree covered with red and white flowers,
growing daily with the blessings of the mõnsoon rains. As a
result, when they came down from the bookshop and Anandi
was about to take the two books out of her bag the alter ego
greedily held out his hand as though he knew in advance for
whom Anandi had bought the two books. Consequently the
manner of acceptance neither remained graceful nor secret as
it should have. However, seeing his outstretched hand Anandi
was vastly amused and shaking her dark hair covered head,
she had a good laugh.

As soon as Anandi took the minibus, Swapna remembered
that he needed to return home. Baba was alone. Of course, he
was frequently alone, but that morning Baba had been running
a slight fever. So it would be necessary to watch him at night.

Sitting in the auto Swapna again touched the two books.
After ages, or for the first time in his life, he had been gifted
something by a woman. Of course referring to Anandi as a
woman was too complicated. Calling her a young girl was more

appropriate. The man next to him was reading the *Evening
News*, holding the paper half open. Unconsciously, Swapnabha
looked at the page because it was rustling against his body.
The news on the fifth column of the right hand page caused his
heart to heave a little. Tanmoy's face appeared clearly before
him. Justice Chaudhuri had passed away this morning after
suffering from a prolonged illness. He had regretfully told a
friend – that his report never got published in his entire lifetime.
The *Evening Newspaper* had in its own style added its own colour
to the news. Was this what one called dying of mental anguish?
Baba's fever had risen in the afternoon, but disappeared in the
evening after profuse sweating. Satisfied with his condition,
Baba had wrapped himself in a thin sheet and was reading
Travel Companion. This was not something to feel satisfied
about and in Swapnabha's opinion it meant a blood-test was
necessary. Baba did not show any anxiety about these things.
At such moments Swapna felt both angry and helpless.
However, since he did not know how to show his anger, his
helplessness was what clearly came to the fore. If there had
been any third person at home apart from Baba and himself,
he would surely have tried to get some support on his side.
Bolu had given him medicine. One had to take it early morning
through a dropper – three days continuously and on an empty
stomach. This was a preventive for malaria. Baba had already
taken this medicine for the season. Hence fevers receding after
a sweat were of no cause for worry for Baba. If a preventive
could stop malaria would so many people die of it?

The neighbourhood shops were still open. Swapna phoned
one of them. They said, 'let us know if the fever recurs – we will
come and take a sample.'

Swapnabha told his father in an angry tone, "Now if the
fever comes again, they will take a sample, I have already

informed the shop." Making a long-suffering face, Baba upturned the *Travel Companion* and kept it aside.

"The food will have to be heated."

"I'll do it. You needn't come."

Swapnabha made quite a racket in the kitchen with the utensils. Baba ate his meal and went to sleep early. It would be natural to have head and body aches – even though he would not admit to it in words. He ate the rotis and vegetables. Swapnabha, therefore, did not have to forcibly tell him "Don't eat rice."

Putting out the light in Baba's room, Swapna made his own bed. Then taking the envelope Tirthankar had given him from his bookshelf, Swapna came and sat on the bed. Justice Chaudhuri. Swapnabha had heard the name in Tirthankar's house. Since he had asked to see Babu and Khokon's letter file, it had been shown to him with a lot of care. Ma and Baba's love and care could almost be felt on touching these papers with one's hands. Every letter written on postcards, cigarette packets or narrow long strips of paper had been transcribed by Arunima in her own handwriting. In some places she had made carbon copies. There had been no Xerox-machines in those days. Once the machines came, Tirthankar had personally carried the papers to the shops and stood there while copies were made. It was as if this was their normal daily practice. Yet this activity did not seem like an obsession at any point. They lived in this world, ran a household, were doing everything, for their neighbours, friends, even their sons' friends. "One letter written by Babu-Khokon's mother, was published by the papers. I have kept many copies of that letter. You can read it later. In these past twelve years the actual paper has become yellow and worn out. Still there is no difficulty in reading it. 'A letter written to Justice Chaudhuri by a Mother.'

'To

The Respected Justice

Sri Chaudhuri,

On the last 14th of April 1975, in the Howrah Jail, my younger son Arunangshu Chakraborty along with five other prisoners were killed. They were beaten up and shot to death . . . yet the newspapers carried the same age old story of a jail break.

On the 13th of April, in the evening, his father and I went to see Arunangshu. At 4.45 pm, when he bid us farewell, Arunangshu (Babu) was healthy and quite cheerful. If he had had the intention of breaking out of jail, would the change in his manner have escaped his mother's eyes?

The papers and radio reveal the news that these undertrial prisoners possessed bombs, knives, sticks in great quantities. Yet it was never possible for us to have an interview or give any food without an SB officer being present. Arunangshu's father once brought back washing powder having been unable to give it – there was such strict regulations. Then how did all these arms and ammunitions get inside?

Arunangshu had been in jail these last four years. He was in Howrah Jail for seven months. Their food entitlement was 75 grams of cooked rice, some daal, and mixed vegetables for lunch, and three rotis and mixed vegetables for dinner. This food had made Arunangshu already weak and boney – how come so many bullets were required to control him and the others? Could not the prisoners have been brought under control by shooting them in their legs or beating them with sticks? They were shot within the compound of the jail – the prisoners had not even gone out of range by then. Then why were so many shots fired?'

* * *

A mother, Babu-Khokon's mother, had questioned Justice Chaudhuri regarding every detail. Needless to say till today no one had answered her questions.

If it was indeed a jail break, then why had a shop keeper at the Howrah market heard screams of "Save us, save us" from inside late at night?

Why was Arunangshu suddenly removed to the small Howrah Jail from the Alipur Central Jail? And Babu passed away even before he could be chargesheeted?

Earlier when a prisoner had fallen sick within the jail, then the Jail Super had said that no Naxal prisoner could be sent to Hospital without a directive from the higher authorities. Then did someone send a directive to kill these five undertrial prisoners?

Having lost her elder son, this mother was awaiting the return of her younger son. In four years the police had not even been able to issue a chargesheet. Babu would have been alive if he had been given a trial. It had been so easy to kill him because he was still awaiting trial. This morning Justice Chaudhuri passed away.

He had survived all these years, but his report had never been published. Hence no one knew how he had answered Arunagshu's Ma's questions.

To Swapnabha this revolutionary struggle, these young men and women with dreams in their eyes – their torture, their deaths, all appeared like some hazy black and white movie screen seen from a long distance. Yet today, after so many years, like the soft yet clear impact of ripples in the sound waves, a mother's voice was touching him. After twenty-four years. "Look I have cooked both cauliflower and cabbage. One Babu loved, the other Khokon loved." This blue-bordered sari-clad, smiling, grey-haired woman had sunk into bottomless waters while identifying her son. Babu's body had bloated up grotesquely with the blows of sticks and bullet wounds. She had not been allowed to remove the cover and see his eyes, as the face had got crushed, rotted and disfigured. Yet Arunima-Tirthankar were still surviving.

Anandi was looking for her father whom she'd never seen. She too would have to survive. None of them would get any answers to their questions. Swapnabha suddenly felt he was a very old and extremely responsible person. In their method of survival, Swapnabha could shoulder the burden of their sorrowful memories like a small load-bearing bridge. He could hold up a light in this dark expedition of their search. Just a small lantern if nothing else.

☜ 16 ☞

The sky was full of clouds. All night there was the sound of thunder, and then it rained till past midnight. Perhaps it stopped after that for a while. At dawn the rain once again washed over the city streets and houses. Arjun had woken up with the sound of rain. Without leaving his bed, he had turned his head and seen the cloudy sky. One would not be able to stick one's neck out of the window, the clouds were so thick! Arjun did not felt depressed, instead he actually felt a kind of joy on waking up. A laden dark sky, without a trace of blue, the rain drowned out the sound of human beings and birds – it aroused pure joy in Arjun's mind. Even though he was not a potter by birth, ever since he was aware he'd lived his life with clay – somewhere in his subconscious perhaps – was engraved the earth's ever-thirsty wait for a long and heavy shower. Maybe this was something every artisan who worked with clay knew instinctively. If the earth did not get water, if the thirst of the soil was not quenched – it was impossible to work life into the clay. It would not take life. With the touch of a potter's fingers, the clay spoke, it began to sing. A potter's story visualised in his dreams, but never told, would then never reach a conclusion. The history of the rain each year leaves its mark on the soil. If it was possible to count then it would surely be evident that much before human civilization, ten thousand lakh raindrops must already have left their mark on the heart of the earth.

A strange joy coursed through Arjun's heart as he looked at the sky. The reasons for this joy were of course not very clear even to him. Amidst the folding up of the job market, the money crunch, the want, people who had gone through all sorts of hardships were left with a sort of restless happiness –"Let what is to happen, happen – let me live the way I please." Maybe he was thinking, at this height of the work season, how many days he had spent desperately hounding the lanes of Kumortuli. He had been looking for artisans. Finally, unable to manage with the money he had, he had either returned without a worker or just booked one person and come back. During the seasonal rush it was very difficult not to go there. Yet, if one looked at things from another angle, that Kumortuli area had not harmed him any less. That he was an outsider, not of a high caste, that he lived in the leather tannery area, and came from there to look for artisans – all this and more had been made quite clear to Arjun by the middle-level owners and artisans, both through hints and insinuations or even unequivocally enough through their language. Still, Arjun had gone there many times, during the months of Shravan-Bhadra, he had not been able to concentrate on his work without visiting the teeming market. "Sarro, O Saree, give me some tea, won't you dear."

Sarayu had barely changed her soiled clothes and raised her

head from its obeisance before the family gods, when her eyes turned to the bed on hearing the call for tea. "Ish, don't tell me you are going to drink tea without washing your face like the Sahibs."

"So what if I do so one day! What's wrong with that?"

Deepu was asleep on his left. A thick sheet was pulled up to his waist. His lips were parted a little. His hair had fallen over his sleeping forehead. Aha, let him sleep. One felt immeasurable love for sleeping children. The boy was in a lot of trouble. Since the last two months he had been hiding from his father. But where could he escape to – the neighbourhood was small. Everyone knew everyone. However far he went, even if his father's eyes were closed, he would notice his son's movements. This was because there was no dearth of people to fill his ears.

Arjun could not shut his eyes forever. Love for one's offspring was strong. He realized now, what must have been Rupen Das' condition, how he must have felt when Arjun started working with clay at the age of fourteen, moulding idols at the entrance of the lane with singleminded concentration. Arjun himself had never wanted to find out. It must have surely struck Rupen Das' heart too – that my son is not attracted to leather work, not interested in carpentry – instead in his school uniform he is running to Kumortuli. If he explored deep enough, Arjun might understand – how obsessed he himself had been, how addicted – in those days of his youth. He could not concentrate on his studies at school – the aroma of straw and clay called out to him, the fear of being yelled at and abused by Ram Pal – everything seemed to cause his whole body to feel an uncanny sensation of love – he only ate one meal at home, and came to spend the night – he would run away again as soon as day broke. Aha! How his mother's heart must have cried out in those days. Rupen Das had calmed her down by making her understand – he is a young lad attracted by something different, one day he will tire of playing his new game and return home, let him go. But the new game did not end so easily, the boy remained outside with his straw and clay. Ma, Baba and Didi stood by him, through his joys and sorrows, and adopted his work as their own. Today, Arjun realized, that if his parents had not been understanding, he would have been free of his addiction to the aroma and colourful beauty of clay ages ago!

However, Arjun had been hurt much more by Deepu's change of mind. Behind Rupen Das there lay the tradition of a calling or expertise of many generations. Even today, Bheem had not given up his father's profession. Therefore, accepting Arjun's differing bent of mind had not affected his heart as much. But in this case Arjun was the pioneer of change. That the obsession in his own blood had not been injected into Deepu's was something he could see but was unable to accept. Would it be over? Would the web of fine dust raised by the hooves of the horses of change, cool, settle down and be exhausted so very quickly? It seemed only the other day that Arjun had taken his first step on the slippery road of this new profession, learnt the skills, and put his heart and soul into his work. He had built up, over the years, a special relationship with clay, jute, wood, bamboo and many other raw materials of this earth, which in turn had begun to change their appearance at Arjun's call. Then came his dedication and with it came criticism, rejection, refusals, bargaining, cheating . . . like so many hailstones. In the midst of these he had kept moving carefully forward step by step as though walking over his very heart . . . till finally, one day, suddenly the strip of earth under his feet was pulled away by the Mahajan he had known for years, by sickness, by expenses, and the burden of a daughter's wedding. All these had come together – was this the end of Arjun and Deepu – was it again a turning back to the old

profession of his forefathers – or wasn't it? It also meant that
Arjun had not succeeded in sustaining his own profession for
even two generations. Like a short-lived child it had died as a
floating bubble did in frothy foam. Arjun's heart was bursting,
he could feel the pain.

By now Arjun's son's application, duly stamped by the local
councilor would have reached the office of the Welfare Board
for Scheduled Castes and Tribes. Deepu had applied for a loan
to start an enterprise for making shoes and selling them. This
was the work his grandfather and great-grandfather had done,
of course using personal funds and loans from money-lenders.
Yes, there were mahajans even in the leather trade. After all in
those days there were no banks or Welfare offices. Having turned
his blood to water for close to thirty years, labouring alone in
this one profession, Arjun had never feared hard work, never
wanted to acknowledge that there could have been what one
would term risks, yet Deepu got scared! Arjun had always
shielded him and protected him with his heart. He had never
sent him to buy merchandise or forced him into delivering the
idols alone. Yes, both of them had had to really work hard.
During the big Pujas, Saraswati or Vishwakarma season, they
had worked day and night without moving from the workshop.
There had been one or two artisans with them sometimes, at
times artisans employed with advance payment had run away,
and never come back. The main reason for making Deepu slog
was naturally the scarcity of money; but there had been another
reason as well. Knowing that his own blood, his own flesh
incarnated with his own arduous endeavour was working
beside him had made emotion leap up in Arjun's breast many
times – Ram Pal too had experienced the same with him –
across the thousands of barriers of caste and creed that stood
between the two.

What this meant was that all the days and nights of slogging silently, of ruining his health, had given Deepu nothing. All he'd felt was that he was merely substituting for another labourer because his father did not have sufficient resources to hire someone. The enchantment of clay had evidently not touched Deepu, none of Arjun's dreams or desires had been conveyed to his son through the magic of clay – so what had Arjun achieved in all these days? Would there be any benefit then in continuing to keep his son tied to his side in this inhuman saga of hard work, half-empty stomachs and sleepless nights?

As a small heartfelt sigh escaped his lips, Arjun recalled the suppressed smile on her face – a face blurred a little now maybe because of the long passage of time. She used to come and sit here at all hours, and with the expert pressure of her fingers she would lift up the perfect, beautiful, soft clay moulds of the Devi face – one after another. Today she was no more – his Didi, Kunti – the imprint of her crimson alta feet – now hung in a frame on the wall. The beloved face tightly enveloped within his heart had now become a tiny insubstantial two-dimensional picture. Even today Arjun thought of his Didi every day before commencing work and at the end of the day's labour. Arjun had not forgotten his Didi even for a day.

Sarayu had brought the tea. She had even floated a teaspoonful of cream in the cup. He liked a mixture of cream and sugar even on his plate of rice, just a handful of cream without sugar would do. He loved cream in his tea – Sarayu knew this, but cream was not always available. In the floating cream today there appeared to be concealed some invisible indulgence, as though in it was hidden the love of a sixteen-year-old girl. "Accha Sarree, do you remember the year of the flood, when we walked the whole night on Nabami, the penultimate day of the Pujas . . ."

In handing over the biscuit, their fingers touched, establishing a divine contact of sorts. "Don't I remember?"

laughed Sarayu. "My sandal straps snapped, just close to the Baghbazar Community Puja, and then I had to carry them in my hands . . . at the corner of Shyam bazar the crowds were as thick as winged insects . . . people were overflowing onto the streets breaking down the restricting bamboo barriers . . . my feet were swollen like a drum the next day . . . "

The next day – not really day – at night, Arjun had forcibly massaged hot oil into his bride's soft feet. Ma had gone to the local Puja venue – no one was at home. Arjun had had no other wicked intentions. Yet, how overcome with modesty Sarayu had been – she just would not let him touch her feet, she kept curling them inward. Oil marks stained the borders of her sari. Her two beautiful soft feet had swollen and turned red. Her long plait was lashing back and forth on the pillow like a python embroiled in a nightmare . . . even after so many years Arjun had not forgotten the desperate struggle of that long black plait of hair . . . yes, love had been aroused, like a flash of lightening or the colours of the season, love had played in this way between them once in a while. . . .

Maybe there was no exceptional closeness, or even the concealment of an age old love – but on quite a few occasions they had at unguarded moments, in embarrassing situations come into very close contact with each other, and had been unable to retract their positions. Undoubtedly on one such occasion, free of all encumbrances, their first child must have been conceived on an autumnal night. They might even have spent some rainy nights or spring nights in close proximity without any thought of possible consequences. Just as the tide waters ebbed, in the same way after such instances of love-making, Sarayu had silently picked herself up, and slipped back again into her still, quiet reticence and her household duties. And Arjun too had gone back to his workshop, to his clay-modelling. Again for many, many days Arjun had gazed at his distantly situated wife, who appeared like a night river, totally lost in the horizon. Not only had he not been able to touch Sarayu, he had not even been able to stand next to her. Arjun's disconsolate, lonely heart had repeatedly questioned 'why, why did Sarree change like this?' Sometimes from within his own heart he had even heard 'Why don't you change yourself? Why don't you request her, break down her pride, beg her on your knees, penetrate the darkness with your touch? All you do is to keep waiting, for when the clouds will clear, and the sun appear or the moon?' Arjun had told himself, 'I don't know why I can't. I have never been able to beg from anyone else, or apply force on anyone – whether wife, mahajan or child'. Today, suddenly, this cloudy Shravan sky was reminding Arjun of those few carefully treasured days of love-making that one could count on one's fingertips. With the Shravan rains it felt as though some of their carefree youthful days had returned. Why did the touch of Sarayu's fingers arouse such sudden joy in his mind? Was that tiny piece of cream floating in the terracotta coloured tea some kind of sign that love was suddenly blossoming between them.

The tea-cup remained untouched – completely oblivious Arjun suddenly pulled Sarayu towards him with his two hands. Savouring the touch of Sarayu's lips and body for a few moments Arjun thought the firmness of the ground under his feet was being restored. Sarayu was either hypnotized or maybe petrified – the backdoor was open, on the bed in front lay sleeping their grown up son. Arjun's body was on fire, as though burning with high fever – maybe just a few moments, or even a tiny fraction of those – yet Arjun in that space of time had traversed the entire shadowy spectrum – from that early morning of the day he pulled out the frames from the burning straw within the bodies of the Jagaddhatri idols, to the morning of the refusal by the mahajan. Maybe only a few moments – soon after which Arjun had let Sarayu go. He had laughed at her fearfully anxious face. The heat that had been aroused for a second in Sarayu's body, had now entered Arjun's blood.

Clay idols are similar, they appear to have no life, but those who think that idols are cold are stupid. The idol is soft, it has the mystery of life within it, it has warmth, it absorbs and reflects the lights of the constellations. The days Arjun had spent with clay on his hands had not been days spent away from human touch or days of loneliness. Instead the new models he was constantly playing with were actually clay creations of his ongoing experiences of human life.

"You must come with me to Kumortuli today."

"Me!" Sarayu's lips looked a little swollen, and had fallen apart as though she had never heard such a shocking statement.

"Well, I'm going today. I always go during the season of the big Puja. This time too my heart is really pulling me. It feels good even if I stand empty-handed watching the bidding."

"They are all your own people." Sarayu seemed to mumble in an undertone.

"You too are my own. It has been ages since you walked with your slippers in your hands, come along today!"

First, Sarayu looked at Arjun, then out of the window at the threatening clouds. Very slowly her large eyes filled with tears, and suddenly, without any prior warning Sarayu began to sob, and sitting down she bent her tearful face on her knees.

"What's wrong, Sarree?"

Sarayu's knot of hair shimmered like rainwashed black granite. Her face was buried in her knees. The sounds of her sobs shook her whole body, running up and down its length as if struck by lightening. These were not tears of hurt pride or because of some small pain, it was as if some deep sorrow had attacked Sarayu's breast. Was this the same Sarayu, the warmth of whose lips were still on Arjun's face and eyes? She appeared to be someone else. A huge broken vessel seen through a curtain of rain. Arjun could not muster up enough courage to touch or console this person. Like an assassin he continued to stand and watch her from afar.

Still weeping Sarayu raised her hand and opened the small box kept on the kitchen shelf to show him the money for household expenses kept in it. A twenty rupee note and some change was lying inside. So what? Arjun was unable to comprehend the problem. There were household expenses, money got spent, so why cry about it?

Sarayu again put her head down on her knees as though she did not want to further explain or justify the reason for her tears. Then, lifting her tear-drenched face, she said in a broken voice, "Bonu-Ma wants to come."

Bonu-Ma wanted to come. Sarayu and Arjun's daughter Bonu was to deliver a baby in the month of Kartik. Their daughter would have to be brought over, Arjun knew that, but had not paid much attention to the matter. Sarayu had asked him to go to the daughter's in-law's house once, but Arjun had not managed to do so. He had thought it would be okay to bring her over at Puja time.

No father was ever going to acknowledge to himself that the main reason for not showing much concern so far was the fear of additional expenses. Money would be required for the girl, one had to carry something to gift when visiting her in-laws, travel expenses, taxi fare . . . unconsciously Arjun had been retreating from offering to go and bring Bonu – maybe he had been thinking, let them first propose the matter. Let some letter come from Bonu's in-laws.

Besides himself now with anxiety he wanted to know from Sarayu, "Has there been any letter from that house?"

Bonu had written. She had got the letter posted secretly by

someone else. She had written to her mother, "Tell Baba to come quickly and take me away. I feel scared."

Seeing the almost empty money box, Arjun suddenly remembered that last week after buying material he had not given Sarayu any money. Sarayu was a very thrifty housewife. Lord knows with how much trouble she had been managing to run the household, buying things in small amounts. Worried about his own means of livelihood and health problems, anxieties regarding Deepu, everything together had made him forget about Sarayu altogether!

But why was his daughter scared? Her due date was still months away. Was her mother-in-law making her do strenuous work? Sarayu said, "No, nothing much. The fear is about something else." The hint of tears still clung to her eyelashes. Seeing them Arjun felt both fear and love.

* * *

"Shakti da, you have grown old."

"You scoundrel! You have grown old too, so why won't I?"

Shakti Malakar roared with laughter. The heavy hair of his youth was no more, his back was bent, two of his front teeth had fallen. For years he had spent all his time extracting flakes from within a pliant yet unyielding plant which sprouted only in marshy lands. Continually, giving these flakes life in the form of flower petals and leaves, Malakar had not noticed when youth, beauty and the pleasures of life had left his own body.

How skillfully and delicately the teeth marks of crabs had to be cut out of the heart of the stem of the sola with a knife was something the young Arjun had watched him doing one day. Shaktinath's shop had not been painted in many years. The work of making bulen, tinsel, zari ornaments was being done and he was holding the hand of a young boy to teach him the work. It was strenuous work and it required a lot of discipline. It took a lot of labour to create each crown, each ornament. Yet, once they were made, no one looking at them in the puja pavilion would have any idea of this. It was precisely because people did not have any understanding that artisans could hardly get a square meal. It was now up to the artist to try and make people realize this. Yet, work would then take a backseat and retreat behind the curtains. The artists who made the ornaments were just not cut out to be players in this particular game.

First the design would be drawn on pieceboard with a pencil. Extremely beautifully, with an easy hand Shaktinath would himself do this. Then would begin the work of decorating and filling up the outline of the design with small beads, gold zari leaves and coloured bulen. Of course, before this, the pencil outlines would have been cut out of the folds of the pieceboard with large scissors to create the base for different crowns and ornaments. Filling up these cut-outs would continue for a long time. To complete a single set of ornaments a person would have to devote himself to it for at least three to four days. Who was going to pay for this hard work? If he did, how would the potter afford to buy the ornaments? If the Puja Committees did not pay him the price for an idol decorated with expensive ornaments, then, like he had to pay for his daughter's wedding jewellery, the potter would have to pay for the idol's jewellery from his own pocket.

"Where are the sola ornaments, Shaktinath da?"

Extracting the roll of tough string from between his teeth, Shakti Malakar said, "This year there has been no sola crop at all. Last time there were such floods that the plants rotted and were destroyed. There is no sola in the market. You take bulen zari ornaments."

The glitter of gold work had never attracted Arjun. Whenever he had bid for bulen ornaments it was under pressure from the Puja Committees. This time he had only one big idol to mould. He would have taken sola ornaments. However, thinking of his daughter's tears, Arjun had dug into the money kept aside for the idol's ornaments and given some of that to Sarayu. With the rest he was going to fetch Bonu the next day. The sky was still heavily overcast with the clouds of Shravan. That sky over the narrow lane appeared like an anxious mother-bird impatiently awaiting the arrival of her babies. The rain was not about to come down just now. On both sides of the lane, at some places were piles of straw, or bamboo poles. A tarpaulin had been mounted on wooden posts. The work on the big idol was almost complete. Now was the time to get orders. On the chest and belly a layer of sandy soil had been applied, under which could be seen the fibres of the strip of thin cloth. This was to ensure that cracks did not appear. The mould of the idol's face had just been fixed, the moist clay on the neck was yet to dry, the fist of the hand was still to be joined, at some places the mould of the fist, and at others the moulds on an open palm were being made. Those who would place orders first wanted to see the way the lion's mane had been moulded. The lion's head was shaped by a plastering of clay over straw. They also wanted to examine the nape of the Asura's neck, raised hand, and the savage look on his face. If all these features were not ready at the time of bidding, how could the rates be fixed?

All around man was the human face of the Goddess. Of course there was also Ganesh and Kartik, and the two girls – Lakshmi and Saraswati – who stood nearby as well. In this family of five were a mother, two daughters and two sons.

Why was it that mankind, who worshipped both these female and male Gods with equal fervour, would not allow their own girls to live? What strange things human beings said. Hand in

glove with the parents of the boy were the doctor and his
machines. Nowadays numerous clinics had mushroomed.
Their son-in-law had taken Bonu to one of these. Today one
could find out in advance, whether the child in the womb was
a boy or a girl. Bonu, it seems, was to have a girl. Her in-laws
wanted a son. On hearing the results of the test, her mother-
in-law's face had turned gloomy. Bonu was at fault for she was
going to become a mother of a girl-child. Her mother-in-law
stopped speaking to Bonu in a civil manner. Bonu's husband
was an extremely quiet type, but it seems even he appeared
disappointed. No wonder Bonu was afraid, and crying
constantly, wanting to come home. She feared for the life of
the child in her womb. Maybe there was not so much to fear.
However she was alone in the house of others. Sarayu's heart
was restless since yesterday – ever since the letter had arrived.
After all she had a mother's heart. Suppose some harm had
come to her daughter in this interval?

How man was changing, thought Arjun! He had money,
doctors, instruments – he wouldn't let anything remain a
mystery, a surprise. He must know whether the child born out
of their mutual love was male or female. If male, his household
would overflow with joy. If female, his face would turn dark.
He who had a wife, a mother, a sister at home, in whose care he
had grown to manhood that man now wanted his girl-child to
be destroyed even before she was born. What kind of change
was this?

Whenever the thought of Putul's half-charred corpse
hanging under the frame of Number Three Bridge threatened
to come to mind, Arjun would try to obliterate the sight from
his eyes with a wave of his hand, as though he was swatting a
fly. It was as though he was not standing under an open sky but
was trapped in the compartment of a train surrounded by the

stench of kerosene and the hideous foul smell emanating from a burnt corpse.

Today, Arjun was acutely aware of the overwhelming sense of anxiety that parents feel when they think of their children. How panic and fears grips their minds at the slightest hint of danger to their offspring. He was supposed to be looking for artisans today at Kumortuli. Maybe it was only a minor arrangement, just one or two assistants for a month and a half. But that question did not arise any more. The money would now have to be saved – however he did this. He would work alone day and night regardless of whether Deepu joined him or not. Not sola, he would adorn the idol with clay ornaments. Not with money, but with hard labour he would make up for the want of beauty. Arjun's fingers still had their intangible tender quality in full measure. Even today his work was flawless, untarnished, beautiful. Even today his moulds, the distinctive mark of his scalpel attracted the eye of illustrious people just as they had twenty years ago. Work was progressing with advance money. Now if he could somehow work really hard and deliver the idol early, he should get full payment in hand. However, this would suffice for just a few days – after which he would have to go into the market again. If he didn't take a loan his household expenses would not be met before and after the Pujas.

There were rows of workshops in the lane. In some places the workshops were flowing onto the streets. The Municipality caught you if you kept material on the streets. Still the hide-and-seek game with the law continued. If one didn't put the Goddess out on the street how would the idol dry? It was monsoon time after all and the work of holding up balls of fire to dry the clay was in full progress. In the midst of all this, one could spot a small green door, its paint faded. On it an old handle and rusted lock were hanging for the last so many years. Twenty-five years ago, Raghu Pal had disappeared from here. Even today no one knew where he was. This was in the days of Arjun's youth. The news had spread through Kolkata. Out of curiosity, even Arjun had come running. On the evening of the sixth Puja day, Shasthi, there were seven or eight small and big idols inside the workshop, complete, faultless yet unsold. That year Raghu Pal had received no orders. Yet he had been unable to stop himself from making the idols. Right to the end, with every grain of his strength and savings he had moulded the idols, he had even decorated them from their feet to the top of their heads. Yet, even till the evening of the fifth day, no one came. Raghu Pal was missing from the morning of Shasthi itself. He had not returned till evening. The whole city was then reverberating with the sound of music and the songs of Puja.

Whenever Arjun came to Kumortuli he could not help but look once at this door. Who knows who was there in this artist's family – wife, son, daughter – where did they go? Were those Goddesses embellished with ornaments, still standing behind the closed doors – faded in colour, their plaster disintegrating, their crowns entangled in cobwebs?

Why did Raghu Pal leave like that – maybe his pride had been greatly hurt by this whole wide world. After having spent thirty years in pursuing one profession with dedication and devotion, if one did not get the order for even one Goddess – one's pride was bound to be hurt.

Arjun just could not think of opting out in this way. If he had been a potter by birth, what he would have done is not known. He had grown up amidst the smell of acid, the colourless sight of wood fibre and rows of drying leather. As soon as he gained consciousness, clay and the game of clay moulding had completely absorbed Arjun. This addiction to

beauty and colour had not left him to this day. Being physically
and mentally wrapped up in this intricate web he did not have
the means to exercise his sense of hurt pride over anyone and
disappear. All the debts and their responsibilities were his alone.
The more he suffered, the more Arjun got involved and took
to the forefront of his struggle. That shut door – Raghu Pal's
abandoned workshop – pained him a lot, but did not show
him a way out of his troubles.

Just a little ahead was Bishamber Pal's warehouse.
Bishamber was a reputed man – his fame extended all over the
city, and even outside the country. Before the partition of the
country, he had come to Kumortuli from Faridpur and taken
a place. His business was as large as his name. Critics said their
business was up to its neck in debt. However, the dazzle and
show of their Goddesses did not reveal this. Arjun stood before
their open door wide-mouthed. "*Aiyee bas*, what a giant-sized
idol" – what huge rounded arms, what a large face mould
placed on a lined neck – and what a face! The two equally
mesmerising eyes, the sharp nose, full lips, all seemed to belong
as much to the earthly world as to the sky. The open mouth of
the lion, its mane, the array of teeth within the mouth, the
attitude of placing its paw – was so real yet divine that one felt
breathless.

"Pal Moshai?" Arjun asked an old artisan in sign language.
He too in a fearful manner indicated the way inside. There
were at least twelve gigantic Devi-lion-Asura ensemble idols –
in two small rooms. It seemed as though the silent music of the
sounds of battle had begun to play. After crossing the outer
room, there were two more rooms inside one after the other.
In the third and last room, sitting on a stool was Bishamber
Pal, working at a table on which was a pile of clay. He was
shaping fingers. A mould of the fist could be made, but the
fingers of an open palm had to be manually shaped. The fingers

of the huge eighteen feet idol were plump and long. One by one
the thumbs, then the four fingers. Shaping and moulding them
in different postures with the pressure of his hands, he was
drawing lines on them with a scalpel. He had eyes for nothing
else. His heavy chin rested on his chest, from his neck hung the
amulet of his childhood days – his spectacles were sliding down
his sweat-drenched nose. Finally he would join them to the
palm. Arjun had seen this sight before as well. Today
Bishamber's age-old absorption stirred his own broken heart
in a strange way. Arjun was watching but unable to move. The
small mountain of fingers was slowly becoming bigger before
his very eyes.

☞ 17 ☜

Dolls made out of unbaked clay got washed away during the
monsoons. Of course they were more durable if they were fired.
Then they lasted for a long time. But in what condition they
survived, what they endured, only the doll could tell. Too much
heat was also dangerous. If a vertical crack appeared anywhere,
then one day it would shatter into smithereens. There were
amazing similarities between man and clay idols. Man was
born on this earth, and with its clay he created the image of a
God, who could neither be touched nor held. However the
image was not actually a God, it was more human really.

Urmi was one such burnt-clay goddess-doll.

Even before she could learn about life and start a family she
had fallen into the fire. By the time she finally emerged scorched
from the blazing fire, Anandi was already in her lap. Little
Anandi, with her tears, her hunger, her sleep, the changing of
sheets followed by her growing up with games, school, music
and various other related activities. Urmi had never been able

to stabilize her own life again. Her whole life had gone by like
a rocking boat on a choppy sea. Her mother had been there, so
had her brother. Because her beloved people had been around,
Urmi had never been without protection. Yet the sorrow, the
deep shame of her solitariness followed her like a shadow.
Urmimala had never been able to share this with anyone else.
By nature she was a strong, self-respecting individual. Even in
acute pain, she was not the kind to speak out about her sorrow,
or resort to a frenzy of crying and wailing.

When Anandi was in her womb, Urmi's condition would
have turned any ordinary girl either mad or deaf to everything
around her. Yet Urmi, seemed to have walked on fire with
ease. However, that a crack was gradually forming within her,
thanks to her proximity and repeated encounters with fire,
was something no one had realized. Much later, one day, Urmi
suddenly cracked into pieces.

In a household, people who suppressed their own traumatic
feelings had a tough time. They looked fine, keeping calm in
the face of other people's troubles. However, if the pain in
their hearts rose up in revolt, then what a sight that would be!
No one would accept it. Every one would be irritated. They
would say, what on earth is this! We never expected such an
exhibition from her. If someone who drank regularly came
home sober one day people would be pleased. But if somebody
who never touched liquor was to imbibe a peg or two one day
people would rise up in consternation. Urmi discovered that
her situation was somewhat similar. The family members were
so used to her never expressing herself verbally, that Urmi's
voice now sounded strange to their ears.

Ma passed away when Anandi was barely ten years old. She
had not suffered too much, she had been unconscious with
high fever for about two days. Internally she had gradually
lost the will to live, the fever was almost an excuse to depart

this life. One could say that overnight Ma's household now became Dada's household. Why was it not Urmi's? Urmi thought extensively about this. There is possibly some deep-rooted fault in the blood of women that finally they are unable to adopt any home as their own. After all, this house was where Dada and Urmi had lived since their childhood. In their manner of living there had really not been any major physical differences! Soon after Ma's death, Urmi had begun to talk of leaving. This was her own fault. If on one's own one kept repeating unreasonable statements, then with the passage of time those same statements would begin to sound reasonable.

Urmi's Dada, Arindam, had reasoned with her several times and told her that there was no need for her to leave. This house was their father's, after all! They could both stay. After Arindam's marriage, the running of the household had undergone a change, as had the interior décor. Arindam's wife, Reena, was an architect. She had taken a small office space on Theatre Road, and did a lot of work from home as well. Reena was of the belief that she was the last word in interior decoration and knew all there was to know about it. Maybe she did. Yet she had poked her nose even into the space which was by right Urmi's – her own two rooms and the small attached balcony. She had placed a durrie, on the floor, she had switched the flower pots, and had changed the telephone stand. These minor changes she had brought about very gradually, with a mixture of curiosity and fun. Urmi had returned from office and seen them, experienced pain and just then Reena had laughingly said, "Ki, how's the surprise!"

Unable to control herself, one day Urmi had retaliated "Boudi, please do whatever you like elsewhere, but I would prefer to keep my room in my own way."

The cheerful, dimple-cheeked Reena's face had changed colour and turned dark pink in a second.

"Your two rooms are part of this house aren't they, they aren't outside!"

"Yes they are, but this space is mine alone – not yours," Urmi had said in suppressed anger.

"Fine. But do take a look at your space sometimes. People can live in a better way than this."

What a minor matter! Insignificant material things! Yet they caused a wall to build up, separating the two families. From outside of course that is what it appeared to be. Along with it many other complaints got mixed up. Urmi had left for office without giving the guard at the gate the keys – the maid was unable to enter and had gone away. At night tension built up on this issue. Anandi had used the phone and not put the receiver back correctly. Arindam had repeatedly tried to get through from office. The line had been engaged. Urmi got angry at Reena's insinuations. She slapped her daughter hard on her back. Anandi, refusing to eat her tea-time snacks had sat the whole evening with her forehead pressed against the window bars. The imprint of the bars were clearly visible on her forehead. Small misunderstandings like these carried on.

Reena actually couldn't understand Urmi at all. Her parents had been against her marrying into this family. At that time she was deeply in love with Arindam. Reena had stubbornly wept and got a Registry wedding done. For Urmi she had felt great love and forgiveness. Aha, poor thing, what was one to do if one's beloved and fiancé died just before one's wedding? She had not aborted her child, she had saved her life, and was bringing her up! If Reena also did not sympathise with her, then Urmi would face a great loss. Before marriage, Reena had seen Urmi a couple of times. She had appeared to be someone very shy or silently sorrowing. That was where Reena had made a grave mistake. In Urmi there was no hesitation, doubt or personal shame, nothing at all. She was cool, spoke little, but was impossibly determined and sharp. What had occurred in her life was just one of the many normal occurrences that one had to face. She was not willing to consider it as bad fate. She felt no shame or embarrassment in bringing up Anandi. Hence Reena's forgiving nature played no significant role in Urmi's life. Instead Reena began to think, 'Ish! is such self-confidence a good thing?' Then Arindam and Urmi's mother had been alive, Reena found it amazing to see that even her mother-in-law felt no embarrassment regarding her daughter. The mother and daughter would be laughing, going here and there as though life was extremely simple, just one long joke.

'What was this?' Reena began to feel angry with herself. 'I came into this family after angering my parents yet my self-sacrifice has not been considered a sacrifice at all. How did that happen?' While making love at night, Reena raised her face from Arindam's chest, and spoke up: "Chchi!"

"What do you mean by chchi?" Arindam asked his brows furrowed.

"You all are awful!" There were tears in Reena's eyes. "None of you feel any shame or disgrace!"

"Shame about what?" Arindam was unable to understand. At a time like this why should there be any question of shame?

"That sister of yours, your mother . . . all the same! You too encourage them. You never say anything to them, do you?"

Arindam finally understood. Having done so he covered his body with clothes. No man could remain aroused after such allegations.

Completely dejected, Arindam continued to lie there. Whatever had to happen in Urmi's life had happened seven or eight years before his own marriage. To save his sister's life with love and affection, to help her to bring her child into this world — these had been the only goals for his mother and Arindam in those terrible days! However, even afterwards . . .

that Urmi could in any way be pitied, or shown sympathy to
... was something Arindam could not even think about. Urmi
was his own blood, his sister from the same mother, his
childhood companion. Whatever Urmi did was correct, it was
right, with everything he had, he had to support her, he had to
stand by her – this was something Arindam understood
completely. It was in his blood.

Arindam had not hidden anything from Reena before
marriage. Any other boy would have made up a few white lies
– my sister had registered marriage – the in-laws did not know
– etc. Arindam had been unable to do so. He knew that Urmi
would never forgive him if he did. Urmi just could not bear
any kind of deceit. At that time Reena's heart was overflowing
with love.

Reena did not seem to find anything very difficult or
complicated. Having been stumped twice or thrice by Reena's
parents questions regarding his sister's life, Arindam was unable
to talk to them any further. He had still tried to make himself
understand that it was but natural for Reena's parents to ensure
the happiness and security of their daughter's married life.
But how could Arindam abandon Urmi? By dying, Tapesh
had forever rendered Urmi's life motionless, still and dark.
Urmi had to bring up her daughter – yet she was left without
any support. That Reena disliked her from the core of her being
was something it took Urmi a while to realize. After meeting
Reena, and for some years after she entered their home, Ma
had been there. There were many things which she had not
allowed her to see, that she had hidden from her. What with
her office work, a small daughter, her untidy room, Urmi's life
was one big mess. In that situation whether Reena accepted
her or not was something Urmi was unable to think of with
any seriousness. After Ma's passing away there was a vacuum
in this small household. The curtain between them was now

suddenly removed and the acute inability to like each other became apparent to both Reena and Urmi. For Arindam there now began a life of suffering.

Arindam was unaware, though Ma knew how much Urmi had had to tolerate when she first went to work. Gradually one got used to many things. Even today, after so many years, when Urmi walked on the streets she could sense the silent prying eyes pricking her from behind. She was not a normal person. When Anandi was five years old she had taken up this new job. She had been summoned by the Head of the office. He was young, educated and good-looking. Urmi had understood as soon as she entered that the atmosphere was explosive. She had been the topic of discussion and those who had been talking about her were now silent on seeing her. The boss had said. "I have heard about you. You are very brave. So I wanted to see you. Congrats! You will have no problems here."

Urmi's eyes had registered amazement. Congrats! For what? She was a dark girl, yet did not think the fates were mocking her. She was an unwed mother, yet had no sense of sin. What courage had Urmi displayed? What choice did she have at that time, as Tapesh's beloved? As the mother-to-be of their child, what else could Urmi have done? How strange!

Yet, having been shown this unsolicited sympathy by the most senior man of the office, Urmi had been forced to say in a low voice, "Thank you." She had not liked it all. She had felt scared. Just as an untouchable feels when given food in new crockery, fearing that he will be marginalized forever. 'You will have no problems' – Why? What problems would she have had? Were there really some hidden dangers surrounding her?

In the same way the Union too had come in to look at Urmi. Urmi had opened her box and was eating her tiffin at lunch-break. Seated next to her were Sanjoy and his girlfriend Monika, who belonged to the same branch. They had stood up in a hurry. On the glass top of the table had been reflected the shadow of Shyamal Dutta. Shyamal was the Vice-President of the Staff Union and he was accompanied by other office bearers.

Unable to fathom what was happening, Urmi too had stood up stupidly. Shyamal had smiled a soft yet priceless smile, and said, "Arrey, why are you standing up, do sit. We have come, because we wanted to see the person who has recently joined. You have nothing to worry about. We will all stand by you."

Shyamal's two sharp eyes had already flicked all over Urmi while she had been still seated, the way eager clients looked at the bodies of expectant prostitutes. On top of the table lay Urmi's quiet, still, soft dark arm. There was no hesitation in it, only a slight fear. Two thin gold bangles encircled it. On her finger was a ring set with white stones.

Urmi was mentally wondering, what there was to see, but she said, "Thank you." Shyamal deepening his voice a little had said, "Your courage, sacrifice – defying society – is like an example to us! This is what is required! Women like you!"

Urmi thought, neither were women like her born in every household just by wishful thinking, nor was it good to have such women in every family. Not understanding what sacrifice she was purported to have made, Urmi gradually grew stiff. "You must tell us if you have any problems of any kind." Shyamal had looked her in the eye.

"I'll take your leave now."

Urmi had lowered her eyes. She was feeling uncomfortable. Taking this momentary lowering of the eyes for modesty, Shyamal Dutta before getting up had pressed Urmi's hand lightly. Urmi had immediately wiped her hand with a handkerchief. Her action had been so quick that there had been no time for thought. Shyamal had felt insulted and not turned back even once. His ridicule and strong hatred of Urmi even today flicked constantly over her in the office. Later in the Ladies Room, Monika had told her, "Why did you go and wipe your hand like that . . . couldn't you wait till Dutta had left?"

Re-doing the wiped off teep dot on her forehead, Urmi had said "I intended to wipe it off in front of him and so I did. What a vulgar man." Urmi, even after twenty-three years had never forgotten her own face, as she had seen it that day in the old dim mirror.

There was Reena's cold hostility at home. And there was the silent curiosity and compassion of the people in the office. Still the office was now gradually growing bearable. The home however was growing more and more cold and complicated. Urmi's only compensation on such days was Anandi. That Arindam was suffering because of her made Urmi suffer too. She then resorted to holding Anandi close to herself even more strongly than before. Anandi was a headstrong young girl. From childhood her behaviour was full of self-confidence. Her speech was absolutely clear and flowing. She was never afraid of voicing her likes and dislikes. At mealtimes, it was her daily task to point out in no uncertain terms things like 'the luchi is under cooked', 'I do not eat bitter things' or that 'The chutney has ants in it', meaning the mustard seeds floating in the syrup. Even after she grew up, Anandi had inadvertently created tension between her aunt and mother by making sharp and bold statements. She had borne her mother's slaps for these no doubt – but that had not reduced their mutual closeness in anyway. In fact, Urmi had instead held her daughter even more tightly to herself.

Yet, gradually cracks were appearing in the body of this clay model – and one day she suddenly shattered into bits.

She was growing old. No more could she work as hard as before. She had just crossed fifty years of age. The weariness pervading her blood was clearly audible to Urmi's ears. This weariness was not merely physical. She felt deeply isolated.

It had been a long time. Tapesh's face and his memories had begun to blur and fade away. How blurred they were was something Urmi had not admitted even to herself. Nowadays, the experience of an unbearable agony had begun to prick Urmi. What had she, Urmi, got out of life? Either by someone's mistake or out of somebody's greed for blood Tapesh had departed this life. After death, the one who dies does not burn anymore. Tapesh remained immortally enclosed in a frame. A handsome, smiling, revolutionary youth. . . .

The one who continued to burn was Urmi. She had thought Tapesh was in her heart. He would look after her and care for her with his whole being and hence she had not thought of anything else. Many other men had offered friendship, love. Urmi had run away. From wherever hints of love and friendship had emanated, she had stubbornly never looked in that direction. But today, where was Tapesh, he was not in her heart anymore was he? Like a burnt-out meteor, Tapesh too had at some time fallen off like a spent force! And what about Anandi?

"Why are you so irritable since morning, Ma? Aren't you feeling well?"

Anandi came and placed her hand on Urmi's forehead. Urmi moved her hand away quickly.

"Where are you going?"

"To the cybercafe."

"Why? What is the need?"

"Come on, what does one do there? I'll send mail."

"Who will you mail?"

"Swapna, Ma!" Running to hug her, Anandi after one loving gesture, became aware that her mother's body was becoming stiff in her embrace.

"You hardly know him, and you begin mailing him! Isn't that being shameless?"

"Why shameless?" Anandi was mortified. "He loves me! Swapna!"

"Loves you! Wonderful! You already know that, do you? Then go ahead and fall all over him! Idiot girl!"

Tears flowed from Urmi's eyes and severe censure from her throat all at the same time.

With one shoe on her foot Anandi remained standing as though struck by lightening. This was her mother – her sensible, controlled, complete role model of a mother! In an old maxi-dress, with graying hair, bewildered eyes, broken voice – this was not Urmi? Who was she?

Yet she did not scream. With bated breath she waited for the next event. Urmi began to throw all the steel utensils from the table to the floor, in anger. She was not chucking down a single glass item. After all, if they broke, she would herself have to pick up all the pieces.

Her daughter was in any case useless.

A strange tenderness came over Anandi's mind on witnessing this strange game of throwing unbreakable things on the floor.

Taking off her shoe Anandi put her arms around her mother. She took her to the bedroom. Urmi bit her hand. Not very hard but with a lot of anger. Anandi once again put the palm of her hand into her mother's mouth. Laughing, she said, "Let's see, bite really hard now!"

Swapnabha stood at the open door completely taken aback. The very person whom Anandi had just been going to E-mail.

On the floor of the dining space, bowls, spoons and ladles of various kinds lay scattered. From within the sounds of laughter and tears could be heard in two different voices.

Pulling the door closed from outside, Swapnabha once again rang the bell.

Anandi now came running and opened the door. Startled she kept silently gesturing to Swapnabha to run away, run away. . . .

By that time Urmi had come out into the passage.

In a voice mixed with tears and irritation, she said "What are you doing Anandi? Tell him to come in and sit."

Gratefully, Swapnabha came inside. He sat down. Serving them tea and chanachur Urmi again went inside. Some of the utensils had been picked up by Anandi, the rest by Urmi. Urmi went to change her clothes and comb her hair, standing before the mirror for a short while. The sounds of Anandi and Swapnabha's laughter and chatter filtered in from the drawing room. Like the rising of water levels in the wells at monsoon time, love was welling up in Urmi's heart as well, but somehow her heart hardened again. Gradually, mutinous thoughts began to develop and grow within her mind. Her daughter Anandi was laughing. She was chatting. One day she would marry that boy. She might even marry someone else. They would go away. They would live in another house. What would Urmi be left with? This room, emptiness, a lifetime of loneliness, a path on which she would have to walk all by herself on bloody feet. Rolling on the bed, Urmi began to cry. She cried endlessly. The unshed tears suppressed for so long. Her body trembled. Urmi was breaking, she was shattering into pieces. She had been excessively scorched by the heat of the fire after all.

Arindam and Reena were not there at that time. They had gone to Ranchi. They were also going to Hazaribagh. What would have happened if they had been there? Seeing Urmi's sudden anger and tears, Reena would have surely said, she was play-acting or dramatizing. A little later, Anandi went out to see off Swapnabha, who was leaving. Urmi then again began to think of Arindam and his wife. Maybe if they had been there, she would have felt better. The house would not have felt so empty suddenly. Why did she feel this way? Tears again began to well up in Urmi's breast. Anandi had gone out. In her room clothes were scattered, some on the sidepost of the bed. Her salwar was lying on the ground. Even her bedroom slippers were left awry. She was quite old now but had learnt nothing. Forget cooking, she hadn't even learnt to tidy her own belongings. Yet she had gone out. Her daughter had gone out to see off an almost unknown, strange boy. She would return in a while. Yet Urmi knew that Anandi would not be returning to her mother any more. Never, ever again. Her daughter's budding wings of independence were beginning to unfold. This very thought caused waves of a strange sense of emptiness to play within Urmi. She was like a series of arches standing on an open field. Only the wind played within her heart. She had no shape, form or body. All she had was the unbearable pain of existence.

↞ 18 ↠

At the crossing of three roads, was a tiny tea-shop. On top of a green painted packing-box a transistor was playing. It played all day. Old Bangla songs could be heard even now. Arati Mukherji was singing. 'Just because I have come without warning . . . do not think . . . I will take my leave without telling you . . . ' The sharp, youthful voice poured out at every turn of the lyrics and brought back thirty-year-old evenings.

The tea at this shop was very good. There was the aroma of thick, creamy milk and not too much sugar. Even if one had several small earthen mugs of tea one did not really feel satisfied. Arjun was drinking tea and listening to the songs. When he came to this locality, it was a special obligation for him to sit on the bench and drink tea at this shop. 'A thousand deaths . . . I have wanted to die . . . I couldn't bear this hide-and-seek . . . ' Arati was singing. A scrawny, black and white cat came and sat close to Arjun's feet. It was possibly so starved that it had forgotten all fear. At the same time Manoj Pal too came and sat, lowering the cloth bag in his hand to the floor. Looking at him, one could see how exhausted he was. He had been out since early morning. He had taken the Krishnanagar local train to Kolkata. Hunger gnawed at his stomach and his head was throbbing with a bad cold. Manoj asked for two biscuits with his tea. Dark complexioned, with an unruly mop of hair, his eyes were full of compassion. He could be twenty-three years of age, or even twenty-eight. While sipping his tea, Manoj was thinking of something, his eyes wide open. Even his lips were moving. The boy was older than Deepu. Yet seeing the hair falling on his forehead and the way he sat down exhausted Arjun felt sympathy for him rising in his breast. He was fighting. The boy was virtually ruined and yet he continued fighting. He had not given up yet.

"Ki, didn't your work get done?" Arjun asked somewhat jocularly.

Startled, and annoyed to some extent, Manoj Pal looked at the man sitting next to him.

White hair, black skin, stark, thick and dazzling, matched each other quite well. At one time, he'd had a very good physique but now just as when the tide ebbs the skeleton of the steps and the sandy banks beside the river are exposed, in the same way Arjun's frame was now visible. In his smile there was still the freshness of morning flowers, there was neither contempt nor ridicule. Seeing it Manoj opened his mouth. A mofussil boy, he still didn't clearly understand the city speech. Once in a while he fell into its trap. This made him even angrier with himself.

"How can my work get done? No one is willing to pay. By reputation they are such big names and very big houses. Yet they have not paid their dues in three years." His burning resentment cooled a little after his outburst. Yet he also felt slightly embarrassed. Rubbing his worn out sandals on the road, Manoj looked at him with a slanting gaze.

Arjun was not startled to hear the name of the big house. Thousands of scandals existed within the depths of this business. The idol would be worth a lakh and fifty lakhs would be invested. Yet the master would be up to his neck in debts. It was as though there was no shame in this, instead there actually appeared to be pride. Meanwhile, the dues of the shopkeeper supplying the decorations would not be paid for over three years. The artisan needed a lot of courage to do this in the clay market. If the rates did not suit him, he would go elsewhere. No artist would dare leave his dues unpaid. But in the decoration market outside the city the situation was quite poor and lowly. The designs were their own, the crowns were drawn personally by them as were the ornaments, the waist adornments . . . yet nowhere would the name of the craftsman be mentioned in the Puja pavilion.

"Who draws the designs? Your father?"

The son of Priyo Pal of Ghurni, Manoj, rubbing his nails on his pants said, "No, my mother draws the designs. Sarayubala Dasi. She is the one who draws. There are piles of paper. They are all rolled up under our cots at home, you'll see." As though he was saying something extremely funny, Manoj said in a lower tone, "Baba all these days did not tell anyone Ma's name. He would say, 'how can a housewife's name be exposed to the outside world?'"

"Baba is now bed-ridden. He cannot walk. Ma in any case has always done all the work, she continues to do so. Of course, I too work but give my mother's name. Look at this, drawn with a free hand, a completely unique design yet he will not allow my mother's name to be written anywhere. It will be three years this Ashwin – all they do is make us go around in circles. We are continuously supplying – we live far away, just suppose they cut us out completely if we don't? Tell me sir, can people like us survive if thirty or thirty-five thousand rupees are left pending in our payments?"

No way. Arjun nodded his head in agreement with Manoj Pal. How could one carry on? Walking along the lanes he could see, kuchcha mud courtyards with adjoining cement terraces strewn with decoration material. In a small tile covered room a group of local girl-wives were working on decoration items. Some were stringing beads, some cutting paper, some were neatly pasting thin coloured paper in the gaps between the designs. The labour was not on daily wages but on piece rate. For a hundred pieces, the rate was between fifteen and twenty rupees. If the big idol-making houses kept their payments pending, then these young women lost their wages. The money to be paid for raw materials to the wholesalers in Kolkata also remained pending. This time Manoj had been unable to face the wholesale dealers out of fear. As a result he was unable to collect supplies quickly.

Next to the window of the room adjoining the terrace was a plain wooden cot. Priyo Pal was half-reclining on it and looking out. Watching, as the rain fell on the kagji lime and on the small white togor flower trees.

Sarayubala would have left his side just a little while back, having bathed him and wiped his head dry. The smell of boiling rice would be wafting into the room. The aroma of the singed spices in oil was yet to have been absorbed by the daal in which they were to be mixed. Sarayubala, after feeding him, and washing the utensils, would lie down for a bit spreading out her sari aanchal. Then she would take yellow paper and pencil and begin to draw. Creepers, leaves, paisleys. Arjun could clearly picture it all. No one had taught her. Drawing freely as she pleased, Sarayubala was slowly but surely pulling her family ahead. Earlier her husband would go to Borobazar,

Kumortuli, to supply and get payments – now the son went. In the courtyard a group of doves were pecking at daal or bits of rice and cooing. Arjun had been to Ghurni. The place was known to him. The picture of Sarayubala and Manoj's household was nothing new to him. What was new was the manner of leaving payments due that the big workshops had adopted, now that they had swollen in size and importance. Man had become arrogant and shameless. The greed for easy cash and to have their names printed in large alphabets had consumed them wholly.

If you took the road to the right, as you emerged from the lane, you came to Hridayballabh's house. Arjun had taken the left turn instead of the right. He was to take a bus home from the same bus-stop, where Manoj Pal would take one to Sealdah. If he had gone down the road on the right, Arjun would have seen a portion of the road and footpath enclosed with ropes and path-dividers. The police themselves had cordoned off the area. Two policemen were taking turns to keep an eye on the place. They were making sure no evidence was lost till the forensic tests were complete. Even in the morning, Hridayballabh's blood stains could have been seen on the road. As soon as the day had progressed particles of dust had blown in and settled over them, while the sun and wind had taken off some portions. Now unless you really examined the place closely it did not appear as if anything had ever been there. That the outcome of such a fall had not been instant death was surprising. Hridayballabh had not died yet.

The boundary wall of the terrace on the fourth floor had not been built. Not even till now. If Hriday's brothers were questioned, they would say we had no idea what Dada had wanted to do. Once in a while there had been discussions on whether another floor could be built, albeit on a smaller scale. After the winters, Hridayballabh had suffered from a cerebral blood-clot. This was followed by the entire right side of his body becoming paralysed. He could not speak. Later speech returned but his words remained indistinct. Strangers could not make out what he wanted to say. His right side was almost useless and as stiff as the trunk of an abandoned tree. Still with the help of physiotherapy, Hridayballabh was able to stand slowly. If one held his hand or gave him a steel stick to hold, he could even walk a few steps. For a sick man, six in the morning was rather early. It took a whole hour till seven, to complete the rituals of making him sit up in bed, brush his teeth, wash his face and change his clothes. The night nurse came from Sonarpur and so she was in a hurry to leave. She wanted to finish all her morning duties quickly and escape. There were two more reasons for the hurry: if the day nurse came late, the night nurse would also have to bathe the patient; that was a complicated and difficult task. Apart from this, there was no morning tea served in this house. Shefali grumbled that there was a dispute every morning on this issue. Who would give the tea? The women of the house had better things to do than to get up so early in the morning just to serve a maid tea!

Hridayballabh would not be able to assume charge of the business any more. The brothers were looking after the work. Not having taken any direct responsibilities in years, they were now at the end of their tether and completely out of their depth. To top everything the markets were down. It took almost four to five months to find out how much money was due and from whom. In a business where the incoming cash flowed immediately into the capital outlay, how impractical it was to hire help both during the day and the night for the care of the patient. This was something the women of the house came to know in no uncertain terms. It was not possible for them to nurse Hridayballabh. He had always kept his distance as their Uncle-in-law. Physical care – even of a sick man – was not something the daughters-in-law could undertake. The nephews came once in a while and stroked his body but they neither had the inclination nor the expertise. Because of this help had to be hired. The money was shared among the brothers. Every month when the money had to be paid, they mentally, almost unconsciously, cursed their wives. This kind of care was taken on by family members in village homes . . . hence so much money did not have to be spent . . . Jagatballabh had once even blurted this out. Only once, of course. For, immediately his wife had heatedly berated him.

"No, nowadays they don't. If they did, there would not be so many agencies all over Kolkata supplying nurses and maids. It is the same in the mofussils as well . . . the rates are a little lower there . . . that's all! Have you seen the local trains in the mornings . . . they're full of dirty, synthetic clad women . . . with cloth-bags in their hands . . . you all only want to save money . . . do the work yourselves. You . . . brothers. He did not marry, we cannot now look after this bachelor Uncle . . . "

Jagatballabh had not been able to resume the topic ever again. He had not had the courage. He had always been a bit of a coward. When the time came to outline the eyes of the Goddess, he would not be found anywhere in the locality – he would hide away somewhere and sit. Hridayballabh had beaten, scolded and taught him the job personally in his youth. Nowadays, Lord knows what was happening – every household had the same malaise. Paralysis, cancer, did one see these patients earlier? Now every household had either bedridden old men or women; or handicapped people walking with the help of sticks. Dada, at least did not have cancer . . . he thought to himself sometimes . . . if that had happened they would have gone bankrupt. They would have even had to sell this house.

"This house?"

"It was the house that proved calamitous, finally, you understand."

Some passerby had possibly made this statement and turned his face and walked on.

On the footpath in front of the house there were rows of shops. Some were selling stationery, two were grocery stores and one was a tea stall.

At the tea stall, people began to come and go, sit on the benches in front of it or read newspapers from six in the morning. Most of the men in the locality drank tea at the stall the whole year round, as they did not dare to ask for tea in their own homes. However, this morning no one had come and sat down, the tea too had not been made because people would have been nauseated if they drank tea there.

On the footpath lay the body, on the road lay the head with the two arms spread out . . . that was how Hridayballabh had fallen, on his front . . . hence no one knew whether there had been a smile on his smashed face at that moment.

"What was such a sick man doing on the terrace so early in the morning?"

"He came out from his room to walk everyday," said someone while reading the papers. "I mean someone took him for a walk. . . . "

"Then who took him for a walk so early in the morning?"

"The old man is tough . . . he hasn't died as yet . . .

"Let's see how much longer he survives . . . "

Just as a famous former artist is painted in a roundabout way by a tea shop crowd with strokes of black colour anywhere and any which way they want to . . . in the same way when Hridayballabh's body fell on the streets either having voluntarily jumped . . . or having been pushed from the terrace . . . he had willy-nilly become a topic of public discussion. In the sixties and seventies his facial moulds . . . the arms of his

Goddesses . . . the paan-shaped faces of his idols . . . had raised
a similar storm in the tea-cups.

From the corner, he had taken the left turn instead of the
right. As a result of this minor change in his daily routine,
Arjun never came to know the news of Hridayballabh's
disastrous fall. Manoj went away, and he too caught a bus.
Alighting a stop before his house, he lit a beedi and slowly
walked home. As soon as he reached home . . . there appeared
before him the wonder of the century!

There was only one single big room in which to sit and sleep.
On one side of it lay the old high bedstead made by Rupen
Das. More than half the room had been occupied by the bed.
Under it lay household boxes, containers, large utensils –
things one did not need daily. On the opposite wall were
Sarayu's gods and goddesses, basket of shells, books in praise
of deities and her needle-work paraphernalia. Close to the wall
adjoining the kitchen were two wooden armchairs. There was
a clothes-stand near the window in front. Outside the window
a rope had been tied on which some more clothes had been
hung out.

A tall, thin man sat on one of the two chairs – Arjun noticed
this first. Perhaps Sarayu was in the kitchen trying to make
some tea. Bonu was already sitting on a stool absorbed in some
filmy magazine. On a wicker mura in front Deepu sat silently.

That Arjun had not recognized the man was clear from the
smooth lines on his face. How could he recognize him, it had
been thirty-four years. Arjun had not changed as much. His
hair had turned grey, his body was leaner, but his dark
complexion and skin was as pliable as in his youth. Tridib Basu
had already been much older then, close to forty years old,
now he had lost his health and also his looks. The shape of his
face had changed a lot when he lost his will power. What had
been a shining mirror now appeared to be a dull frosted glass.

Tridib Basu stood up . . . almost like a blind man . . . slowly he extended his right hand towards Arjun. Arjun was still staring at him unmoved . . . the darkness was lifting, yes, he recognized him now.

As he stared at him unblinkingly, it was as if Arjun in a few seconds traversed three whole decades and returned to the present.

This was the same Tridib Basu . . . the artist babu – holding whose hand the nineteen-year-old Arjun, hoping to gain entry into the elite market had in fact stumbled at the very threshold itself. Just as dark alleys reveal their deep hidden secrets in flashes of lightening, if Arjun had not tripped up at the very outset like a fool, he would have knocked at all the wrong doors with the broken bits of his dreams in his heart. The lesson had been so illuminating that he had got his direction for the rest of his life. Of course even till today he had not had the time to figure out whether that had been a good thing or bad. One of the big bosses of an aristocratic Puja Committee . . . was this the same Tridib Basu . . . he had not come even once in the interim . . . in these thirty-four years . . . he had never bothered to come and see how Arjun had spent these long years, what he had got to eat, whether he'd survived or had to go back to the leather trade. . . . That's how it was. These educated, gold-rim spectacled babus lifted you on to a tree and then snatched the ladder from under you. The man had now come again. . . . A strange thought came to Arjun's mind . . . he came at the beginning and was now there at the end . . . had the end arrived? What nonsense came into one's head! In his childhood there used to be a small familiar lane which he went to see regularly . . . blocking the lane suddenly now, was a wall, a blind wall . . . how a wall could block a road, Arjun was unable to figure out. Tridib Basu was saying, "I actually went to your studio at first, but I found you were not there. I have been looking for your house . . . I haven't come in a long time . . . one cannot recognize the streets . . . "

The printing press on Pottery Road had closed down. Asim Sen was not alive. The boys had emptied the old press room and were planning to set up a cyber cafe. In this press a lot of Tridib Basu's work had been printed. He had an amazingly artistic way with letters and sketches, and had introduced a new style in cover design. The business relationship had developed into friendship. Gradually Asim Sen too had got involved in the secret play of letter-creation. Tridib Basu, wanting to involve his friend, purposely asked for his opinions. He brought over different samples of new kinds of work. Towards the end, Asim Sen had become quite well-versed in art, he even searched out books to read on such abstruse subjects as calligraphy and typography. With the death of Asim Sen the friendly relationship between the two old men also came to an end. The weeds around the press room had grown as high as the windows. It would not be surprising if in this jungle of high grass there were snakes lurking around.

Tridib Basu, of course, had not been able to stop working, even though the income was abysmally low. With the arrival of the computer he had initially gone into shock, then eventually he'd picked up computer language and other software. Commercial art was no more a brush and pen affair. Now it was the age of multimedia and Adobe Photoshop. One could still accept the profusion of software, but the new girls and boys believed that there was no requirement any more for hand drawn skills. Instead of wasting time learning how to draw, it was more than enough if one learnt how to use the software. The appreciation of beauty, awareness of perspective, sense of balance and so much else inherent in art, which one picked up in the learning process, they had no idea of. They, in fact, did not even have the time to go into such details. In the

world of advertising now drawing was secondary, what was
required much more was computer generated designs. In spite
of this Tridib Basu was carefully hanging on to one corner of
the world of drawing and handmade designs, and had not let
it go.

"What do you want, do tell me!"

Arjun pulled a folding chair and sat down. The chair was
normally kept next to the bed, against the wall, for lack of
space. Deepu had got up and left.

Maybe he should not have spoken in this manner, Arjun
thought as he sat down, seeing Tridib Basu's anxious face but
what else was he supposed to say? 'Why didn't you come in so
many days? What were you doing? Do you know what all has
happened in these long years, what paths I have had to
traverse?' Tridib Basu was by now part of a hazy, strange time
– barely even perceptible – how was he supposed to address
him? Tridib Basu was wondering what he should say. Why
had he not come for so long? If that calamity had not happened
consequent to Arjun's dressing the Asura in animal leather,
then there would definitely have been an ongoing relationship!
If Leena, his wife had not left him and he had not got so involved
in the care of his small son Manuj – he was just an eight-year-
old boy – what did he understand of the letter his mother had
written him, which he read on waking up in the morning –
"Dear Manu, I am leaving you and Bapi. Stay well!" To him
the whole thing had initially appeared to be a joke, and
subsequently remained an anxious expectancy within him.
Gradually at the age of twelve-thirteen the boy had
understood that there was no point in waiting any more.

People got late for various reasons. Sometimes one thought,
let me just finish this job at hand, then I'll go. But then some
other job would come up or some other person. At one point,
one thought, it's got really late one couldn't go now. But

perhaps it wasn't really all that late then. But this was how things kept getting more and more delayed. In the end, neither the reason for going nor the intention to do so remained.

When Tridib was standing knee-deep in the quagmire of a family crisis, battling mainly to save Manu from being scorched, didn't he too once or twice reflect with hurt pride at the fact that Arjun never came back? Even if he did not know his residence, if he had enquired at the club surely someone would have directed him. Alternately, he might have felt at peace with himself thinking that by not returning Arjun had surely saved himself from certain insult. The age at which Tridib Basu had discovered Arjun was not an age at which one could develop social relationships in a hurry. An eighteen or nineteen year old boy, with a forty year old man. The difference in class between the two, by this country's standards, separated them by miles. If there had been constant interaction, whereby a mutual sense of dependence had developed, of course, there would have been no obstacle to such a relationship growing strong. However, Tridib Basu never again got the opportunity to initiate this.

⟨ 19 ⟩

If not at the peak of his career, at the age of forty Tridib was certainly moving towards a midpoint in that direction. As a design artist in the world of advertising and non-commercial art, his originality was being accorded vast respect. He, together with Asim Sen, designed covers and made illustrations for the entire Little Magazine group and for small book publishers. They worked late into the night, taking a lot of care. Needless to say, Tridib and all did not even ask for money from this lot. This creative hobby kept them occupied for several hours in the evening, and they also thoroughly enjoyed themselves. In Tridib's professional world also there was plenty of security, money too. His small family was picture-perfect, beautifully laid out. That Leena was suddenly going to disappear through an undetected crack in this photo-frame, was something Tridib had not been able to fathom.

How come he had not?

He realized later, just after Leena left, that there was no reason for him not to have known.

His work and his hobby both satisfied him to a great extent – it swallowed up fourteen hours of Tridib's day. He fulfilled his responsibilities to the family by providing the necessary finances but never showed any interest in them. This was not on account of lack of affection or annoyance, it was just an inability to show he cared. Later, sitting by himself and thinking over things, Tridib Basu had found many things – bits, broken fragments, wood shavings, all of which could be easily used to fill the empty spaces in the outline – like Leena's behaviour, her conduct, glimpses of her reactions and responses. . . .

The very profession and hobby which had almost torn him away from his family and had made him so inattentive to household matters, were the two things he discarded like old toys and returned home when the cracks appeared in his family life. Unused to taking any responsibilities in household work, he had never had any idea of what went on at home between bringing the milk in the morning and drinking his nightly cup of coffee. Like picking up scattered grains of rice in order to eat, Tridib had now to learn every tiny detail.

Who watered the pots in the verandah? Who picked up the dry clothes in the evening? Who wiped the kitchen floor all these days – why did it feel sticky when one stepped on it? Where were the strings of the mosquito nets tied up? What was the name of the sweeper who cleaned the bathrooms, on which days did he come? There were thousands of simple questions like these which Tridib was in no position to answer!

There was a part-timer at home who had been there since Leena's time. However, that the person was not a clock which worked by itself, but had to be made to tick, a person whose work had also to be carefully monitored and reviewed, were things Tridib had not known. He was therefore in a state similar to one who had fallen into the deep end without preparation.

Little Manuj however knew quite a few things, as Tridib could see. Even if a lot of time was spent at school, the rest had been devoted to his following his mother around and vice versa. Manu began to enjoy seeing his father's state, despite the vast uncertainities that confronted them. Just to shock Tridib, he voluntarily produced facts and techniques out of his pocket at regular intervals as if they were marbles or tops. When the nails that held up the mosquito nets got loose and fell down they were kept in a box on the dressing table. Tridib discovered this one day. The plants in the verandah had to be watered only after the afternoon sun had lost its intensity. Only Manuj knew where the clothespins were kept. The two of them together began to look out for savoury snacks and filled them in containers so that Manuj never felt hungry in the evening. In this way, Tridib would hold Manuj's hand and involve himself in some new game, in search of some new happiness. The word happiness is probably not correct in this context but one needs to give some name to the small joy that the heart feels when it finds a half melted candle in the midst of deepest darkness.

Walking along with Manuj in this way Tridib discovered that within his heart had opened many new windows and doors. He discovered a new country. His house seemed newly painted, his plants shining. The pathways, the landing ghat at the river, the bridge over the canal were all newly built. The books for Manuj, the toys, the cotton wool, glue, broom-sticks, even the marble paper required for his project work, Manuj's report card, and of course the Parents Meet at the school. Tridib was walking along the strange pathways of a totally new world, and thinking, the boy had grown up completely without his help, what kind of upbringing had that been?

Once again Tridib began to make up stories for Manuj and to illustrate children's books. Manuj too would sit near his father with colour pencils, brushes and Chinese ink. Of necessity all this had one effect on his profession. His evenings were now transported from being at Asim Sen's side to his own home. As a result, his contact with young boys and girls, the writers and publishers of Little Magazines automatically reduced. In some places it was discussed that Tridib Basu's sense of self-importance had increased, he no more took up work without payment. When he met Asim Sen, and Asim expressed his sorrow, Tridib Basu did not even bother to refute these allegations. Tridib carefully did all his office work to the best of his ability. He did so in spite of knowing that the lightening glow of creativity grew dim when he concentrated on his work too deeply. Whatever was required to survive in that niche – hard work, concentration, learning new techniques – at the end of the eighties, computer software, later the know-how required for multimedia work – Tridib had mastered it all – so that Manuj and he would never have to worry about the expenses involved in their personal upkeep.

Leena had asked for a divorce after about a year. Almost like a silent, inevitable victory she had got it as well. For Manuj's sake, Tridib had told his lawyer to make sure there were no contentions or arguments of any kind, so that in no way even one spot of dirt spattered out of this. Leena, therefore, married her former lover after the divorce without any problems or obstacles.

Tridib had feared, that after her second wedding, Leena's

love for Manuj would grow uncontrollably. She would come, stake her claim and another round of battles would commence. The apprehension of an impending battle had itself caused Tridib to turn lean and thin. However, it was evident that Leena, in that sense, was not one you could gauge or comprehend easily. She had neither shown distress for Manuj, nor had she come running to take him home. Of course, she did send him clothes for the Pujas. Also a birthday card. Her new husband Dipankar was a manager in a multinational. Travelling with him within the country and abroad, she had sent colourful picture postcards. Tridib had felt that it would have been better if she had not done all this – if she had completely cut off the bonds, Tridib would have been much more relieved. Igniting memories like this once in a while could hardly be anything but a kind of cruelty.

The gullible boy would be leaping up the stairs with the card in his hand, saying –"Ma's letter, Ma's letter." This broke Tridib's heart every time. However, he had understood that to say nothing at such times was best. In a way it was a good thing – not being able to see her and on special days remembering her had created a certain rhythm – the inexorable distance, the inevitability of separation was a rhythm that had helped Manuj, to both hold his father's hand and at the same time to grow up on his own.

Today Tridib was relieved, free and at the same time he felt as if he were completely drained out.

Manuj had now reached that age when Tridib had been forced to pick up the threads of his torn, broken and utterly devastated life, put them together and start again, after Leena's departure. Manuj was much more successful, wealthy. By earning a design technology and management degree together he had earned immeasurable credibility. Already he had his own company and personal art studio. He had begun to step

into the world of audio-visuals, and his contacts with the
television channels were being set up. Very soon he would have
established himself as a Production House. An absolutely
modern, commercial production venture.

Leena's second husband Dipankar, had passed away five
years ago. Leena had now returned, wanting to stay with
Manuj. Manuj would inherit the entire property on Lee Road
owned by her in-laws, as there was no second claimant. Leena
owned the whole house. Leena and Manuj, Manuj's wife Trina
and their son Somdutta – all of them got along wonderfully
well with each other. Their household was a full and lively one.
It was as though Leena had always been there, and had never
gone away! She had an amazing capacity to abandon people,
and win them back as well. Well, hadn't Manuj and Trina too
accepted Leena so beautifully? They didn't have any sense of
loss or pride did they? Trina was a newcomer to the family, she
could not be expected to feel anything about the past, but
Manuj? Had Manuj forgotten his childhood days, the unhappy
days spent with his father, in these happy times? Whenever
such thoughts took control over his mind, Tridib felt that all
the members of the house were strangers to him. He felt like a
resident tenant, kept at bay – a marginalized human being
living far away from the mainstream. His conscience of course
tried to play its age old role and opposed him. It told Tridib-
'Chhi! don't be so small-minded – everyone is happy, look at
them and feel happy yourself, stay well.' The moral
murmurings of his conscience irritated Tridib even more, and
he tried to find a way to quieten it. Needless to say, the unseen
voice had no throat that he could strangle.

Today, Tridib Basu was free, satisfied and empty – all at one
go! Just as he was thirty-four years ago! To have a single life
rendered empty and void twice by the same person must also

be some Divine destiny. A pathetic laugh arose in his mind
when he thought this.

Completely empty, the first person who came to mind when
Tridib came out of his initial weariness, was Arjun. Did man
return to the soil when there was nothing much left to get out
of wealth and software? The world of clay-straw-bamboo had
kept Tridib hooked till his middle years. There was no
opposition between his profession and this fascination. He had
gone around seeing the work of idol-makers, he had undertaken
clay-modelling, he had split hairs with his friends while
discussing details of work. These kind of discussions were
possible only amongst the intellectual middle-class, as the
potters and Pals had no time to even talk in the work season. It
was at that festive time that he had found Arjun, brought him
into the limelight and then had had to end everything in
heartache and mortification.

Tridib shuddered as soon as he remembered Arjun. The boy
was alive surely? Did he still mould idols? He had obviously
not become very famous because if he had then his name would
have appeared in the papers. But was he still persisting? All
these years – where had he been, what was he doing, were details
he would have liked to know – but behind the wish also came a
fear. Suppose he went and didn't find him – suppose he had
been felled by some blow? No promise had been made of course,
but to pick up a chamar's son and bring him to the Sanskriti-
Sansad did make one answerable to some extent. In such an
invitation obviously lay a hint of the future, a development
which only an upper-class artist like Tridib Basu could bring
about in the life of Arjun! As soon as the doors of the Sanskriti-
Sansad closed, Tridib Basu also disappeared – for a completely
different reason of course – but that too was also a kind of
sabotage. Not to be with or stand by at the time of social

disgrace, not to offer a hand. The social-worker within Tridib Basu, the young comrade was suddenly aroused, he just had to go to Christopher Road. Just now, today, at this very instant!

It was with this thought that he had come out just on a whim.

The pond was not there any more and Arjun's workshop which had stood on its banks too had disappeared. He had changed his house and his work place as well. The neighbourhood appeared impossibly small and littered at first sight, after so many days. Cobwebs were visible on the electric wires hooked up in the lanes of Christopher Road. In every house in the slums there were now televisions, cable connections and all were lit up with electric lights. There were still queues for water – but the vessels had changed in shape and variety – in place of tin buckets and canisters, there were now plastic ones. The clothes of the girls had also changed – one could now stand in the queue wearing thin maxidresses and small blouses, without pulling one's sari aanchal over them. The language people used to quarrel with others had also changed – Bangla had been ousted and the Mumbai-chawl Hindi had come in. Tridib observed all this as he walked along.

He felt that if Arjun still lived in this neighbourhood then by now he would have become a 'hero' among these people. Looking for Arjun's new house and constantly asking people for directions made Tridib realize that Arjun was possibly still poor and hence insignificant. The people of the neighbourhood had no grudge in their minds because Arjun had broken the family tradition and had tried to take up a more high class profession. This was because his attempt had not brought him any benefits at all nothing that common people could look at and envy. If he had a lot of money or fame on the strength exclusively of his artistic skills, then people would have envied him, or have talked ill of him. Now they just about tolerated him.

Even though the middle-aged tolerated Arjun, the young

and old even today loved him a lot – this Tridib had gauged. Those above the age of fifty possibly looked at Arjun's solitary pathbreaking attempt with respect. The young still looked at him and thought of freedom. The factories choking in their death throes, the lack of jobs in the offices, the unemployment of the sixties was again spreading like the cow-dung cakes covering the walls of the city. A sultry, stifling atmosphere seemed to be spreading, engulfing the city. In the midst of this scenario Arjun would, with single-minded concentration, be painting the curved wings of the swan with his fine bamboo scalpel or marking the tongue of the lion – completely engrossed yet detached – as if he were somewhere else or this was some other time!

"What do you want, sir?"

Arjun's apparent snub was completely ignored by Tridib Basu. This was Arjun! Tridib was staring wide-eyed at Arjun, and it seemed as though he too could not stop staring.

Tridib remembered the physique of the eighteen-nineteen year old boy and his sharp face. His shiny black hair, the deep curve of his spinal column like an animated snake on his back, an impossible self-assurance in his fingers. Yet, the one who came in now with a bag in his hand had gray hair, though there was no evidence of fat on his body. He wore spectacles, his eyes and mouth were sharp, he wore a full sleeved shirt with pyjamas – the outlines of his two shoulders appeared a little loose, possibly because of the exhaustion of old age!

Who was this strange person? Could time change someone so much? If he did ask him his business, there was nothing to be surprised about that.

Lowering the bag full of golden wire to make ornaments to the floor, Arjun had sat down on the chair.

"Do you recognize me, Tridib – Tridib Basu. Years ago I had taken you to a place known as Sanskriti-Sansad. . . . "

Within a minute of entering and seeing Tridib Basu – Arjun had collected together all the fragments of his life and joined them together. It seemed as though the chemical fluid required to accomplish this joining came from within. Arjun had recognized Tridib. Although his looks had deteriorated a lot, even after thirty years, the shape of a forty year old man's face did not change so much – not like a nineteen year old boy's face had. As soon as he saw him a needle-like pain had pierced through his ribs and spread through all his veins and arteries. . . .

At the same time like light filtering through an open window an autumnal dawn had spread through his mind with the aroma of the sheuli flowers. . . . This Tridib Basu . . . this was the person who had first held his hand and taken him from Christopher Road to the centre of the open world – a place where Arjun would never have been able to reach on his own.

In the space of a minute, a smile appeared on Arjun's face. Touching his joint hands to his forehead he said –"Of course I recognize you, babu. Tell me, how come you have remembered me after so many years? Are those at home well?"

Tridib Basu stared at him through his spectacles – "I had not expected to see you in such a bad shape. The boy said that you had got only one order for a big idol this time . . . that the mahajan has not lent any money. . . ."

"Sarree, do make some tea." Sticking his neck out to call, Arjun again leaned back in his chair.

He said, "This giant wheel has gone up, come down and gone up again many times – now that it is about to touch the ground you have come and are saying I am in a bad shape. . . . At one time, single-handedly I have moulded fifteen Durga idols, twenty Kalis, eighteen Jagaddhatris . . . The money does not last in this profession, you know that . . . Earning and spending, I have managed to sustain the family so far . . . only now it's a little . . . " Calling in the direction of the kitchen, "What do you say, I haven't starved you all have I? Say – I have fed you, of course not biryani and pulao! Daal and rice at least."

Sarayu said something from the kitchen, but couldn't be heard. Bonu's suppressed laughter came floating out. Tridib Basu was tapping the arms of his chair uncomfortably.

"In this business there is no other way out, babu. Where there is no surety of the selling price, how can one keep to a budget? To whom are you going to explain the value of the work you have done, how much labour was required, how much the decorations cost. The Puja Committee will come and start bargaining at half the price of the last year's rate – an idol built with clay cannot be kept at home, you have to sell it – one who knows this fact, why should he pay the legitimate price for it? We are like thieves who get caught, because of this helplessness, and every year end up in this bind. It seems, the babus' salaries increase, D.A. or something like that also increases, the expense of pandals, tents increases, lakhs of rupees are spent on lights, the labour cost of moulding clay idols does not decrease and yet never does the price of the idols fully cover the cost of production – tell me, who will pay for the potter's household expenses? Still we are somehow surviving, possibly because we are made of stone, anyone else would have given up the ghost by now."

☞ 20 ☜

It was the dawn of Mahalaya, the new-moon day immediately preceding the autumnal worship of Goddess Durga. Since the past ten days or so, the hues of the sun had begun to change. The yellow rage visible in the sun from mid-August now gradually seemed to acquire some shades of bronze. With the onset of late autumn, the sun appeared to take on the colour of fresh sheaves of paddy. Once Bijayadashami, the finale of the Durga festival was over, and the millions of saal-leaf plates, paper and plastic packets lay in entangled heaps in all Puja venues, whether of the low or high class, then suddenly the atmosphere turned still and grave. The sky then even more blue silently descended closer to the earth, the white coloured kash flowers, turned light nutty brown and bronze which became even more pronounced in the sunlight. Arjun did not get too many orders for the Goddess Lakshmi. The one or two he did get were always completed in advance. Hence just after the Pujas, like the sky, it was Arjun's time to sit quietly with his face resting on his knees.

The thought of Mahalaya now spread dejection in Arjun's heart. The rustle of fallen leaves could be heard on the paved footpaths. The Mahalaya dawn was different. In his almost forty years of working with clay, there was not a single year when Arjun had been able to sleep through the night before Mahalaya. The whole night strange dreams troubled him. Various scenes were mixed up with clay and covered in the colour of the earth. In his sleep he was constantly fearful that he would be late, that he would be unable to wake up early. Just as he felt in his childhood, adolescence and youth so did he feel soon after being wed – and now having crossed his fifties he still felt the same. The early morning breeze came wafting in mixed with the aroma of flames emanating from burning wicks – every year. In his childhood, his mother always lit an oil lamp the night before and kept it near the seat of the house Gods. Didi and Sarayu had kept up the tradition out of habit. At dawn, the flame of the wick would splutter as the quantity of oil rapidly reduced till finally its breath choked and it lost its battle against the breeze and darkness. The dawn of

Mahalaya. The sun in its bronze image, the aroma of the sheuli leaves and along with it the smell of the burning wick.

Waking up at dawn on that day, Arjun neither took the smoke into his chest nor drank any tea. Being able to take a bath depended on several factors. If there was no water or the public washrooms were too crowded with women then he was unable to bathe. However if he was able to fast, he felt physically clean and light.

This year there was only one big idol. He had to write only two eyes. Guru Ram Pal called it 'writing' – he did not call it 'drawing'. So Arjun too said the same. It was in this writing that his handwork gained life and his struggle to survive joined together with his work and worship. The clay began to talk. Going beyond all the pain, sorrow and scarcity all around, Arjun himself too seemed to develop and spread his branches up in the sky like a tree. Sitting on the scaffolding with the pot of paint invariably made him recall the wonderful details of the first time in his life when he had written the two eyes – how he was caught red-handed thanks to Surapati and gang. How, for the first time, with fear and shame, he had written the eyes, shaking all the time. He had been only a fourteen or fifteen-year-old boy. On his return, he had been beaten by his mother, a beating that had split the skin of his forehead. He still carried the scar. Unknowingly his fingers would automatically touch it on the Mahalaya morning. It was as if he was just reliving a lost time in his life.

This time he did not require any scaffolding. There was only a small idol. Under his feet was a mud and paint covered stool. He was going to draw standing on it. He was not feeling good, there was no joy this time. There was only one Durga idol. As if it was there just to remove the lethargy settling into his hands. The workshop was filled with the unending void of emptiness. In the midst of this stood only one big Goddess. If he stood up, her chin was a little higher than Arjun's head. Face to face, she was on level with him. It was as though some woman was looking at Arjun with a sightless smile and without fear. After so many years, at the end of such a long arduous path, and after having crossed so many hurdles on that path, there was only this tiny needle-like place to stand in – and on it just one big Goddess. This had never happened had it, even during the days of his youthful struggles? Was the female figure standing before him, gradually spreading its soft aroma, its low heat into Arjun's blood? Was she Didi? Sarayu? The faces which Arjun had not really looked at very carefully in this life were the ones who from behind had protected his lamp of life from the winds till now! It was strange, this feeling of fearful joy! The empty workshop, suspended from the scenic blue sky, were cobwebs and last year's old strings – in the midst of which stood face to face this motionless woman in close proximity – who seemed to be saying 'I am here, I am here'. With an invisible embrace, she lovingly stroked Arjun's head and body with something beyond mere touch. Arjun noticed while putting his brush into the bowl of black paint, that the mopping-cloth had got left behind in the earthen jar in the corner. In the beginning, Bishu used to stay with him. Bishu did not have to be told, he handed everything to him automatically. After him many artisans had come and gone. Sometimes two, sometimes three. Some came back after five-six years. They were like part of the family. They ate their meals together and bathed at the tap on the street.

Before the last pujas, during heavy rains, the artisan Padmalochan had left Arjun sunk in waist-deep water without notice. This bout of getting wet followed by fever left Arjun's health close to breaking point. Artisans sometimes proved treacherous! They stayed with the artists, slept and sat with them, ate with them too, yet they did not allow any extra passion to enter into their work. 'Take my work, but give me the money, after all I am not your enemy, am I?" Any slight differences, led them to change places. And why not? Their childhood days were spent half-hungry, working without wages either lured by false promises or out of fear of someone's anger. The artisan trusted no one. He was always alert, rough and out to save his own skin. At Hridayballabh's workshop an old artisan called Bir had once said, "Dada, no relationships develop in this work with clay. I am in it for so long yet there is no conversation between two people except regarding money. Quite strange!"

Well, this time Arjun had no artisans. He did not have to hire any. Where was the boy? Even Deepu hadn't come near him, somewhat out of shame and also to some extent for his own convenience – after all, his leather loan officials might spot him when they came for investigations. In the meanwhile Tridib Basu had come twice. He wanted to give two things, one of which Arjun was unable to accept. He sat and looked at albums of Arjun's old and new work. The earlier ones were in black and white, the later ones coloured. All of them were taken by the local photographers. Even so the temperament of the work, the flawless finish could not be missed by the eyes, from the footwear of the Asura to the ear-piece of the Goddess. A man had shrunk with his prolonged struggles yet he had not lowered the standards of his work by even a jot. Whether the Goddess was due to go to Phalpatti or to Auto Road under the bridge was of no consequence to Arjun, his creation had to be beautiful in totality. There would be no flaw in his work. He had taken the responsibility of making good any shortcomings in the product through physical hard work and the magic of his fingers – in so doing even a rich owner would sink, so how could a small fry like Arjun survive. Tridib Basu kept looking at the pictures and thinking! Arjun had not gone down. He was alive. He had survived in some unbelievable way.

Tridib could remember reading a couplet by the poet Kabir in his school text. The poet expressed his sorrow at seeing the relentless revolving grindstone of life in motion, in which not a grain survives when crushed between two stones.

'Between two stones' – was what Tridib very often felt he himself had been in life, a mustard seed imprisoned between two stones.

It seemed Kabir's unworthy rebellious son Kamaal, had laughed on hearing this couplet. Maybe to point a hook at his own method of survival, he had coined a contradictory couplet.

Seeing the whirling grindstone Kamaal had wanted to laugh. The opening on top of it through which the mustard was poured in, always hid a seed or two in its inner-side, which never got ground and hence survived. Through that opening fistfuls of new mustard were poured in – yet a couple of seeds hid and made a niche for themselves to survive, even in that rapid push of grains. In his childhood, Tridib felt happy when he heard this. There was obviously liberation somewhere from oppression. In Class Seven, Bimal Babu, while teaching had said, this mustard was nothing but a path to reach God. It was good for mankind to stay close to this path.

This reference to God had not attracted the mind at that age. Instead it had reminded him of the round, blue sky seen from the bottom of a well. There was a way out which he would have to find.

Today the same thought came to mind as he looked through the pictures of Goddesses created by Arjun. At the end of the day, the meaning of familiar words changed. Strange words came close to being understood. To survive – to be free of that churning grind-stone – was something Tridib understood the meaning of today. It was to live naturally – to have the freedom to remain involved in whatever search one was interested in.

Arjun had survived and not died till now because he had been able to do so. He had not earned name, fame and renown. Of the initial requirements of a potter, Arjun had not had even one.

One, capital on low interest, or money saved.

Two, a place to stay and a workshop in Kumortuli, the potter's colony.

Two and one in some cases were also linked together. If Arjun had been able to step into a place in Kumortuli, he could have become a member of the co-operative. He would then have got a loan on low interest in the month of Baisakh with which he could have bought raw materials and have employed an artisan in good time. He would not have then had to almost sell his own hair in order to buy goods at high prices in Shravan. Bank loans could have been taken. Although the paper work was tedious, the interest at least was low. Where he lived, there were no potters, so Arjun was unable to change his money-lender. Thirty percent of his life's earnings had always gone in paying interest. The Mahajan's house, car and money all bloated and swelled up. Then, one morning in the month of Chaitra, he dropped Arjun with one shake of his hands.

Arjun kept stepping backwards, and was now standing at the edge of the ditch. Yet he had not changed at all. The fingers, arms, the shape of the throat, the muscles – in fact even the wings of the swan, the feathers of the owl, the nail of the mouse, moulded by Arjun remained the same as thirty years ago, as flawless and full of beauty. Even today, Arjun applied his mind in the same way whether he was moulding a Durga worth fifteen thousand rupees or a Vishwakarma worth two hundred and fifty. Hence, Arjun had been able to remain natural and that was why poverty had taken his wealth but had not been able to stifle the pulsating beat of his life. It was in this that Arjun had been victorious as an artist. Whereas Tridib, even with the

ideal combination of brilliance and education, had lost. The
artist within him was not alive anymore. Meaningless ties,
contemptible yet unchecked pride had ruined him and
destroyed him totally. Arjun was his past. Therefore, like a
lightening struck tree can still hear in its dreams the rustle of
its destroyed leaves, so too Tridib could still hear the beats of
Arjun's heart.

Tridib had offered Arjun two proposals. It had been difficult
to utter the first, although he had still done so. "You do take
loans, so on interest only, I will give you the same. About fifty-
sixty thousand. Now I have the money. It is in the bank. You
can return it to me after a year." Arjun had looked at the ground
and shook his head. Later he had raised his face and said, "No.
You took me personally to the big pandals. By my own fault, I
was unable to keep their respect. However, it was you who
took me there after all. I have roamed those streets and worked
. . . whatever had to happen has happened. Yet if I am in debt
to you, I will not feel good babu, I will feel really small in my
own eyes."

The second proposal was different; maybe a little premature
as well considering the times. Manuj had just started to do
audio-visual productions. His friend Supratik was the new
director. They were making several episodes under the title of
"The Unknown Faces of Kolkata." Supratik wanted Arjun Das
to feature in one of them. Completely off-beat. A chamar's
son, who was an idol-maker. His fight against society and
poverty. His long struggle on this path. The recording would
be in the studio itself. Arjun would have to go there. Arjun felt
curious hearing about it – and felt it would be fun as well. His
face on the TV screen. The old and young of the neighbourhood
crowding around to hear him. Just the fun of it. It was as though
it had nothing to do with Arjun's life or work. It was similar to
the fun children use to have in his childhood with a tin-box, or

when watching a film on a screen hung in the middle of a field. However, as he listened to Tridib Basu's words a different kind of wish had grown deep in Arjun's heart. The wish to talk about himself. No one really knew. No one had ever wanted to know either, what Arjun actually desired.

Not what Arjun, the person, wanted but the history of an artist's creative desires. The river that came out of the heart, went from land to land and finally flowed into the sea, it was that story. No one knew it. Poor Arjun. It was a twenty-five minute episode with three questions. He had no idea that hardly anything could be told in this limited time or within this framework. He was not familiar – either with the inside story of this light and shade medium or about programme ratings in the market. On the basis of this indistinct understanding itself Arjun had nodded his head and agreed, "Then I will go." He had refused the earlier proposal hardly a week ago, now to say no to this one again would not appear very courteous.

On the dawn of Mahalaya, suddenly, Arjun was reminded of this incident as he stood with the paint bowl in hand, in the artisan and Deepu-less workshop. Tridib Basu had been satisfied with his agreeing. At the same time, he had been fearful. The ball was now in Manuj and Supratik's court, and possibly Tridib would not be able to do much. Still, hiding his doubts and fears, Tridib had affectionately placed his hand on Arjun's shoulder and spoken to him. Thinking of those words, joy returned to Arjun's mind as he stood close to the clay image.

So what if Deepu was not here?

The little son of Santosh the plumber, was roaming around outside. He called him and said "Go home and tell Mashi and Didi to come."

Sarayu had come after putting aside the vegetables she had started chopping. The heavily pregnant Bonu had come and

handed him the brush and the mop. Arjun's brush had begun
to move. With the assured self-confidence of over thirty decades
of painting hundreds of eyes, Arjun's brush spoke up with joy.
The two dark brown iris' were as deep and flawless as they were
thirty-four years ago. In the very fine black pupils at their
centre, was evident the pure darkness of their days in the womb.
In the whites of the eyes could be seen the emptiness of a field
which had just been harvested and the weary veins and arteries
hinted at the weariness following many victorious battles. No,
everything was fine, unchanged, assured and very much his
own.

Kolkata had changed so much in that fragment of time, the
false posturings to mitigate the shame of poverty, the
inequalities in life-styles – these too had changed. The glories
of comfort and luxury had assumed even more varied colours.
People's language had changed, as had their personal
relationships – what had not changed at all was the artist and
his creation. His understanding too remained as it had been in
his childhood days – this girl who would soon be a mother,
this Sarayu, both appeared to be like two light-posts of this
unchanging time. They stayed close and waved fans to give
Arjun some air. They stayed close in order to wipe the sweat
off his brow and stem the blood streaming out of his heart.

Under his own spell, Arjun saw the two eyes on the clay-
image come to life. Taking up the white paint brush to put the
last finishing touch on the heart of the black, like before, Arjun
felt he was a weightless, bodiless entity. As though from time
immemorial, apart from Arjun and these two eyes, given life
by his own magical mantra, and this seriously melancholic
face – there were no other seafarers in this ocean of time.

Hearing the soft sounds of Bonu's tears, Arjun came out of
his trance. Bonu, though not as dark as her father, was still

darker than her mother. She had light curly hair that fell to her back – which was not like either her mother or father's. She did not have a very sharp nose, but had two large eyes and slightly full lips. Tears were streaming down her cheeks. The scents of the imminent Pujas were now all around. Bonu was not happy. Her husband, Jagat, had not visited in two months neither was there any letter or telephone call. Bonu could make out that her yet unborn daughter was the reason for the disaffection. Her in-laws did not want a girl-child. Jagat may love her very much but he was being influenced by his mother and her elder sister. Bonu had not listened to them. Not only had she not agreed to the plot to abort the girl-child, she had instead broken out of their scheming in a way causing their suppressed anger to acquire a face.

Bonu was feeling awful after coming to the workshop. There was that corner – didn't pishi, their father's sister sit there? She had returned from her husband's house – although Bonu had never seen her, she had heard of her from her father.

Suppose Bonu too came back home like that – chhi, why like that – let Jagat enjoy a long life – suppose Bonu returned with her daughter and Jagat never came to take her back – then Bonu too, like her pishi, would sit in that corner and mix clay, and lift moulds. Jagat had not come as yet, but how could it be true that even after the birth of the baby he wouldn't come. Just thinking of the possibility caused more tears to flow from Bonu's eyes and her sobs shook her whole body. . . .

Sarayu had hugged her daughter. On her fingers was the astringent juice from the inner stem of the banana tree. The tips of her fingers were scarred with cuts from her kitchen chopper. She hugged her daughter close so that outsiders would not be able to see her daughter's tears, and kept saying, "Don't cry, come on Boni, I will send for your husband today itself – you will soon have your lap filled with a treasure, you will forget everything then . . . just wait I will send for him today itself . . ."

Arjun had quickly wound up the work at hand. He said, "Come on, I too will go home with you both. Bonu, will you have fried sweet jalebis? Ghose's shop has become old, Hari is not there any more, but still their jalebis haven't changed much." Her mother scolded, "Stop it, there is no need to feed her stale jalebis at this odd time. Let's go home. It is time for lunch . . . "

The girl's feet were swelling up slightly. So were her ankles. Arjun's heart broke on seeing her tear drenched face. Soon she would deliver. There would be various expenses for the baby. Money was required. Why were the girl's feet swelling? Was there water retention in her body? No hospital had been fixed yet, although the local doctor had checked Bonu thrice. What if there were sudden complications? The son-in-law was not showing any concern, the in-laws were angry, would he be able to save Bonu? At this moment, in Arjun's mind there was no thought for Bonu's baby, he was only worried about the life of his own daughter. This was his actual life, his real world – those magical writing of eyes, the paint and clay were all part of a spell of fantasy – which extinguished itself as soon as he climbed down from the scaffolding. One had to stand with one's feet firmly planted on the ground. Those who floated on air could not be depended on – neither for themselves, nor for others.

Arjun went out after his meal. He returned well past sunset. Thirty thousand rupees, in new crisp notes. Tridib Basu had withdrawn the money with his own ATM card. He had been worried a little at Arjun's change of mind. Was there some problem or danger? No, that is not it, Arjun had laughed and assured him. "There is no fault in being a debtor, I realized, in order to save my daughter's life. Who else does she have? There is a lifetime left to become an artist."

☞ 21 ☜

The clouds of Kartik prevailed. For the last few days, it had been raining heavily. The sky was overcast, heavy with clouds which did not clear up for days. There was a mild depression over the sea, and consequently the brassy sunrays which helped to dry the nappies and sheets of babies and handkerchiefs of old people in the bylanes of the city, were also wiped out by these moody, unseasonal clouds. Every year it got cold a little before time, although it normally passed off till the real winter cold set in at the end of Agrahan. However, this time the rains had caused the chill to set in quite strongly and ones' hands and feet had begun to feel the effect as soon as the sun set.

Sarayu didn't sleep well. Her daughter too was unable to sleep – at least that's what Sarayu felt. Her pregnancy was now full term and she wasn't very happy. Her blood-pressure was a little on the higher side, and her hands, feet and face swelled up if she did the slightest work. Sarayu did not allow her to come anywhere near the kitchen. Earlier she wrapped a thick sheet around her, now Sarayu covered her with a light blanket. It was a very old blanket, mended all over with scraps of cloth taken from old clothes. It had been kept away all these years, as it was not adequate protection against the cold. Now, in order to contend with this early chill, Deepu had pulled it down from the high shelf on which it had been kept. Bonu was not really conscious of the cold or heat. As soon as she was covered, she'd kick off the cover with her feet. That was why, Sarayu had to keep getting up and covering her at night. Despite this, at dawn, often Bonu had nothing covering her body and lay all curled up like a ball. It appeared as though it was she who was the foetus inside her mother's belly.

It was very cold at dusk. Bonu had pulled a low stool inside the kitchen and was sitting close to her mother. On her knees was a plate of rice for the evening meal. Once in a while she picked out stones from the rice and threw them on the ground. Next to her feet was a huge pile of potato and gourd skins. Bonu kept pushing her mother with her hand from time to time and asking her in a whining tone, "O Ma, tell me, won't you, where you went for my delivery – you went to Dida, didn't you?"

"Dhat, where did I go to Dida's? You were born at the Kamardanga Hospital."

"Why didn't you go, didn't Dida ask you to come?"

For a few seconds, Sarayu shielded her nose from the sizzling spices to be mixed in the daal. Like a burnt-moth without wings, the dry chilli was circulating in the hot oil, restlessly. As soon as it turned from dark red to black, the strong pungent aroma, which was its dying siren song would spread throughout the whole room. Then everyone would begin to sneeze. The work of a good housewife was to protect her family and neighbours from the sneezes which were activated by the sizzling of these spices.

"Dida did ask me to come. She had wanted me to stay for a few months. I was the one who wasn't happy to be there."

She was not happy at her parent's home – this was a little difficult for Bonu to believe. Could this possibly be true? Wide-eyed she looked at her mother's face. From the side she observed her mother's nose, forehead, the slightly tired pair of lips which still presented an inseparable, almost unbroken line. Her two eyes were huge, as though they would fill up immediately with the incessant downpours which occurred during the month of Shravan. On her nose, she wore a small cheap red stone ring.

Ma is beautiful, thought Bonu suddenly, and realized that she had never before really looked at her mother carefully.

As soon as she conceived Bonu, Sarayu had felt a call from that house at Chapadanga where the rows of banana trees swayed in the breeze causing the ripe yellow banana leaves to constantly tear into shreds. That call had been as emphatic and powerful as was her mother's invitation. After the monsoon, when the flood waters went down, the smell of muddy-wet soil that pervaded the air in that part of the country seemed to have transformed into a small baby and was causing a restless throbbing at the base of her navel. All the fear, shame and panic she had experienced before she left Chapadanga it seemed had flown far away like fallen leaves out of her sight. Sarayu had again become the little girl who used to eat fish and forget to wipe off the crooked fish-bone stuck on her forehead. Arjun had not wanted to let her go at this time. In their marital relationship, there may not have been any ardour and closeness, there may have been many moments of silence, but there was no cheating or neglect. Arjun and Sarayu loved each other in their own way, even though the burden of various memories, thoughts and lack of language skills had prevented them from clearly expressing this to each other. Even if there was no transparency in this house, there was no lack of attachment and care. Her father-in-law, mother-in-law, husband, everybody tried to protect Sarayu. However, her mother's letter had caused Sarayu's heart to turn topsy-turvy. It had been decided that as soon as she had delivered the baby safely Sarayu would return to her husband's home. She would not stay on for long after her confinement.

Sarayu had gone to her parents. Her mother-in-law had carefully filled a trunk for her with clothes to wear at home, petticoats, teep to adorn her forehead, kajal for her eyes, gamchha, powder, a new copy of the *Panchali*, and a pair of rubber sandals – she had repeatedly warned her not to go into areas where there was water or mud, and if she just had to then she should wear her rubber sandals. She had even given her a bottle of sugar globules. Sarayu loved these. She had also got Arjun to get a big bottle of Horlicks. Sarayu, however, returned before either the globules or the Horlicks finished.

Janardan Mandal had never been just an ordinary harmless family man. He had fed and clothed his wife and daughter all right but had never thought to go beyond his duties and responsibilities. Even while fulfilling them he had many things to say. He made pointed comments and constantly reminded those he had benefited of what he'd done for them and when. Giribala remained on edge all her life. However, since Sarayu's marriage, she had not been keeping good health. She had lost some of her will power. The iron content in her blood was depleting and malnutrition was causing the hair on her head to fall rapidly. Agitated she asked her daughter to come, not so much because she wanted to see her daughter but because she herself required moral support.

Her daughter was shocked to see her. "What have you done to yourself Ma? Your eyes have dark shadows under them, your forehead is like a broad open field, your cheek bones are sticking out – you are not far from becoming a skeleton."

In the banana forest the torn leaves swayed and their rustling sound could be heard in the peaceful afternoon. In the deep of the night this sound permeated one's sleep. Sarayu felt that the song of the leaves had changed somewhat. In her childhood, Sarayu could hear some imaginary green-yellow calls of the forest. In the sounds and movements of the breeze there was an outpouring of joy. Now it appeared as though the breeze was moving around in a deserted, isolated place where the emptiness aroused eerie feelings in the mind. Her unhappiness increased as a consequence.

It had not been very long. About four years or so. Sarayu had visited her parents twice in this period. Once accompanied by Arjun. It had only been a short visit. She had been treated formally like a guest. The family secrets had not reached her through any cracks or crevices. The biggest thing was that Giribala's health had not been bad then – she not only kept herself busy with work, her daughter too followed in her footsteps. This time, within fifteen days, Sarayu was able to make out where the cracks were beginning to appear. Baba was now a different person. While he would eat meat and fish cooked in hotels, at home the true Vaishnav style would be followed. Now along with him were his cronies. They were used to frequenting the brothels. The Janardan Mandal who had begun life dealing with the wholesale vegetable business had now taken a bank loan and was even planning to start a poultry farm. Dark, slippery and slimy like the Magur-Shinghi fish were some of the friends he had acquired who belonged to dismal backgrounds. They came home. Surprisingly, most of them were younger than Janardan. Was it to feel young and adventurous that he mixed with these younger men? Was this what was called breaking one's horns in an attempt to enter the herd of calves? Sarayu felt awful. She was clearly pregnant physically. The child in her womb was increasing its demand for rest daily, and required food at short intervals. At this time one wanted isolation, one did not enjoy excitement. The house had never been a big one. There was an inner verandah which was quiet. That was where, Sarayu on returning from school, performed her ablutions from a water kept in a pot. From there the thick forest was visible, a mixture of drumsticks, the ever-green flowering bakul tree, the banana and gum trees. Now a party gathered on that verandah. After dusk, the local louts and middle-aged men got together. The smoke of six-seven beedis, the calls for tea, the noise of laughter and merriment filled the house. Where was Sarayu to sit or sleep amidst all this? Baba was very often not even present. Ma had to supply them with tea and matchsticks. With Sarayu's arrival, their license seemed to have increased. "*Ayee* Sarree, come on, come here, come and sit," they would say. Sarayu felt very irritated. Before the afternoon got over, Sarayu noticed, that the bitter gall of irritation would begin to rise up in her, burning her throat and chest in the process.

"What is this you all have started, Ma?" Not finding her father at hand, Sarayu attacked her mother instead.

The swollen veins on her mother's hands never got any rest from work. As harmless as a cow, Giribala raised her two scared eyes and said, "What can I do, tell me. Your father has invited them. Now if I say something there will be hell to pay."

"I can't do anything I'm warning you. I will not go and serve them tea and cigarettes."

Giri bit her protruding tongue in shame.

"No, no, why should you go? Why would I even allow you to do so? Lord knows what my son-in-law will think if he gets to know."

Sarayu's eyebrows wrinkled in a frown.

The man who was sitting in Kolkata concentrating single-mindedly on his clay idols would be least interested in all this useless gossip. It was true that the man knew nothing except his work, he did not look at anything else. He did earn money no doubt, but it was as though he had no love for it. And how strange! In his hands, the clay seemed to speak – he could create a lotus on the backdrop, lift the flawless beauty of a facial mould, shape a finger, paint the soles of the Goddesses' feet . . . If not exactly in this language, these thoughts did come in this way to Sarayu – the man obviously had some personal equation with beauty . . . whatever he desired, exactly that appeared from the clay he was moulding.

Having come far away from Kolkata, Sarayu was able to plumb the depths of her heart and perceive things more clearly. In the city the noise and various unpleasant details of daily life in a small room did not allow her to see or think of them. She was only driven by them from dawn to dusk, and from the night towards another morning.

Just before Bonu's birth, when she had come back to Chapadanga, she suddenly realized that over here all those who came to their house and the people of this neighbourhood were very different from Arjun. As different as blood is from water. Arjun had neither the time to joke and gossip like them, nor the inclination. He was like a bee drowning in the scent of the lotus flower – spending his whole day, with his mind and heart wholly surrendered to the meditation of beauty. Before she had left Chapadanga, Sarayu had no idea such men existed in the world or that such individuals were to be found anywhere.

After spending day after day in this uncomfortable, irritating manner, finally one day Sarayu blew up. She was sitting in the corner of the small room adjoining the verandah. She sat looking through her belongings in the trunk under the bed, when suddenly from inside her breast there arose a trembling. There was a boy at the window, grinning at her, saying, "Sarree, come outside, Bappa da is calling you!"

The name felt like a shower of muddy water being sprayed over her body.

Bappa had come on his own having heard from other people of her arrival. What had occurred had got buried many years ago. What was his one-time victim doing now, what did she look like after marriage were things he was now eager to know.

Sarayu gathering up all her inner strength began to scream, "Ma! Tell that vulgar lot to leave immediately."

Janardan was in the verandah when Sarayu's scream was heard – as though a wail had arisen straight from her belly-button. The puffed rice and brinjal fries scattered from the father's hands out of fear.

Sarayu by then had collapsed in a faint, the box open before her, her hands and feet cold, her forehead sweating.

On hearing her daughter's call, Giri had come running from the kitchen. She screamed and cried, her hands beating at her forehead. "Someone please call the doctor, the girl has fainted!"

The boys on the verandah disappeared on hearing this commotion. They were such good for nothings they did not even have the sense to either arrange for a doctor or to stand by the dazed Janardan, they had so little sense.

The discontented, irritated Janardan, hired a car and a day later left his daughter at her in-laws. She was now another's responsibility, so let him take charge – what was it to him?

Sarayu had never gone back to Chapadanga. Now she felt, she had done something very wrong – she had not looked at her mother's face even once since this incident. Her mother had wanted to see her before she passed away. Her mother-in-law had told her, Arjun had begged her, but Sarayu had only shaken her head, while tears flowing from her eyes had wet the clothes on her breast. Of course she had had to go after the fourth day rituals – her father had sent the message that the tenth day ceremony would be held at home, which his daughter and son-in-law should definitely attend. With a three-year-old daughter, Sarayu had gone that time as a couple. Instead of sorrow, strangely, her mind was filled with peace. The child in her womb was now in her lap, had learnt to walk, and was gurgling with small talk. Along with her was Arjun, Ma was no more, she had suffered a lot, but at the same time her death had severed all ties for Sarayu. Like a snake that had lost its poisonous sting, she too would now never return to this house of her father's.

They had reached at night. By the end of autumn, dusk fell rather quickly. Not hearing the rustle of the banana palms, Sarayu had not immediately thought anything amiss – Ma was gone, the emptiness of the house lay doubly heavy on her. Moreover, she was rather anxious at that moment to feed her half-sleeping daughter. Unlike on other occasions, at dawn Sarayu's sleep had been disturbed by excessive light pricking her eyelids. It was then that Sarayu remembered that this time she had not heard the leaves rustling in her sleep! Immediately she saw that the banana forest had disappeared, trunks, leaves, flowers, fruits, aroma, everything had vanished. Except for a weak drumstick tree, the entire jungle at the back had vanished too. The bakul tree had been chopped from the very base of its trunk. The drumstick tree appeared like a painfully thin beggar standing, its leaves trembling at intervals, as though in fear of a death-sentence. Baba had sold this entire piece of land – some Kolkata firm had bought it. They were going to grow flowers in this whole area. There was a lot of money in the floral business. The unpaved road in front of the house would now be tarred; the village Panchayat was taking up the work, stone-chips and heaps of sand were being piled up on both sides. The two events coming together caused Sarayu's heart to lurch in a strange manner – those who were going to grow flowers had just chopped a young flowering bakul tree and toppled it on the ground. How could they do it? The road was to be built. Now, no one would have to enter the house with muddy feet, but who was there left to enter? Dada was lost, Ma dead and Sarayu would never come back. Baba too would take this road and venture forth forever, never to return. The paved road would join Baba to his business, his market and all his friends and associates.

Sarayu had returned home. The void in her heart had

gradually filled up. Within a few months she knew she had conceived Deepu.

* * *

"Don't put your hands into the bowl, Bonu!"

"Should I throw away the gourd peels?"

"Just don't touch the bowl! I am not doing anything more today. There is rice, potato and egg. These peels will not taste good in this monsoon weather. Should I fry some brinjal?"

Bonodevi. This was the fancy name given to her by her father. Thank God he hadn't named her Bonobibi. How would Bonolakshmi have sounded? Finally Arjun's preference won the day. Just thinking of all this, Sarayu seemed to shiver in this unseasonal cold! God alone knows what was in the girl's fate. They had thought the family and groom were good, they were not in penury like Sarayu and all. Yet, just because Bonu was expecting a girl-child did her husband have to frown – this sort of thing had never happened before in their kind of families!

The maladies of the rich had now entered the blood of the poor. Their daughters and wives showed themselves to doctors a hundred times, saw their unborn babies in machines and even got rid of them if required. That married girls aborted their babies was something Sarayu was unable to believe. In poor households like theirs a child meant love. There was want but no neglect. That people were now choosing the sex of the unborn foetus, deciding between a girl and boy was a thought that made Sarayu's body shudder with disgust. She had mentally begun to hate her own son-in-law. If the boy troubled their daughter, or refused to take her back – Sarayu would bring up her grand-daughter herself. Sarayu had the courage to do that. She had no doubt that Arjun would agree to this as well.

With these thoughts in her mind Sarayu finished cooking

moong daal. Bonu was sitting, her two lips compressed. The blank look in her eyes was directed steadily at the wall in front of her. Lord knows from what and when all this had happened. How distant the plait-swinging daughter of the house had become – who would now be able to fathom the bottomless depths of her sorrow?

Lord knows what Sarayu suddenly thought of when she screamed for Deepu.

Deepu had just arranged all the papers for his new scheme on the bed and sat down. "Bring a paper and pen, will you?"

Bonu stared at her mother.

"What are you going to do with pen and paper?" she enquired, her eyes anxious. "I won't do anything, you will do it. Write what I ask you to."

Bonu understood, and immediately began to twist her head away like a stubborn horse. "No, I can't do this."

"You will have to. Those who silently accept beatings are never given their rights."

Bonu still remained silent and glum.

Sarayu encircled her daughter's back with one arm and pulled her head down to her breast.

Bonu kept bursting into tears.

"I can't Ma. Why should I write – he will not understand. He has forgotten all I have done for them all, worked hard, cooked, served, just as though they were my own people." Stupid girl, she still thought if she worked physically hard and cooked and served people they would think her one of their own. Like a steady flame, Sarayu sat with the pen and paper on her lap. Leaning a little, she turned and whispered into her daughter's ears, "You will have to, Ma. Otherwise, just suppose the newcomer blames you ultimately? What answer will you give to her, tell me? You at least have a father's home, which home will you give your daughter? Yes, of course, if the father does not come, one never can say, that will be a different matter. Then your mother's home and mother's lap will always be there. But why should you give up your rights so soon? You yourself are saying you slaved for them as if they were your own people – can that be measured in monetary terms?"

* * *

Bonodevi finally wrote. Hiding from her mother and brother. Completely without reason, she covered the lined sheet with her hands. Leaning over her full stomach, her back muscles began to throb. Her milk engorged breasts began to ache. Yet despite all these discomforts she wrote. She wrote to that husband of hers, Jagat, with whom she had spent the last one and a half years and to whose family she had devoted herself as her own, the poor innocent girl. She did not write of the ups and downs of the last few months. The two of them had had a small room of their own, some hens, a fish pond, it was these memories that she tried to offer to him through her language and handwriting. She wrote about the baby to be born, the little girl. She wrote of how she would look, completely from her imagination. How she would put her to sleep, swing her cradle . . . were some of the things she wrote about. The paper finished. Laughing, Deepu gave her more paper. At the end finally, Bonu asked him to come. 'You have to come. Otherwise you won't be allowed to get away.' She wrote 'she is a life created by both you and me. You have to come.' At the end of the letter, fell a few tear drops. Some of the alphabets became hazy. Bonu still wrote. Since some of her spellings were wrong, Bonu had scratched some portions to the extent that there were holes. Through them the red floor of the room was visible. Using her saliva to stick the holes up, Bonu continued to write. . . .

The rain fell heavy in Kamardanga. The roads were waterlogged. The Jagadhhatri Goddess had been sent off. Now rain water splattered the door of the empty workshop. . . .

Sarayu had taken out the old-fashioned quilt today. She was sleeping, having wrapped herself and her daughter nicely in it. It was very cold today. The house was two-storeyed. Otherwise, like the old frames of the idols, water would have been slapping against their feet as well. Bonu was sleeping. The sunken circles of her eyes were dry at long last. Sarayu touched them with her fingers to check. So were the eyelids. Maybe she was now feeling a little more at peace. Maybe today she had had the courage to dream of her old household. She was also possibly able to hear the gurgling laughter of a little baby.

Arjun and Deepu were on the bed spread out on the floor. Arjun had kept an old envelope under his pillow. He had found it after a lot of search. It was lying in the middle of some old papers. He had told his daughter he would post her letter first thing in the morning. It was a luxury to keep an envelope at home. When did they ever write letters? When the mahajan babu had suddenly refused Arjun he had thought of writing a letter of pride and complaint to him. That letter of course had never been written. Arjun's own struggles had become so acute immediately afterwards that he had not even remembered the letter. That envelope would now come into use. A complaint would now go to another mahajan. Before going to sleep a slight smile came to Arjun's lips – one never knew when one needed to use what.

☙ 22 ❧

Arjun was surprised to see Sarala at the workshop so early in the morning. Sarala had housework to do at this time. She was alone but there was enough work for her to do especially filling water. They had to store water for the whole day. Standing in the queue, making two or three trips to fetch water made Sarala's hip bones ache. Moreover, these days her comings and goings had decreased. Her grandson had been running a slow fever for the last one month. The doctor was not able to really diagnose the reason for it and her son and daughter-in-law were very upset. Staying up nights had exhausted them too. Sarala went over once in a while and relieved them at night. Sarala stayed awake, while the boy's parents took a nap. Of course, it was very painful for her to leave the bed in her room and accept her lot once again. Her daughter-in-law had given strict directives – her mother-in-law was not to assume permanent residence in their home under any circumstances.

Sarala had had no option but to come in the morning. Unable to tell his father himself, Deepu had personally come to request her to do so last evening. This afternoon the people from the loan office would be visiting. They wanted to see the premises.

"Pishi, please tell Baba."

"Haven't you told him anything as yet?"

"I just can't. It feels strange. I have never even mentioned the loan to Baba."

"Never mentioned . . . ! Very sensible of you. Your modesty has beaten even a young girl's!" Sarala grimaced. She said whatever she felt she had to. That this was not some female bashfulness, but fearful self-torture of proving to be an ungrateful son to his father was something too complicated for her to understand.

Hence Sarala came bustling to tell Arjun. She stood with her hands on her hips at the door of the workshop. Arjun, of course, came every morning out of sheer habit. He had done so all his life. The frame building work for Goddess Saraswati would be commencing in a few days. As of now, the place was empty. Lying around was some straw and small piles of entel clay. Apart from these, there were a couple of unsold ancient idols of Vishwakarma and Kali. Since they had been there for quite a few years they appeared warm and animate like living beings. They listened to everything, thought about and worried over things. If required, one could hang one's clothes or towels on the shoulders of their escorts; on the raised fingers of the Gods one could hang up one's watch.

"Have you thought of something for the boy, Dada?"

"Who's boy?" Arjun was unable to understand at first.

"Who's boy? Listen to yourself. Deepu of course! Officials are coming to see the room for him today."

"Which room?" Arjun was still making a mental estimate of wood, bamboo, sticks and strings, whatever else would be required for the framework from the outside; he was finding it difficult to gauge from which angle Sarala's question was being fired. Actually, the three weeks following the Pujas had been very enjoyable. Almost in the same way as street urchins enjoy any festivities in the city. After two years he had got orders for four big Jagadhhatri idols and had been able to deliver them on time. The local people had stood and watched, even those who came along with the truck to take delivery were absolutely thunderstruck! What stunning workmanship.

"Aibaas, just look at the shoe of the Asura, there are white dots on it . . . "

"This one's face is absolutely different, have you noticed –."

"Such a big Thakur! Will you be able to carry it under the bridge?"

With Tridib Basu's money, Arjun had shown Bonu to the doctor, bought medicines and kept most of it away for expenses at the time of delivery. With another fifteen thousand he had made advance payments for the Jagaddhatri idol-making work.

Since Deepu was busy, he had kept another boy from across
the canal as an artisan. The rates across the canal were even
now lower than Kumortuli.

Deepu had suddenly become rather busy – his papers had
now become one big file. The whole day he was making rounds
of various places – the bank loan office, the councilor's office
. . . Arjun was well aware that his pre-occupation was not so
total, most of it was shame and hesitation to come in front of
his father. For no reason at all Deepu was tiring himself out
roaming the streets the whole day.

Badu, the boy who had worked on the Jagaddhatri idols
was very restless. He talked a great deal but he had a good
hand. The clay cover over the frames was enough evidence of
the skills of the hands applying the coat. Deepu had come twice
and watched from a distance, he had not come near. Badu
could really make one laugh. Arjun was almost a stranger but
even then he could not stop talking, one had to almost scold
and shut him up. The idol was a big one, one had to sit on the
scaffoldings and work – could one afford to be so restless?
Arjun could understand to a certain extent why Deepu had
merely stood and watched and had not come close. That he
was a leather worker and was not interested in anything else
was something he had to demonstrate. The neighbourhood
was watching his behaviour, the staff from the councillor's
office were keeping an eye on him, the clerks from the loan
office too came around once in a while.

However Arjun had been so immersed in preparing the
Jagaddhatri idols, that while he knew what was happening
around him in a hazy fashion, he was unable to concentrate on
anything because of a special reason. After a very long time
Arjun had undertaken a work with great pleasure – and had
with complete happiness exhausted himself in the process.
Apart from which there had been a tremendous paucity of

time as well. Getting the money in hand, getting the order and making the delivery were events like three stations which a mail train just touched while speeding past. Arjun had noticed Deepu, he had guessed Deepu's plans but had not been able to completely take in the events taking place outside his own special world.

Was Deepu jealous of Badu? Who knew? When Arjun and Badu sat down to their mid-day meal, Deepu was never there. This too could be a sign of jealousy.

* * *

Hearing Sarala's words, his thoughts were given a sudden jolt just as a rickshaw and its passenger leap into the sky when the rickshaw hits a bump on the road. People would be coming, the loan officials would be arriving to see the room. Was that why Arjun had to vacate the room? What next? A small hand machine would be set up on one side of this room. On the other side would be processed leather to be cut. The pieces would be sown together on the machine. On the loan application, this room with its measurements had been shown with outlines drawn. Deepu had already spoken to the landlord, he too had no objections. Arjun found Sarala turning into a stranger. In the artistry of Sarala's words the face that repeatedly rose up before him – Deepu's face – also seemed strange to him.

Yes, Deepu was certainly a very responsible boy. He had not just talked to the landlord regarding opening his business in the workshop area; he had even told the guardians of the locality that the small enclosed area on the road which was of no use for anything would be used by his father. By setting up a tarpaulin shade he would be able to mould idols the year round. Taking the idol out of the narrow lane would no more be the problem. Deepu knew that this was where his Baba usually kept his thakurs – whenever there had been more orders the workshop area had not sufficed. For big idols Baba would arrange the frame out on that strip of land on the roadside. Except for the last two years, the inside of the workshop and the footpath outside had both been used for the work. Now this space was more than sufficient for the few orders that Baba was getting. Of course this was a fact Deepu had been unable to tell his father. He had kept it close to his heart. However, just because it remained unsaid, did it make the fact untrue? No, it was not untrue. Those were the facts that Sarala Pishi had carefully put together and was trying to make Baba understand. If there was something wrong would Sarala Pishi have been able to speak? Sarala the foolish woman! She called herself a member of Arjun's family, yet she had no sense whatsoever. She was arguing Deepu's case with all good intentions yet had no sensitivity to the fact that every word she spoke was piercing Arjun's heart like a pointed missile.

When Arjun returned home just before midnight, Sarayu who had been sitting like a crazy woman at the kitchen door came running and held him in her arms. The hair on his head was tossed by the river breeze, his cheeks sunken, eyes red – what had happened? The man who had never touched liquor in his life – had he come home drunk today? Arjun had been sitting at the Baghbazar Ghat, from evening to night. Having forgotten both hunger and thirst he had sat just watching the movement of the waters, watching the changing lights on the crest of the waves . . . the waters were flowing towards the sea, but where was the sea?

Seeing how late Arjun was Sarayu had repeatedly asked Deepu, "Where could your father have gone, can you tell me?"

Deepu's tongue and throat were turning dry. His heart was palpitating. This afternoon the room had been inspected. Baba was not required to be present. That his presence was not mandatory was the message he had sent in a roundabout way through Sarala Pishi. Baba in fact had not been there in any case. After the inspection, Deepu had taken the officials for a meal to Ghosh's shop. Tea, sweets and the savoury shingara. After spending the evening with friends, he had returned home after dark. Deepu had known that his father would suffer a blow to his heart. However, being inexperienced in household matters he had been unable to gauge to what extent it would change the tide of events.

"I was feeling breathless and my heart was constricting every time I thought of the room – Lord knows who was snatching away the air from my breath. What could I do? So I ran away to the ghat and sat there. I never realized when dusk descended. Finally a policeman began enquiring. He must have thought that I was waiting to jump into the river – many people do, you know . . . "

Arjun was laughing. After midnight he sat down to eat a small portion of daal and rice with a spinach and potato mix heated up for him by Sarayu. Spinach was very cheap this season. In his laughter there was still so much fun that it made Sarayu shiver in apprehension. God, it was sheer luck he had not gone close to the waters. They were two individuals who had always hidden more than they had revealed in speech. In such a small room, in front of the children it was not possible to openly demonstrate one's feelings otherwise Sarayu would have taken Arjun into her arms and with the heat in her breasts have endeavoured to re-kindle the smouldering straw that was gradually petering out within his frame.

"Do not give that room." While picking up the used dishes Sarayu could feel the insides of her throat choking up with pride.

"Do others have rented rooms? How do they start their business?"

"Their fathers give them money. I don't have any. Only the room is there. The boy is my own son. He is taking up a good project, shouldn't I give him something? Thankfully the landlord has agreed. Otherwise what could I have done?"

"Then why did you say you were feeling breathless, and there was a pressure in your chest?"

"Shouldn't I say that? After all that too is true, wife! This room has been with us for so long – how many sleepless nights I have spent in it! So many attachments!"

* * *

The next day, all the paraphernalia of the old workshop was moved to the footpath, carried by hand or on top of heads. Forty years of Arjun's world. Arjun did not allow Deepu to remain glum. He said, "You've managed to reduce your father to a refugee, now come on lad, give us a helping hand. The straw and strings are kept in jute sacks. The pile of entel clay is to be put in the big iron karhai. It would be better to leave the old thakurs." Deepu agreed to this. On top of the shelves, were kept sets of hair-pieces, borders of saris, stitching kits, old decorations, useless falchions and other odds and ends. Where would they keep all this? On the road? One would have to buy a trunk immediately. Shyamal Maity of Kamardanga who was now one of Deepu's guardians, advised him to keep all this in a bundle at home. Even though nothing was clearly said Arjun understood that the whole thing was following the pattern of the Sanskriti Sansad Puja. This was to prevent what had happened when animal leather had touched the body of the thakur. For Deepu's work animal leather would be brought here. If one left these dresses, ornaments and other things in the workshop, would Arjun be able to use them again? People would consider them impure.

It was better that these things were taken home and stored there. To look on the brighter side of things, thanks to the lack of orders in the last two years and the resulting paucity of funds, there was hardly any material stored anyway. Otherwise it would have taken the whole day to carry the stuff out.

However, just as hands and shoulders were beginning to get stiff, Arjun's back was starting to sweat and droplets of sweat were dripping from Deepu's forehead, then from behind the straw mat stacked against the wall peeped out the old clay and paint covered wooden shelf and on it arranged in piles – countless moulds. So many faces – peaceful, ancient, still, shapely, silent . . . piled one on top of the other. For years these ever-changing moulds piled up and waited for the sculptors to look back at them. Every year the colour of the sun, the aroma of the breeze changed. Fresh orders came and the sculptor thought anew of the beloved face which would finally emerge from his meditation. He ultimately lifted out another mould from within his heart. The next year, this face lay still, inert. Like the waters of a river never return, in the same way an artist never returns to his moulds. The signs of his progress kept piling up one over the other, along the wayside. The sight of the shelf seemed to suddenly hold up in the fresh air many years of Arjun's life. Like fossils, these days had remained preserved in a time that had been forgotten. For a few seconds, or was it years, Arjun stared at these faces steadily.

He then signaled to Deepu to come close. "These, together with the shelf will go out of the workshop, on to the footpath. More people will be required." Deepu, along with some friends, would take some of them. Arjun too would take a few. At the moment in his hands was the mould of 1971. A slightly square

face, wide eyes, lips a little on the fuller side. Kunti was there.
Kunti would always be there in her fixed corner – for all times.
She was of course now only a spirit dissolved in air but neither
destitute nor homeless. Lifting the mould in his hands Arjun
brought it very close to his eyes. Was the long ago scent of the
dry and granulated soil still emanating from it? Didi with her
slim yet strong fingers would press the soft clay into the base of
the moulds.

The torn out roots still seemed to be breathing life at places.
With hunger in his eyes, Arjun looked once more at the room.
What was the need to do this really? Close by, on the footpath,
Arjun would be working – and he could come anytime and see
the room. Why was he feeling as though he would never again
see that cobweb hanging from the ceiling? Both Bonu and
Deepu, had crawled around this earthen floor and filled their
toothless mouths with this mud. Were the marks of their tiny,
tiny knees and feet hidden here somewhere?

Yes, these worn out walls also concealed the picture of one
more person just as moth-eaten sheets were used by the poor
to shield against the cold. Sarayu. How many nights, in full
season time, had Sarayu worked with Arjun. She had glued
bunches of hair on the heads of the thakurs, hung ornaments
and painted the fingers with a fine brush. Small thakurs with
their innumerable tiny details that just didn't seem to end.
Many touched these up in the manner of somehow completing
a job as the cost of production did not make it worth their
while. Yet, just out of fear and shame, in case a knowledgeable
person saw and found fault, artists like Arjun almost killed
themselves trying to work these details beautifully as far as
they could. This was done a whole day and night before delivery.
Sarayu spoke little and when at work she became even more
quiet. Her two lips would be set even more firmly, her eyelids
did not blink, like one under a spell her fingers kept working

continuously. In the still of the night, when there were no sounds except for the fading whistles of passing trains in the dark and cries of baby crows awake at night, then this Sarayu, calm and pre-occupied, felt very close to him. Everything seemed meaningless without her, yet there was no conversation between them. Around their hearts flowed countless unseen waves of lightening. The night breeze bound them together and yet caused them to scatter apart into fragments. The memories of all these feelings would linger on.

A few days later, Arjun got a call from the Director of Manuj Basu's serial. The whole thing seemed unbelievable. His own hesitation was keeping him apart from his life.

The first to arrive was the camera team. They came and began to wail. They had no idea that the workshop had shifted from inside the room on to the footpath. Outside, under a tarpaulin covered corner of the road there was nothing much to show. Of what were they to take pictures? There was hardly anything left to provide a visual effect. These people did not understand the seasons, to them the rhythms of an artist's life were totally unknown. Realising this Arjun kept silent, thinking it was meaningless to talk of such things. Finally, one of them used his brains and got Arjun to work on some frames for Goddess Saraswati while they took close shots. Along with these would be put together some old pictures collected from Kumortuli. Very reluctantly they took long shots of the by-lane and the slum. Actually the team was unable to figure out the importance of taking pictures of an almost destitute man amidst so much poverty and so much filth and gloom. In the Kumortuli sculptors' colony, every house was full of work and colours – in fact even across the canal it was better than this. Those who thought a camera could capture all the delightful realities were facing defeat in this case, at every step.

Manuj had later told the Director, "That is the essential

point – that solitariness, that detachment, that inability to find a place in the crowd, the struggle for existence. It is okay if there is a lack of visuals. You can always make it up with the interview."

They had left a paper with Arjun for the interview. On it was given the address of the studio, the day, the time etc. Wearing clean clothes, a good dhoti and polished shoes, Arjun reached the place and found utter chaos. "Dada, you are here. Good." Saying this, one person handed him a paper cup of tea.

In the group would be a prominent expert in fine arts, a writer and the Director. The other two eventually came in one by one. The set was being prepared. A little later, the Director came and spoke a few words with everybody regarding make-up, and pulled the buttons of the writer's panjabi.

Still there were delays, long delays. After an hour and a half, when Arjun couldn't make out whether he should stay or go, a person called Boltu bustled in and said a connecting chord couldn't be found, it would have to be bought from the market. The recording fixed for eleven in the morning began at two in the afternoon. Arjun had, by then, half collapsed with hunger, exhaustion and the weariness of waiting.

He answered a few questions after which the art discussant said a few things till the writer pulled the thread of the conversation towards himself. The final question again came back to Arjun. Initially Arjun had found it difficult to pick up the points of the discussion, but still over all Arjun was finding the whole thing quite a lot of fun.

When they finally let him go with Rs 250 in his hands the sun was setting. After reaching the bus-stand he suddenly realized that he had forgotten to find out when it was to be telecast. There was no colour television at home. He would have to speak to someone in the neighbourhood in advance.

Tridib Basu had come home in the evening one day just

after the recording. By that time Arjun had fabricated quite a few Saraswati frames – maybe to make his working area on the roadside appear a little more presentable. Apart from this Arjun had got the order for a cement idol to be made for the Lokenath Mandir. Tridib Basu had been unable to be present on the recording day. Possibly it would not have looked very good if he had come and stood there. He actually wanted to ask him in detail about the question-answer session. He noticed that Arjun's enthusiasm had already abated and was reduced now to zero level. However, Arjun did ask when the programme would be telecast. Deepu, Bonu and Sarayu had been asking him repeatedly. The people in the neighbourhood had also come to know. They too were very eager.

"Oh, I will come and tell you about that. Don't worry." Arjun had hesitatingly told Tridib Basu that he would not be able to start paying back the installments of his loan before the following month of Baisakh. That meant, almost six months of interest. . . .

"Arjun, I know nothing escapes your notice. But please don't cause me anymore distress. You can always pay back my money along with the interest. Let the girl deliver safely first, you can take your time . . . My money would in any case have just lain uselessly in the bank – I have no one to spend it on."

Arjun was unable to open his mouth and question him – Why, what had happened, where had all the people who used to be in Tridib Basu's household gone? Or maybe he was unable to understand that many a time man became lonely even in the midst of men. Then nothing mattered. Nowadays, when Arjun saw Tridib Basu, two black and white opposing streams of thought and awareness arose in his breast – one was gratitude. He felt amazing gratitude towards Tridib Basu, a gratitude he had rarely felt towards anyone in his own life. No one had so far come and stood by his side with unsolicited help in this way. At the same time, in his mind pain and the deep dark music of dependency began to play. He thought, what was all this? Was this the outcome of so many years of struggle? No shelter, no money. At home a pregnant daughter. The boy had got a strip of land to stand on – but even for that he had been required to show the space, otherwise he wouldn't have got it. Bonu would have taken to the bed with swollen feet and face, and her baby's time of birth would have been uncertain. Arjun's work would have finally got stuck in a blind alley. Was this the result of forty years of walking the streets? Tridib Basu's presence, made Arjun's feelings of personal defeat doubly strong.

In his shock and dismay regarding his own life Arjun had actually spoken out when Tridib Basu was about to step out to the road. Tridib had the stance of looking down for a few seconds and laughing to himself. Arjun recalled that he used to laugh like this even in his young days. He said, "So many years have passed Arjun, in this poverty. Just think, you are still a true human being, a pure artist. You have not died of starvation and even have a roof over your head. I am finding it difficult to say this – but without changing yourself, you would not have achieved much more. If you had taken up another profession, or changed yourself, maybe you could have avoided this loss of capital – but you would have remained here!"

Arjun had merely said – "I have understood, babu." There was no smile on his face.

Tridib felt restless on his return home. What he had just said – was that not a surrender of his self in order to maintain the status quo? Examined in detail, the pressure of various events relating to his personal life had not allowed him to be completely absorbed in his art. Without losing his freedom completely, however, Tridib was still on a highly elevated path. House, car, servants – all that the upper middle-class possessed, he too had. In the last fifteen years, this city had hoped to survive the various dangers to its existence. The rise of a large section of the middle-class and the rich businessmen had been thanks to fatka, hawala, dalali, promoters and trafficking in women and children. The status quo in their lives had changed . . . was that only because one had changed oneself from inside? Most people were better off than Arjun because they had compromised with their true self. Tridib had been lucky in managing to retain most of his freedom while succeeding by not being completely true to the artist within him. Today some special event was being celebrated at home, he could smell the aroma of good coffee and freshly baked cake on the landing. The light from the glass lamps bounced off the leaves on indoor plants. Leena's pet terrier had rushed out but went away again on seeing Tridib. It was amazing how even such creatures had a strong sense of the near and the not-so-near.

As he untied his shoelaces Tridib thought – was this just a question of personal likes and dislikes? He had given his opinion and left. In the fight to grab financial power, Arjun and his kind had collectively failed. Power did not change hands. Instead what was reserved for the people too went into the hands of the select few. Television for the masses, completely removed poverty from the screen. Tele-serials were thickly peopled with fair girls sporting glass and gold bangles which encircled their entire arms. The money from the Unit Trust, the nationalized banks vanished in the share scam. If the banks had to give Arjun and his ilk a loan they asked for property papers, over and above which one had to get a government officer to become a guarantor. In the latest financial scheme of things, all that remained for Arjun and his kind were the mahajans. If the mahajan, Badribabu, turned hostile then a Tridib Basu would have to appear. Even if Arjun had wanted to shake off his artistic integrity, what could he have done? He, along with his whole family, would have possibly become extinct even earlier.

Leena's terrier was going back with its head down on seeing Tridib. People always, unfailingly recognized rejection.

☞ 23 ☜

If one imagined the scene it didn't appear too bad.

Swapnabha was now standing near the dining table. As he buttered a cold piece of toast, he was looking towards the kitchen.

Inside the kitchen, there were three people at three different places. Bolukaka was slicing onions with a knife, his head and neck were turned completely away – for fear of the zing. Baba was wiping plates and arranging them. Urmi Mashi was pressing rice grains with her finger tips on top of a ladle, to check whether they were cooked. The scene was attractive – Swapnabha felt like laughing just thinking of it. In these thoughts where was Anandi? Anandi would never be found anywhere in the vicinity of the kitchen. Instead if she were given a bookshelf or a clothes cupboard to tidy, Anandi would be very comfortable.

"Why are you laughing?" Baba said from behind. Then he went past Swapnabha to switch on the light in the kitchen. There was bread in Baba's hands. Placing two slices in the toaster he said. "Leave that alone. You can't eat cold toast."

Lowering the cold toast, Swapna said, "Baba, how much rent do you expect if we let out the other portion?"

There was a balcony with two rooms side by side. The ground floor verandah could not really be called a balcony even though it was a good six inches off the ground. As a result fallen leaves, dried simul petals, the feathers just shed off newly born crows and a lot more accumulated in a confused heap under the verandah. In the grounds in front, Dadu had planted a few trees. Due to some strange reasons connected to the life giving nutrients in the soil these were not particularly healthy, but they bore fruit. Melons, guavas, custard apples, chilli-shaped hibiscus – all bloomed in great numbers.

Baba replied distractedly, "It depends on who the tenant is . . . they have to be like family . . . after all, the kitchen is common."

That was true of course. Instead of using the kitchen if someone wanted to cook and eat in his room . . . it would be like a boarding house.

Anandi had visited quite a few times. Anandi had made good friends with Baba. Bolukaka too was happy to get a quiet listener. Anandi was extremely transparent. She had a strong will and she had an amazing capacity to enter into the world of others. Now, at this age, Urmi mashi was just the opposite of Anandi. Her pride got hurt rather easily and she harboured her anger and resentment for a long time – and then suddenly she would begin to scream, almost like Booth Saheb's child, in Sukumar Ray's famous collection of poems *Abol-Tabol.*

Anandi had discussed her mother's present problem with Swapnabha. Ma was just unable to live in that house – Mama said nothing but Ma still felt that Mami's behaviour had Mama's support: they were both not keen to let Ma stay. They seemed to want her to leave.

Anandi knew in her mind that this was not correct. The way Ma had been protected by Mama since before Anandi's birth, that love and care had not been destroyed even today. But men were unable to speak about family matters – the wife would most likely misunderstand. A husband who failed to show single-minded devotion to his own family, for all practical purposes finally lost their faith in him. Often, to remain neutral was the only sign of dependability. Arindam had tried to remain unbiased. If Urmi's pride had not been aroused to such an extent then maybe Arindam would have been able to clarify his position a little better. Perhaps because there was very little expectation from the people around them, young people of today understood much more than what their parents attempted to even in their middle-age. Anandi knew that they could not expect anything more from her Mama.

Hearing of Urmi's problem, Swapnabha had told her about these two rooms and verandah. If they would like to rent it, then Swapnabha would talk to his father. One day when Baba was not at home. Swapnabha had unlocked the two rooms and verandah to show them to Anandi. A unique memory from his childhood was in these rooms. Swapnabha had then been so tiny that his head did not rise above the verandah wall. Through the iron grill he would look at the hazy trees and plants and hear the sounds of the street.

There was very little kept in these two rooms – an old harmonium wrapped in curtain cloth, an ancient sewing machine and a solitary table. If Urmi and all came Swapnabha was wondering, what might need to be moved and what they needed to keep. If Anandi stayed in the corner room, what could he organize to put on her walls – these thoughts crossed Swapnabha's mind. Standing on the verandah next to Anandi, he thought suddenly – Arrey, if Anandi and all were to live in this house itself, then every morning as soon as he woke up, even before he brushed his teeth he would meet Anandi . . . this was an amazingly blissful thought. . . .

He was standing on the ground floor verandah while Anandi was standing next to him leaning over the wall a little in order to catch one of the branches of the custard apple tree. The idea that this was a scene he might be able to see now for a long time to come brought a blaze to Swapnabha's eyes. Suddenly with

out any premeditation he enveloped Anandi in his arms very
tightly, just as a drowning man clings to another for support.
Anandi must have been a little taken aback as a suppressed cry
escaped her throat. But within seconds she too put her arms
around Swapna. Anandi's freshly washed cardigan, the scent
of grass and dry twigs, the touch of the light and soft body of a
young girl swept Swapna away on a crystal clear green sea
wave. Gradually his body shed all the rejection, the humiliation
of the past . . . Avinash Samtani . . . the inability to find his
mother . . . Swapna had never wanted Avinash's company. He
had however wanted Sree, only to be hurt in return. For many
days he had, with closed eyes, waited in the room filled with
the body scents of his mother. Ma had not come. Yet Anandi
on her own had come to Swapnabha. She, too, had set out to
search for someone. The search for Tapesh was still far away
on the horizon, indistinct. Yet Arunima and Tirthankar were
there. They were as clear as the light of day, real.

Anandi was real, not an illusion, one could touch her by
extending one's hand – this discovery had stirred up feverish
shivers in Swapnabha's body. On trying to lift Anandi in his
arms, Swapnabha found that she was almost as light as a feather,
and that tears had wet both her cheeks. On that deserted, dusty
winter afternoon, in the emptiness of that unfurnished room
both Anandi and Swapnabha discovered each other. Two
separated physical halves of the same childhood – who had
been scattered in two areas of the city – now returned to each
other. They emanated the same scent, the same touch and the
same pulsating blood. At the onset of evening, Swapnabha was
shyly pouring black tea into Anandi's cup. Anandi was sitting
silently with a biscuit in her hand. If one touched her skin it
was as though one would still be able to touch the marks of his
caresses. Both were simultaneously thinking the same
thoughts. Surely, and no mistake, their search was over.

After that day, Swapnabha just never wanted to go to the other side of the verandah. As though something self created would be spoilt with the sound of his footsteps, or some other unwanted colours would get splattered on a newly-painted canvas. On that verandah there still remained the clay figures of a lonely man and woman bound to each other. Swapnabha could see them as soon as he closed his eyes. He had not told Baba about Anandi's visit – Swapnabha realized this only today.

In the morning, when Swapna had not been at home, Avinash had sent him a letter through someone. Baba had kept that letter in one of the pockets of the jute bag hanging on the wall for this purpose. Even before he opened the envelope Swapnabha could make out the language of the letter. A similar hint had been conveyed earlier by phone as well. Avinash wanted him back. Avinash was neither getting the work nor the attitude Swapna had displayed from the new employees. Swapna should come back. The letter also mentioned the proposed amount that was going to be offered in the new pay scale.

Swapna felt even the effort required to tear up the letter would be a waste of energy. He dropped the letter with its envelope into the kitchen dustbin.

"When are you joining the new job?" Baba wanted to know.

"From the fifth of next month. Before that I will have to go to the field once. Jayanta will accompany me." Swapna seemed to say this in order to put Baba's mind at rest.

"Be careful of malaria. Carry a mosquito net with you."

"Don't you have some liquid for it – that Bolukaka gave you?"

Seeing Swapna's faith in Homeopathic medicines Baba felt a little reassured.

Anandi had shown him the advertisement for this New Policy Research Institute.

"Will you apply?"

On Swapna's question, Anandi went into spasms of laughter.

"They will never take me. You try. You have a degree in Economics. It will help you."

Swapnabha had not expected to get an interview call. Nowadays there was a scarcity of jobs. His bio-data was not very impressive – but maybe because he was young, and having heard the reasons for leaving his last job, the Board must have decided that Swapnabha was a young man with ideals. The institute had taken up a very big project, primary education and a review of the results of Operation Barga, the drive to give ownership to sharecroppers – in three districts. It would be elaborate statistical work, then a paper had to be written. Swapnabha would have to tour and co-ordinate the work of the research team. Whether any input would be required from Swapna in the writing of the paper would be decided after seeing his entire work and point of view. The pay was less than his last had been. There was a five year contract. However there was a separate allowance for his tours, which if not very generous, at least would suffice for Swapnabha. Jayanta Biswas was their district level co-ordinator. The boy was healthy and sharp. He would himself accompany Swapna in the first phase. After that Swapna would be able to manage on his own.

The job involved research and debate. With this opportunity, the thought that he would get a chance to explore the rural areas gave Swapna great joy. Yet the fact that he would be alone on a night train was not such a happy feeling. He would have to stay outside Kolkata for almost fifteen-twenty days a month. To be involved for the next five years in this kind of a life was not something Swapna's mind was favourably inclined towards. Glaring at him Anandi had said, "Am I supposed to leave my data-entry work and roam around with you? Who will look after the old folks in Kolkata?" Anandi had still not found any permanent job. She typed the data of one of the resource centres of the Open University. She was a piece-rate worker. With this she had enough pocket money and quite a bit of savings. Anandi's logic was also very strong. No one was getting any younger. On one side Urmi, on the other Baba, Bolukaka, Debika-Vikram. Just a few days back Urmi had taken voluntary retirement – even if the amount was the same, pay and pension was not the same thing. This was something which Urmi was just discovering, as was Anandi. Maybe, if Ma still had office, the house would not feel as uncomfortable as it did. But Urmi had lately not been keeping well. She had been forced to take leave for minor reasons. Ma's office-head here was very crotchety. Even if one had leave due to one, he got irritated. Everything put together, Ma was finding things unbearable. Anandi had thought she'd tell her mother that it was not correct to leave one's job just on the whims of the boss. However at that time Mama-Ma-Mami all together created such chaos that Anandi couldn't get her voice in edgeways. Of course mentally she was also pre-occupied then with Swapna.

In the month of December, Anandi and Swapnabha roamed around a lot. On the following fifth, Swapna would be leaving on tour. At this time Kolkata looked beautiful. The leaves from the neem on the roadside were flying around. There was sunshine, the aroma of new jaggery, the colours of vegetables in the early morning markets and kids in colourful caps and socks. Many hawkers had taken to the streets with clay and string musical behalas, paper crocodiles, drumbeating toy cars, and a variety of services. . . . The sound of the gins shredding cotton had begun to ring at the opening of the lane. . . .

The two of them took to the streets soon after having tea and toast for absolutely no rhyme or reason. They then roamed around . . . they sat in Deshapriya Park in the mornings, took a metro-rail ride between Dumdum and Tollygunge two or three times, in the afternoon they sat somewhere and ate either idlis and sambhar, or dosa and sambar or potato paranthas. One day they went to see a matinee show. . . . There was nothing fixed about where they would go and that was the fun of it. However, very often at dusk, they went to Tirthankar and Arunuma's place. Arunima waited for them anxiously. She made snacks for them in anticipation. On some days they met Tanmoy or one of the others. Anandi's heart felt at peace when she visited Arunima. She had wanted to bring Urmi. But partly out of embarrassment and partly out of internal rebellion, Urmi did not want to come. Arunima and all were not so familiar with Tapesh's name. Tapesh had not participated so wholly in their politics, he had been an eager theatre worker who had been able to stay with the party only for a short time. Smart, always smiling, his appearance at that time had attracted common people to him. The hard core believers also did not dislike him. Tapesh wrote poetry. Between 1968 and the middle of 1972, many Little Magazines carried his poetry. During the evenings, Arunima, Tirthankar, Anandi and Swapnabha would build up an image of Tapesh by putting together all these various scraps of information. Gradually Tapesh would grow into a complete and real person: someone who had never been Anandi's father but a revolutionary-minstrel singer who had suddenly vanished. Getting to know Tapesh in this way, along with Arunima-Tirthankar, Anandi would feel she was one with them. She too had given up a lot, her childhood, the freedom to grow up as she pleased. Her mother, even now, was carrying on her fight with herself and those around her like a solitary tree surrounded and consumed by fire. The effect of an event that took place thirty years ago might even arouse the young of today to some self-sacrifice. Instinctively, Swapna and Anandi found themselves getting closely involved in Arunima's household matters. Without any hesitation, Arunima was now able to show them the hole in the pressure-cooker valve or

Tirthankar's X-ray plate. There was a small white patch on his left lung. Anandi too was able to give her opinion without hesitation on why it was not healing.

Before passing away, Justice Chaudhuri had given a small interview to an evening daily. The interview would have had no significance if he hadn't died soon after. Following the Justice's death, the piece reached small papers and magazines in some mysterious way. In spite of repeated requests to the Government, Justice Chaudhuri was unable to get them to accept his own report. As a result, all those who were responsible for the bloodshed, escaped scot-free. Those who had died, been injured – their families had not only not been given any compensation, even a verbal apology was far from forthcoming. For two months after Justice Chaudhuri's death, there was again a surge of feelings between Arunima and Tirthankar. By bringing back various bits of memorabilia, Boltu-Tanmay and all only served to further stir the already churning pot. Gradually even those waves disappeared. Arunima and all had come back to their normal lives. Tirthankar once in a while showed himself at the outdoor patients' department of the Eastern Metropolitan Hospital. The doctors had advised that he should get himself admitted and undergo a full check up. It was not a critical ailment nor an emergency hence no bed was available right now. However, taking Boltu with him, he would have to go and get admitted, such statements were made once in a while. Anandi said – "When Dadu goes to hospital I will take food from home. Thakuma will cook it."

* * *

The first telecast was on Tuesday at 9 p.m. The previous day, Tridib Basu had sent a handwritten note to inform them. Even so, they were unable to make the necessary arrangements. At home there was a black and white TV which was just about alive. Once in a while it had to be banged at and woken up from sleep. Very often, during an interesting Bangla movie, there would be snow on the screen, or crooked lines and the sound would become inaudible. Sarayu was not particularly bothered by this, if the TV shut down she too got up. However, Bonu who had come from her in-laws' home, was keen that there should be a good colour TV in the house – but seeing her father's state, she had not been able to say anything. Sarayu did not talk of it – it was a mother's superstition – the girl had only come for a few days, suppose the purchase of a coloured TV closed the path to her return? It was better she went back to her in-laws – there she could live her own life.

Arjun had thought that they would be able to see the show at home. Hearing this Deepu laughed loudly. Baba did not understand Cable TV!

"This will not do, we will have to get a cable connection."

"Then get it, if required!"

"Dhoor, why should we take it for just one day? It would be a useless expense."

"It would be better to see it in Rafiq's shop."

"What about us?"

Sarayu spoke. She was concerned for Bonu. She could not be taken anywhere and everywhere now.

Still, an expense of six-seven hundred rupees at this time! The proposal to sit at home and watch seemed very costly. The mind could not support it.

Arjun, in his own way, tried to distract Sarayu and Bonodevi.

"This is not a movie or something. There is only talk and more talk. What will you get out of seeing that? When it is telecast again. . . "

"Ish, as though they will call you again!" Bonu said pouting her lips.

The expected baby, the swollen feet of the mother, these were very real worries and right now these were the most important things on his mind. Therefore, Arjun did not really notice the pouting lips. He had to be strict with the money, it would not do to be otherwise.

In the evening, Arjun and Deepu waited outside Rafiq's shop and came back. Some neighbours were also there. Rafiq's shop was right at the entrance of the alley. Past the alley on the right footpath was Arjun's workshop now. His old room stood yawningly empty, waiting for Deepu's loan to be sanctioned, for the leather cutting machine to be set up. Some more neighbours had come and were peeping in, it was almost nine 'o' clock. In the cold of December the roads were dreadfully gloomy and dark. In a strange way, the channel vanished from the screen. In spite of turning it around, pressing buttons, seeing various jungles and hearing movie songs, Arjun's programme just couldn't be found even though every channel on the TV was searched. After waiting till nine-twenty, Arjun and Deepu began to return home. Rafiq's face looked disgusted. He kept saying, "Did you hear correctly? Are they actually showing it today? Why, this has never happened before. My TV is a new one, hardly two years old – just the other day the whole locality saw the cricket match on ESPN!"

The road was deserted. On the way back the road divided into three lanes at one point. Taking the path on the left to go home, Deepu suddenly asked, "Accha Baba, do you know any senior government official?"

"No, I don't. Why do you ask?"

"Unless I get a guarantor, they are saying, they will not give the loan."

Something inside Arjun which had been filled with air like a balloon burst immediately and crumpled up.

Again a guarantor! Here too?

"They are a government office themselves! They give loans. They came for an inspection – they made estimates, then why should you need a guarantor?"

"That is also required." Deepu's face appeared gloomy. "They will not take any risks. Do you know anyone?"

This was a strange matter, really! They were schedule castes after all weren't they? For them there were different loan forms, different offices. There had been an inspection, they had already discussed the rate of interest, when it would be paid up, everything had been calculated. The workshop had been emptied, the rent receipt for the room, the schedule caste certificate, all had been checked. Now one had to find a big government officer to stand guarantor! Did Arjun know anyone?

To how many houses had small thakurs had been supplied in the last forty years, to how many clubs had Arjun supplied big thakurs. In those houses and Puja Committees, had any big officials been hiding? Should he have found out? Arjun had not really paid much attention to big officials. Were they the ones who drove by in white ambassador cars accompanied by uniformed police with red lights rotating on their bonnets even during the day – as though in some corner of the world, some major disaster had just taken place? If these cars got stuck in a jam, the occupants got agitated, as though they did not belong to this city. Inside their cars were to be found boxes of face tissue, unopened newspapers and colourful magazines.

What was their connection to Arjun? Why would they sign the papers for Deepu who belonged to the dirty lanes of Christopher Road? If they wouldn't sign, then why were Arjun and all being asked to look for them? The inside of one's head felt quite empty – trying to match two completely opposing arguments was a dilemma. At the same time, while feeling bad for his son Arjun himself experienced the failure of Deepu's efforts and felt completely helpless. He could make out that it was all a very complicated game. This was a very fine trick to incite the poor who were without any support. In the snakes and ladders game, the snake at ninety-nine, in a second caused the counter to go down to the lower numbers. This was no different from being told after fulfilling all the requirements for getting a loan to get the flowers at the feet of some supernatural God called a guarantor. How would Deepu manage to do this? Or maybe he would, since he was a boy of this modern age?

"What will you do now?"

"Taraka da, has said he'll take me to someone, let's see. I will go tomorrow."

Arjun could catch the false hope in Deepu's statement. He would go to someone, who was he? Some middle-level official, or dalal, a broker. He would provide the underground path to the guarantor's house. Through this tunnel, Deepu would reach the windows and doors of the big house. Then what? Would this unknown person take on the responsibility of paying back the burden of Deepu's loan? Why should he? He would be stunned at the amazing daring of a chamar's son. The brows of the house servants would crinkle up. Bow-wow would bark the carnivorous dogs of these people. . . . A desolate Deepu would spring back – the insignificant loan papers would be blown away by a breeze. . . . Seeing all this clearly in his mind's eye Arjun began to shout and his voice, which usually never reached a high pitch sounded strange – "No, no, you will not go, you don't have to go anywhere. I am forbidding you – remember that."

Deepu stared at his father in shock.

The street dogs were sleeping under the lamp-post all curled up. They would wake up in a while and go out on guard duties.

The huge and shabby Rail Quarters and Arjun's room lay sleeping in the smoke enveloped pale moonlight. The bushes and the playgrounds were hidden in the darkness. The only thing shining was the rail line. The soft clay that wrapped the world tightly in its layers was also as invisible to the eyes of man. Man crossed over paths with his feet, he slept on the paths as well, yet the hopes of the soil never became clear to him. The clay was there. Under his feet. In the ten fingers of his two hands. Under his head. In his blood.

"Don't go anywhere. The soil is there." Arjun mumbled the words. "The soil is ours." In Deepu's ears the words sounded like – "I am there for you."

Deepu laughed a little and just as he used to as a child he caught his father's hands. His fingers intertwined with his father's.

The Eastern Metropolitan was a huge hospital – not very old. After a decade of independence, when money suddenly flooded in for health purposes, the hospital then extended its premises and completely covered the entire area around it. It was now not so posh, the walls were dirty, the mattresses on the beds were tattered, on one bed there were two patients and dogs roamed the corridors. Still, quite a few good doctors manned the outdoor patient ward and were responsible for the treatment given there.

After a point, Arjun did not think it sufficient to show Bonu to the local doctor. Arrangements had to be made for the delivery as well. For the last two months, Bonu had been brought here to the outdoor patients' ward – Sarayu brought her, with Deepu accompanying them.

In the outdoors, a salt and pepper haired old doctor attended, assisted by a younger doctor. Bonu had come four times. After taking an iron tonic and resting a lot she was now much better. The swelling of her feet had still not lessened however but she had become much more calm and relaxed. This was because affection and reassurance dripped from the tongues of the doctors. Fear spread its wings and flew away. On the wall there was only one picture and a green calendar. But in the poster of the medicine company was the picture of two beautiful babies sitting shoulder to shoulder. Bonu could already picture her daughter walking, moving and laughing. Then instantly she would touch her forehead in reverence and appeal to her gods. It was not auspicious to anticipate so much in advance or to want so much.

Jagat came one day without his mother's and sister's knowledge. It was for one night. Sarayu and Arjun gave up their bedroom to their daughter and son-in-law and slept in the kitchen. Deepu was sent off to a friend's. Sarayu was delighted at her son-in-law's arrival but was unable to sleep a wink. She tossed and turned restlessly the whole night. Not, of course, because she was sleeping in the kitchen. As a mother, how was she to tell her daughter not to indulge in sex now, only talk to each other and stay far apart! How could one possibly say such things? Yet, she was very scared. If the boy had come now, why hadn't he done so before? In between her daughter's tying her hair, applying collyrium to her eyes and changing her clothes, Sarayu had come close to Bonu, placed her hand on her head without reason, on her back, as though she was trying to warn her to be careful, not to displace the foetus floating in the amniotic fluids. They were meeting after a long time, but they shouldn't forget the baby in their own hearts' delight. . . . After a long time her daughter's voice could be heard humming a song, her eyes were animated and the joy of life had returned to her feet. . . .

That everything was not running smoothly at the hospital was not something Sarayu's inexperienced eyes had understood. It had never been her responsibility to take care of outdoor work. Hence, what was happening outside or on the roads, what the signs meant, was not something she gave much thought to. From the following month, the helper ayahs were going to be laid off from the hospital. Hence they were often to be seen demonstrating in front of the hospital wearing black armbands. Sarayu passed by them each time but did not think it was any cause for worry. The internal staff and these ayahs were bound to each other. If the outside help stopped then there would be tremendous pressure on the permanent staff and so after-care would become a problem. Sarayu had of course never thought of these possibilities. The permanent staff had a fixed pay. Like any government servant they got paid on time – whether they worked or not. They now felt that the extra work that the ayahs did would now fall to their lot without any increase in pay. This was making them very agitated and, in turn, making them behave very badly with the patients. They did not go on strike or wear black armbands so their anger was largely invisible. But, was there anything more dangerous than invisible anger on a deep dark winter night, when the streets were empty and rain soaked?

Jagat had come on such a night. Although happy, Jagat's arrival had filled Sarayu with apprehension as well, she was full of doubts and fears. According to the doctor's calculations there were still ten days left for Bonu's delivery. These ten days had to be spent carefully. However, they had decided not to keep Bonu at home for all ten days, they would admit her in the hospital at least seven days in advance. That was as much as the junior doctor had said. Bonu would be admitted during the day, she would be required to bring a small bag with her personal belongings. This was surely the safest thing to do at such a time.

On Jagat's arrival, Bonu's heart had leapt up in joy, and

Sarayu's had paled with fear. As long as her son-in-law had been far away, there had been a different fear and anxiety. Now she knew that Jagat wouldn't be able to stay away. Hence like a tigress protecting her cub, Sarayu's desire to safeguard her daughter had become very strong. Why had her husband come now?

"You only ask him! You did not ban him from coming did you?"

Her daughter was red-faced and speaking with her eyebrows crinkled up.

"It will not be possible to send Deepu to his friend's house everyday. Let your Baba, Deepu and your husband sleep on the big bedstead tonight – you and I will sleep on the floor, okay?"

This arrangement was not to Bonu's liking. Her angry pride overflowed in her every move and word. Utensils fell from her hands, and made a loud clattering noise.

Sarayu kept glancing questioningly at Jagat, while doing her work. The boy had not come for any specific purpose. He had not carried any of the gifts his mother and aunt had said they would send for their daughter-in-law, the sari, sweets and other foods. It was true that he had come to find out how his wife was but actually he was after all a starving man. Following a long interval the last time, there had been a shower of rain. This time however the thick clouds seemed to be hovering close overhead on their own volition.

* * *

The roads were wet with the drizzle. The breeze was pricking one's body like needles. Resting her chin on her mother's shoulder, Bonu was shaking severely. Arjun and Jagat were seated in front. On her side was Deepu. Sarayu's eyes were wet

– in front of her she could see how raindrops were falling on the glass thanks to the inadequacy of the broken wipers. One side was hazy, the other wet but clear – the old taxi driver was driving looking straight ahead at the road. According to Sarayu's instructions, he was trying to avoiding the bumps and potholes on the road as much as possible.

The anger that had initially arisen at Jagat, had now turned cold with the night breeze. Sarayu could hear her own suppressed anger growling within her. Why hadn't she insisted then, why had she listened to Bonu, she was young, a child, what did she understand? If only they had all made a long bed on the floor and slept in the same room!

Bonu had been banging on the kitchen door and one could hear the bolt being opened in one's sleep.

"Ma, what's happened Ma!" Arjun had woken up calling out in fear. In such a small house, it was impossible to keep one's dignity or modesty under cover. Initially Bonu had not realized it was the onset of labour pains and was frightened when her bed and clothes got soaked. Jagat was fast asleep, as though at this very moment he was a complete stranger with no responsibilities whatsoever. Having finished his job, in spite of having to overcome the minor obstacle relating to the swelling in his wife's heavily pregnant body, he was now sleeping, his eyes shut tight.

Sarayu had understood that Bonu's water bag had burst. The helpless, innocent baby who, with complete trust in its mother, was lying all coiled up inside her womb, suddenly found the watery atmosphere surrounding it attacked and all the water flowing out over clothes and beds. The mother was not aware that the small area in which her baby could swim was being destroyed, and immediately it would become homeless and detached, and would very soon be unable to breathe. . . .

In her sleep a slight nagging pain had begun in her underbelly which Bonu had not understood at first. It was as though she was dreaming. It came, stopped and went away. Then the pain became more acute and remained for a longer span. Her throat began to dry up with thirst. Before one wave of pain could subside, the wave of another one raised its fangs – even in her sleep Bonu realized there was no escape from this, or there was only when the baby was born. This acute pain, the cries of the baby in its ineffectual grief at being confined in this airless void of darkness, had to be given its freedom, had to be brought out into the world. . . .

Jagat was sleeping. Deep snores emanated from his slightly open lips. He seemed to be sleeping on some calm, sandy beach at the edge of a stormy sea.

A hospital in the middle of the night is quite different from what it looks like in the morning or even how it was in the afternoon or evening! Those who could not be seen in the light of day returned as guardians of the night. The ward lights were visible from the road. Somewhere a patient was groaning in pain, somewhere else a small child could be heard crying continuously near his mother. Dogs were cautiously moving about the vicinity, a mad vagabond was eating bread dipped in water. As soon as the taxi stopped in front of the Emergency signboard, the man standing at the gate turned his face and went away. It was as though the huge, ugly house was displeased and the sudden arrival of Bonu was something they had not liked at all.

"Will you be able to stand, Ma?"

Turning his head to ask, Arjun immediately realized that his daughter almost unconscious with pain, was not even capable of raising her face.

"A stretcher will be needed, wait let me see . . . "

Jagat remained standing like a moron, sleep still dominated

his entire body. He had accompanied them all right, but had no idea of what was happening.

Inside, there were corridors on either side but there was not a soul around and neither were there any iron stretchers on wheels. Arjun came back perplexed and agitated.

A Nursing Sister had been sleeping with her head on her arms. On seeing him, his appearance and clothes, she went back to sleep having estimated his status.

The man who had turned away from the gate, a hospital staff member, too looked at Arjun with irritation. Bonu was almost being carried in on a human stretcher, created by the outstretched arms of Deepu and Sarayu. The taxi wouldn't wait, it had to be released.

Where could they lay her down? On the cold floor? On the bench-seats? On the table on which papers were to be kept?

"Nowhere. Get out. None of us are working here. Don't you read the papers or what! No admission will be made."

"A doctor must be here on duty at least?" Deepu picked up courage enough to ask. He now realized that if a couple of neighbours had been brought with them in a separate taxi, it might have made a difference.

"There are no doctors. No one will call them. Can't you see, the strike has begun . . . "

Arjun in desperation said, "It is to start in the morning, bhai! It is only midnight now! Can't you see this is a delivery case . . . "

It was past midnight. The day technically began as soon as midnight was over. As soon as the clock struck twelve, the dawn of the New Year had been heralded. Hence the strike of the protesting staff-workers came into effect rightfully at this hour.

Tears flowed from Sarayu's eyes.

Deepu told Jagat, "At least hold Didi! What are you looking at!" Walking ahead he directed his continuous cries of help at the sleeping Sister, "Listen, Didi, please wake up, O Didi. . . . "

The Sister woke up. Initially she stared at him sleepy-eyed. Then fearfully she said, "Ayee Poltu, let them come in won't you, it is a delivery case . . . "

Emerging from both sides of the corridor, Poltu, Badan, Shyama, Ghoton and others came forward angrily, ready to fight. As though for its own protection this huge building had hidden them in its cracks and crevices . . . as though they had anticipated some attack soon after midnight. . . . The iron shutter that was rolled up at the entrance of the hall . . . with a loud clanging was brought down, shutting out the hospital from the rest of the world.

When the iron gate came down, Arjun and the others stared at the hospital in shock. They'd been left outside! Bonu's hands were cold, there was sweat on her forehead and she was writhing like an animal in pain. Her pitiful cries would start, touch the stars and fall . . . just like the pain. In front of the closed gate stood just one person, whose back was to the gate. The person was not connected to the hospital. Arunima was walking down the corridor from the ICU. Tirthankar was admitted. He was being treated for his lung infection. He could have been treated in a normal ward. Possibly he had been taken to the ICU to be taken care of by some senior doctor. Outside either Boltu or Tanmay would be waiting.

'Didi, O Didi . . . ', on hearing these calls for help, Arunima had come out. Then, after seeing Bonu's condition, she was unable to return.

"They did not let us enter . . . " Sarayu was weeping loudly. Laying down the thick shawl she was wearing, Arunima spread it out on the floor. In front of the closed doors on the paved floor . . . there was no end to the dust from the feet of people and paws of dogs, still it was less cold than the grounds outside.

"Nothing to be afraid of, she will deliver right now, you hold her, no, put your arm under her shoulder . . . you men, move to the other side . . . "

"Take slow breaths girl, take in your breath and release it slowly . . . a new life is coming, a new soul is being born . . . " Bonu's grip was hard, her two eyes were red like a sacrificial animal. Her screams rent the night . . . Strike Zindabad, long live the strike . . .

It was seven-thirty in the morning. Arjun was going to call the local doctor. The baby had been washed and dried, now she and her mother were sleeping. With quick movements, Sarayu was arranging for clothes to be washed and new sheets to be made. Deepu and Jagat too were sleeping. The umbilical cord had been cut, with a new blade of course, but still it was best the doctor came and checked her up. . . .

At dawn, Arjun had shared a cup of tea with Sarayu in the kitchen . . . the tea had tasted like ambrosia. Sarayu's look was a mix of tears and laughter, very much like the light and dark of the dawn sky; there was no discernible joint to mark where the two met. . . .

Rafiq had opened his shop very early in the morning. As soon as he saw Arjun, he called him. . . . "They are telecasting your TV show again, see it now Dada . . . it is a morning repeat programme, maybe that's how they telecast, who knows when and how they will show it."

Arjun saw himself on the TV screen for the first time – he was amazed. He had never before seen his own two eyes, sharp nose, chin, his style of talking with his hands raised. It was as though another man was being revealed in layers, a strange, unknown Arjun. . . .

Bending a little, the man of letters said something – only the last bit came on the screen . . . "Afterwards" . . . Arjun's laughter then filled the screen. . . .

"No, no, afterwards no contact was kept . . . "

"I hear they performed an 'Akal Bodhon Puja'. Since I had draped the Asura with animal leather . . . a sin had been committed. . . ."

"No, I do not think myself guilty. . ."

"That was the first big thakur I had sculpted . . . I was only eighteen years old then, it was the Sanskriti-Sansad Puja . . . I was so enthusiastic, I had poured myself into the work, with my life and soul I moulded . . . "

"I don't understand much, I'm not literate you see . . . all I know is that the struggle of the artist is a very crucial one, not just to survive, but to remain unspoilt, keeping one's self respect in one's own hands . . . while continuously trying to do this, I never realized when my life was drawing to its close. . . . See that Rail Bridge . . . at one time Puja Committees used to say, make the thakur four feet lower than it in height, otherwise the lorries will not be able to pass under . . . initially they said so . . . then when I made a name for myself, I sculpted thakurs of any height I chose to make . . . they carried the images on push carts lying horizontal, or slanting, and crossed the bridge. . . . They never raised any objections. . . . This time no thakur could cross the bridge . . . I have seen so many different kinds of days. . ."

The screen then filled up with footage of Kumortuli thakurs, and Pal thakurs. . . .

Arjun had no visual material with him . . . so the camera had to find its own material. . . .

Arjun told Rafiq, "I am in a bit of a hurry. I am going to call a doctor, you watch, Rafiq . . . "

"They are telecasting at such a time . . . I can find no one to show it so early in the morning . . . " Rafiq was looking around disgustedly; as though the repeat telecast time had been fixed by a mistake on his part. . . .

The screen kept shifting away from him for in his minds-eye he saw only the red-fisted new born sleeping baby girl . . . next to whom lay her sleeping mother . . . it was imperative the doctor was called now, at least once. . . .

Arunima was standing on the road waiting for a taxi. She had sent word to Boltu that in her absence he should sit on a bench in front of the ICU . . . next to it there was an open door . . . maybe they would lift the shutter in front. . . . Meanwhile she needed to go home, have a bath and change her clothes. If there was no one close by, Tirthankar would become restless if he couldn't see Arunima.

Arunima's hair was disheveled and her head felt heavy in the early morning chill. On her shawl there was dust and dirt from the street. Even her sari was covered with the grime of the road. Its front was soaked in blood and the juices of the mother and child. How surprising! She did not feel impure at all! Arunima had not allowed Bonu's child to be born on dust under an open sky. She had offered her lap at exactly the right minute. After how many years since Babu and Khokon had passed away, had blood soaked her lap in this way. It was after ages that Arunima had actually taken life into her two hands – restless, angry, pulsating.

* * *